Table of Contents

Chapter 1
Bad Joke

Charmaine parked her new Kia Sportage SUV in front of the two-story home. Both levels had a porch. The trendy neighborhood looked deceptively quiet. No wonder, since it was almost four in the morning. She glanced at her sister. Jessi had already managed to strap on her backpack of ghost-fighting tools. Charmaine took in a deep breath and let it out. She pulled her faux shearling jacket collar up against chilly late-January night air.

"I hope Diamond called the cops," Charmaine muttered. "God only knows what we're walking into. I wish you'd gotten more sense out of—hey!"

Jessi had stepped out of the passenger side of the Kia. She didn't say anything, simply jerked a thumb for Charmaine to follow before she kept going. Jessi strode up the paved walkway leading to the house. "Talk later. Bestie needs us. Now."

She read her sister's thoughts as clearly as if she'd spoken aloud. Charmaine's telepathy had kicked in. She whispered a prayer that her ability would stay consistent as she scrambled after Jessi. Hearing the mental monologues of people could be hit or miss. Especially if Charmaine was stressed. And based on the high pitch of Diamond's frantic voice on the phone before the call dropped, this was going to be a bumpy night. Or rather early morning. Jessi had already climbed the six steps of the first-story porch. She pushed on the red front door with long rectangle glass panes on either side. Charmaine sprang up the steps to catch her.

"Jessi," Charmaine hissed. "Don't just bust in!"

Her warning was too late; Jessi was already inside. Despite her unease, Charmaine followed. The spacious foyer had two stuffed chairs. Jessi went to their left before Charmaine could grab her by one arm. With a whispered expletive, Charmaine jogged after her. She bumped into Jessi's back because her sister had skidded to an abrupt halt. A chaotic scene lay before them. Bodies lay in various positions around the otherwise lovely living room. Jessi stepped over a woman in a bunny suit. Charmaine stood frozen in shock for a few minutes. But Jessi wove her way quickly around prone figures looking for her friend. A soft sniffling and whine made Charmaine spin around. She followed the sound. Diamond sat on the fifth step up of the stairway to the second floor. She was dressed like a belly dancer, with diaphanous light green harem-styled pants. Her top was gold lame and cropped above her midriff. The low neckline showcased Diamond's cleavage. Her feet were clad in gold ballet-type slippers. Thick gold thread had been woven into a long braid of hair that draped over Diamond's left shoulder. Baby hairs circled her forehead.

"I didn't know what else to do. I hid when I heard footsteps, but then I thought it might be y'all. So I came out of the closet and... and..." Diamond's voice hitched and she shook her head. "But then I thought it might be the police so maybe I shouldn't."

"You didn't mention we'd be walking into a mass murder," Charmaine blurted out. When Diamond let out a gasp, she regretted it. "Just calm down, take your time, and tell me what happened."

"Don't take too much time," Jessi said over Charmaine's shoulder. "Not if she called the cops. They'll be here any minute."

Diamond sprang off the stairs to hug Jessi. "I didn't do anything but my usual act. I swear it."

Jessi patted Diamond's back and made a few soothing noises before wiggling free. She grabbed both her shoulders. "Did you call 911?"

"I told them someone had passed out," Diamond said with a nod. She pressed the wad of tissues to her nose.

"Okay. Okay." Jessi paced in a short circle. She'd shifted from panic to problem-solving mode now that she knew Diamond wasn't among the fallen.

"NOPD might take exception to her leaving out the detail that everybody is *dead*." Charmaine shivered. "We're in a house full of corpses."

"Well, it's not my fault. I was upstairs with what's his name when the lights flickered, and then..." Diamond waved her hands around. "Then he slumped over. I tried to pull his pants up but he was too heavy. And—"

"What's his name?" Jessi stopped pacing.

Diamond blinked hard. She rubbed her temples. "A state legislator, or at least he was. Buddy is his nickname. Shit, I can't think straight."

Charmaine shook her head. "Let's get out of here fast. All the police know is an anonymous caller reported a problem at a wild party and—"

"Miss Law-Abiding Social Worker wants us to bounce?" Jessi raised both expertly shaped eyebrows at her sister.

"Uh… y'all. I might have gave them my name," Diamond replied as she twisted her hands.

"You did what?" Charmaine yelled. "Diamond, what the fu—"

"What I was I supposed to do? The 911 guy was shooting questions at me!" Diamond started crying again.

"And how the hell will we explain being here. Oh, this is bad," Charmaine said.

"We can figure this thing out." Jessi put one arm around Diamond's shoulder.

"Have you lost your damn mind?" Charmaine looked around as she spoke. She took out her keys to her SUV. "Diamond, grab your stuff. We can explain why you left later. After we get you a lawyer."

"Stop. Forensics. Smart alarm system." Jessi jerked a thumb at a corner of the foyer ceiling.

A compact camera attached to the crown molding blended in so well it was almost invisible. The black lens seemed to stare at them like an accusatory eye.

Charmaine resisted the useless urge to run and hide. "Shit. Is it monitored?"

"The alarm hasn't been triggered. Which means the security company doesn't have an alert. NOPD is seriously understaffed. It's gonna take a while before anyone responds to a party with some drunk passed out. They got other priorities," Jessi said and faced Diamond again. "Show us the guy."

"Okay." Diamond swiped her nose with the soggy tissues and led the way up to the second floor.

"Great. We're going to hang around a house full dead white people. Dead rich white people. This furniture is from West Elm. High end," Charmaine muttered as she glanced around.

Framed art prints lined the wall of the staircase. The top landing had three chairs in a seating area. A table held glasses of wine. A woman dressed as a Greek goddess sat in one, her head back and mouth slack. Charmaine let out a gasp. Jessi grunted as her only response. They went down a hallway to a closed door. Diamond swallowed hard and pointed to it.

"In there. I just want to first say, Indyah goes to St. Mary's and I needed extra money." Diamond's little girl had started first grade at the pricey private girl's school.

"Right." Jessi gave her friend's shoulder a squeeze along with a look of understanding.

"Tick-tock." Charmaine tapped the bracelet watch on her right wrist.

"Whew." Diamond huffed out a long breath and pushed the door inward.

"Damn." Jessi surveyed the room.

A clown lay stretched across a king-sized bed. It sat in the center of the expansive primary suite. He wore the full costume, including white facial paint. Wide red lips had been drawn over his mouth. A shirt with lemon and green checks had been pulled up. his clown pants were around his knees along with boxers. Glasses of wine sat on one of two matching side tables on either side of the bed. A fancy ashtray held two cigars. Charmaine tilted her head back and sniffed. She turned to Diamond.

"Special blend with a bit of lavender," Diamond murmured. "Top grade stuff."

"Girl." Charmaine shook her head and sighed.

"Well, I didn't know he was gonna die on me. He looked healthy. Last time—"

"He's your regular?" Charmaine clicked her tongue in dismay.

"The last six months," Diamond said. "St. Mary's fees are sky high."

Jessi paid little attention to their conversation. Instead, she stood over the clown. His flaccid penis lay on one side. "How far did you get?"

"I was dancing topless in my panties while he... you know." Diamond pumped one hand in an up and down motion. "Then he made a grunting sound. I thought he was about to finish before we got to the next part. He's done it before. Really upsets him. I try not to get him too worked up with the foreplay. Anyway, he grabbed at his throat and went limp. All over I mean."

Charmaine kept her distance from the prone figure. She craned her neck as if trying to get a better look. "Is he dead?"

Jessi leaned close to his face. "He's not breathing. Bluish color to his fingertips. Welp, no more happy meals for old Ronald McDonald."

"Seriously, Jessi?" Charmaine hissed. "Remember, we've got a house full of trouble here."

"Not the first time folks with more money than sense mix expensive liquor with drugs. Oh, and they're not dead. At least not all of them. One or two might be coming around." Jessi took out one of her gadgets. She aimed it around the room.

"You might have mentioned that before now!" Charmaine shouted. She flinched at the loudness of her own voice.

"Cleared the kitchen. One or two of 'em woke up," a female voice came from downstairs.

"I hear noises. Up there," a male voice responded. Foot falls muted by the carpeted staircase followed.

"What do we do?" Diamond whispered, her eyes saucers full of fear.

"We're in the third bedroom, unarmed," Jessi called out as she gestured at Diamond and Charmaine not to moved.

The male police officer appeared, pistol in hand. He glanced at the three women quickly and then the clown. "Move away. Against that wall. Hands where I can see them."

"On my way," his female partner yelled over the sound of a siren and more arrivals. Seconds later she came into the bedroom. "Emergency guys are looking at the people downstairs. What the hell we got up here?"

"A mess by the looks of it. Party got out of hand, did it?"

The male officer jerked his head at the trio as a signal to his partner. He kept his gun pointed at them while she used flex handcuffs to bind their wrists. Diamond's quiet sobs soon followed. Jessi looked furious but didn't resist when Charmaine gave her a warning look.

"Sir, our friend entertains at private parties and—" Charmaine started.

"I'll bet she does," the female officer retorted.

"She became concerned when the gentlemen seemed to have respiratory distress. So, she called for help," Charmaine pressed on, straining to keep her voice level.

"Sit," the female ordered.

She took a step back and watched Jessi, Charmaine and Diamond comply with awkward movements. They were lined up along the wall. The female officer wrote their names down on a small notepad. A third officer appeared with a tablet computer. He tapped in their information, a check against the police database no doubt. An hour dragged as they went over each one of their statements.

Diamond had recovered enough to fill in the blanks. Charmaine and Jessi were just as interested in getting the full story as the cops. They hadn't had time for details.

The male officer holstered his pistol when his partner said they were secure. The clown's name was Bernard "Buddy" Kennedy, a former Louisiana state senator. He was a member the Krewe of Misfits, one of the newer social clubs that threw balls and parades during Mardi Gras season. Diamond had been hired as "entertainment" for part of the evening. Her role was to play the fictional Goddess of Wild Revelry, one the krewe created. The police officers wore various expressions of suspicion and amusement. As they questioned the trio, emergency medical staff worked on the clown. After a few minutes they confirmed what everyone already knew. Chuckles the Clown, aka Buddy Kennedy, had blown his last kazoo.

"He was fine all evening. He did drink a lot. I mean a lot." Diamond glanced over at Buddy and then quickly looked away.

"Looks like they all did. Plus, these." The female police officer held up two clear plastic baggies in each hand. One had what looked like a large cigar, the other multicolored pills.

"All I brought was my karaoke mike and costume. I don't know anything about that stuff," Diamond said as she shook her head.

"Look, the man obviously died from natural causes," Jessi spoke up. "Our friend called us for help when things got crazy.

By the time we got here, the poor guy was beyond help. Diamond tried CPR but he was too far gone."

"Yeah, and I called 911, too. I was trying to save Buddy. What they sniffed or swallowed partying ain't got nothin' to do with *me*," Diamond said, her voice shrill with stress.

"And she called you two because..." The male officer squinted at Jessi and then looked at Charmaine.

"We're here to support our friend," Charmaine said. "I'm a social worker with Mid-City Mental Health. My sister is a legal professional."

"So, she called a lawyer and therapist so she could get her story straight before we got here." The female cop shot a glance at her partner.

"If you contact Chief Detective Bryan Harrison, he'll tell you we're not criminals," Charmaine said. "He knows us well."

"I wish I didn't," a deep voice responded.

Detective Harrison looked impeccable even before the crack of dawn. He wore a dark green cable sweater over a crisp light green shirt. His black Dockers straight-leg pants looked pressed to perfection. Harrison's square jaw clenched as he did a full scan of the scene. Two members of the NOPD forensic unit moved around the room. They placed labels with numbers on items and took pictures. Then a young woman entered. She wore a jacket with the coroner office's logo on it.

"You really know these two?" The female officer raised both eyebrows when she glanced at Harrison.

"Yeah," was Harrison's gruff reply. He scowled at Jessi, Charmaine, and Diamond in turn. "Finish getting their statements."

"What about these cuffs? They're cutting off my circulation. Hey!" Jessi held up her bound wrists.

Harrison turned his back on them and strode from the room. They heard movement from the police activity downstairs and other voices. Another thirty minutes passed with the trio still seated on the floor. An officer had graciously draped Diamond's jacket on her shoulders. She'd shivered in the scanty outfit for hours. The first two officers took turns standing over them. Finally, the female officer used a pair of scissors to cut the thick plastic zip ties and free them.

"About damn time," Jessi muttered as she rubbed both arms.

Charmaine, stiff from sitting, slowly stood. She planted a palm on the wall as she rose. "Thanks, officer. I'm sure this will all be cleared up soon."

"Uh-huh. Y'all still got a lot of explaining to do." The female officer gave them a final look of suspicion before she walked off. "Detective Harrison is waiting for you downstairs. Good luck talking your way out of this shit-show."

"I didn't do any drugs, y'all. I swear. Okay, maybe smoked a little weed, but no pills or whatever powder they was sniffing." Diamond stuck her arms in her coat as she talked. A female tech gestured to her.

"Ma'am. The team says you're clear to get your items from the hall closet. A pair of pants and a pink sweater I think?" the woman said.

"Yeah, and my duffle. It's a Vera Bradley bag with purple and blue flowers all over it." Diamond glanced at Jessi.

"Go on. We'll meet you in a minute. Did you drive here?" Jessi said.

"Buddy, Mr. Kennedy, paid extra for my ride share," Diamond called over her shoulder as she scurried behind the tech.

Charmaine grabbed Jessi's left arm and yanked her close. "I thought Diamond had given up sex work," she whispered.

"Yeah, cause being a receptionist at a hotel pays so well." Jessi pulled free of her hold.

"So, you knew? Jessi!" Charmaine started to say more but stopped at the look from the male police officer.

"Some people have limited options, remember?" Jessi kept a close eye on the activity around them.

The cop walked over and handed Jessi her bag. "Here. Sure you weren't part of the act? Strange-looking gear in there."

"You don't have a warrant or probable cause to search my personal belongings." Jessi looked at him through narrowed eyes. She snatched her bag from him and examined its content.

"Pain in the ass lawyers," the cop mumbled as he walked off.

Jessi started after him. "Thick headed pain in the—"

"Oh, hell no." Charmaine grabbed a fistful of Jessi's jacket sleeve and jerked her back. "We're close to spending a night in jail as it is. Don't push our luck."

"Yeah. Whatever." Jessi smoothed the fabric of her quilted jacket. "Don't be grabbing on my shit. I paid good money for this."

"Look, we—" Charmaine broke off when Harrison appeared in the doorway. He jerked his head as a command that they follow him.

Charmaine and Jessi exchanged a look before they followed him down the stairs. Partygoers in various states of consciousness were being tended to in the foyer and living room. Harrison led them out to the porch and down the front steps. He gestured to a corner of the yard away from the flow of traffic in and out of the house.

"Looks like everyone else is alive. That's a good sign," Charmaine said, forcing an attempt to find a positive spin on things.

Harrison continued to gaze at the house for a few beats. Then he faced both women with his arms crossed. "You two are ass deep in every bizarre mess in New Orleans. Why is that?"

"Not *every* single one. C'mon, Bryan. We gotta sleep sometimes," Jessi wisecracked. Her sardonic smile didn't fade despite the heated look he gave her.

"Detective Harrison to you, Ms. Joliet. You're at a scene with illegal drug use, what looks to be overdoses, prostitution, and a suspicious death." Detective Harrison ticked off the list on his fingers.

"Boo-Boo the Fool finally died doing something stupid. Didn't see that one coming." Jessi shrugged.

"Not funny," Harrison growled. His dark brown eyes appeared to gleam with rage.

"Yeah, his last gag fell flat." Jessi yelped when Charmaine slapped her arm hard. "Ouch."

"Cut it out," Charmaine barked.

"Sorry, but the jokes just write themselves!" Jessi waved a hand at the commotion going on around them. Two people dressed in white and purple togas limped by. A woman wore a green, gold, and purple Mardi Gras cape over a bustier. Other costumed partygoers were led or carried out by various ambulance attendants.

"The poor man is dead," Charmaine snapped aside to Jessi and then faced Detective Harrison. "Of natural causes while engaging in consensual... fun."

"Pay for play is still illegal," Harrison said in a dry tone.

"Diamond has a side hustle dancing at parties. Not against the law last time I checked," Jessi put in.

"Entertainment with a 'happy ending' is." Detective Harrison waved a hand at Jessi. "I'm not going to argue with you. We'll sort through what happened. So, tell me. What ghost or monster brings you two out tonight?"

"We told you the whole truth," Charmaine protested. "Diamond called us because this poor man collapsed. She also called the authorities, which is easily verified because it's recorded."

"No ghosts, goblins, or gargoyles?" Detective Harrison looked from Charmaine to Jessi with a skeptical squint.

"We do more than investigate paranormal phenomena," Charmaine replied with an irritated frown.

Harrison started to retort when a steady beeping sound started. He cast a quick glance at the lawn. "What's that noise?"

"Damn!" Jessi unzipped the largest section of her bag. "My EMF meter is going off. Or maybe it's my anemometer. The tones sound the same. See—" Jessi stopped when she looked at Charmaine, who chopped one hand in the air.

"What the hell are you talking about?" Harrison followed her gaze to Charmaine.

Charmaine affected a neutral face. "No, sis. That was my cell phone. Probably Scotty calling me."

"Her boyfriend," Jessi added with a nod. She smiled when Harrison looked at her.

"I know who he is. You must be joined at the hip if he's calling you before the sun comes up." Harrison's dark eyebrows pulled together.

"It's our thing; a morning routine. He always calls before his early workout. You know, ex-military. Those habits stick." Charmaine strained out a smile when the beeping started again.

"You gonna answer?" Harrison cocked his head to one side as he gazed at Charmaine.

"Oh, it's fine. Scotty knows I keep strange hours sometimes. If he calls and Jessi doesn't reply, he'll know we're together." Charmaine pointed to her sister and then herself with a short laugh.

"Spirits never sleep, ya know," Jessi quipped. She cleared her throat loudly when Harrison stared at her.

"Not that we're here because of anything supernatural," Charmaine rushed to add. "Like I said, just plain old helping out a friend."

"Why is your phone in her bag?" Harrison's gaze ping-ponged between them.

"I, uh, asked Jessi to hold it cause... her bag is bigger." Charmaine's voice pitched up as if her answer was a question rather than a statement.

"You two are up to something." Harrison studied the two sisters in turn. He was about to speak when they were joined by the female uniform.

"Sir, the victim's wife is demanding to talk to whoever is in charge." The officer grimaced. "Making a big stink about who she knows, blah-blah."

As if on cue, a strident female voice rang in the night air. "You will give me answers right now! My husband is in Mobile on business. There's been a mistake!"

"Okay," Harrison replied. He looked at Charmaine and Jessi. "I'll deal with you two in a minute."

"Aw, c'mon. We gave our statements. It's obvious the guy had more fun than his old heart could stand. And you know Diamond is innocent," Jessi said with heat. "We've been here for freakin' *hours*, dude."

"What Jessi means is—" Charmaine chopped off her excuse at the granite frown on Harrison's face.

"I said, stay here. Right here." Harrison stabbed a forefinger at the dew-moistened grass beneath their feet.

"But we'll just be in the way," Charmaine pressed on bravely.

"Do you know who I am, officer?" A basso male voice cut through the night.

His protest was followed by a more voices joining him to argue with the female cop's partner. He stood surround by a group of four in an opposite corner of the front lawn. A handful of neighbors had emerged from their homes. The outnumbered officer wore a stiff mask as the lead speaker lectured him. The beeping from Jessi's bag started up again. She clutched it closer to muffle the sound. Although Harrison looked at Charmaine and Jessi again, the debate dragged his attention away. With a grunt, he marched over to rescue his colleague.

"Let's go find Diamond." Jessi pulled Charmaine by the arm. They went down a side path.

"What are you doing?" Charmaine jogged to keep from being dragged in Jessi's wake. They ended up in the backyard.

"Looking for a way past the crowd. Here we go." Jessi pointed to door with a glass upper half. "Only one cop in there. Okay, she left."

"Harrison is going to blow like a pipe bomb if he catches us," Charmaine whispered.

"He's going to be busy for a minute. Lucky for us."

Jessi pulled Charmaine along up the steps. Charmaine peeled her tight grip away from her arm when they reached the top step. She took a second to look around. Tan wicker furniture was in a corner of the back veranda. A short square of grass made up the backyard. A smaller cottage painted to match the main house sat at the end of another paved path.

"This place is luxe. Wonder color that is? I'm thinking about painting my house," Charmaine murmured.

"Girl, dead clown. Drugs all over the damn place. This is no time to go all HGTV," Jessi spat. She shoved Charmaine into a crouch. "Get down!"

Harrison followed the forensic officer into the brightly lit kitchen. "Okay. Check samples of the food. Rule out deliberate poisoning or something like salmonella."

The tech, her hands covered by gloves, put a sample in a tube and held it up to the light. "Should get results fast if we're not backed up."

"Hear that?" Harrison's handsome face twisted into a sour expression. Raised voices formed a background chorus. "That's the sound of important people expecting special treatment. Fast results will be much appreciated."

"Gotcha, boss," the woman said with a short laugh.

Minutes later they left. Jessi tried the gleaming polished brass door handle. She smiled when the lock clicked open. They moved with stealth across the hardwood floor, pressed against walls. Jessi peeked around corners before they'd proceed. Harrison's voice receded. Charmaine tried to calm her nerves so her telepathy might kick in. She squeaked at the cacophony that clanged in her head. Too many frightened, guilty voices. Once again, Charmaine wished her ability came with controls like Jessi's tools. She couldn't turn it on and off like a spigot. She rubbed her temples. At last, a few voices faded. She jumped when Jessi tapped her arm. She hadn't noticed that she was alone in a hallway.

"Harrison's out front dealing with the Karens. There's an alley between this place and the house next door. We'll circle around, get to your SUV, and go," Jessi said.

Diamond clasped her bag against her chest. "Sounds good to me."

Charmaine shook her head. "Harrison will—"

"We're not leaving the country, Char. He knows where to find us," Jessi hissed.

"Right. And we did cooperate by giving our statements. We're not running from the scene of a crime. Are we?" Charmaine looked over her shoulder and then at Jessi.

"The cops have a shit load of witnesses and forensic samples up to their noses. I don't think we'll be their priority. Now move," Jessi replied in a hushed voice.

She pushed Charmaine ahead of her to cut off any debate. Diamond didn't need convincing. She scurried in the lead as they returned to the kitchen. Minutes later they were out into the chill morning air. The sky had begun to show faint signs of daybreak. Short barks came from inside the neighboring house. They froze for a few seconds before trotting on toward the street.

None of the police officers or emergency medical attendants noticed them. Charmaine used her remote to unlock the Sportage. They slipped inside with Diamond scrambling in the back. She lay down on the seat. Charmaine held her breath as she turned the ignition. The sound didn't draw interest in their direction. She pulled away from curb into the street. A horn blast made her stomp the brake pedal.

"Shit!" Jessi sank down in the passenger seat as if that would help.

Charmaine waved an apology at a white Volvo sedan. "Sorry."

"Oh, Lord," Diamond whimpered from behind them.

"Stay calm. Wait! Don't go by the house," Jessi said.

"I'll attract attention if I try backing up and turning around. This street is crowded with all these vehicles," Charmaine replied. She dug a knit hat from the center console and covered her hair. Then she put on sunglasses.

"Right. Slow. But not too slow. But not too fast," Jessi breathed.

"Shush. I'm nerved up enough as it is." Charmaine gripped the steering wheel as she pulled onto the street.

They drove past the dwindling crowd in front of the house. Curious onlookers gawked at the commotion and not them. They were just another vehicle of early morning commuters going to work. At least that's what Charmaine prayed they looked like. She risked a darted glance at the red-doored house.

"You see him?" Jessi whispered from a hunkered-down position. Her bag of equipment had been shoved to the floor next to her feet.

"He must still be inside," Charmaine said.

Then she concentrated on taking slow breaths and watching traffic. Twenty-five minutes later they arrived at Charmaine's Esplanade Avenue home. Scotty's gray GMC Terrain was parked out front. All three heaved a sigh when Charmaine pulled into her driveway and cut the engine. Scotty opened the back door. He held up a mug and gestured for them to come in. As they entered Charmaine's cheery yellow and spice-orange kitchen, the welcome aroma of fresh brewed coffee greeted them.

"I figured something was up when you didn't answer my call or text," Scotty said. He put a full mug on the butcher block surface of the kitchen island. Then he hugged Charmaine tight and let her go. He gave Jessi's pal a look of curiosity. "Diamond went on a case?"

Jessi went to the spinning mug stand on the countertop. She grabbed one for herself and filled it. "You got time for a short version of the story or the long one?"

"There is no short version." Charmaine sighed as she sat on one of two bar stools at the island.

Diamond went to the small breakfast nook. She dropped her bag without looking to see where it landed. Then she plopped onto a chair at the table. Her heart-shaped, girlish face had a morose expression. "Shoot. Buddy was my golden duck."

"It's golden goose, girl. Here, I'm going to make you a cup of tea." Jessi put down her mug. She turned on a gas burner under a kettle on the stove. Then she found tea packets Charmaine had in a decorative basket.

"Thank y'all for showing up. No telling what the cops would've done to me if you hadn't. I've never been in jail for longer than a couple of nights." Diamond shivered and wrapped both arms around herself.

"Hey, it's not so bad after the first time," Jessi said with a grin.

"Well, I don't want to have a first time. My mother wouldn't keep Indyah long-term, not that I'd want her to. I don't believe in spanking. But that leaves my sister or my great aunt. Auntie Tee loves Indyah to pieces, but she's almost seventy and—"

Charmaine took her mug with her to sit at the table next to Diamond. "Honey, slow down. You're not going to jail. The police have no evidence you killed the clown."

Scotty choked on a mouthful of Louisiana dark roast. He coughed hard. Jessi rapped his broad back and handed him a napkin. He blinked hard as he wiped his lips. "I'm clearing my morning calendar to hear this, however long it takes."

"I want Indyah to have nothing but the best in life. That means a quality education. Her early years are the most formative, so I had to make sure she started off right. She'll get that at St. Mary's Academy," Diamond started. She wore a determined face.

"Nothing too good for our baby girl," Jessi put in with a sharp nod.

"Whew, those fees though. My boy Donnell's ex insists that his twins go there. His child support is a *lot*," Scotty replied.

"St. Mary's is worth it." Diamond heaved a sigh. "Mama says I think I'm so damn much, trying to be better than everybody else. Says that's what I get hanging out with boojie-ass Charmaine and—"

"Say what?" Charmaine's eyes widened in shock. "She was nice to me the times I met her."

"Oh, shit. That slipped out. Mama didn't mean it in a nasty way," Diamond rushed to explain, a hand on Charmaine's shoulder.

"Stop making excuses for her, Diamond. The woman is toxic. Always has been, always will be," Jessi retorted. "I know what she says behind my back. You don't have to tell me."

Diamond sighed. "Yeah, apologizing for mama is a bad habit of mine."

"So, what's her honest opinion of me?" Charmaine said.

"Well... that you think you're so much because you got a master's degree and wear secondhand designer brands." Diamond grimaced as she spoke.

"And she was all full of 'bless you' and 'you girls are so sweet' to my face." Charmaine shook her head.

"Belinda may go to church on Sundays and Bible study on Wednesdays, but she's all venom. Like a lot of so-called Christians," Jessi said with a grunt of derision. The kettle whistled as steam came from its spout. She poured hot water over the tea bag in a cup and handed it to Diamond.

"Thank you." Diamond sighed. "Anyway, Tranisha has an event company, Crescent City Entertainment."

"The dominatrix who used to work with y'all at the strip clubs? Oh, Diamond," Charmaine blurted out. "She's bad news."

"Harrison says the same about us, don't forget," Jessi said with a crooked grin. "Tranisha has always been good at business. She was the first one of us to get off the pole."

"Yeah, she made a fortune on her own first selling pics even before Only Fans blew up. She started with them way back in 2016," Diamond added.

"Right. A real pioneer," Charmaine mumbled and drank coffee.

"So, you started working for her to earn extra money," Scotty prompted to keep the story on track.

"Right. Flexible hours see. I can work my regular job at the hotel and pick up gigs on off hours. That's how I met Buddy."

"Buddy?" Scotty asked.

"Bernard Kennedy. Buddy is his nickname. He spoke at a Rotary Club luncheon at the hotel. Buddy recognized me from a party I'd booked a few months before. He was impressed that I didn't out him or anything. We got friendly and you know..."

"He became your private client." Charmaine worked to keep disapproval out of her tone, but she knew it came through.

"He likes to dress up and fetish play; armpits and feet are his thing. *Were* his thing. Poor guy." Diamond sighed and gulped tea.

"Old Buddy was a bundle of kinky," Jessi said. When Charmaine shot a look of reproach she added, "Rest in peace."

"Hey, I remember him. He served four terms in the legislature until 2016. A typical family values conservative." Scotty leaned against the kitchen counter, staring at his phone's screen. "Married for twenty-five years to his wife Loreen. Four kids, six grandchildren. Has a real estate outfit and an insurance company that specializes in property coverage. Commercial and residential."

"His oldest son and daughter took over when Buddy decided to run for office. Then he retired to spend more time with his family," Diamond said.

"And more free time for his other hobby," Jessi joked.

"His wife didn't understand his special needs. That's how he put it." Diamond shrugged when Charmaine raised both eyebrows in response.

"Typical trick. Justifies his craving for wild sex with no emotional involvement by blaming the wife." Jessi perched on bar stool and drank from her mug.

"He talked to you a lot, huh?" Charmaine gazed at Diamond.

"Buddy was okay. Like Jessi said, he was like a lot of men we meet. Anyway, I think he was working up to asking me to do the whole girlfriend experience. He liked that I was discreet and polished. That's how he put it." Diamond exchanged a knowing look with Jessi.

"Right. He didn't go for the rough street type," Jessi replied with a nod. "A lot of respectable white guys enjoy the 'urban Black girl' thing. Loads of cussing and dirty talk."

"Buddy loved to watch me dance to 'Back That Thang Up.'" Diamond giggled when Scotty's mouth dropped open.

"This guy?" Scotty held up his phone. A photo of Buddy in a suit looking every bit the straightlaced family man. An American flag served as a backdrop.

"Yep." Diamond and Jessi giggled harder.

"Okay, but how did he end up dead?" Scotty lowered the phone but continued to stare at the picture.

Diamond grew somber in seconds. "I think he had a heart attack from the excitement."

"But the police are keeping all options open, including murder because..." Scotty looked at all three at his prompt for more information.

"There was party favors at the place. Not me, and I didn't bring the stuff. I mean, a bunch of socialite types," Diamond said.

"Go figure. It's not just us hood types who do drugs," Jessi drawled.

"So, he died when he was with you." Scotty let out a slow whistle. "Bad."

"Second-degree murder is possible if drugs contributed to his death. But Diamond is in the clear," Jessi said.

"Right, she didn't provide the drugs. Though a negative might be hard to prove. Those upper-class types won't confess to supplying them," Charmaine replied.

"Yeah, and who better to take the heat than the hired entertainment," Scotty added with a frown.

"With a sketchy background. Oh Lord." Diamond squeezed her eyes shut.

"Stop the doomsday talk, folks. We're Gucci. I know who killed Chuckles." Jessi grinned at the round of shocked gasps her declaration produced.

Chapter 2
Prime Listings, Ghosts Included

Two days later, Charmaine sat before Det. Bryan Hezekiah Harrison. His office at the New Orleans Police Department District 5 station had a military kind of order. Files in a neat stack on one corner of his desk. He scowled a warning at her when she stretched her neck to read the labels upside down. Charmaine slid back in her seat with a smile. They needed to be on Harrison's good side. "They" meaning her, Jessi, and most especially Diamond. He was on the phone when Det. Ricky Ward led her to their meeting. Despite her silent look pleading him to stay, Ricky withdrew. He'd closed the door behind him with a decisive thump.

Harrison sat behind his desk, silent as he held the phone up to his ear. He gave monosyllabic answers to whoever was on the other end of the call. Yet his steely gaze stayed fixed on Charmaine. Jessi had a meeting at the law firm where she worked as a paralegal, so she hadn't come along. A fact that put Detective Harrison in an even more foul mood. Diamond was Jessi's best friend. By extension, he seemed to hold Jessi equally accountable for Diamond's involvement.

"Right. Thanks for the update." Harrison tapped the phone's screen and put it down with care on the desk. Then he rocked in the black executive chair for a few seconds, his fingers steepled.

"So, anyway, you have full statements from Jessi so her being here wouldn't change anything. We went over everything in detail that night, well morning. And the next day. You questioned Diamond yourself. I mean, she doesn't have motive." Charmaine cut off her flood of rationales when Harrison raised one large palm like a school crossing guard. She blew out a slow breath.

"How long?" Harrison transferred his gaze from a point on the ceiling to Charmaine's face.

"S'cuse me?" Charmaine blinked at him.

"How long have you and your sister been withholding information on a possible homicide from my investigator?"

"Now wait a minute. I know we've had our bumps in the road over the past year or so—"

"Years, plural. More than I want to think about. I've fished you two out of hot water too many times, Charmaine," Harrison shot back. He pointed a sturdy forefinger at her like a father lecturing an errant child.

"And we've helped you figure out tricky cases. Who have successfully kept supernatural-related crime out of the news? Us, that's who. Your professional reputation is intact because you haven't been laughed out of this nice office over ghosts and goblins." Charmaine pointed back at him. They now had dueling forefingers.

"Which I wouldn't have to think about if it wasn't for the Joliet Sisters. Sticking your noses all over New Orleans looking for..." Harrison dropped his hand. "Now Jessi says she knows who killed Kennedy."

"Not JFK. Now that would be a blockbuster." Charmaine smiled but let it fade at the heated look Harrison wore. "Sorry, too early in our case for a lighthearted moment, I guess."

"This isn't 'our' case. See, that's what's wrong with you two," Harrison grumbled.

"Look, I know the last time we worked together—" Charmaine cleared her throat at the groan from Harrison. Best not to touch the sore point of their collaborations. "I mean, we were involved with the whole Senator O'Donovan thing and it got messy."

"What is it with you and Louisiana politicians? You and your sister seem determined to ruin the entire legislature. And take my career down with em." Harrison picked up a pen from his desk and threw it down again.

"Commander Murphy has full confidence in you. He's grateful you kept details about the mayor's friends from being anything more than rumors. Those people did themselves in. They didn't deserve the cover you gave them," Charmaine said with a nod.

"Yeah, well." Harrison drummed his fingertips on the desk for a second. He squared his shoulders as if preparing for a blow. "Okay, spill it."

One sharp rap on the door was preceded by Jessi pushing it open. She held a tall paper cup from MoJo Coffee House. "Great, you're still here. Wrapped up the meeting early. The client agreed to settle. Lawsuit I helped work with one of the partners. So, where are we?"

"Maybe we should serve you a muffin, too. I mean, since you seem to have the run of this place," Harrison snapped.

"No thanks, but sounds like you could use another shot of caffeine. Here. Got this for you. A double shot Madrugada espresso with caramel. Just the way you like it."

Jessi planted the cup in front of him. She pulled a second chair from a small table nearby until it was next to Charmaine and sat. She dropped her compact purse on Harrison's desk and shrugged out of her dark brown leather jacket. She wiggled her butt in the chair to get comfy.

"I swear..." Harrison muttered something under his breath but picked up the cup. He drank it, swallowed, and closed his eyes in appreciation for a second. "You'll need to bring me more than espresso to get out of this mess."

"So, you can be bought," Jessi quipped with a grin.

"Not funny," Harrison snapped. "Not after what the department has just gone through."

Jessi adopted a serious expression. "Hey, you weren't part of police officers fiddling with their timesheets. I mean the head of the NOPD Public Integrity Unit of all people."

"Jessi, please," Charmaine whispered aside to her.

"I'm just saying," Jessi went on. "Bryan here has cleared some high profile cases. Hell, they should give him a promotion and a medal. If anybody plays by the rules, it's *you*."

Harrison took another large gulp from the cup and set it down. A deep chuckle rumbled from his throat as he loosened his dark gray tie. Two single thin red stripes gave it a touch of debonair. Jessi and Charmaine exchanged a look of surprise at the mood shift.

"Fancy coffee and butt kissing. Just the thing on a Monday to set my week on the right track." Harrison barked another short laugh.

"I'm a little hurt by the trace of cynicism in your tone, Bry—" Jessi flinched at his sharp look and course-corrected. "Detective Harrison."

"Everything points to Mr. Kennedy dying as a result of cardiac arrest. He had a heart condition, according to his doctor. But he made the mistake of mixing alcohol, drugs, and kinky sex with a woman young enough to be his granddaughter." Harrison spoke as if he was preparing a speech to his superiors.

"Check again," Jessi said.

Harrison's jaws clamped shut. His lips pressed into a hard line as silence stretched. "Meaning?"

"I have reliable info that he was given a dose of something on purpose. Have the labs runs tests for..." Jessi grabbed her purse to root around in it. She pulled out her cell phone, tapped the screen and nodded. "Phenobarbital. It's an old drug first use to treat seizures. Sometimes used during alcohol detox."

"Seizures are possible and can be intense enough to be fatal," Charmaine added. "I worked in a short-term psych unit. Doctors would use the drug when we admitted people with an addiction. Including alcohol."

"No mention made of Kennedy being an alcoholic," Harrison replied, his face neutral. "And that fancy address had more drugs than a pharmacy. At any rate, like I said. He had a heart condition."

"Actually, Bernard Kennedy, age sixty-three, had mild CAD or coronary artery disease. He was diagnosed in 2022. His health and his age became an issue last year when he ran for Congress. His opponent was thirty-two at the time. Kennedy spoke openly about his healthcare. A combination of diet and exercise resulted in a reversal of some of the damage." Jessi read notes from her cell phone like a reporter on the morning news. She looked up at Harrison. "Old dude was in fairly good shape. Sort of like you."

"I'm forty-seven," Harrison snipped.

"Exactly." Jessi smiled at him. "Great looking and solid for a middle-aged guy."

"The espresso isn't *that* delicious." Harrison's dark eyebrows pulled together to give his handsome face a sour look. "Now skip to the explanation about how you got this information."

Jessi tapped her cell phone against her chin for a few seconds. "Ah, the part about his health is public. News articles all over Obama's Internet."

"Uh-uh. So, Kennedy was in good health for a man his age. He was obviously up for vigorous fun with your friend..." Harrison paused and flipped open the top folder on his desk. "Diamond Phillips. Two arrests for soliciting at age eighteen and twenty-one. Judges in both instances took into account a 'troubled childhood'. She worked a few strip clubs."

"And she had no motive to kill the guy," Jessi said with force. "His wife has a long list of reasons to see him gone for good. Don't believe the grieving widow act she's putting on. Oh, and she has her own political ambitions."

"Here in NOPD and at the DA's office, we are picky. We need evidence, not crazy allegations. Having a rotten marriage doesn't cut it," Harrison countered. "His wife wasn't at the party. Insists she didn't even know he was there. Kennedy told her he was going to be at a real estate conference in Mobile for the weekend, which she also suspected was a lie. She knew he was having an affair. Fact is, she didn't care."

"Oh, she cared alright. Check into her Internet searches. Loreen Kennedy killed her husband. She ordered pheno-whats-it from an online drug site. Replaced it with his little pills to keep his joystick going for hours. Boom! Sleaze-ball hubby problem solved. And it looks like he had a heart attack," Jessi said.

"Hacking is illegal," Harrison replied in a flat tone. His stony gaze went from Jessi to Charmaine. "You need to keep an eye on your sister. She's going to land you both in court. Not to mention get your private security license pulled."

"I didn't misuse or share any information for the purpose of fraud. I read the statutes, you know. Plus, any knowledge I've gained is in the pubic interest of catching a killer. Not that you could prove I hacked Kennedy's Wi-Fi." Jessi snapped her fingers to get his attention. She raised an eyebrow when Harrison looked at her again.

Harrison heaved a sigh. "Look, I don't have the time or resources to chase down the tricks you pull."

Charmaine blinked at the flood of info bombarding her brain. "You got the tox screen results just now on that phone call. Bernard Kennedy had a lethal dose phenobarbital in his system. There was powder cocaine at the party and blunts. No barbiturates."

"How did you come up with the wild theory about his wife?" Harrison continued to stare at Jessi with a frown. He ignored Charmaine's burst of mind reading.

"Hmm, you're going to like the answer even less than the bit about her computer searches." Jessi gave Charmaine a side glance.

"Might as well rip the bandage off," Charmaine said as she rubbed her temples. She pushed Harrison's inner voice, the same baritone as his speaking one, from her head. The sensation brought on a short bout of wooziness.

The detective leaned back in his chair. "If you say—"

"A ghost at the house told me, yeah. Now before you lose it let me explain. Delilah only pointed me in the right direction. She heard him having an argument with his wife. Loreen called his cell phone and for some strange reason Kennedy answered. If you're cheating on the wife, wouldn't a guy just ignore the call?" Jessi looked at Charmaine.

"Not necessarily. I mean, he's going to keep up the lie that he's at a conference. Makes sense the husband would answer and act like he's where he said." Charmaine and Jessi looked at Harrison.

"Don't ask me," Harrison shot back with an irritated frown.

"Anyway, the convo was hot. Kennedy called his wife a few choice names. Something about she'd better not touch the investment accounts. There you have it. Money, jealousy, revenge for humiliating her. Case closed." Jessi nodded as she looked at Charmaine.

"Let me get on the phone right now with the DA. Let him know a ghost is going to be his star witness. A judge will have no problem issuing an arrest warrant," Harrison said and threw up both hands. His voice got louder as he ranted. "We'll form a support group. Former criminal justice officials thrown out of their jobs because they listened to ghost chasers."

Det. Ricky Ward stuck his head in the door. "You okay, boss?"

"Oh, it's always a fun time when these two show up to my office," Harrison hissed.

"Hey, you invited us," Jessi retorted.

"Because you were at the crime scene, and it wasn't an invitation. You're being questioned as persons of interest. Then you come in here with a crazy-ass story about a prominent man's wife killing him. Wait, Ricky. It gets better. They had a séance and a spirit from the other side told them."

"We don't hold séances. Spirits are energy, Bryan. It's science!" Jessi squinted at him. "And I followed solid leads to give you people the goods. You're welcome."

"Listen, Bryan, we're just trying to help..." Charmaine placed a restraining hand on Jessi's arm, afraid her sister would leap across the desk.

"Stop calling me Bryan like were old school mates," Harrison growled.

"Good point. We were still in diapers when you joined NOPD," Jessi replied with fire in her tone. "And we're still better investigators than you."

"You know what, I'm going to get you booked." Harrison stood and glowered at the two women.

"Uh, let's think about that for a minute," Detective Ward entered the office and shut the door."

"I'm not going to go quietly, Bryan," Jessi replied, her voice raised as well. She stood and planted both palms on Harrison's desk.

"We all need to take a break and consider reasonable options," Charmaine put in using her best social worker voice. She looked at Ricky for help.

"Right. Loreen Kennedy is well connected," Detective Ward answered on cue. "Anything involving her has to be solid and documented."

"Do you really want word to get out that psychics are saying NOPD uses ghosts as informants?" Charmaine spoke in a normal tone in an effort to stop the shouting match. "If this discussion gets any louder, you might as well issue a press release."

Harrison's eyes narrowed to slits. Then for a few moments he paced in a short circle. Charmaine spoke low to Jessi, her tone an urgent whisper to calm down. Detective Ward chose to let his boss cool off without interference. After a few minutes Harrison, Jessi, and Charmaine sat in their chairs again. Detective Ward stood at the right corner of Harrison's desk. Charmaine wondered if he was showing support for his boss or stayed close to keep Harrison from trying to strangle them. Probably both. After a few more seconds of charged silence, Harrison blew out air.

"This department doesn't follow leads based on messages from ghosts," Harrison said, his deep voice sounding strained.

Jessi glanced at Charmaine before she spoke in a level tone. "Of course, we understand your position, Detective Harrison. Which is why we dug deeper. I'm sure your officers would have turned up information about problems in the marriage. And the autopsy would confirm that Kennedy died of barbiturate poisoning."

"Given the circumstances, naturally you were going to look at everyone connected to the case," Charmaine added. "I know our unique approach to private investigation is bit... tricky for you."

"Understatement," Harrison rumbled.

"So, that's why we make it a point to get facts you can actually use," Charmaine went on despite his crack. Then she looked at her sister.

"Sorry for blowing up." Jessi winced and hissed a sigh. She pressed her lips closed as if the terse apology was all she could manage.

"We've been bullied most of our lives about having extrasensory skills. Kind of a sore spot. Anyway, Jessi didn't break any laws." Charmaine didn't flinch at the sharp look Harrison gave her. "You were going to look at the wife anyway. Those closest to the victim have to be considered. Prominent family or not."

"Examining digital devices is standard procedure." Detective Ward nodded assent.

"You knew about this so-called ghostly lead?" Harrison at Detective Ward and then at Jessi. He knew they were dating.

Charmaine read them both. Harrison had advised Ricky against any involvement with Jessi, especially a romantic one. In fact, he'd warned him to avoid both sisters. Harrison gazed at him with an impassive expression. The attractive redhead turned a shade of light pink.

"Jessi told me about it this morning." Detective Ward gave a slight shrug under Harrison's glare. "Not about her web search though."

"Gee thanks. Throw me under the bus, Ricky," Jessi muttered.

"Look, we're all after the same thing. Getting to the truth." Detective Ward looked at Charmaine.

"Right. We share info and cases get solved. Win-win." Charmaine smiled at everyone.

"Okay, Miss Sunshine Social Worker," Jessi joked.

"Get Mrs. Kennedy's computer, tablet, or whatever. Phone records as well," Harrison said to Detective Ward.

"Officers are at the Kennedy home as we speak, sir. I sent Olstead. She's from one of those old families and speaks their language. Oh, and we gave the family attorney a heads up," Detective Ward replied in a crisp all-cop business tone.

"Hmm, the mayor hasn't called our super," Harrison murmured, referring to the superintendent over the 5th District. He cast a glance at his phone as if expecting it to bite. "Otherwise, I'd have heard from them bright and early."

"The mayor and his buddies got burned the last time with Senator McDonald. He's learned a lesson from jumping in too soon." Jessi smirked when Harrison grunted.

"Yeah, keeping them off my ass is the only silver lining. They do step lightly these days," Harrison agreed.

Jessi stood and took a bow. "Again, you're welcome."

"Don't push it. Give Ricky the name of Kennedy's alleged lover. I want to follow up on potential hidden cracks in their publicly solid family life," Harrison said.

"Sure," Charmaine said before Jessi spoke. She heard the protest forming on her sister's lips. She shot a warning glance at Jessi. "We're in full cooperation mode."

"She might talk to one of us more freely though," Jessi pressed on. She made it a point not to look at Charmaine.

"You've done enough. Am I clear?" Harrison enunciated each word as he stared at Jessi and then Charmaine.

Charmaine stood next to Jessi. "As plastic wrap. We don't have any more information to share but if we come across anything else—"

"I don't like to repeat myself," Harrison broke in.

"Meaning, details we already uncovered or documented and haven't shared," Charmaine added quickly. "I'll review our notes and inform you or Detective Ward ASAP."

"Yeah. This thing has a lot of moving parts. Plus, Diamond is still shook up. She might remember something else," Jessi added.

"In which case we'll make sure you hear about it first," Charmaine added. She forced a smile in the face of Harrison's stone-faced stare.

"Let us know what you find out from the digital forensics..." Jessi stopped when Harrison's steady gaze fixed on her.

"Information will flow one way. From you to my officers." Harrison looked from Jessi to Detective Ward, who nodded.

"Have a great Monday, Detective Harrison." Charmaine nudged Jessi with an elbow in the direction of the office door.

Detectivew Ward followed them through the door. None of the three risked a look back as they left. Minutes later the trio stood in a corner of the narrow lobby. Activity bustled around them. Ricky let out a long breath as if he'd been holding it inside Harrison's office.

"Almost got my ass chewed. Again. The boss hates cases that involve rich, connected types," Ricky said.

"Yeah. Way to save yourself and leave me open to get blasted." Jessi jabbed a forefinger in his chest.

"But you didn't tell me about the internet search, Jess."

Ricky put a hand over hers. He brushed a light kiss over the back of her hand. Dressed in a navy-blue sweater over a light blue dress shirt and tie, he looked like a young community college professor. His reddish-blond hair was brushed into a neat short cut. Ricky wore a look of affection as he gazed at Jessi.

Jessi smoothed the indentation her finger had made in the knit fabric. "Whatever. You still better make it up to me."

"I can order in food and you can meet me at mine," Ricky spoke in a low, intimate tone. "Doubt I'll have to work late today."

"Because we basically solved the latest sticky case for you guys. Again. Huge debt, sir." Jessi wiggled her eyebrows at him.

"I'll pay more than the minimum, I promise." Ricky grinned as they shared a laugh.

"Oh, pu-leeze." Charmaine rolled her eyes.

"Hey, I put up with you and Scotty mooning over each other," Jessi stuck her tongue out at Charmaine.

Charmaine took out her buzzing cell phone. "I need to hustle if I'm going to make my first therapy appointment. Lucky for me, my schedule is flexible."

"I gotta head over to UNO to do some research." Jessi pulled the clasp on her purse strap until it was long. She looped it over her head cross-body style.

"I don't want to hear anymore," Ricky said to Jessi as he backed away, both palms up.

"Scaredy pants," Jessi teased. "Anyway, it's got nothing to do with your delicate case."

"Great. Text you when I head home." Ricky gave a parting wave that included Charmaine and strode off.

"Nothing to do with Kennedy?" Charmaine snorted as she looked at Jessi. Then she headed for the glass public exit doors of the 5th District station.

"Stay out of my head," Jessi shot back with an annoyed frown.

"Lord, don't I wish I could turn this thing on and off," Charmaine muttered.

"We might have a new client. A lucrative one at that." Jessi followed Charmaine to the visitors parking lot.

Charmaine arrived at her SUV, hit the remote to unlock it, and faced Jessi. She held out a palm. "Good. You need to pay for your expensive ghost-busting toys. Give it."

"The upgraded full-spectrum HD cam will pay for itself," Jessi protested. When Charmaine's implacable demeanor didn't change, she heaved a sigh. She searched a pocket in her bag for a few seconds. Then she slapped a slim company credit card onto Charmaine's hand. "Putting me on restriction like I'm a kid."

"Because you spend our money like one." Charmaine put the card in her own purse. "Stay out of Harrison's case."

"Yes, mama. Whatever you say, mama."

Jessi pouted when Charmaine flipped middle finger at her. She mumbled complaints mixed with expletives. Jessi's phone rang, the ringtone a neo-soul tune. She smiled at the profile photo that showed on the screen and answered.

For the following two days both sisters were busy with their respective day jobs. Charmaine had left her job working for the local health district. She now worked for a private behavioral health clinic. The salary boost had been a nice part of the employment package. Jessi did contract work for two law firms, preferring not to be an employee. By Thursday afternoon they finally met up at their agency office, a room attached to Charmaine's house on Esplanade Avenue. A breezeway separated the business from her personal space. On occasion they saw clients there but not often. Today was different. Jessi had declared her as "harmless." Not because they were concerned about their physical safety. Because they dealt with the supernatural, sometimes disturbed entities followed people. Those consulting the sisters weren't always truthful or blameless. A particularly vengeful spirit might attach itself to a target. Charmaine didn't want her cute cottage to become haunted.

At five o'clock on the dot, the plump brunette arrived. She wore a black suit jacket over a houndstooth pencil skirt. Gina Garcia-Shaw sat across from Charmaine, taking in the décor. Gina held her genuine leather satchel purse on her lap like a shield. As usual, Jessi was running late. Which left Charmaine with the task of extending hospitality to their potential customer. Charmaine poured hot coffee from a decorative ceramic pot into a matching cup. She had bought the set especially for the office. Cold wind blew against the window and Ms. Garcia-Shaw started. She let out a nervous titter when Charmaine looked up at her.

"Horrible weather. Thank God for short Louisiana winters, right?" Gina accepted the cup. She stared down at it instead of drinking for a few seconds. Then she raised it to her lips and took a dainty sip.

"Right."

Charmaine resisted the urge to sarcastically assure her the cup was clean. She didn't need telepathy to sense the woman's unease. Gina Garcia-Shaw wasn't used to regular contact with Black women. At least not those who weren't service workers.

Gentrification had sunk its claws into New Orleans after the destructive force of Hurricane Katrina. The pace had quickened with two subsequent storms in the following two years. Poverty prevented a lot of those who lost everything from rebuilding. People lost homes that had been in their families for generations.

The lack of clear property titles resulted from a succession of owners not leaving wills. That, combined with no money to pay taxes, led to property being acquired by developers. Like Ms. Garcia-Shaw. Charmaine had visited her slick website. The woman even had a short-run reality show about restoring and flipping luxury homes in the Greater New Orleans area. Still, Charmaine needed to push down her distaste over the first impression.

"Charming home," Gina said to break the heavy silence. She looked around. "Transitional in the main house?"

"Sorry?" Charmaine blinked at her.

"The décor. Like modern, farmhouse, traditional," Gina said, ticking off home design styles. The real estate agent in her seemed to take over. She rose and went to a window. "Great how you separated your office from the residential portion. Did you inherit?"

"Hmm. My great-aunt didn't have any children. She left it to our mother. This was originally her beauty salon back in the late seventies." Charmaine listened to appraisal values being calculated in Gina's mind.

"Very unusual," Gina murmured.

"Yes, Aunt Mamie actually did estate planning with a lawyer and everything." Charmaine smiled with Gina left the window and resumed her seat.

"Lovely restoration. Was their much damage after the storm?" Gina had lost interest after sensing a quick acquisition was unlikely. She picked up the cup again, sipped, and put it down on the edge of Charmaine's desk.

"We were lucky. The flood waters didn't touch it. So, you mentioned using our investigative services related to your business. How did you find us?" Charmaine asked.

Her telepathy had annoyingly switched off. Sometimes it was unpredictable as a cat; came and went as it pleased.

"Well... I work with Buddy Kennedy. Worked with." Gina took up the coffee cup. Her gulp was less refined this time, as though she needed the caffeine to continue. "You and your partner were listed as witnesses on the scene. I did a search and found your Instagram page. For Joliet Investigations."

Jessi came in using her code to unlock the outside door. "Sorry I'm late. Work got a bit crazy and... Oh, she's here early. I thought you said six." She glanced at the decorative clock on one wall.

Charmaine suppressed a sigh. She'd asked Jessi to arrive early so they could talk about the potential client. "It's okay. Ms. Garcia-Shaw was just starting to explain how she found us."

Jessi dropped her satchel on the floor. Then shrugged out of her deep red leather moto jacket. Her slender black slacks were a nod to the need to dress professional for law offices. She wore a light gray button front shirt tucked into them. Jessi brushed her long braids over one shoulder and sat in the extra chair, flashing a brief professional smile at Gina.

"Great. I haven't missed anything."

"I was just saying, this is awkward." Gina broke off and fiddled with the strap of her purse.

"Ms. Garci-Shaw—"

"Gina is fine."

"Sure," Charmaine replied with a nod. "She knew Bernard Kennedy. And that we were at the house the night, he, you know."

"Was murdered," Jessi said with blunt force.

Gina flinched the lack of gloss put on his demise. "The lawyer we use is friends with Mrs. Kennedy's family attorney and, long story short I learned who was there. I wasn't familiar with you or Ms. Phillips, so I did a bit of research. When I found your agency profile, I decided to contact you."

"Because of Mr. Kennedy's death?" Charmaine wore a baffled frown.

"Not directly. You see Mr. Kennedy, Buddy, invested in my firm. We've been very successful in helping buyers find homes locally. We'll definitely miss him."

"Yes, he had an insurance business specializing in residential and commercial properties. He also was into real estate," Jessi said.

"His family has owned lots in New Orleans for over one hundred years. His great-grandfather had a small carpentry business and ran a hardware store," Gina said. "His family and mine have known each for years."

"The haves," Jessi mumbled.

"Pardon?" Gina blinked at her.

"I said I'll have a coffee, too. Go on." Jessi poured the dark liquid into a third cup. She avoided glancing at Charmaine.

"Yes, please," Charmaine put in. She would have the umpteenth talk with Jessi about her smart mouth later.

"I admit I did some digging about your unusual specialty. Prior cases, I mean, involving..."

"Ghosts," Jessi replied.

Gina jumped as though Jessi had yelled "Boo!" She squeaked when coffee spilled on her skirt. "I'm sorry. Your nice floors."

Charmaine grabbed a handful of paper napkins from the tray holding the pot and cups. "Let me dab some water to keep the stain from setting."

Charmaine and Gina got into a minor tussle over who should apologize for the mishap. Gina insisted on wiping up the tiny puddle from the laminate. Charmaine hurried to the house to get a damp cloth and stain remover. She helped clean Gina's skirt until the brown spot was hardly visible. Jessi watched it all without lifting a finger or offering. She took her tablet computer her satchel and scrolled through screens for a few seconds. When Gina and Charmaine had settled into their seats again, Jessi looked up.

"We don't investigate criminal matters. The police kinda get annoyed when folks cross their turf." Jessi lifted one shapely eyebrow at her.

"What? Oh, no. I understand that. The police have their job to do. Loreen is quite upset." Gina looked from Jessi to Charmaine. "According to her lawyer."

"Umm, yeah. Questioning the people closest to a victim is standard procedure," Charmaine put in. She didn't need to read Gina's mind to know the woman wanted the inside scoop. "So, what can we do for you?"

"NOPD been in touch?" Jessi gazed at her with interest.

"Yes, but I'm not a suspect, naturally," Gina blurted out and blinked rapidly. "We went in together on three properties Buddy owned, yes. Our business dealings went smoothly."

"Okay," Charmaine replied quickly to head off the wisecrack forming on Jessi lips.

"As you probably know from researching my business, we represent about sixty homes. Twelve we own outright. They're historic properties, including in Plaquemines, St. Charles and St. Tammany Parishes. Those are in various stages of restoration. We have a lot of interested buyers. The cost of living here is more affordable than other places. Now with remote work, people aren't tied to an expensive city," Gina said.

"Yeah." Jessi's dry tone spoke volumes.

Charmaine shot a warning look at her sister. "Sounds lucrative."

Jessi's judgmental scowl softened at the mention of money. "How can we assist you?"

"Several of the homes are problematic. Workers won't return to one because of unusual activity. Of a supernatural nature. My partner Conner thinks it a bunch of superstitious nonsense. But we have competitors willing to hire our contract staff and the delays will cost us a lot of money." Gina heaved a sigh. "I'm not saying I believe in apparitions or anything. But we have to *do something.*"

"You need us to complete a paranormal investigation," Charmaine said.

"Ghostbusting services," Jessi added.

"I noticed you were able to keep talk of spirits out the media on at least two prior cases. This has to be kept... discreet. Reputation is everything in our business. Never mind stories about haunted mansions would scare off buyers." Gina grimaced as if losing money frightened her more than ghosts.

Jessi smiled. A nice payday always improved her attitude. "We specialize in flying under the radar."

Chapter 3
So Many Spirits, So Little Time

The next day, Charmaine settled into her office at the clinic. She had a hard time concentrating. So, she took a few minutes for a mindfulness exercise. It wouldn't do to be distracted during a therapy session. By lunchtime she felt drained. She'd have to speak to reception again about scheduling depressed clients back-to-back. After a light meal of chicken and sausage gumbo at a nearby deli, Charmaine felt refreshed. The rest of the early afternoon went by quickly. She managed to finish notes from her morning sessions before the last appointment of the day at three o'clock. Charmaine sighed at the name on the calendar app. Andre Fisher, aka "Dray-Dray." Speaking of challenging sessions.

"Let me talk to Sharon right now," Charmaine muttered. She picked up the handset of her office phone. A knock on the door made her put it down again.

Andre stuck his head in the door and winked at her. "It's your favorite schizo guy. May I enter?"

"You're almost in anyway." Charmaine couldn't help but smile. When he was stable, Andre could be a real charmer.

"I know, I know. Boundaries, blah-blah." Andre ambled in. He did a quick turn, arms outstretched. "You like the fit?"

Charmaine's clinical observation mode activated. Bright colors in multiple layers was one sign Andre was decompensating. But he was dressed in an olive-green sweater with a green checked shirt beneath. His brown slacks looked threadbare but clean. His short locs looked neat as well. At forty-seven, the tall, lanky man cut a handsome figure when he was well groomed. When his symptoms were acute, Andre walked with a shuffling gait and muttered to himself. Though harmless, his odd appearance frightened strangers. Charmaine worried that his agitated behavior might get him hurt by the police one day.

"Very nice. Who helped put that outfit together?" Charmaine gestured to the chair next to her desk.

Andre sat and crossed his arms. His thick dark eyebrows drew together in a serious look. "You trying to say I'm too nuts to dress myself?"

"Of course not. I—" Charmaine stopped when he chuckled and waved a hand at her.

"I'm just picking at you, Ms. C. And stop making me feel even older than I look. Call me Andre."

"We talked about this." Charmaine glanced at the screen of her office laptop. Then she switched to wallpaper image.

"Right. I deserve to be addressed formally. You're almost two decades younger than me. And it helps my sense of self-worth," Andre said, ticking off the points they had discussed in several previous sessions.

Two more positive signs, Charmaine noted. Clear thinking and a good memory. "Tell me what's been going on."

"Well as you already know, I've been keeping my appointments with Dr. Mendoza," Andre said, referring to his assigned psychiatrist.

"How's the medication change going for you?" Charmaine leaned back in her chair, relieved that he was doing better. And if she was honest, she was relieved for herself, too. She wouldn't end her taxing day dealing with the intense paranoid ramblings he exhibited when he wasn't.

"No drooling. The nausea is better. Sometimes it's better to be crazy than to feel like shit all day, every day. Y'all need to come up with something better," Andre quipped. He raised a palm at her again. "Don't worry. I'm not going off the meds. I've lost too much already." His lighthearted expression dimmed.

Andre had been married years ago. His descent into psychosis and resistance to treatment led to divorce and limited contact with his two children. His career as an engineer had also suffered.

"But now you have an understanding employer and a supportive network of family," Charmaine said in a gentle tone. "Dr. Mendoza can always adjust the dosage if the side effects become too much."

"Yeah. Glass half-full, huh?" Andre sighed.

The rest of their hour together was spent going over his Wellness and Recovery Plan, or WRAP. They reviewed the signs that his symptoms were escalating. His father and older brother were the two people to be contacted in the early stages of trouble. Charmaine was encouraged by his determination to maintain his progress.

"You should feel good about where you are right now," Charmaine said as she began to end their time together.

"I do. I do. I'm glad to be reconnected to my family. I even talk to Aunt Lydia. She's my godmother, too. I had Sunday brunch with her this past weekend." Andre wore a wide smile.

"That's wonderful."

"She's forgiven me for scaring her and knocking holes in her walls thinking somebody had planted listening devices in them. That wasn't one of my finest moments. Four years before she even spoke to me again." Andre shook his head. "She was even able to joke about it. Said it forced her to get rid of that ugly old wallpaper and redecorate."

"Sounds like she cares about you." Charmaine smiled.

"That's why I was thinking maybe you could help her," Andre replied.

"Sure. We can schedule a family session with just the two of you and—"

"No, no. That's not what I mean. I'm talking about your side hustle. See, Auntie has this property that developers are trying to get at but she doesn't have clear title."

"Sounds like she needs a lawyer."

Andre leaned forward. "She needs to prove this land has been in the family. See, my great-great grandparents didn't leave a will. But we've had relatives living in the house for decades no problem. Then Hurricane Katrina happened. Both houses were knocked flat. The city forced demolition, health and safety ordinance. We finally paid the back taxes. Well, almost all of the full amount."

"Again, this all sounds like a legal issue, Mr. Fisher."

"But see, with some historical research we can establish ownership at least by occupation by the same family. Plus, and don't think I'm hallucinating again... my aunt feels like my great-grandmother might be able to tell us where documents are hidden."

Charmaine blinked at him in confusion. "You want us to interview her? Where does she live?"

"Nowhere. Um, she died in nineteen sixty-six. Aunt Lydia has been trying to contact her. My dad and other family have tried talking her out of it. She's been scammed out of over three thousand dollars so far by fake mediums." Andre made air quotes with his fingers around the word.

"Okay." Charmaine started to speak but his raised palm stopped her.

"No, being delusional doesn't run on that side of the family. Anyway, dad and Uncle Roger, that's dad's younger brother, says maybe she'll listen to me. No go. Her only son died in an accident when I was a kid. Maybe that's why we became so close. Anyway, she's set on trying again. I don't want her to go broke and lose her property."

"Listen, Mr. Fisher—"

"I know your private detective agency handles special cases, you know, with spirits. Not that I believe in that stuff. I'm not that crazy," Andre said with a chuckle and then grew serious. "No offense. I mean, I'm not making fun of your business."

"None taken. I'm not sure getting involved is a good idea." Charmaine frowned in thought.

"She can afford to pay," Andre put in quickly.

"Our fee isn't the issue, Mr. Fisher. My getting involved could be seen as a professional conflict."

"Just say you'll think about it at least. Those folks at Shaw Real Estate are coming after her with big guns. Please."

Charmaine gasped in surprise. "Did you say Shaw Real Estate?"

"Hell, yes, we'll take the case. Three great reasons." Jessi raised three fingers. "One, we'll get more intel on our client Gina Shaw. Two, we'll help a little old lady in distress. And three, more money."

"Sounds reasonable to me," Diamond added.

They sat around Jessi's eat-in kitchen table enjoying Greek takeout. White paper bags littered the counter where they'd unpacked the food. Diamond was still considered a "person of interest" in Bernard Kennedy's death. So, she joined them for dinner to get an update. Her little girl Indyah sat cross-legged on Jessi's living room floor. The five-year-old nibbled on pita bread and roasted chicken while watching Tab Time on YouTube. The adults could see her across the space of the open kitchen.

"Don't you think this is another wild coincidence? First, Gina Shaw shows up and now this. Both connected to a murder." Charmaine said the last sentence low with a glance in Indyah's direction.

"Could be. On the other hand, that's reason number four. Somebody is trying to play us. But how would Gina or anyone know this guy sees you at the clinic? You won't even tell us his name." Jessi stuffed a forkful of gyros in her mouth.

"Good point," Diamond said with a nod. She looked at Charmaine.

"You'll find out if we do. No way around it. Look, this could be an ethical conflict for me. I don't want to be accused of using the clinic to drum up business for Joliet Investigations," Charmaine countered.

Jessi wiped her mouth with a paper towel. She swigged down a gulp of Lebanese tea before answering. "So, what if we learn who Mr. X is? First off, he's not our client. Is he going to pay Joliet Investigations?"

"He says his aunt will," Diamond put in before Charmaine had a chance to speak.

"Right. Which means you're not using him for profit. Does he have an ownership in the property?" Jessi turned to Charmaine.

"I'm not sure. He didn't mention it, but it's family property and he's obviously family." Charmaine clicked her tongue. "I should have asked, but he caught me off guard. I try to keep our agency separate from my therapy practice at the clinic."

"I can check public records. Unless he's in her will or something, then he's not a direct descendant. You already said even his aunt doesn't have clear title. I'll act as your legal rep if anyone files an ethics complaint." Jessi grinned at Charmaine and dug into her plate of food again.

"I don't want there to be a complaint in the first place. Let alone a hearing before the licensing board. Oh, and let me remind you Joliet Investigations isn't stable enough for me to go full time. Besides, I *like* being a social worker." Charmaine fed her anxiety with a mound of moussaka.

"Relax, sis. Use one of those yoga things you're always rambling on about," Jessi quipped. She sighed when Charmaine glared at her. "Your do-gooder career is safe. I promise."

"Not that you haven't dropped me into big trouble before, right?" Charmaine muttered around a mouthful.

"Run it by the licensing board if you're so worried. Meanwhile I'll check on the property. The Orleans Parish Assessor's office is a good place to start. Then I can track down land sales, mortgages, and building contracts. You said there were at least two houses, right?"

Charmaine nodded. She washed down the food with tea. "City forced demolition. Floodwater made them total losses."

"So that's settled. You'll take the aunt's case." Diamond waved a hand as if the subject was closed. "Let's get back to the more important problem. Me being a murder suspect."

"Harrison doesn't seriously consider you as a suspect, Diamond," Jessi said.

"We talked to him. He's looking at a few other people with stronger motives. You wouldn't benefit from his death," Charmaine added. When Diamond avoided her gaze and fidgeted with her fork in her hand, Charmaine stared at her hard.

"The police will probably be glad to leave you out of it. Old Buddy boy had low friends in high places. They want to avoid a scandal. Plus, we put Harrison onto Mrs. Kennedy. The spouse is always considered first." Jessi started to go on but paused. She glanced from Charmaine to Diamond. "What's going on?"

"I think Diamond has something to tell us." Charmaine squinted at Diamond before she glanced at Jessi. "Can't quite make it out, but something is up."

Jessi studied her long-time friend. They'd known each other since the sixth grade. "She chews her bottom lip and can't look you in the eye when she's guilty."

Diamond took her takeout plate to the kitchen trashcan and tossed it in. Then she got busy throwing away bags. When she started wiping down the counters with a damp dishcloth, Charmaine left her chair and pulled it from Diamond's hand.

"Stop using that magic stuff on me." Diamond turned away from her only to face Jessi.

"You might as well tell us. Like you said, magic." Jessi pointed her forefinger at Diamond's nose.

"I met Buddy when I was looking for an affordable place to stay a couple of three, maybe four years ago. He may have paid my rent for a few months." Diamond cleared her throat. "And maybe got me a good price for my little house. Then the stupid pandemic happened and things got tight. Maybe he paid my mortgage a couple of times."

"*Maybe* you got thousands of dollars from the man? All of a sudden, your memory is fuzzy on the details. Lord have mercy," Charmaine blurted.

"Change maybe to for sure he paid those bills. You became his sugar baby." Jessi pursed her lips and frowned.

"I got a job and stopped taking his money though. Then a spot opened at St. Mary's for Indyah. Tranisha offered me a job. Buddy was one of her customers and... well, long story short we hooked up again." Diamond lifted her chin. "I don't have to tell y'all all my personal business."

"No, but it might help since you were at the scene of a *murder*. Us knowing everything about your relationship to the victim before the police could help," Charmaine snapped.

"A hell of a lot for damn sure." Jessi put both hands on her hips.

"Maybe they won't find out. I mean, him helping with my house situation was a long time ago. And why would I kill the guy giving me money?" Diamond waved both arms to punctuate her argument.

"The cops will find out. They're not all stupid," Jessi said.

"Not Harrison and Ricky," Charmaine agreed.

"The police wouldn't pick on me. You said his wife is the one. She'll get houses, land, a piece of his businesses, and bank accounts. He was always cheating on her, too." Diamond's voice went high from stress.

"Which is exactly what we pointed out to Harrison. Wait a minute. You know a lot about who gets what." Jessi's raised both arched eyebrows at Diamond.

"Buddy had a lot on his mind what with running multiple business deals and his political career." Diamond crossed her arms in a defensive posture. "I can't help if the dude confided in me."

"That cute naïve face always did have men spilling their secrets," Jessi said. "When we were in the life, Diamond's little girl charm in a sexy body worked wonders."

"And got you two arrested for extortion and rolling a man. Both of those guys were too embarrassed to press the cases. Lucky for you. It's the only reason you didn't get jail time." Charmaine gave them a scowl of disapproval.

"We've changed our wicked ways. Now we're respectable law-abiding citizens." Jessi cackled at the prim expression on Charmaine's face.

Charmaine blinked rapidly and gasped. "Wait a minute. Something he said might point the finger away from you. Did he talk about enemies or anyone out to get him?"

"Buddy was a tough negotiator is how he put it. Honestly, he sounded downright gangsta if you ask me," Diamond said with a snort.

"Which means plenty of suspects willing to take him out." Jessi grinned at Charmaine. "You're sharp, sis."

"Diamond, you have homework. Think back over what Kennedy told you. Anything about fights or arguments he had. Deals that were cutthroat," Charmaine said. She turned to Jessi. "Give her a tablet to write it down."

Jessi waved away the suggestion. "Old school. Type it up on your tablet and print it out. But don't save it in a file. Just in case you become a suspect and the cops seize your electronic devices."

"You think I might be arrested?" Diamond's brown eyes went wide with alarm. "But I'm a single mother. I need to take care of my baby!"

"Plenty of parents are in prison, girl," Jessi said.

"Don't say stuff like that," Charmaine blurted.

"Facts." Jessi gave a shrug. "Which means you don't hold back from us. Got it?" She pointed at Diamond again.

"Yeah, yeah. I understand!" Diamond added when Jessi continued to glare at her.

"If the police investigation gets politically sensitive, they might look for an easy target to take the blame. Not that I'm saying you would even make it to court," Charmaine said at the panicked expression Diamond wore.

"Yeah. Those rich folks have low friends in high places. So, get that list started so we can point Harrison and his bosses in multiple directions. If they come after our friend with flimsy circumstantial evidence, we'll go public." Jessi wore a fierce expression. "Just because we don't have deep pockets or connections doesn't mean they can push us around."

Diamond let out a sigh. "Thanks guys. I swear, you'll get everything I know. So, are you going to take the aunt's case?"

Jessi looked at Charmaine. "Yes."

"Under one condition. If at any point I see a conflict, we pull out."

"Let's call Miss Lady and get this party started." Jessi turned to Diamond again. "And you get to work on that assignment. I have a feeling these two cases are going to make life interesting!"

"Drama junkie," Charmaine muttered to herself. She finished tidying up the kitchen as Jessi and Diamond excitedly talked about their next steps.

To their surprise, Mrs. Chatelaine was eager to talk to them despite having no idea her nephew had asked for their help. They set up an appointment for Friday evening, The elderly woman sounded quite lucid on the phone. Also, a surprise given Andre's odd turns even when he was stable. Charmaine's heart dropped when they pulled up to the address Mrs. Chatelaine had given them.

The cottage-styled house on Vallette Street was painted in bright blue with purple trim around the windows. The front yard was crowded with crosses and garden decorations. A three-foot-tall statue of the Virgin Mary, her face and hands painted brown, stood on one corner of the porch. Three wicker chairs matched a swing attached to the ceiling. A gray cat, its tail curled around the statue's base, reclined as if keeping Mary company. Jessi parked her Jeep on the street in front of the cottage, but they didn't get out.

"Girl…" Charmaine shook her head as she gazed at the riot of colors and shapes. "I think we need to take everything she says with a mound of salt."

"I'm already getting vibes. And look." Jessi reached into her backpack on the rear seat. She pulled out a small black box. "EMF meter readings are registering."

"That thing stays beeping or crackling. This is New Orleans. Hell, all over Louisiana it would jump into a two-step dance," Charmaine said. "I still don't like it."

"Oh, stop. I think it's kinda cute myself. What could go wrong?" Jessi gave a short laugh when Charmaine made a face. She got out of the Jeep, the backpack slung over one shoulder.

"Here we go," Charmaine mumbled and followed her.

Potted plants and flowering shrubs were covered with old sheets to protect them from the cold. The temperatures of late January had dipped to freezing several times. Mardi Gras Day promised to be chilly this year. Charmaine was encouraged by the care Mrs. Chatelaine seemed to have taken with her yard. Once on the paved walkway leading to the cottage, she noticed there was a kind of symmetry to the garden décor.

"You're right. It doesn't seem half as weird once you look closer," Charmaine admitted. "Maybe I was wrong and—"

The darker blue door swung open. "Aha, the cavalry has arrived to save the day! Come, come! I have hot hibiscus tea with ginger to chase away winter's chill. I also baked my Mississippi great-grandmother's tea cakes. We'll have such fun."

"Mrs. Chatelaine?" Charmaine shot a side-eye at Jessi and looked at their hostess again.

"Who else could I be but me?" Mrs. Chatelaine let out a musical laugh and beckoned them inside.

Her light brown skin had a delicate web of lines on her forehead. Those and the slight crow's feet when she smiled were the only signs of her age. They knew she was at least in her seventies, if not older. Yet she had a spring in her step as she continued her animated welcome. She chattered on as Charmaine and Jessi gave polite answers. When she bustled off to her kitchen, the sisters ogled what they could see of the home's interior. The living room was furnished with vintage furniture. A large chaise lounge covered in a tea rose fabric dominated one corner. Sofa and chairs also looked antique. Tables of ebony, oak, and cherry were polished, their surfaces covered with lovely porcelain and crystal figurines.

Jessi went over to a landscape of an old house. A line of oak trees draped in Spanish moss flanked the two-story mansion on both sides. "Your art is amazing."

"My first husband was Jean Paul Vasquez. You may have heard of him," Mrs. Chatelaine said when she returned carrying a tray.

"Let me help you with that," Charmaine said, remembering her manners.

"Thank you, hon, but I'm quite capable no matter what my nephew might have told you." Mrs. Chatelaine breezed by Charmaine and set the tray on the coffee table.

"You were married to the famous artist?" Jessi sat on a stuff chair that faced the sofa.

"Lovely home." Charmaine sat in the matching chair.

Mrs. Chatelaine smiled as she settled on the sofa. She handed the sisters cups of tea and pointed to the plate. Golden brown cookies were piled on it. Charmaine looked at the rich red liquid content of her cup and took a small sip.

Mrs. Chatelaine glanced at the painting in question. "Hmm. Jean Paul had a melancholy disposition, but the man was a stallion in the bedroom."

Charmaine choked on her second mouthful of tea. She coughed as Jessi patted her back. "Ah, wow."

"Compensates for a multitude of masculine flaws," Jessi quipped.

"We had a wonderful five years together. A fling put an end to wedded bliss." Mrs. Chatelaine gave a slight shrug and nibbled on a tea cake.

"Same old story, a cheating man," Jessi replied.

"Oh, not him, dear. I met the drummer in Kid Valentine's Creole Jazz Band and fell head over heels. He was good, but no Jean Paul. I regretted my foolish impulse until I met my second husband. Great-aunt Ella was right. Men are like St. Charles Avenue street cars. Another one will come along any minute." Mrs. Chatelaine picked up her own porcelain cup and drank.

"Wow," Charmaine murmured a second time. She lifted the cup to cover her stunned expression.

"But enough about me. Darling Andre says you might be able to help me. I appreciate the dear boy's thoughtfulness. My favorite nephew." Mrs. Chatelaine looked from Jessi to Charmaine in expectation.

"So, you're fighting developers over two lots you own is what we understand," Jessi put in when Charmaine seemed still at a loss for words.

"Actually, I own four lots. Two of my aunts had no children, you see, and left their property to me. Three generations of family lived in the houses on those lots. Until they were destroyed in the hurricanes, that is." Mrs. Chatelaine's expression turned somber. "So many lives lost."

"You say they left the homes to you," Charmaine put in.

"The whole family knew. They told everyone. I have letters they wrote saying as much to family. My cousins sent them to me. Both my aunts loved writing to family. Anyway, when these grubby, greedy developers started up, my cousin Harriet in Metairie remembered her grandmother's letters. My aunts loved to travel and gossip."

Mrs. Chatelaine pointed to an antique rectangular tin box on the coffee table. The side panels and lid were painted. Men and women in nineteenth century dress were shown in New Orleans street scenes. Two depicted a Black woman selling wares on a street corner. Another showed a man driving a horse-drawn carriage with a white couple as passengers. Mrs. Chatelaine opened the box. Letters bound with blue and green ribbon were inside.

Jessi picked up one packet. "Okay if I take a look?"

"Go right ahead." Mrs. Chatelaine gave a regal nod and turned to Charmaine. "So, tell me about your ability to find supernatural beings."

"In most cases we end up debunking claims of ghosts and such. We're private investigators. Gathering facts is our main job." Charmaine smiled at her in hopes her sidestep wouldn't be too obvious.

"You're reserving judgement in case I'm a loopy old woman. Are you religious at all?" Mrs. Chatelaine tilted her head to one side.

Charmaine ignored the soft grunt from Jessi. "Yes, ma'am."

"I'm a devout Catholic, as is most of my family. Faith means we believe in the supernatural. That said, I've lived long enough to know people will use anything to line their pockets. I'm not one of those people," Mrs. Chatelaine said firmly.

"I wasn't implying—"

"The spirits of ancestors, angels, loa; all are guides, messengers, or protectors from another realm. My vivid dreams of my great-great-great grandmother led me to gather these letters. And then there is this." Mrs. Chatelaine stood and left the room.

"You finding anything that might help?" Charmaine said quietly to Jessi.

"Hmm, interesting. I'll have to do some legal research. Try not call our paying client delu-lu." Jessi giggled at Charmaine's pained frown in response.

I didn't!" Charmaine cut off the rest of her self-defense when Mrs. Chatelaine returned.

"This family heirloom appeared in this very living room after one particular dream two years ago. The next morning, I was sitting here chatting with one of my nieces. I'm also her godmother. She said, "Auntie, you've been buying new antiques. I've never seen this before." Mrs. Chatelaine placed a ceramic figurine on the coffee table.

"I see." Charmaine didn't at all, but didn't want to risk offending her again.

The statue, six inches tall, was of a woman. She wore a long dress, shawl, and a colorful hat with feathers. Delicate folds of blue and ivory made up the skirt of the dress. She carried a small purse.

"What are we looking at?" Jessi raised an eyebrow at Mrs. Chatelaine.

"I'd never seen it before," Mrs. Chatelaine said.

"Don't take this the wrong way, but you have a lot of what our grandmother calls knick-knacks in here. You could have forgotten you even had it." Jessi picked up the figurine. She turned it over it her hands and put it on the table again.

"That is the woman in my dream. Obviously, I never met my great-great-great grandmother. But here she is!" Mrs. Chatelaine pointed to the object in question.

"I'm afraid finding this, collectible as it might be, isn't proof that—" Charmaine blinked when a series of sharp raps sounded through the house. Rapid beeping followed soon after.

"Hold that thought, sis." Jessi transferred the packet of letters in her lap to the table. Then she dug in her backpack. She removed the EMF meter.

"Probably a package being delivered," Charmaine said. She rose and crossed the room. The porch was empty. She didn't see anyone walking down the path or a box.

"Amazing! I've never had such clear communication before. Only in dreams. Clearly Grandmother Euprosine wants you to listen. I wasn't sure when Andre told me about you two, but now I'm convinced." Mrs. Chatelaine clapped her hands together.

"The readings don't lie," Jessi said before Charmaine could respond. She held up another one of her tools. This one looked like a tiny cell phone. She plugged a miniature fan into it. "What I got before we walked in could have been from anything really. But I don't think these are random."

"Are you picking up anything specific?" Charmaine shot a glance at Mrs. Chatelaine and then back to Jessi.

"I don't see or hear granny, if that's what you're asking," Jessi replied. She focused her attention on the two screens.

"You can talk to the dead? We'll have a séance! With your legal expertise, you'll know exactly what to ask." Mrs. Chatelaine rose to her feet with the agility of a woman half her age. She pulled Charmaine to her feet, taking her along for the ride. "I have everything you'll need—items left over from Madame Rose's session."

"Ma'am we don't—"

Charmaine stumbled alongside the older woman, surprised at her strength. They arrived in the formal dining room adjacent to the front parlor. Mrs. Chatelaine opened a drawer in an antique sideboard. She arranged a deck of Tarot cards, a large crystal rock, and a locket on the polished table.

"The readings are going down, but definitely still hot." Jessi appeared with both devices. She looked down at the table. "What we got here?"

"What you'll need to reach across the divide," Mrs. Chatelaine replied. Her dark brown eyes sparkled with excitement.

Jessi laughed. "Props used by scammers. We use scientific methods. Well, I do at least. My sister is the church girl."

"I don't understand." Mrs. Chatelaine transferred her confused gaze from Jessi to Charmaine.

"Jessi doesn't believe in... religion. She thinks—"

Jessi cut in. "What we think of as 'spirits' are forms of energy we don't fully understand. Matter, living things, leave traces that we can detect. All phenomena that one day will be explained. And not by superstition."

"I apologize, Mrs. Chatelaine. My sister doesn't mean any disrespect toward the faith of others." Charmaine gave Jessi a pointed stare.

"Humph." Jessi went back to fiddling with her tools again.

"I like your straight-shooter style," Mrs. Chatelaine said with a laugh. "Andre and my brother told me more than once I was wasting money. Still, Madame Rose did find my missing silver service."

"Probably after she stole it in the first place," Jessi retorted.

"Oh, you think so? But I enjoyed our talks."

Charmaine flinched at sudden pressure on her temples. Mrs. Chatelaine desperately needed to believe in Madame Rose. She hoped to reach her son. More tried to come through, but Charmaine couldn't get a clear picture. Despite her lively disposition, Mrs. Chatelaine was lonelier than perhaps her closest relatives realized. Con artists looked for such victims.

"I'm sure you did, ma'am, but you have people who care about you. I don't think their concern is totally off base. Of course, we don't know Madame Rose," Charmaine said in a gentle tone.

"You agree with Andre that she's probably a fraud." Mrs. Chatelaine sighed as if let down.

"Ninety-nine point nine percent sure she's phony," Jessi blurted out. She tapped a button on the EMF meter, oblivious to the dark scowl Charmaine aimed her way.

Mrs. Chatelaine lifted her chin in a "soldier on" gesture. "What are our next steps?"

"Let's go back to the living room to talk." Charmaine smiled at her.

Another hour passed with Mrs. Chatelaine making the case for being contacted from the "great beyond," as she put it. Jessi asked for and got permission to explore the rest of the house. Charmaine stayed with Mrs. Chatelaine to discuss their fee structure, how they worked, and a preliminary scope of work.

"We'll email you the contract for electronic signature no later than Monday morning," Charmaine said. "In the meantime, use this weekend to think of any family records that might be helpful."

"You have quite the business-like approach. Very different from the others," Mrs. Chatelaine, reading glasses perched on her nose, stared at the iPad screen Charmaine had handed her. She handed it back to her. "But I don't do email or that other electronic stuff. Well, my niece Angela set me up an account on something called Google."

"You have Gmail. Perfect," Charmaine replied.

"Angela set up a computer and a printer. She can print out sheets without even being in the house. Seems such a cold, distant way to keep in touch." Mrs. Chatelaine gazed at the offending technology with mild disdain.

Charmaine followed Mrs. Chatelaine to her kitchen. A small desk sat in a nook. Mail and other papers were neatly piled in a tray. A laptop sat open. Next to it was a compact all-in-one printer. Mrs. Chatelaine sat down in the chair at the desk. She tapped the keyboard and the screen saver disappeared. She pointed to it.

"Do you open the browser at all?" Charmaine asked.

"Only to read emails. Sometimes I get messages from princes and foreign ministers They say I've inherited thousands, even millions of dollars. To get these vast estates, I should send them my bank information. Even I know that's a bunch of nonsense." Mrs. Chatelaine snorted as if amused at the idea she'd be taken in.

Jessi came in through the kitchen door from outside. She clicked the locks. "Nice yard out back. I like your old Buick. You still drive?"

"Not very often. I like walking in my neighborhood. You see much more on foot. And make human connections. You can't experience life zooming from one place to another," Mrs. Chatelaine replied.

"I explained how we work and showed Mrs. Chatelaine our boilerplate client contract. She has email." Charmaine pointed to the laptop.

"What do you mean electronic signature? It sounds like something a robot would do." Mrs. Chatelaine chuckled at the joke.

"We can send the contract to your printer. Sign it and email it back?" Charmaine studied the older woman for signs for confusion.

"My nieces showed me how to scan and send things. Not too different from the fax machines I used when I worked. All these gadgets would look like witchcraft and magic to our ancestors. Your arguments about science make sense, young lady," Mrs. Chatelaine said to Jessi.

"Exactly. Well, I'm all done." Jessi slung the strap of her backpack over one shoulder.

"What did you learn from the spirit world?" Mrs. Chatelaine asked.

"I'll analyze the data later. In the meantime, I'll research if these letters can add weight to your ownership claim. It would be helpful if you dreamed about a will," Jessi quipped.

"I'll notify you immediately in the event I do," Mrs. Chatelaine said in all seriousness.

"Yeah. Right." Jessi cleared her throat. She turned to Charmaine and nodded they should leave. Fifteen minutes later they were in the Jeep outside.

"Now you can tell me what you found," Charmaine said.

"Not much. If you don't count the ghost of a murder victim hanging out in her garage apartment," Jessi replied.

Chapter 4
Reality Bites

Later that Friday night, Jessi followed Charmaine back to her house for dinner. Charmaine's boyfriend Scotty had let himself into Charmaine's house. He'd brought over soul food from the restaurant he used to own. He sold it to his friend, a chef. They dined on fried catfish and shrimp.

"The good news is, she didn't kill her. The bad news is, our new ghost says Mrs. Chatelaine is lying to us. Or..." Jessi paused to gulp down cola before she continued. "At least she's holding something back. We need to find out more about this family."

"Sounds to me like y'all should do enough work to collect payment and move on. The aunt sounds about as off as her nephew if you ask me." Scotty gave his matter-of-fact assessment.

"She's eccentric, not crazy. My professional opinion," Jessi joked. "Besides, we strive to give our very best for every client."

"Plus, Jessi found out Mrs. Chatelaine has a nicely padded net worth," Charmaine said with a side-eye at her sister.

"Hey, did you forget there's a connection to our other new case?" Jessi reached for a cornbread muffin as she talked.

"The real estate client? What's she got to do with anything?" Scotty looked at Charmaine.

"Her company wants Mrs. Chatelaine's property. Gina Shaw's partner builds the houses, and she sells them to high-end buyers," Charmaine replied.

"Gentrifiers. Back-to-back hurricanes or floods from 2005 to 2007 destroyed homes that were in families for generations. The blood suckers swooped in to take advantage. Especially after Hurricane Katrina," Jessi added.

"The problem is no wills. Homes and land were passed on to succeeding generations by tradition or informal agreements." Charmaine shook her head.

"The succession process can be expensive. My Uncle James left a will, but the lawyer wanted over twelve hundred dollars to handle the court process." Scotty shrugged.

"And guess who wrote the laws. Louisiana has a simple succession process that costs a lot less. The value of the estate has to be under $125,000. That includes everything. Most people don't know that though," Jessi said.

"Anway, legal expenses aren't an excuse for Mrs. Chatelaine's relatives. I'll bet there's at least one lawyer in the bunch," Charmaine said.

"Two, but they're in Texas." Jessi smeared tartar sauce and ketchup on fried catfish. She hummed in satisfaction as she chewed.

"There are a lot of houses being renovated or built in the Greater New Orleans area. I know a couple of guys who do security for construction sites. I might get some information about the developer. Maybe even the real estate lady, what's her name," Scotty said.

Jessi covered her full mouth with a napkin and mumbled, "Gina Shaw."

"Text me the deets on both and I'll ask around. I'll be sure to tell Kat you approve. She's had a tough time since the pandemic, but I think she's turned a corner. Some Instagram food influencer gave her a great review. Yesterday she had customers lined up." Scotty said with a smile.

"I'm so happy Kat has put a lot of sweat and blood into your old place." Charmaine smiled back at him. Scotty had decided to focus on his private security business.

"I sold the two lots next to my aunt's café to developers. Guess I'm part of the gentrification problem," Scotty said. "The buyer gave me a good price though. Tried to lowball me, but my daddy didn't raise no fool."

"You weren't desperate for cash. And your aunt and uncle signed the property over to you while they were alive," Jessi pointed out. Her cell phone rang and Jessi wiped her hands before taking it from her sweater pocket. She walked out of the kitchen as she answered.

Scotty watched her leave. He leaned close to Charmaine, voice low. "Did you hear from the doctor?"

"Follow up test are fine. I'm *fine*, babe." Charmaine squeezed his muscular bicep.

"You should tell Jessi, Charmaine." Scotty's worried frown eased. He put an arm around the back of her chair.

"I will. I just didn't want her to get upset. You know why." Charmaine started to say more but stopped when Jessi strode back from the hallway.

Jessi grabbed her red leather jacket draped on the hook of a wall-mounted coat rack. "Diamond is going in for questioning again Monday. I'm going over to her house to prepare."

"Okay. Call if you need us." Charmaine exchanged a look with Scotty.

"I'm taking this. I can eat the rest on the way over." Jessi grabbed the takeout out plate with her food. "Bye y'all."

"Bye," Charmaine called after her as the door bumped shut once Jessi left.

"You should tell your sister we're expecting, Charmaine. The longer you wait..." Scotty pointed to her tummy.

"I will. But we're in the middle of two cases and—" Charmaine broke off when he cocked his head to one side. "Jessi says she doesn't want kids, but she can't get pregnant. I'm not sure how she'll react."

"Her best friend has a kid, though, and she's good with it. I see how she loves on Indyah," Scotty replied.

"On the surface she seemed okay. The truth is Jessi spiraled into depression and relapsed. It took six months for her to pull out of it. Besides, a friend is one thing. Your sister is different." Charmaine rubbed her belly with both hands. "I don't want to hurt her."

"Give her more credit. She's come a long way in the past few years. Remember when she was on the pole? That girl was a mess back then. Now she's a paralegal, has her house and friends."

"And Ricky. I was skeptical about her dating a cop, but they seem happy," Charmaine agreed.

"Speak up before you start showing. Or she'll definitely be hurt," Scotty said.

"I'll find the right time. Promise." Charmaine rested her head on his broad shoulder.

The weekend went by with no drama. Jessi managed to reassure Diamond that a followup interview was standard police procedure. Still, she ramped up her research on the other partygoers, all persons of interest as well. The Monday workday for Charmaine at the clinic was busy. By the end of the day, Charmaine felt drained. She hoped the extra vitamins she started would help. Once again, she went over in her mind the way to break the news to Jessi. She'd confided in her old therapist, a licensed social worker she'd seen in the past. Monica had provided wise counsel that made Charmaine less anxious. That evening she would tell Jessi over traditional red beans and rice. She'd set up the beans to be done in her slow cooker. By the time Charmaine got home, the scent of spices welcomed her like a hug. Andouille sausage medallions filled the pot as well. She cooked the rice and warmed up a French bread loaf with garlic butter.

"Damn, it smells good in here. I'd say just like mama's cooking except she didn't," Jessi joked when she arrived. Their mother hadn't been the homemaker type when they were children. Not the maternal type either.

"I've got everything you like. Louisiana Hot Sauce, sweet tea, and I put in extra sausage."

Charmaine scooped rice onto a plate and piled red beans on top. The table was already set. Sweet tea filled a pitcher on the table. Jessi took the floral plates and silverware to the large slow cooker with a matching pattern. Folded napkins completed the place settings. She stood, hand on one hip, as Charmaine chattered on. Once they were seated, Charmaine whispered a food blessing. Jessi waited in silence for a few moments.

"Okay, now you're going to tell me what's going on. And don't act like you don't know what I mean," Jessi added when Charmaine opened her mouth to answer. "Monica is up to some shit again. I'm not going to rescue her ass. Not after that stuff in Memphis. You can save that speech. I swear, the woman—"

"It's not about mama." Charmaine stopped pretending to be hungry. She pressed her lips together.

"Shit, you sick with something bad," Jessi blurted. She shoved the plate of food away.

"Not unless you count morning sickness," Charmaine said quietly. Nerves and racing thoughts prevented her telepathy from reading Jessi. She watched her sister's face for some sign.

"Oh." Jessi said. Then she beamed at Charmaine. "I'm going to be an auntie again! Wait, are you okay with it? I mean, you want the little crotch goblin?"

"Don't call him that!" Charmaine gave Jessi shoulder a playful slap. "Yes, we very much want a baby. Scotty is thrilled."

"You said, 'him'. You know it's a boy already?" Jessi stared at Charmaine's stomach. "I don't even see a bump yet."

"No, and I'm not going to find out. We want to be surprised. Are you..." Charmaine let her voice trail off.

"You forced me to have my head examined, so I'm good," Jessi laughed when Charmaine winced.

"Therapy is not 'getting your head examined'," Charmaine said with a grin. "I'm serious, Jessi. Be real with me."

Jessi's expression turned thoughtful. "You mean what happened when Diamond got pregnant with Indyah. Yeah, I'm over it. Triggered flashbacks to... you know. What happened. Not being in control. But I faced it. Turns out I got the 'not the mother type' gene from Monica. It wasn't really the part about not having a baby that really bothered me. If that makes sense."

Charmaine studied her for a few moments. "Yeah, I think I do actually. So, in other words, I was right about therapy being a good thing."

"Whatever," Jessi said with a grunt.

"Go on and admit it. Big sis was right. Next thing I'll have you going to Sunday services." Charmaine poked her shoulder with a finger.

"In your dreams. What about you? Last time we talked about kids, you were fine being child free."

"I had fun switching out men in my teens and twenties like I changed purses," Charmaine agreed.

"And girl, you got a *lot* of purses."

"Shut up. I saw our cousins getting tied down with babies young. Wasn't for me. Plus, my boyfriends tended not to be good father material. And don't you dare comment or I'll put names to your trifling body count." Charmaine shook a forefinger at her.

"Ugh, I'm def in a glass house on that one, sis."

"Scotty is different. I'm different." Charmaine placed a protective palm on her abdomen. "I'm in a better place to do what's best for a child."

"So, in conclusion, we're both good. I'm ready to be an auntie, too. Now let's talk about getting this money. Baby's gonna need more than a new pair of booties," Jessi said as she gazed at Charmaine's belly. "And I want a new tool I saw on a tech website."

"See, that's why we can't build up a big cash flow cushion. You and those thingamabobs!" Charmaine blurted. Her stomach rumbled, signaling her appetite had returned. She speared a succulent piece of sausage with her fork. "Eat your food before it gets cold."

"My equipment has saved our asses more than once." Jessi dug into her food.

For another thirty minutes they ate and tossed around ideas on how to approach both cases. Charmaine still hadn't heard back from the licensing board on her ethical enquiry. She had consulted a more veteran colleague; the social worker who had supervised her as she prepared to take the test for her license. Eva didn't see a conflict.

"Nothing Mrs. Chatelaine has told us so far says he'll benefit. He's not our client and doesn't seem to be in line to gain anything should she hold onto the family land," Charmaine said, giving a short summary of her former supervisor's opinion. "Eva should know. She served two terms on the board back in the early aughts."

"Hmm." Jessi, mouth full of red beans and rice, nodded. She drank ice tea and sigh in satisfaction. "I missed lunch today. Busy day at the office. But I managed to do some research on Mrs. C's land. I still need to search records in the Notarial Archives Division. Those have conveyance records that go back to the year seventeen-thirty-five."

"Lord, I hope we don't have to reach into ancient history," Charmaine replied.

"Nah, but it's helpful to know we could try. Mrs. Chatelaine is sure her ancestors left a paper trail. Oh, and she does have a will on file. Your client inherits items in her art collection and some family heirlooms. Also, land she owns on the north shore. But that's property she inherited from her second husband and isn't part of our case."

"Whoa, you got a lot done. Good work. I don't see how Gina or her developer buddy could get their hands on Mrs. Chatelaine's property.

"She missed a few tax payments. The city jacked up assessments after Hurricane Katrina. Values went up with all the hipster types moving in the years after the storm. She and her two nieces managed to catch up. Then Mrs. C. got sick and missed another one," Jessi said. "Bottom line, local city officials would love to let developers take over. Higher payments once certain tax breaks expire. It's a mess. Tax incentives after the disaster didn't help most low and moderate income residents. But those incentives lured a lot of developers. Still does because the incentives are still on the books."

"So, there's no motivation for shady officials to be on the side of people like Mrs. Chatelaine." Charmaine let out a tiny burp. "Ugh. I'm getting gassy already."

"There's more to come. Just ask Diamond."

"Can't wait." Charmaine nibbled a corner of French bread. "Add murky land title questions and you have a perfect storm of gentrification."

"Most folks lost everything in Hurricanes Katrina and Rita. They didn't have money cushions before; sure as hell couldn't afford to hire lawyers to fight after," Jessi replied.

"More than a few people are still dealing with the emotional trauma of loss. I see it at the clinic, and I'm not the only one. My social worker friends say the same thing. Look what happened in our family. We're scattered. Two uncles died, probably younger than they would have, from the stress. Mama decided not to come back like a lot of people."

"Or they couldn't come back even if they wanted to. That said, I want to make sure Mrs. C. holds onto her property. I—" Jessi stopped when her cell phone played a lively rap tune. She answered the video call. "Hey Diamond. Wait a minute, slow down."

"I'm still at the police station. And they might arrest me any minute. I told them about the glass and then that Detective Harrison said he couldn't help me. They gone charge me with obstruction or tampering with evidence," Diamond's words seemed to spill over one another in her rapid-fire outburst.

"Glass? Obstruction? What the hell?" Jessi blinked at her distraught friend's image. She used the phone's kickstand to place it on the table between her and Charmaine.

"Just come help me," Diamond pleaded. "This is my phone call."

Jessi stood. "On our way."

"Not how I wanted my Monday to end," Charmaine muttered.

"Hold up. Maybe you should stay here. Get some rest." Jessi put a hand on Charmaine's arm.

"Don't start treating me like I'm made of glass or something. I'm not on bedrest. Let's go before Diamond talks herself into a murder charge."

Charmaine moved with precision, stacking dirty plates and silverware in her dishwasher. She hurriedly poured the red beans into a large lidded container and put it in the fridge. Jessi came in already dressed against the January evening chill in a dark brown leather jacket. Charmaine rushed to put on boots. Already dressed in leggings and a sweater, all she needed was her wool jacket. Jessi drove, which meant Charmaine white-knuckled it for the fifteen-minute trip. They arrived at the Fifth District Station in record time. After a whispered exchange with Detective Ward, he took them to a holding area where Diamond sat. More an alcove—at least it wasn't a jail cell. Diamond launched an incoherent flood of verbiage at the sight of Jessi and Charmaine. Ricky stood to one side, arms folded.

"Okay, Diamond, take a few deep breaths in through your nose. Then exhale slowly through your mouth. One in. Slow out. Again." Charmaine coached her through the anxiety reducing exercise. She and Jessi sat on either side of her on folded chairs.

"Girl, it's been a day. And Indyah decided to act a fool at St. Mary's after a girl took her favorite pencil with a giraffe on top. You know the one we got her when we went to the zoo. I shouldn't have let her take it to school and—" Diamond stopped, took another deep breath as instructed and let it out.

"Don't take out your frustration on my baby," Jessi warned.

"Her little butt is in timeout. She's getting dinner and bed. I can't have her popping kids upside the head. Well, she shoved her and the girl tripped over a mat, but still." Diamond stopped when Charmaine raised a palm.

"Don't get wound up again. Is the little girl okay?" Charmaine asked.

"Oh yeah. She's fine. The other mother isn't upset or anything. But getting that call after the morning I had with the cops." Diamond shook her head and closed her eyes briefly.

"Tell us what happened," Charmaine said before Jessi could speak. She sensed Jessi was about to light into Diamond about saying too much to the police.

"Okay." Diamond heaved a sigh. "I went in and they started asking me the same damn questions. Going over what happened that night from the time I rang the damn doorbell to finding Buddy conked out. I just thought he was drunk or high or something. He liked to party. When he wouldn't wake up, I took the glass and tossed it. I gave him the drink."

"Buddy would mix certain drugs with alcohol for more energy during sex," Jessi said.

"Not from me," Diamond said with force. "I didn't give him Fantasy or Liquid Ecstasy!"

"But you knew he took that stuff to keep it up. Why didn't you tell me that shit!" Jessi blurted.

"Not helpful, Jessi," Charmaine broke in. Diamond's large brown eyes looked glassy with tears.

"I didn't know what else to do. I didn't think he would die on me. He'd played around before. He could go for hours, like he couldn't get enough. Said his wife wasn't down to satisfy him like his favorite playmate. That's me. I always used condoms though," Diamond added with a nod and sniffled.

"Points for safe sex. Did he always dress like a clown?" Jessi asked.

She raised an eyebrow when Ricky let out a chuckle. He took a call on his police-issued cell phone. He moved away to talk but didn't leave them alone.

"Please," Charmaine cut in. "I don't want those images in my head."

Jessi grunted at her sister's prim reaction. She lowered her voice. "Okay, so you panicked and threw the glass away."

Diamond nodded. She leaned forward and whispered, "Before I knew he was dead. The police found the glass, tested the contents. My fingerprints and Buddy's were all over it."

Harrison strode in. He frowned at Ricky, who kept talking into his phone with a shrug. Then Harrison turned his irritated scowl on the young women. He looked like a harassed high school principal about to deliver punishment. "It's always something with y'all."

"Okay, before you go off, listen to what we know," Charmaine said, a palm raised.

"Here's what *I* know," Harrison snapped. "One Ms. Diamond Phillips attended a party to provide a striptease performance."

"Interpretive sensual dance," Diamond shot back, her chin raised in defiance. Her bravado wilted in the face of Harrison's thunderous expression at being interrupted. "I'm just saying."

"Ms. Phillips has a history of drug use, and illegal substances were found in the murder victim's system. She had a history of providing him with sexual services. And we found text messages suggesting she might be blackmailing him." Harrison's deep voice sounded like the gong of doom in the small anteroom.

"What? I never did!" Diamond turned to Jessi and Charmaine with eyes wide with terror. "I swear it on my baby's life!"

Jessi stood to face Harrison. "Let's see those texts. Right now, I'm Ms. Phillips' advisor until she hires an attorney."

"No," Harrison said. "I don't have to show you anything at this point."

"Well then, I'll get Fannie Wilkens to deal with you," Jessi said, naming the most prominent Black criminal lawyer in New Orleans. Wilkens had won two high-profile cases, embarrassing the DA and NOPD. She had uncovered gaping holes in the investigations.

Harrison's eyes narrowed as he gazed at her. "I don't care if you resurrect the spirit of Johnny Cochran. Your friend is in big trouble. Unless she decides to stop lying through her teeth and tell us everything she knows."

"Humph." Jessi studied him for a few seconds in the heavy silence that followed. "Something else is going on."

"Like, like her fingerprints on the glass Kennedy drank from with traces of a drug. Witnesses confirmed she handed him a drink," Harrison countered. "Now what really happened, Diamond?"

"Stop talking," Jessi clipped when Diamond opened her mouth wide to spill more information.

"Sir, a moment," Ricky said and gestured to Harrison. He shot a glance at Jessi and shook his head.

Harrison hissed like a boiling teapot before stomping away. Ricky turned his back as he spoke low to his boss. Harrison nodded a few times, rubbing his jaw in thought. Charmaine tried to make out what they were saying. To her annoyance, outside the interview room two officers had entered the station. They marched a young man between them loudly protesting his treatment. The racket acted as interference with Charmaine's telepathic abilities. Diamond's distress didn't help either. She caught only snatches, but it was enough.

"Jessi," Charmaine said softly. She had to tap hard on Jessi's shoulder to get her attention.

"What?" Jessi turned to her.

"Let's talk." Charmaine tugged the sleeve of Jessi's coat.

"Wait, you're not going to leave me here, are you?" Diamond squeaked.

Charmaine rubbed Diamond's shoulder in an effort to soothe her. "Of course not. We're just going over here for a minute. Try to be calm. Breathe."

"Okay." Diamond sucked in air and huffed it out

"Harrison is bluffing. He's catching heat because Kennedy's wife is making a fuss. Well, her well-connected lawyer anyway." Charmaine spoke fast to get it out.

"To avoid backlash from his bosses, Harrison needs to find another suspect. I don't think he's got anything solid on Diamond. We better get back over there before she does something dumb." Jessi jerked a thumb toward her friend. Diamond did appear to be eyeing the nearest exit.

Charmaine followed Jessi's gaze. Diamond's jumbled thoughts of an escape plan came through clear. "She's thinking of making a run for it."

"Shit, all we need," Jessi replied and shot a glance at Harrison and Ricky.

Charmaine and Jessi marched over to Diamond. Charmaine moved to block her path toward the glass double doors a few yards away. Jessi put both hands on her hips as she stared down at Diamond.

"I didn't do anything," Diamond squeaked. She chattered on, words coming out so fast nothing made sense.

The sisters spent another few minutes reassuring Diamond. Jessi's warning that talking too much would land her in jail finally seemed to get through. Charmaine held one of Diamond's hands. She tried to counteract Jessi's brusque warnings of dire consequences with words of reassurance.

"Sorry. I got so flustered when they brought up the drugs and stuff." Diamond sniffled and rubbed her nose with tissues supplied by Charmaine.

"Um, what about these texts Harrison mentioned?" Charmaine said in a gentle tone.

"Yeah, dumbass move to put that shit in writing—"

"Jessi, please," Charmaine hissed at her.

"I don't know. We did the phone sex thing sometimes." Diamond's face screwed up as she blinked in thought.

"Give us access so we can read any direct messages you sent him," Charmaine said quietly. "Did the police take your phone?"

"Not the one I used for my freelance work with Tranisha. I had a separate little phone for that. It's at the house in my lock box to make sure Indyah doesn't find it. Oh, damn, my cousin will be pissed. I was supposed to pick Indyah up from her house hours ago." Diamond looked on the verge of panic again.

"Give me her number and I'll send a text." Charmaine took out her phone. At Diamond's instructions, she sent the cousin a message. Seconds later a reply. "See? Keisha's not mad."

Diamond sniffled. "Thanks. I know I made of mess of things."

"Mess ain't the word, girl. You should have told me about the glass that night. I would have told you to wipe it clean," Jessi muttered.

"Yeah, so I could arrest you, too," Harrison said over Jessi's shoulder, causing her to jump. "Please tell me you're involved. I've had a holding cell with your name on it for so long."

Jessi exchanged a glance with Charmaine. They'd been too preoccupied to notice Harrison's approach. She recovered from the surprise and quipped, "You wish. Is Diamond going to be charged?"

"Unless she can convince me she was just cleaning up and didn't specifically mean to hide evidence of a crime," Harrison said.

Charmaine held up a hand to thwart what was sure to be a tart response from Jessi. "Witnesses saw Diamond helping the catering staff clear up. And there was at least one other set of smudged prints that can't be identified."

Harrison's jaw muscle visibly tightened as he gazed back a Charmaine. Then he spun to glare at Ricky. The younger detective raised both hands and shook his head no.

"Ricky hasn't told us anything. Sounds like you ain't got shit. In my professional opinion," Jessi said in a dry tone.

"Don't try that voodoo magical BS on me. You have a source. I know you two," Harrison clipped.

"You mean we're damn good investigators. Why, thank you." Jessi smirked in the face of his dark glower.

"Go away. All three of you. But not before Ms. Phillips stops at the desk to get her summons." Harrison transferred his stern gaze to Diamond.

"Sir, yes sir. I didn't tamper with evidence." Diamond clutched her purse against her chest.

"Out." Harrison pointed to another section of the station.

Jessi started to say more, but Charmaine yanked her away. She dragged Jessi along with one hand while pulling Diamond from her chair with the other. "Don't poke the grizzly bear. Not on his turf."

An hour later they'd dropped off a still shaky Diamond at her cousin's home. The police had scooped her up as she arrived to pick up Indyah, so Diamond's car was still there. They left as Diamond launched into a spirited account to a wide-eyed Keisha. Charmaine yawned widely as Jessi drove them through the Mid City streets. By the time they arrived at Charmaine's house, it was close to ten o'clock.

"You need to take it easy. I don't care what you say." Jessi pointed to the hallway. "I'll stay while you take a warm shower and get in those corny pajamas you like to wear."

"Don't make fun of my pink PJs with cute sheep. They're perfect for cold, damp weather." Charmaine's words were garbled by another big yawn.

"The baby is telling you to get your ass in the bed," Jessi quipped. "By the way, how did you know about the witnesses?"

Charmaine tapped her right temple. "Not sure if it was Harrison or Ricky thinking I heard though. That's what Ricky was telling him."

"The look on Harrison's face was priceless when you threw that plot twist. He hates anything supernatural."

"Don't antagonize Bryan, Jess. He's a good guy. A little hard-headed and judgmental," Charmaine added when her sister grimaced at her defense of the dour detective. "But he tries hard to do the right thing. We could do worse when it comes to cops."

"Yeah, whatever. Go get settled." Jessi waved her away as she sat at the table in the breakfast nook.

Forty-five minutes later Charmaine padded back to the kitchen. Her favorite fuzzy slippers made slapping sounds with each step. She rubbed the small of her back as she walked. "Just what the doctor ordered. What have you been up to?"

"Research." Jessi didn't look up from the screen of her tablet. Minutes later she continued to read as she picked up the mug and drank. "Eww! What is this stuff?"

"Herbal chamomile tea with peppermint and honey to soothe the nerves. We had a trying night." Charmaine sat next to her with her own cup.

"Yeah, well don't poison me with that healthy new age crap. I'll take an Irish coffee next time. You have to swear off liquor, not me." Jessi drank more tea in spite of the complaint.

Charmaine waved a hand, dismissing her sassy retort. "What have you found out?"

"Not much about Mrs. Kennedy. News sites are still reporting her hubby 'tragically succumbed to an underlying heart condition while attending a party.'" Jessi kept scrolling through search results.

"She's doing a great job of controlling the narrative. I'm surprised the media isn't skeptical about the details though. You'd think some reporter would sniff out the faint whiff of scandal." Charmaine sighed as she sipped more tea.

"Quiet as it's kept, the powerful influence what makes the mainstream news. But indie news hounds are definitely talking." Jessi pointed to a few results with headlines from digital political observers. "Buddy made noises about running for mayor of New Orleans. Says here he told this interviewer he was 'exploring all options'. He had one big-time political foe. Seems this guy backs another candidate."

"Killing him to keep him off the ballot is a stretch." Charmaine stared at the photo Jessi pointed to. "Garrett Vincent. Never heard of him."

"He stays in the background, pulling strings to make things happen. But get this." Jessi opened another tab. The digital edition of *New Orleans Magazine*. She pointed to a photo of Garett with a group of well-dressed, smiling people at a social event. "See anybody familiar?"

"Gina Shaw. So, she hangs out with the upper crust of New Orleans. Not surprising. She specializes in luxury properties." Charmaine shrugged.

"They look a bit too cozy. I'll bet the hand you don't see is cupping her ass." Jessi cocked her head to one side.

Charmaine laughed. "From a picture of them standing together? C'mon."

"One episode of her reality show was selling his fancy house on the West Bank. He built it for his son and daughter-in-law, but they moved to Las Vegas. Junior got a job with one of Elon Musk's companies. He's an engineer or something. I watched a few minutes of the episode. Vincent showed for the walk-through since his son had already moved."

Jessi opened the YouTube app. They watched as Vincent and Gina giggled their way through large rooms. He kept touching her arm as they talked. The house had five bedrooms, five bathrooms, a powder room, and pool. The landscaped lawn added to the curb appeal.

"Wow. Some place. When was this?" Charmaine asked.

"Seven months ago. Gina signed a contract recently for more episodes. Folks in other states love anything New Orleans. A little heavy on the Big Easy tourist talk, but it sells tickets as they say," Jessi joked. "We can ask her about it in a couple of days. We're going to meet her at one of her 'problematic properties'," Jessi said, making air quotes.

"Right. I'd forgotten with so much going on at the clinic and my last doctor appointment." Charmaine continued to frown as she watched the now muted video continue. "She's doing business with both men, but... nothing to do with politics. Or Bernard Kennedy ending up dead."

"I don't know. Diamond said Kennedy liked to talk. He tells Gina something about Vincent that gets him killed? Or—" Jessi raised a palm when Charmaine gazed at her with skepticism. "Or Vincent told Gina too much during some pillow talk. She repeats it to Buddy, who's going to use it against Vincent, and..." She drew a finger across her throat.

"Harrison would laugh us out of his office if we told him. Well, not laugh since he's so pissed off with us right now."

"What else is new? He'll love us again when we solve Kennedy's murder and let NOPD take credit. *Again.*" Jessi snorted and went back to scrolling.

"Love us is an even bigger stretch," Charmaine said with a laugh.

Chapter 5
Six Bedrooms, Four Poltergeists

They arrived at the three-story home on Audubon Boulevard on Thursday. Charmaine drove straight from work to meet Jessi at the address Gina had given them. Late-afternoon sun slanted across the red tiled roof. The day was still cold despite the bright sunlight. The long front porch stretched the length of the house. Painted pale yellow, grand double steps led up to it on either side. The top floor had a balcony with an iron railing that matched the one on the porch. She got out of her Kia and locked it with the remote. She'd left her handbag in the center console. Her cell phone was in the pocket of her jacket so she could be hands free.

"Not bad." Jessi joined Charmaine on the sidewalk after getting her large duffle with equipment.

"It's a mansion. How much?" Charmaine's gaze took in the mature magnolia trees that stood to either side of the lawn.

"You could be the happy owner for the mere price of seven million. Small change you and Scotty could scrape up in time to welcome Scotty, Jr." Jessi grinned at Charmaine and looked at the house.

"I'm gonna buy ten Mega Millions lottery tickets when we leave here."

"You'll need it for this address." Jessi jerked her chin toward the house. "There's our new client. At least she has the money to pay us well."

Charmaine saw Gina Shaw's outline in one of the floor-to-ceiling windows facing the street. "Commissions must be real sweet."

"Yeah. Plus, she's signed a contract for another reality show. This one on renovating and interior design. Read it in an entertainment online magazine." Jessi nudged Charmaine with an elbow and marched ahead of her. "Let's go get this money."

Gina opened the front door as they climbed the wide steps. She wore a tense expression. "I'm so glad you're here. Please tell Carlos and Jamal they're being silly. I have three weeks until I need to start showing this home."

"Good evening, fine thanks," Jessi replied with a smile.

"Jessi," Charmaine whispered but Jessi refused to look at her. Instead, she came around her sister all but pushing her aside. "Hello, Gina. Sorry we're a few minutes behind. Traffic slowed us down."

"No problem. I didn't mean to launch into complaining before you could even catch a breath. It's just..." Gina blew out a sigh and flapped a hand in the air. "The kitchen and main suite need updating. Jamal needs to get the drywall up and the painting done before staging. I have three premium clients interested. One is flying here in three weeks to do a walk-through with his new wife. These people are very busy. I can't keep putting them off and—"

"Excuse, but we need you to take a look at the cabinets the vendor delivered," a stocky Hispanic man said.

"Please tell me it's not another screw-up!" Gina blurted. She muttered under her breath when the man shrugged. "Sorry, I have to deal with this."

"No problem. We can start our assessment," Charmaine said in her most reassuring therapist voice. Apparently, it didn't work.

Gina stomped off beside the workman. "What the hell is it *now*, Carlos?"

"Sis?" Jessi looked at Charmaine.

"I'm not sure. Lots of interference from other workers in the house. But I don't need to read minds to know things aren't going smoothly," Charmaine replied. She glanced around at the foyer. "I do read a lot of anxiety about getting out of here before dark."

Jessi glanced at her smartwatch. "Four forty-eight. Sunset will be in less than an hour. Should take us a good twenty minutes to walk through this McMansion."

"Hmm."

Charmaine tried once again to sort through the jumble of thoughts coming at her. She shook her head in resignation and followed Jessi into the first living room of three. They split up to cover more square footage in less time. Jessi handed her one of three EMF meters she'd bought. Electromagnetic field meters measured the presence of paranormal energy. One also contained an anemometer to measure rushes of cold air, sometimes associated with spirits. Though Jessi preferred more scientific language.

"I hope all the money you spent on this thing is worth it," Charmaine said, turning on the digital display.

"More sensitive and compact. And it has my playlist on it so I can jam while working." Jessi laughed when Charmaine's mouth flew open. "Just kidding. New let's get to work. Hopefully the entities will show up soon."

"Hopefully they won't," Charmaine muttered.

While Jessi fiddle with dials on her tool, Charmaine went through an arched opening. She entered a long formal dining room. A tall, light-skinned Black man with thinning brown hair was applying the last two sections of wallpaper. She nodded a greeting to him as she walked by.

"I'll try not to get in your way," Charmaine said.

"No worries. I'm about done." The man continued to press a roller on the wall.

Charmaine stepped back to look at the floral pattern on a soft white background. Sage green, pale yellow, and delicate pink flowers bloomed along winding branches. "This is beautiful."

"It should be at five hundred bucks a roll," the man said.

"Good Lord. You definitely don't want to mess up a spot at that price." Charmaine gave a slow whistle.

"Which is why they hire me. Twenty-five years of experience," the man replied. "You can't just pick up some guy in a Home Depot parking lot to work on expensive homes."

"Gina says there have been a few delays." Charmaine glanced at the EMF screen. Nothing registered within sixty square feet.

The man stood back to examine his handiwork. Then he turned to face Charmaine for the first time. "You considering the place?"

"The banks would laugh me right out the door if I tried. This house is way out of my league. Gina hired us as staging consultants," Charmaine explained at his curious expression.

"You the ghostbusters, eh?" He laughed when Charmaine blinked in surprise. "Yeah. I've heard the carpenters and electrical guys talking about things moving and stuff, and saying we need to get out before dark or else." He grunted and rolled his eyes.

"You haven't noticed anything though," Charmaine replied.

"Nothing but a few clumsy guys dropping their tools. The brave ones step up to work later hours. It's a scam to get more overtime pay if you ask me. They know Gina is desperate to move it off the market. Brad, that's the contractor, has two other big jobs. I figure he's pulling his guys to work on those. Spooks are handy."

"Gina didn't mention anything to us." Charmaine looked at him with interest but he didn't need encouragement.

"I'm Harold Green, by the way." Harold gave Charmaine a friendly nod and glanced around again. "I'm not surprised. Reputation is everything in this price range. The house was built in 1902 by Thomas Billingsley, a banker. His family came to New Orleans right after the Civil War. Family traded in sugarcane and lumber. Supposedly there was at least two suicides and a murder over the years. They say a great-uncle killed his wife and jumped from the roof when cops tried to catch him."

"Not the kind of history you want to get out for sure." Charmaine looked around at the lovely room in a different way. Still, the EMF meter stayed quiet.

"Bunch of nonsense. I haven't seen any floating objects or disappearing people. Brad just stoking the superstitions of his employees, if you ask me. But I stay out of it." Harold raised both palms before he turned to reposition a ladder.

"Thanks for the info."

"Hey, you didn't hear it from me," Harold said in a conspiratorial voice and winked. Then he climbed the treads. At the top he used a wide brush and applied glue to the wall.

"Understood," Charmaine called up to him.

She went through another opening, which led into the kitchen. Gina gestured in frustration yards away. Carlos pointed to boxes on the floor that workers were opening. The expansive room was a hive of activity, so Charmaine retreated into a hallway. She followed the path of protective construction paper out down applied to protect the wood floors. She crossed the foyer to second living area. Nothing jumped out at her as unusual. Literally. Charmaine went outside through a side door in the kitchen. Gina and Carlos, still having an intense discussion, didn't seem to notice her. The driveway led to a backyard. Vines covered a pergola left of a patio. With trepidation, Charmaine entered the garage and went up to the second floor of it. In the past, this would have been called the chauffer's apartment. Charmaine remembered Jessi finding a ghost behind Mrs. Chatelaine's house. She glanced at the EMF meter constantly as she made her way through three rooms. The apartment had two small bedrooms, a bath, kitchenette, and a living room. Vintage furniture was scattered about. She sneezed a few times from the dust. Nothing living had occupied the space for a long time. Finding nothing but spider webs, Charmaine headed for the main house. Harold waved to her as he loaded his gray pickup truck and she waved back. She entered through the same door and made her way to the second living room again for another look. Then she headed to the foyer.

"Up here," Jessi called from the second-floor landing.

Charmaine climbed the first few treads. The stairway went up and then branched off at a ninety-degree angle. "You got something?"

"Keep your voice down. I'm guessing Gina doesn't want us to scare her people," Jessi said low.

"Yeah, well, according to Harold they already know what's up. Which is why she hired us." Charmaine admired the polished banister as she went up.

"Readings up here are high. I mean, look." Jessi held up the EMF meter in her hand.

"Remind me again what the numbers mean. I—" Charmaine's meter emitted a series of sharp beeps.

"Put the damn thing on quiet mode," Jessi clipped.

She clicked her tongue in irritation when Charmaine fumbled with the tool. Her own meter was attached to a lanyard around her neck. Jessi snatched the meter from Charmaine and pressed a button on the side. The beeping stopped.

"Excuse me. I don't play with these things all day like you," Charmaine shot back.

"Remind me to instruct you like a toddler before our next field operation." Jessi handed the meter back to Charmaine. "Forget the numbers. All you need to know is this red light means supernatural trouble. Didn't light up until I went to the third floor."

"But not on the second floor at first?" Charmaine glanced around with a frown.

"Nope. Which means—"

"Uh-uh, me and my guys are leaving. Sorry. It's getting dark. I don't care." A raised male voice came from downstairs.

"My power drill just flew the fuck out my hand. What the hell?" a second voice rang out.

"Which means," Jessi continued. She pulled Charmaine close to whisper. "Something is on the move."

"Or following *you*. Did you shake something loose with one of those whats-its?" Charmaine darted a look around.

Jessi dropped her tote bag and searched through it. "No. Maybe. I—"

"Don't be ridiculous. The deadline to complete this work is in your contract," Gina's voice was pitched to a shriek. "You have any idea how much these delays are costing me?"

"I'm talking about a safety issue here. We—" The man's voice was drowned out by a loud crash followed by heavy footsteps. "That's it. We outta here."

"You'll pay a penalty. It's going to cost you. The contract clause is clear," Gina yelled.

Jessi and Charmaine raced down the stairs where the action seemed to have moved. They were almost mowed down by four men and a woman. They made a beeline for the front door. Charmaine stepped aside just as the woman spun back.

"Damn. I left my phone," the woman said as she patted to pockets of her cargo work pants.

"Leave it. Get a new phone," one of her co-workers said without slowing his sprint for the exit.

"We'll go with you to look for it," Jessi said with a nod at Charmaine.

"Oh, good. Confront the poltergeist right off the bat," Charmaine mumbled.

"What?" The woman's already-wide eyes got bigger.

"She said we'll find where it's at." Jessi jabbed Charmaine's side with a sharp elbow.

"Right," Charmaine winced but then forced a tight smile.

"Shit. I dropped my bag. Here, hold these." Jessi shoved the EMF meter and another device in Charmaine's hand.

"What... okay." Charmaine stood with both hands full. A thump made the woman spin around in a circle. "Um, it's okay. Just probably the house settling?"

Before the scared woman could reply, Jessi raced back downstairs, skipping treads in her haste. Jessi placed her bag against a wall. She took the two of the devices from Charmaine. She dropped them in the bag and handed her a different one.

"You think we can trap it?" Charmaine asked.

The woman gasped "Trap what? Look, I don't—"

"Let's go." Jessi pulled the woman along.

At first the woman was beside her. With each step toward the kitchen, the woman fell behind. Charmaine nodded encouragement when the woman looked at her as if for help. They entered the kitchen. Unboxed shaker-styled white cabinets sat in the middle of the floor. Lights flickered on as they entered.

"Oh shit, it's happening just like Carlos said." The woman pulled to get free of Jessi's grasp.

"The lights are on a timer." Gina jangled keys as she entered the kitchen. She frowned at the woman. "You people are acting like superstitious— OMIGOD!"

Gina ducked as a mallet flew at her head. It stopped and hung suspended for a few seconds before clattering to the floor. Then all sound stopped. A strange quiet descended around them. Tapping, like metal against metal, started, followed by a muted chuckle.

"Fuck a phone."

The woman ran to the back door. She cursed as she fumbled to get it open for a few seconds. Then she was gone without bothering to look back or close it behind her. Gina let out a howl of anger.

"Sabotage!" Gina stomped a foot. "There's no such thing as ghosts."

A cabinet nearby slid across the floor to bump against the back of Gina's knees. She squealed and grabbed Charmaine in a tight bear hug. Charmaine let out a surprised squeak of her own. Not at the paranormal activity but the vise-like grip. Gina's hold pinned Charmaine's arms to her sides.

"Calm down and let go." Charmaine pushed against Gina but she didn't budge. Expensive perfume, too much of it, made Charmaine sneeze. "Jessi, some help over here."

But Jessi was gone. Beeping from one of her devices came from a distance. Charmaine managed to shove Gina away finally. She followed the sound with Gina on her heels. The woman grabbed the hem of Charmaine's jacket. They arrived at the bottom of the staircase. Jessi came from the larger of the two first floor living areas.

"Well, this is really interesting. I've never had such high readings but no appearance. At least one usually shows up to yell at me." Jessi shrugged as she looked up from the tool she held. "Didn't get to use the FCT or the neutralizer."

Gina panted as she blinked at Jessi in confusion. Then she turned to Charmaine. "Wha-what is she talking about?"

Charmaine tugged her coat until Gina finally let go of it. "Short answer, you have a haunting and we can most likely resolve it."

"Well, why didn't you do something before my sub-contractors ran out on me? I'm losing thousands a day. And that's just on this property. No. No, I don't believe in spirits or spooks or whatever you call it. Maybe you set this up to increase your fee." Gina's eyes narrowed as she her gaze went to Jessi and back to Charmaine. "Or you work for Uptown Realty."

"Who?" Charmaine blinked at her.

"Did Frank Young put you up to this?" Gina spat.

"Look, woman. You came to *us*. Remember? We don't know a Frank whoever," Jessi snapped.

"Young. He's got his own show on property flips," Charmaine put in. When Gina gave her a sharp look, she added, "Not that I know him personally. I just like watching home design series."

"Really?" Gina's professionally arched eyebrows lifted as she studied Charmaine.

"Yeah, really. The settings don't lie." Jessi raised the EMF meter she held in one hand. She glared at Gina. "Neither do we. We don't need your money."

"We kind of do because of your spending," Charmaine mumbled close to Jessi's ear. Then she faced Gina. "Let's all take a deep breath and regroup."

Jessi shook her head. She marched over to her duffle bag and packed away her devices. She unsnapped the lanyard and stuffed the EMF that had hung around her neck into it as well. "We not takin' crap from anybody at any price. Our contract states either party can terminate at any time. You'll be billed for the time we spent tonight."

"Uh, listen. I apologize. It's just... I'm so stressed out over this. I've poured my entire life just about into my business. I have two children to support. Flying tools, workers abandoning sites." Gina placed a trembling hand over her mouth. Then she burst into tears.

"Shit. I know what comes next." Jessi cast a glance at Charmaine. Still, she went back to arranging items in her duffle.

Charmaine landed tentative pats on Gina's right shoulder as she sobbed. "I can imagine the strain it's been juggling so much. A demanding job, motherhood, a television show."

"My husband recently confessed to having an emotional affair with a twenty-year-old grad student. Timothy," Gina wailed. "I'm not sure how much more I can take!"

"How awful for you. There, there now."

Charmaine continued an empathetic exchange with the distraught realtor. She darted glances at Jessi, who rolled her eyes in response. Her sister made it clear she was indifferent to Gina's plight. Yet Charmaine also knew Jessi well. That dramatic speech about ending Gina's agreement was phony. Jessi wasn't about to give up a lucrative client over one outburst.

"I need your help." Gina dabbed her nose and turned from Charmaine to Jessi. "Please."

Jessi blew out a sigh. She stood, hands on her hips. "I can do without the 'Karen' meltdowns."

"What she means is trust us," Charmaine said when Gina frowned. "We understand you're under tremendous pressure. We're here to find answers."

"Yes. Of course," Gina replied after a few beats. "Well, now what?"

"We'll neutralize the AEBE at this property. Do a full sweep, including any outbuildings." Jessi knelt next to her black duffle bag and rummaged through it.

"AEBE?" Gina blinked at Jessi before she looked at Charmaine.

"Most lay people say spirits or ghosts. Jessi calls them 'alternative electromagnetic biological energy'. In other words, alternative forms of electromagnetic energy with a biological origin. AEBE," Charmaine explained since Jessi didn't answer.

"Hopefully, we won't have to damage fixtures or anything. Sometimes these entities get attached to solid objects." Jessi stood with the EMF meter back around her neck. She positioned her newest anemometer on a section of the wall.

"Oh, no! But we've finished most of the renovations. I've even scheduled the stagers." Gina looked close to tears again.

"Dismantling any part of the house is a last resort, if everything else fails, action," Charmaine said quickly, patting Gina's shoulder once more. "We're several steps away from making such a decision. Right, Jessi?"

"Sure. Didn't mean to suggest otherwise. I like to inform clients of all possible outcomes." Jessi spoke in a professional tone as she flashed a brief smile for Gina.

"Going forward you need to disclose complete information about the history of each property. I mean *everything*." Charmaine removed her hand from Gina's shoulder as she stared at her.

"What are you implying?" Gina's mouth formed a tight line.

"Several tragedies happened here over the decades since this house was built. Suicides. At least one murder." Charmaine glanced at Jessi, who grunted in response.

"Left out a few details, huh?" Jessi continued to adjust her instruments.

"Who told you..." Gina frowned.

"We're investigators, remember."

Gina tugged on the front of her wool and silk-blend jacket. "Um, every home has a past of some kind."

"If we're to do a thorough job, we need full disclosure from the client," Charmaine put in before Jessi could jab with a sharp retort.

"You discredit claims of ghosts and hauntings. Supernatural legends are great for tourism, right? But we know it's nonsense." Gina seemed to have regained her composure.

"Not all of it," Jessi shot back in a bland voice. "Flying hammers at your head didn't convince you?"

"Scammers have all kinds of ways to fake that kind of thing. I assumed your equipment could find hidden cameras, thin wires that aren't easily seen with the naked eye. Like magicians in Las Vegas." Gina looked from Charmaine to Jessi.

"We can. Our equipment also detects true AEBE," Charmaine said. "You want to tell us what you know about this house?"

"It was built in 1902 by a banker for his young family. They lived here happily for a number of years. Though"—Gina cleared her throat—"their youngest two children died soon after childbirth. Mrs. Billingsly, the wife, never got over the losses. Some say she killed herself, but it's not clear. He remarried and had three children along with their oldest, who survived. About a decade later a visitor suffered what appeared to be a heart attack during a banquet."

"And the murder?" Jessi asked.

"In 1930 a nephew was living here. He accused his wife of cheating on him with their Creole chauffer. He slashed his wife's throat and tried to hang himself. The wife survived and so did he.

He claimed self-defense and was acquitted. It was quite a scandal at the time since they were a prominent family. But stories like that are common," Gina protested.

Jessi stared at Gina in silence for a few seconds. "It's unusual to know that amount of detail about a house over one hundred years old."

"Part of the appeal for new owners is knowing background information, especially homes here. I have a part-time employee do the research."

"Smart business move. Folks moving here love New Orleans lore." Jessi nodded in appreciation.

"It's what sets me apart from most other real estate agents, particularly when it comes to luxury historic properties." Gina smiled with satisfaction.

"As long as the history doesn't have too much blood in it?" Charmaine put in.

Gina's smile faltered. "Yes."

"Not to mention having 'Casper the Not So Friendly Ghost' throwing things around every once in a while," Jessi quipped.

"Whether potential buyers believe those stories or not, that kind of talk can affect a sale. If I can even get workers to finish renovations. I never expected them to be so susceptible to superstition." Gina frowned as turned to examine the home's interior. "They do such fine work, too."

"Is there more?" Charmaine prodded gently.

Another thud from the second floor made Gina jump and seemed to loosen her tongue. Two more people died in the house, of natural causes from what her student found in obituaries in old newspapers. Darkness had fallen and the house was chilly. Not from spirits. The new furnace was not turned on. Charmaine reassured Gina that they would give her a report the next day. Gina seemed to have lost a bit of her skepticism. Though she did express hope they'd find evidence of tampering to simulate the presence of apparitions. By six thirty Jessi and Charmaine were alone in the house.

They decided to stick together since whatever hung out in the fancy house had a temper. They went to the third floor. A modern main suite stretched its length. A floating painters' sheet looked like a cheap horror film from the past. Charmaine let out a shriek as the thing drifted towards her. She moved back as Jessi stepped in the from the hallway. She flipped a switch on the EMF disrupter. An angry hiss filled the air before the cloth collapsed to the floor. They made their way downstairs to the second floor and repeated the process. They used the disrupter twice before reaching the first floor.

"I think we're done here. Look." Jessi held up her EMF meter. The digital display backlight showed a number.

Charmaine stared at the screen. "Hmm, .06. Not bad. Mine says .049. Gina can get back on track to earn a hefty commission."

"Yeah, only we'll take a healthy cut into it. I say we calculate a percentage of what she's going to get. Strike a blow against gentrification." Jessi took the meter when Charmaine handed it to her.

"That's not in the agreement, Jessi," Charmaine chided.

"Subsection C, paragraph four says we can assess additional fees based the difficulty or unexpected hazards. Most people don't read every word of contracts. Especially when they're desperate to get rid of unwanted dead guests."

"We're not going to use shady fine print to jack up prices. I'm going to go over that new template you created and make revisions. So, you might as well tell me if you included anymore 'gotcha' clauses." Charmaine scowled at Jessi. She gasped when lights went off.

"Timer," Jessi said with a laugh. "It's set to lower the lights to only one or two for security after seven-thirty. There's a manual override in case they work late."

"Oh, right." Charmaine retrieved an EMF meter and turned it on just in case. The low value hadn't changed.

"Told ya." Jessi opened the top flap of her bag. "Surging hormones got you."

"Oh shush." Charmaine stuffed the device back into the duffle and zipped it closed.

Jessi giggled as she slung the wide strap over one shoulder. "I promise to keep the preggo jokes to a minimum."

"Sure you will," Charmaine said over her shoulder. "I'll just double check the kitchen door is locked."

Minutes later they were on their way. Charmaine went straight home to Scotty waiting for her. Jessi said she was meeting up with old friends from her days on the strip circuit. The evening went by with no more excitement. Friday morning temperature dropped to forty-six degrees. They looked forward to the weekend kicking officially kicking off Mardi Gras season. Having Three Kings Day or Twelfth Night land on Saturday, January sixth, was an added bonus. Mardi Gras balls, with elaborate attire for kings and queens of Krewes, would be held. King Cake parties were planned around town at local event spots and popular restaurants. Charmaine and Scotty planned to attend one at his former restaurant. Kat, the new owner, had built a reputation for having some of the best King Cakes in the city. Everyone was in a festive mood. Until Harrison spoiled it. Scotty had just left to check on one of his team providing security at a Krewe of Fat Cats private party. Her cell phone rang just as she put her feet on an ottoman to Netflix and chill. Charmaine tapped the icon to put it on speaker.

"Hey, you had fun with your girls and now you're calling me for bail money. Right?" Charmaine laughed. She'd had to rescue Jessi more than a few times.

"I got you on three-way," Jessi said.

"Mmmf, okay." Charmaine nibbled on a corner of the praline and cream cheese pastry in her hand. "Kat sent me samples. I'm going to save you some. You really should come by—"

"We got a problem. Tell her what you did, Harrison," Jessi's voice sounded taut with suppressed fury.

"I know she's your pal, but the evidence places Diamond squarely in the frame for this murder." Harrison's deep voice came through the speaker. "The DA is taking it to the Orleans Parish Grand Jury."

"They're going to indict Diamond for murder. Damn him," Jessi blurted.

"I'm not the entire freakin' system, Jessi."

Jessi shot back a switchblade-sharp accusation. Harrison shouted a rebuttal and the verbal boxing match took off. Charmaine struggled to sit up. Crumbs sprinkled from the front of her Southern University long-sleeved t-shirt. She cursed at the mess she was making.

"Y'all slow down." Charmaine brushed at her leggings. "Hey, I can't understand either one of you."

"I told you it's a fuckin' setup. Loreen Kennedy is the one you should be dragging into court," Jessi spat. "What's the point of Black cops if they get co-opted into a racist criminal *injustice* system!"

"That's way over the line. Don't you dare question my integrity as a police officer or a Black man. I gave you a heads up. The facts are the facts. Do what the hell you want. I'm done," Harrison shouted.

"Oh, you're done? You have no idea. Listen Harrison... hello?" Jessi's enraged huffs came through loud and clear.

"He hung up, Jessi. What did you expect?" Charmaine heaved a sigh.

"I'll see you in a few," Jessi replied.

"Hey, wait. Scotty is coming back to—" Charmaine stared at the phone, realizing Jessi had ended the call. "Spend the weekend here. Damn it."

Thirty minutes later Jessi sat brooding in Charmaine's living room. The girls' night out had been cancelled. So her pals partied on without Jessi. Charmaine tried to coax her with shrimp fried rice left from her and Scotty's early dinner. Jessi waved away food. Almost two hours of watching Jessi stare at the television passed. Scotty arrived in a good mood. He had a black and gray weekender bag in one hand.

"Hey. My crew has everything under control. I love Mardi Gras season." Scotty dropped the bag in a corner and rubbed his large hands together. He planted a kiss on Charmaine's forehead. "Great for my bottom line. Oh, hey, Jessi."

Charmaine raised both eyebrows at him. "Harrison called. They're taking evidence against Diamond to the grand jury. Murder."

"Damn. That's tough. How can I help?" Scotty looked from her to Jessi.

"See, that's why you're my favorite brother-in-law. Ready to take action." Jessi gave him a brief grin that faded back into a pensive scowl. "We've got to get enough on other suspects."

"You said it's circumstantial." Charmaine sat on a long sectional sofa. She scooted over when Scotty joined her.

"We know the wife had motive. But so far, it's just not enough."

"Cheating husband, sure. But she put up with it for twenty-five years," Charmaine agreed. Her mood started to dip as she considered the consequences for Diamond.

Scotty rose and went to the kitchen. He handed Jessi a bottle of Abita Amber, a popular local beer. He had one for himself. Charmaine got a tall glass mug of Barq's red crème soda. He remained standing. "What do they have on Diamond?"

"It's bullshit!" Jessi slapped a sofa cushion with one fist.

Charmaine reached out squeezed her arm but answered the question. "A glass with traces of the drug that killed the victim. Her fingerprints were on it."

"That's bad." Scotty took a swig of beer and frowned.

"Witnesses from the caterers say Diamond helped them in the kitchen. They found her prints on maybe two other glasses. She hung out with them before her dance and after the main performance," Charmaine said.

"Okay. Something to work with," Scotty replied.

"Harrison claims they have text messages between Diamond and Kennedy that suggest she tried to blackmail him." Charmaine glanced at Jessi when she blurted out another expletive.

"So, why would she kill him? He couldn't pay up if he was dead. That doesn't make sense," Scotty said.

"Exactly what I told Harrison. Thick-headed tool of the system wouldn't listen!"

"Well, if you called him names, I'm not surprised. Harrison hung up on us before he shared more details." Charmaine shared a knowing look with Scotty.

"Look, he's made it clear. Harrison isn't on our side." Jessi squinted as if the formidable detective stood across from her. "Ass-kisser."

"Harrison is stubborn. A bit of a color-in-the-lines kind of guy, sure. But we've never known him to throw a defendant under the bus to appease his bosses," Charmaine argued.

"He's always impressed me as a stand-up dude," Scotty agreed with a shrug.

"First time for everything. Don't forget he has political ambitions." Jessi clenched her jaws tight and crossed her arms. She went back to staring at the television.

A few moments of morose silence stretched as all three contemplated the challenge ahead. Charmaine convinced Jessi to eat her favorite, wonton soup. Scotty and Jessi teased Charmaine about eating dessert before and after dinner.

"My doctor says being so hungry is normal. I'm hoping it will taper off in the next few months. Luckily, I like snacks like raw carrots, celery, and apples. I don't want to gain too much." Charmaine picked up another small portion of King Cake.

"So that cake has a veggie filling?" Jessi teased.

Charmaine stuck out her tongue in response. Still, she put the slice back in the box and closed the lid. "Back to Diamond's case. What about the alleged blackmail text messages?"

Jessi's playful mood evaporated. "Tranisha is going to get us the archived DMs."

"Tranisha?" Scotty asked.

"Tranisha Lee. Diamond has a side gig working for her," Charmaine explained.

"Diamond works for the dominatrix Tranisha? They call her the Iron Claw."

"And how do you know so much about her, down to her stage name?" Charmaine slapped his muscular arm.

"I've got a guy who work security at clubs. Hey, don't give me that look. Getting spanked ain't my thing. Unless you're up for it." Scotty leaned close to Charmaine and winked.

"Showing you who's boss might be fun for a minute." Charmaine giggled.

"Oh, please. I'm eating." Jessi grimaced at them. "The text messages. My friend on the hook for murder?"

"Ahem, right. Poke holes in the theory that Diamond had a motive. Oh, my friend called me back. He had guards at two sites for Gina Shaw's business partner. He didn't get along with Kennedy. In fact, they almost threw hands one time," Scotty said.

"Now we're talking. Diamond's lawyer can use that plus anything we can dig up on Loreen Kennedy." Jessi nodded with a smile.

"Harrison might have told us more if you hadn't insulted him." Charmaine gave a one-shoulder shrug when Jessi glanced at her.

"Well, we don't need him." Jessi went back to slurping soup.

"I hope you're right," Charmaine murmured.

Chapter 6
Walkthrough

Charmaine spent the rest of the weekend resting at Scotty's insistence. Jessi continued to gather information without Charmaine. She also put effort into reassuring Diamond they had a good chance against the DA. Charmaine and Scotty still went to Kat's party on Saturday. Charmaine and Scotty went to church in the morning. Jessi declined to meet them for lunch served at the church's diner attached next door. Sunday passed quietly. The cloudy day turned into night. Charmaine curled up next to Scotty by eleven o'clock. Scotty woke her eight hours later. She stretched and yawned when he rubbed her back until her eyes opened.

"Babe, there's a crazy woman on the phone. You shouldn't give patients your cell number." Scotty shook his head. "She keeps calling back. I think she needs to get picked up. Made no sense."

"Don't call them crazy. They're human beings just like us. Emotional and mental health is on a continuum, and—"

"Okay, Miss Social Worker. You still shouldn't hand out your number to 'em,"

"What time is it? Oh, Lord. My alarm didn't go off." Charmaine scrambled out of bed.

"I turned it off. Figured you needed the extra sleep." Scotty brushed and patted his short cut coils as he stood in front of her dresser mirror.

"I don't give *clients* my home number. Wait, which cell phone?" Charmaine paused in the act of rifling through blouses in her closet.

Scotty didn't answer. Instead, he walked out of the room and returned. "Here. Damn, she's called three more times. Probably left a crazy, I mean odd voice message."

Charmaine swiped the mobile phone from his large hand. "This is our Joliet Investigations cell phone, Scotty. Pay attention."

"I was too busy making you breakfast, my darlin'. Scrambled eggs, grits, and toast in the warmer for you. I've got an early meeting." Scotty smoothed down the front of his dark blue pullover sweater.

Just as Charmaine tapped the voice mail app to retrieve the message, the phone went off again. Gina Shaw Realty appeared on the screen. She hit the accept call icon and the speaker function. "Good morning, I was about to call you back."

"Never mind about that," Gina huffed on the other end.

"Are you okay?" Charmaine glanced at Scotty, who had paused in picking up his keys and turned to listen.

"Listen, they're here. The workers left. I dropped my keys I was so nervous. I can't find them. Oh God. Everything is falling apart. I'm going to lose my business. Someone is deliberately trying to destroy everything I have—"

"Slow down. I don't know what you're talking about. Tell me... hello?" Charmaine stared at phone's screen.

"I get it. Your detective agency clients are the real crazies." Scotty chuckled despite the hot look Charmaine gave him in response.

"Something is very wrong." Charmaine stopped when her phone rang again. This time Jessi's ringtone and face appeared on the screen. "Jessi, I just—"

"Yeah, I'm on my way over to the property. Shaw says a monster flew out of the attic of a house and she's trapped. Something like that. She was babbling a mile a minute. Couldn't get any damn sense out of the woman. I'll take care of this."

"Text me the address." Charmaine pushed passed Scotty on her way to the bathroom.

"Char, no. You don't need to be out in the cold air chasing whatever's got Gina pissing her pants," Jessi replied. A car horn blew in the background. "Screw you, too, bruh!"

"The address, Jessi. I'm not made of glass." Charmaine managed to push down her panties and sit on the toilet. She put the phone on the counter with a sigh of relief. "Speaking of which. Gotta ask the doc if my baby should be pressing on my bladder this early. Whew!"

"You okay?" Scotty appeared, one hand on the doorframe.

"I'm going to get a booklet on pregnancy so you both can stop acting silly," Charmaine huffed at both. Then she glared at Scotty. "You, go to your meeting. Jessi, if you don't send me the address, I'll call Gina or her office to get it."

"I better drive you..." Scotty held up both palms at the way Charmaine glared at him. "You may not be made of glass, but you're not made of steel either. And neither is our baby."

Charmaine's scowl melted. She looked down at her round belly. "Sorry. I'm getting a bit grumpier, too, huh? The point is I'm physically fit."

"You have work, too," Jessi broke into their exchange through the phone.

"I left today free to catch up on clinic notes. Just send me the address, Jessi, and pay attention to your driving," Charmaine said when she heard another vehicle horn blast.

"No use arguing with a hormonal preggo." Jessi ended the call.

"You better had hung up. I'll get you later." Charmaine waved at Scotty to leave. "I have no restrictions, honey. Now go. I've got a case."

"Fine." Scotty glanced at the cell phone. He tapped to open her message app. "Not too far from where I'll be. Maybe I'll swing by."

"Wow, what a coincidence. I'll see you this evening."

"Call me, bae. Let me know if you need help. Or that everything turned out okay," Scotty wore a serious expression.

"Deal. Carrying a baby doesn't make me incompetent to do either of my jobs." Charmaine had finished and washed her hands. She went to Scotty. "I'm doing good. Okay?"

Scotty brushed a lock of hair from her forehead. He planted a kiss on her lips. "Okay."

Charmaine gave him a quick hug before going around him to the bedroom again. She pulled out a pair of tights. Then she stepped into a pair of jeans. "You know we can take care of business, hon."

"I trust you. I even trust Jessi, wild as she can be. I don't trust those goblins or whatever it is you're about to run up against,"

Scotty replied as he followed her out. His mobile phone buzzed on the dresser top where it lay.

"See? You've got things to do, too. Move it, Mr. Minor. We both gotta make some stacks to pay for this kid." Charmaine's voice was muffled as she pulled a sweater on over her camisole. Then she shrugged into a short fleece jacket to ward off the chilly morning air.

"You win. Don't forget to—"

"Call you. Yes, yes. Now shoo." Charmaine flipped her fingertips in the direction of the door. "My grandmother made her famous jambalaya so I wouldn't have to cook. Her way of celebrating her first great-grand."

"I get a son and Miss Etta Ray's cooking? Life is good." Scotty grinned at Charmaine.

"Who said it's a boy?" Charmaine shot back.

They had a playful debate about the sex of their child as Charmaine finished getting ready to leave. Despite her reassurances, Scotty insisted on staying until Charmaine got into her SUV. After two more promises to update him, he finally waved goodbye. Still, he sat in his dark gray GMC Terrain. Charmaine sighed but knew arguing with him would be useless. He waited until Charmaine drove off before he turned to go in the opposite direction.

Twenty frustrating minutes later, the bland female GPS voice announced she'd arrived. She'd cursed Monday traffic the entire way. She didn't know what Jessi had walked into alone, and anxiety pushed her patience to the limit. Charmaine pulled up to the address, a rundown two-story home on Andry Street in the Lower Ninth Ward. Something tickled at Charmaine's memory as she looked around. Jessi's Jeep Compass was already parked on the street. Her nerves spiked when she didn't see her sister. Loud voices pushed through her reverie. She rushed up what looked like fairly stable steps onto the porch.

"Get in your fancy Volvo and bounce, girl. You're in the damn way," Jessi said in her usual poor customer service way.

"Lord, be a fence," Charmaine mumbled as she opened a rickety storm door. She squinted into a dim interior, her eyes adjusting from the winter sunlight outside. "Hello? Jessi, I'm here."

A crash and squeak of fright made Charmaine jump. Lucky for her she'd moved away from the door. Seconds later, a terrified man in white coveralls blew past Charmaine like a runaway bus. He hit the door and didn't stop or look back. A string of expletives from Jessi followed. Charmaine held the compact EMF neutralizer Jessi had given her out like a flashlight, hand on the trigger. The LED beam from the neutralizer cut through the dim interior. Sunlight from outside seemed not to penetrate the house; a bad sign. Malevolent supernatural entities sometimes darkened interior spaces they inhabited.

"I got ya. Little nasty fucker!" Jessi yelled with triumph ringing in her voice. "Oh shit."

Another crash sent Charmaine running to find her sister. "I'm coming. Hold on."

Charmaine stumbled over a heap of rags or tools in her way. She caught her balance and kept moving. Sounds of a struggle pushed her forward into what looked like a gutted kitchen. Jessi, back against a wall, had one hand wrapped around the neck of a weird creature. It hissed at her as she held up a small notebook with the other hand.

"What the—" Charmaine only paused a second in shock. Then the instinct to fight for Jessi kicked in.

She'd always defended her baby sister. When they were growing up, people made fun of Jessi's unconventional behavior. Calling her names like "psycho" because Jessi heard voices. Teasing them about their mother's hot girl rep. Or the cruel comments about Jessi's own questionable life choices. Alive or dead, bullies going after Jessi had to go through Charmaine first.

"Elements of the sun, elements of the day, I summon thee. Elements of light, elements of righteousness come my way. I call upon thee to protect me!" Jessi chanted the phrases in quick succession.

Charmaine saw Jessi's duffle bag. She rushed over and rummaged through it. She used the light from her compact neutralizer to find the heavy duty one she knew Jessi carried.

"Damn it, where is... Here!"

Charmaine held up the larger version. She dropped her smaller one. Then she pressed the green button while aiming it at the creature's head. Jessi continued to struggle as claws swiped at the arm holding it away from her.

"Seven times seven the pattern repeats!" Jessi shouted.

A popping sound vibrated the air around them. The thing Jessi held convulsed, went limp, and then vanished. Smoke curled around Jessi's arm. An acrid scent spread rapidly. Charmaine waved at her face with one hand to catch her breath. Jessi coughed hard as she stumbled to a window. She had trouble raising it for a few seconds. When she finally got it up, Jessi leaned out of it, taking in gulps of air.

"Phew! Good thing I didn't eat breakfast," Charmaine said as she joined Jessi at the window. "It would be all over these floors right now."

"Shit. You okay?" Jessi seemed to forget her own distress. "You shouldn't be wading into fields of negative energy. We don't know how my niece might be affected."

"Scotty says it's a boy," Charmaine said in between clearing her throat of the acid taste.

"Screw him. I say it's a girl.

Jessi pulled Charmaine by one arm out of the room. They went through a back door with wide concrete steps. Charmaine leaned against one of two iron railings, Jessi the other. Both inhaled deeply and exhaled, their faces tilted up to the sky. Cars went by. The brick house next door looked undisturbed. After a few moments birds twittered.

"Girl..." Charmaine looked at Jessi, eyes wide.

"I think it's an undocumented New Orleans cryptid." Jessi's eyes lit up with excitement. She still held a leather-bound notebook in one hand. She went to open it and grimaced. "Ugh. I hope the water is turned on in this place."

"Cryp-what's it? Jessi—" Charmaine blinked but Jessi had already gone back inside.

Jessi went to the kitchen sink. She let out a whoop of relief when water came out. She found a rag and scrubbed her hand. Then she pushed up her sleeve to repeat the process on her wrist and forearm. She unzipped the red sweatshirt hoodie she wore, shrugged it off, and shoved it at Charmaine.

"An animal that some claim to exist but there's no proof. Like Bigfoot."

Charmaine put the hoodie and the neutralizer on the counter, but within easy reach. "That didn't look like any Bigfoot I've even seen. In pictures I mean."

"Louisiana versions are the Honey Island Swamp Monster or the Sabine Thing." Jessi strode to her duffle bag. She found a bottle, removed the cap, and sprinkled the corners of the room. "Obviously this one is a different variety."

"Obviously." Charmaine mimicked her sister's dry academic tone. "We just got our butts kicked by a... I don't know. An extremely pissed-off hellcat with demon eyes!"

"Good observation. Feline in nature. I'll write that down. Hey, there might be hairs from it on my hoodie. We can get those analyzed." Jessi dried her hands on a discarded painter's cloth as she talked.

"Will you please explain what just happened? Sheesh, I'm going to need a therapy session myself after this morning." Charmaine grabbed the neutralizer. She found an old folding chair and plopped onto it.

"Don't worry. I just sprinkled repellent, my own blend. That, combined with the sequence I repeated, should keep it from coming back. All we have to do is put some in the walls. Another sweep with the EMF neutralizer will give this place a clean bill of health." Jessi found an empty vial and tweezers in her duffle. She placed particles in the vial before packing it away again. Then she faced Charmaine with a look of concern. "Maybe you should take the day off."

"Jessi..." Charmaine glared at her.

Jessi assumed the posture of a professor giving a lecture. "Gina called me. Girl, she was losing her shit on the phone, but she managed to describe the cryptid, sort of. Well, she didn't use the word. I think old girl isn't quite the skeptic anymore. Anyway, my brain kicked in as she screamed. Thanks to my own extensive research into legends of so-called supernatural animals, I figured an AEBE had taken up residence here. I'm going to look into the history of this area. Back to the days of indigenous tribes before Europeans showed up. Whew, child. We earned those fees today."

"So, not a ghost or poltergeist. We're dealing with solid creatures now that can claw us to death. Great news." Charmaine jumped at a noise.

"My life is in danger? Oh God!" Gina leaned against the doorjamb. Her smart wool jacket had dirt smudges on one arm. One leg of her slacks was still pushed up on her left ankle. She looked frazzled. "I think it scratched me. I could have rabies!"

Jessi looked Gina up and down. "It didn't even get close to you. You got that little boo-boo when you passed out. You're fine. Now back to the infestation—"

"Feral cats. They can get really mean and territorial," Charmaine broke in. She shot a look at Jessi, who was ready to terrify the woman even more. "And big. Right, Jessi?"

"Yeah, and disappear in a puff of greasy smoke," Jessi mumbled. She shrugged when Charmaine mouthed at her to shut up.

"Do I need to hire an exorcist?" Gina replied, her voice squeaky with fear.

"Don't be silly. There's a science-based explanation for anything that seems supernatural. For example, mathematical patterns in nature. Ever heard of the Fibonacci Sequence. Well, basically there are self-repeating patterns in plants like cauliflower or ferns."

"Cauliflower?" Gina blinked at Jessi and then turned to gape at Charmaine.

"Basically, we got rid of the problem. We'll alert one of the animal control agencies in the area to come over," Charmaine said before Jessi could.

Gina gasped and stood straight. She rubbed her left ankle. "You mean, there are more of those *things*. Something kicked me. See, I have a bruise."

"It's gone. We made sure." Charmaine put the neutralizer on the floor and stood. "You go on with your day. We'll finish up here, contact your work crew and get things back on track."

"I'm not sure..." Gina brushed a hand across her forehead.

Charmaine realized what she'd almost tripped over earlier was Gina out cold on the floor. She went around the distressed woman and found her Louboutin leather tote. "It's not even ten o'clock yet. You can get plenty done. We've got this."

"Yeah. It's handled," Jessi added.

Harold, the carpenter and wallpaper expert, appeared in the open back door. He stood on the top step. His gaze swept the room until it settled on a disheveled Gina. "Sorry I'm late. Traffic was a pain on the way over. What's up?"

"Nothing much. Just mean abandoned pets," Charmaine said quickly before Gina or Jessi could reply.

"Yeah. Last job I did for a realtor a pack of stray dogs had made the house their new playground. Animal welfare folks had a time rounding those mutts up." Harold glanced around at the walls. "Sure everything okay? I don't want any wild animals jumping out at me."

"Fine. The rest of the workers will be back soon," Jessi said.

"You mean they're not here yet? That's weird." Harold raised both bushy eyebrows at Gina.

Charmaine put a hand on Gina's arm when the realtor started to speak. "Anyway, we're done. Just another day on the job."

Jessi glanced at Harold. He stared hard at the neutralizer. She packed their devices into her duffle. Then she strode off toward another part of the house. "Just get on with whatever you need to do. I'll be right back."

"Right, I left my phone in the other room. Thanks for getting it for me," Charmaine called after Jessi. She plastered on a bland expression. Harold gave her a sharp side-eye when Charmaine's phone trilled a ringtone from her pocket. "Never mind, Jess. I found it. So, Gina, you were telling me about the other two houses."

"Um, right." Gina brushed at her clothes. She accepted her tote bag from Charmaine. Then she looked muddled again as she turned to Harold. "We're not ready for paint. I sent the schedule for each phase on the calendar app."

"I decided to get a jumpstart by taking a look around. I'm going to the house on North Rampart once I leave here. Shouldn't take me long." Harold's long strides took him in the direction Jessi had taken minutes earlier. His brow furrowed when Jessi walked past him the opposite direction.

"All done." Jessi looked into Charmaine's eyes and jerked her head toward the door.

"We'll get out of your way." Charmaine tugged the sleeve of a still-discombobulated Gina. She pulled her along as they walked out of the house and into the sunshine.

Gina pressed the fingertips of one hand to her temple. She blinked in the sunlight. "I'm confused. What is happening?"

"We're one step ahead of whoever is trying to delay your projects, that's what. We'll take a closer look into your business rival. Won't we, Jessi?" Charmaine looked at her sister.

"Hmm, right-o," Jessi replied in a chirpy tone.

"I'm sure you have a busy day ahead. We'll visit the house on North Rampart. Then head over to North Claiborne next. All in a day's work for us. Like I said, most of the time we don't find anything scary. Just plain old ordinary explanations."

Charmaine chattered as she walked Gina to where her SUV was parked. After a few more baffled questions, Gina seemed more oriented. She even smiled at a corny joke Charmaine told. Something about the cats being out of the bag. As the vehicle backed out, Charmaine waved goodbye with a confident smile. Once the SUV disappeared around a corner, Charmaine turned to find Harold studying them. The lanky man stood at one of the two vertical windows that flanked the front door. He moved away after a few seconds.

"Well, this was a way to start the week off with a bang. Why did you cut me off back there? I was about to let ol' girl know how effective we are at vanquishing monsters." Jessi wore a pleased expression. "What?"

"Our supernatural cases have been under the radar for the most part. Let's keep it that way." Charmaine glanced over her shoulder as she spoke low.

Jessi followed her gaze with a frown. "What's up?"

"Gina is dramatic. I don't trust her not to blab to her friends. Harold likes to gossip, too. He's the guy that told me about the first house."

Charmaine kept her voice down as they walked to where their SUVs were parked. Harold had parked his pickup truck along the cracked driveway of the empty house next door.

"So what? Most of what we do is considered bogus anyway," Jessi said with a laugh. "Nobody but a few crackpot vloggers take paranormal investigations serious."

"All the same, I think we should be low key. I like playing up the whole line that we mostly disprove ghost sightings. Talking about ghost creatures won't help." Charmaine blew out a long breath and leaned against Jessi's Jeep for support.

Jessi opened the rear cargo door of the Jeep and carefully placed the duffle inside. She shut it with a thump before walking back to eye Charmaine. "You already look worn out, sis. I'll handle the next call alone. Scotty will be on my ass if you even break a fingernail."

"Oh, crap. Speaking of which." Charmaine pulled out her phone. She sent a text message to Scotty. His answer came a few seconds later. No doubt he'd been watching his phone.

"You gonna tell him about the cryptid? That was something else."

Charmaine squinted into the sunshine. "Yes, I don't keep secrets from him. We have an agreement."

Jessi snorted. "Girl, everybody keeps secrets."

"We're open with each other. I'll give him a less intense version of what just happened." Charmaine raised both eyebrows at Jessi.

"You mean scrubbed of all the creepiest details." Jessi replied.

'I mean without you making it sound like we just faced down a raging Bigfoot," Charmaine retorted.

"In other words, you gonna lie." Jessi barked a laugh when Charmaine scowled at her.

"*Certainly not,*" Charmaine protested. "Anyway, tell me about that thing."

"I think we're about to get famous in supernatural circles. We may have found a previously undocumented cryptid. I'm going to search the archives for legends from local indigenous tribes. Probably should look into African American lore as well. Super exciting." Jessi grinned as she put on her sunglasses.

"Yeah." Charmaine looked at Jessi and then past her to the house. She fished her own sunglasses from her jacket pocket but didn't put them on.

"Look, I'm not going to mention anything about the werecat to Scotty. I'll let you break it to him gently. Logan will be thrilled to come along if Gina calls all stressed again. You can sit the next one out."

"Hmmm, no." Charmaine squinted harder at the house.

"Okay, I'm not the mind reader so spill it." Jessi turned to face the house as well.

"Doesn't this location seem familiar to you?" Charmaine looked down the street and back again at the house.

"I know two people who live around here. Monica used to come party over here," Jessi said.

"Nah, that's not it. And it's odd Harold showed up when he did." Charmaine tried reaching across the distance between her and the man in the house. She couldn't make out his thoughts, only a general strong curiosity.

"You think he's up to something?" Jessi adopted a casual pose as she turned sideways to face Charmaine.

"I don't know. There's more to him, but I can't quite get what it is," Charmaine replied.

"Gina gave us a list of all contractors and sub-contractors working on listings under development," Jessi replied. She took out her smartphone and tapped an app. "It has enough details for me to do a deep dive."

"Hmm." Charmaine stood straight and snapped her fingers. "I knew it. Mrs. Chatelaine's properties."

"Huh?" Jessi continued to enter notes.

"Two lots are in this area," Charmaine said. She looked at Jessi. "Could be a coincidence. But like you always say..."

"Coincidence my ass. I'm going to the Land Records Division for one of the lawyers. Perfect chance for me to do more digging around. Have to stop by their office first." Jessi got up close to stare at Charmaine. Then she stepped back to scan her from head to toe. "Sure you okay? That was some crazy action in there."

Charmaine blew out a noisy sigh. "I really have to deal with you smothering me for the next seven months?"

"Uh, yeah," Jessi said. "While you're incubating my niece for sure! Drive careful now."

"Me? I'm not a menace behind the wheel." Charmaine huffed as Jessi opened the door and waited until she was in her SUV.

"I'll check on you later." Jessi waved goodbye, then scurried to her Jeep and drove off.

They went in different directions from the St. Andry address. Charmaine headed to the clinic. There she settled into a mundane routine of clinic notes, consultations with colleagues, and answered texts from two patients. The Monday ended quietly, which astonished her given how it had started out. Gina didn't call again. Jessi texted with the details on the next building they would examine. A boutique hotel on Royal Street.

After checking in for assignments, Jessi sat at her office laptop. She signed into the Clerk of Civil District Court's online records search. The law office paid the annual subscription. The rest of her morning was spent staring at deeds, mortgage filings, and conveyances. Jessi felt like an expert on all things related to buying, selling, and transferring land in Orleans Parish. By noon her shoulders ached from sitting too long in front of the computer. She took a break. The three-block walk to a local deli revived her. Brisk winds whisked away what little warmth the weak winter sunshine tried to provide. As she munched on a roast beef sandwich and people watched, her cell phone rang. Jessi was tempted to ignore it, especially when she glanced at the call ID. Ricky.

They'd had what could be considered close to an argument. Jessi told him he was having a midlife crisis, even though he was only thirty-two. Ricky wanted them to move in together. The cost of living was one reason he gave. Yet Jessi knew he was pushing for a more permanent kind of commitment. She sighed deeply as she let the call go to voice mail. He'd been dropping hints about wanting to take their relationship to another level. Stories of happy days with the parents and siblings would pop up in their conversations. Jessi noticed the change after she told him Charmaine and Scotty were expecting. She dreaded Ricky making a "We need to talk" announcement any day. A bell notification announced she had a new message. Jessi frowned, put down her sandwich, and tapped the icon to listen.

"Hey, call me. It's important," Ricky's voice said through the speaker. And his name lit up the phone screen again with another call while she listened. Jessi took a long pull of her cola. She quickly plugged in the phone's earbuds and accepted the video call.

"Hey. I was just about to call you back," Jessi said. "How's your Monday going?"

"Hectic. Listen, don't do anything impulsive after I tell you what I'm about to tell you. A lot can change before a trial. Preliminary hearings alone can take months to get scheduled..."

"You're stalling and it won't work," Jessi broke in. She glared at his handsome yet tense face. "Don't tell me. You no-good tools of the militarized police state are going to arrest my best friend."

Ricky's reddish-brown eyebrows bunched together. "Name-calling is unnecessary, Yes, she's been booked. Mrs. Kennedy is screaming about her husband's killer walking around free and—"

"She's got more motive to want her potbellied politician husband on a slab than Diamond," Jessi blurted out. She ignored the startled glances from the other diners.

"Calm down. You know Harrison will make sure our investigation follows all avenues and—"

"Save the bullshit for your granny's vegetable garden. What's the charge?" Jessi swiped at her mouth to get rid of crumbs. "Is she sitting in jail?"

"She bonded out. It was all very routine." Ricky cleared his throat.

"Answer the damn questions, Ricky." Jessi huffed as she studied his face.

"Involuntary manslaughter. The DA is getting pressure to switch it to murder based on the evidence. But we pointed out that their text messages were more like sexting, role-playing than Diamond having a real motive. Like you said, she doesn't have a solid motive. It's not all bad," Ricky added. "Honey, I'm just the messenger."

"Tell that to the five-year-old girl who might lose her mother. I can't talk to you right now." Jessi tapped the phone's screen harder than necessary to end the call. Then she wrapped the uneaten half of her sandwich and headed back to her office.

Two hours later she finally got through to Diamond. Her friend tended to isolate when things were bad. Being charged with killing a white guy certainly qualified. Jessi held off on calling Charmaine. They'd already had enough of a stormy Monday. When she finally went to Diamond's seventh-ward home, her friend looked strangely calm. Jessi let herself in with her key; given for emergencies. She followed the sounds through the shotgun style cottage through the compact kitchen and out of the rear door. Indyah played in their small backyard with a little boy who lived next door. Diamond puffed on a cigarette as she sat on a large lawn chair. She was wrapped against the cool day in a chunky cable sweater.

"Hey, don't pull me off the wagon with you," Jessi said.

She walked over to stand next to Diamond. She reached out a hand and Diamond handed her the cigarette. Jessi puffed once. She grimaced at the bitter taste on her tongue. Then she ground out the burning end on a saucer Diamond had used as an ashtray.

"What I really want is a king-sized blunt with an extra kick added." Diamond's lower lip twisted when she tried to smile. "Not like I don't know where to get one. Or three."

"Girl, look—"

"Save the 'it's gonna be all right' speech. This is my life. One kick in the ass after another. I started a new savings account to buy the house next door. Couldn't decide if I would make it part of this one or rent it out. Money started to be right working for Tranisha." Diamond sniffed as she pressed the heel of her hand against her eyes. "Stupid to think anything would change for me."

"Stop it. Okay, so this shit looks dark right now. But don't we always pull off a win?"

"I'm tired, Jessi. Tired of fighting to get crumbs only to have it blow up in my face."

Diamond smothered a sob. Indyah looked away from her play and at her mother. The large bright orange ball her playmate had tossed bounced off her chest. Instead of chasing it, Indyah ran over, up the three steps, and patted her mother's shoulder. The touch seemed to shake Diamond. Jessi stepped into the kitchen and returned with a paper towel. When she returned, Diamond wore a smile to reassure her little girl. The little boy continued to throw the ball around, oblivious to the drama playing out.

"I told you that smoke was gone make your allergies act up," Jessi said.

"You right. These things are poison. Can't believe we ever liked this crap." Diamond's voice held a strained light note. "Go on. Finish the game. Hey, I'm gonna fix your favorite dinner, fish sticks with mac and cheese."

Indyah eyed her mother. "I don't like fish sticks any more. You were crying."

"I forgot you got wore out on fish sticks. Meatballs with those curly noodles and tomato sauce. Chocolate pudding for dessert." Diamond stroked Indyah's smooth brown cheek with one finger.

"Yay!" Indyah threw up both arms and jumped down from the top step to the small square of grass.

"Nice fake out. She's growing fast." Jessi applauded when the kids took turns doing awkward tumble moves.

"I don't want her to have to grow up fast like we did. But if I go to jail..." Diamond whispered the dreaded words. Her fragile composure started to fail.

"Hell the damn no!" Jessi said with force. "I'm already working on fixing this shit. You hear me? Take some time off. Meditate. Smoke a joint—just one, if you have to. But we are not going to roll over."

"Okay." Diamond blinked away tears and squared her shoulders.

"Okay," Jessi repeated with all the conviction she could put into the single word. Now all she had to do was deliver.

Chapter 7
Shady Appraisals

Harrison drummed the fingers of his right hand on his desk. The solid digits made a steady thump-thump in the silence. He'd agreed to meet with Charmaine and Jessi Tuesday morning. Now he gazed at the sisters, who wore matching hostile glares.

"Yeah, and you had Ricky do your dirty work breaking the news to us. Like we haven't pulled your butt from between a rock and a hard place multiple times." Jessi shook a finger at him.

"Blowing up at each other won't help your friend." Harrison glanced sideways at Charmaine.

"You know, *Bryan*, I've found getting pissed to be very helpful. Clears the mind and any delusions that the system isn't bullshit," Jessi snapped before Charmaine had a chance to speak.

"How did that work out for you the umpteen times you landed in jail?" Harrison's voice was level but one hand clenched into a fist.

"Fine since I have no felony convictions," Jessi tossed back.

"Okay, don't let me hold you up any longer. You can deal with this mess without me. There's the door. Don't slam it on your way out." Harrison glared at Jessi, who scowled back at him.

"Jessi, Bryan, shut up!" Charmaine yelled when Jessi started to reply. The sharp volume of her voice made them both jump.

The door eased open and Ricky slipped in. He glanced at his boss and then at the sisters. "Just thought I'd better..." His voice trailed off. He stood against the wall and said no more.

"I could use the backup." Charmaine nodded at him. She turned to Jessi. "Detective Harrison doesn't have control over his bosses or the DA. Not to mention Mrs. Kennedy's influence."

"Not just her. Bernard Kennedy had powerful friends as well. But I fight the deadly three," Harrison said with a heaviness in his tone.

"The deadly three?" Charmaine blinked at him.

"Motive, means, opportunity. Text messages between Ms. Phillips and the victim suggest blackmail. She served him alcohol, possibly mixed with drugs. Witnesses say she spent most of her time entertaining him during the party." Harrison ticked off the points using the fingers of one hand.

"Shit." Jessi slumped in the chair.

"A good attorney could poke holes in each one. But..." Ricky said.

"Yeah, it's a toss-up if a judge or jury will buy it. They can't bring up Diamond's arrest or conviction history, but an assistant DA can mention her sex work," Jessi said in a morose tone. Then she looked at Harrison. "You don't think she's guilty?"

"Too neat. Like you said, those texts could also be sexy talk. He kind of enjoyed being submissive. Am I right?" Harrison raised at eyebrow at her. "I mean, you're the expert when it comes to..."

"I didn't specialize in BDSM if that's what you're asking. Diamond looks like a sweetheart, but she has done the dominatrix thing. Nothing dark. Some guys like being ordered around by a cute 'wouldn't hurt a fly' looking young thing.

Buddy liked dressing up and being treated like a naughty clown," Jessi replied.

Ricky burst out laughing and then stopped when Harrison looked at him. "Sorry. It's just... I got a visual and. Yeah, no. sorry."

"So, like Ward said, a smart attorney could probably make a good defense. Sure, she served him drinks, but so did the wait staff hosts hired," Harrison said.

"His wife is acting like she didn't know about his playing around, but c'mon. I don't think it will take much digging to show that's a lie. She gets his assets now that he's gone," Ricky pointed out.

"Their oldest kid, a daughter, is going to inherit the business. Seems there's a bit of family drama over that. The next eldest, a son, is pissed about his sister being put in control," Harrison added.

"So, you've been investigating someone other than Diamond?" Jessi blinked at Harrison, her scowl in his direction easing.

"I've been doing my job. Looking at everyone with a possible motive," Harrison replied. "Plus, according to witnesses his wife could have been at the party without anyone noticing. Once things got *lively*, no one paid attention to who was who."

"They were all wearing masks. People were arriving and leaving for hours. She said she didn't go, but they both had invites. So, the valet would have let her in." Ricky nodded.

"They had a valet? Wait, of course they did. Rich folks." Jessi shook her head.

"You're saying the valet did double duty as security?"

"Yeah, to keep out any strays," Ricky said.

Jessi looked at Charmaine. "Maybe Scotty can talk to the guy."

"For sure. Give us the details." Charmaine took out her phone.

"Don't step all over my investigation. And by the way, I got a call from a colleague about some weird disturbance over on Andry Street. You two were there." Harrison looked from Charmaine to Jessi.

Jessi crossed her arms. "Our client—"

"Gina Shaw, a sometime business partner of Bernard Kennedy," Harrison broke in.

"Our clients and their cases are confidential," Jessi shot back.

Harrison transferred his gaze to Charmaine. "Okay. What details did you just ask me to give? The NOPD has the right to keep information from the public if it compromises our investigation."

"The DA has to share all discoverable evidence to the defendant's counsel, so we'll find out anyway," Jessi clipped.

"You're not a lawyer, let alone her lawyer," Harrison replied.

Ricky spread his hands in a peace-making gesture. "Look, let's not—"

"I'm her lawyer's investigator. I'll get the information to look into all possible witnesses and evidence," Jessi said.

"Great. Then we can let the process take its course. Once her attorney of record notifies the DA, then said defense counsel can make a formal request." Harrison flashed a tight smile that vanished one second later.

"Or we can get the info from the party's hosts." Jessi leaned forward with a scowl.

"Those folks will close ranks in a hot minute." Harrison wore a smug expression when Jessi fumed at his answer.

"Gina Shaw wants us to clear out ghosts at properties she's developing," Charmaine blurted before Jessi gathered steam to lob another volley at him.

"Oh boy," Ricky mumbled from his position behind Charmaine.

"What—" Harrison blew out a slow breath. "No, don't say anything more. Just swear it doesn't have anything to do with my murder case."

"Nope," Charmaine said. "Not a thing."

Harrison eyed Charmaine steadily for a few seconds. His expression implied he was skeptical but didn't want to press it. He nodded to Ricky. The junior detective stepped forward and pulled his phone from an inside pocket of his jacket. Harrison wrote on a sheet of paper and pushed it across the desktop to them.

"Here is the company that catered the party and the valet's name." Harrison frowned and pointed at them with a large forefinger. "Don't mention my name and *do not* cause any kind of chaos with these people."

Charmaine grabbed the paper fast as if afraid he'd snatch it back. She folded it neatly before slipping it into her handbag. Then she smiled sweetly at Harrison. "Who us? Never."

"Geez, you two... Look, something smells off about this whole thing." Harrison frowned at no one in particular.

"Yeah, and we know what the criminal justice system does to marginalized people," Jessi said.

Harrison shook his head. "I wish I could argue with you but it happens."

"The good news is you know top attorneys that can be on the case. And you're damn good investigators. If anyone can turn over a rock and find skeletons, it's you, babe." Ricky squeezed Jessi's shoulder.

"You got your metaphors mixed up, but I get it. Thanks for the vote of confidence." Jessi patted his hand.

"Look, you're upset about your friend. I get it. But I'm not in the habit of arresting anyone because some socialite screams loud. I'm keeping an open mind." Harrison stood as a signal their meeting was over.

"That's all we ask. Right, Jessi?" Charmaine spoke quickly and nudged her sister with a sharp elbow.

Jessi winced. "Yeah, right."

As they left Harrison's office, Ricky seemed poised to kiss Jessi goodbye. Harrison cocked his head and squinted at him. Ricky gave Jessi's right hand a quick squeeze instead as she walked by. Once outside, Charmaine walked to her SUV with Jessi following. Instead of getting in, Charmaine leaned against the driver's side door. Jessi blew out a long breath as if decompressing.

"Don't say it. Harrison ain't the enemy and he's trying to help us in his own way," Jessi said.

"As usual your temper got outta pocket. But I know what you're feeling. Diamond is like my second little sister." Charmaine frowned and put on her sunglasses even though the late January day was overcast.

"We can't let them frame her with this bullshit," Jessi said with force.

"Hey, wait a minute," Ricky called as he jogged across the parking lot to them. "Listen, the boss wasn't going to say this but he had feelers out on other principals in the case. One thing to know, our deputy superintendent had no love for Kennedy. Something political. Mrs. Kennedy or his pals don't have the pull they think they have."

"Thanks, Ricky. At least that will make me sleep better." Jessi planted a kiss on his cheek.

"Don't tell Harrison. He's in a tricky position. Plus, you know how he is. I'm going to check on which ADA will get Diamond's case. See you tonight maybe?" Ricky stepped close to Jessi.

"Sure, but call me. We might be chasing ghosts," Jessi said with a grin.

Ricky pretended to shiver. "I'd rather run after criminals than do your job."

Jessi laughed. "Thanks again, babe."

"Bye, love." Ricky strode back into the office answering his cell phone as he walked.

"See? Now stop poking the bear; Harrison I mean." Charmaine elbowed Jessi's side again.

"Ouch! Pregnancy has made you a menace," Jessi complained, taking a step away from her. "What now?"

Charmaine took out her cell phone and checked the time. "It's almost ten. I can't put off another appointment. Baby or not, the clinic director won't be pleased."

"Okay. I'll be done at about four today. We can meet up at your house by five. Hey, why don't we all go out for dinner? Double date," Jessi replied.

"Deal."

Their plans were thwarted by the universe and job demands. Ricky had to work late and Scotty did, too. Tuesday evening found Charmaine and Jessi sharing Creole, Asian, and Indian fusion cuisine from Nirvana restaurant on Magazine Street. Scotty treated as an apology for working late once again. Charmaine dug into her chicken biryani with enthusiasm. They sat in Charmaine's living room on large pillows as they ate. Their paper plates were spread buffet style on the long coffee table. A news broadcast played on the television in the background. An attractive couple reported on the usual mix of mayhem and feel-good local stories.

"Oh, so tasty!" Charmaine said around a mouthful basmati rice.

"Well, at least you have a healthy appetite." Jessi eyed her as Charmaine stuffed a piece of naan into her mouth.

"Umm." Charmaine chewed and swallowed. "My ob-gyn says I haven't gained too much weight."

"Wow." Jessi watched as Charmaine reached for a fried milk ball dipped in rose syrup. "You got me beat."

Charmaine paused and drew her hand back. She wore a sheepish grin. "Guess I should slow down, huh?"

"Well, at least finish the main course before you gobble down dessert," Jessi said with a laugh.

"I don't know what's gotten into me." Charmaine patted her lips with a napkin.

"First Scotty and then his baby," Jessi quipped.

"Oh, yeah." Charmaine and Jessi shared a loud laugh. "Good news. I heard back from the licensing board. Taking Mrs. Chatelaine's case isn't a conflict."

"Helpful seeing as how we're already working for her. I would have bucked if they'd said anything else. There's something funky about her case and Gina's, like there's a connection," Jessi replied. She licked sauce from one thumb.

"Speaking of which, what about Diamond?" Charmaine shifted to get comfy on her pillow.

"I let her know what we found out so far. She's holding up. Tranisha has been helping her get more online work. I got her lined up with an attorney I know. She's a pit bull for her clients."

"Cool."

"Yeah. I'm feeling a little better about this whole thing, but it could easily go left. I didn't say that to Diamond though." Jessi sighed.

"You didn't have to. Diamond knows what she's up against." Charmaine felt a chill despite the cozy feel of her home.

"We're going to look over the texts between her and Buddy Kennedy. The couple that threw the party has outside cameras at the entrance and back of the house." Jessi sipped tea.

"I already asked. The wife politely told me to eff off when I called about getting the footage for that night," Charmaine said. She'd made the call between appointments.

"Diamond's lawyer can ask for it in discovery. Matter of fact, let me tell Ricky so Loreen's bestie won't try 'losing' the recording." Jessi hopped up to retrieve her phone. She paused after a few moments. "Or maybe..."

Charmaine studied Jessi's expression. "You've got that shifty look. What trouble are we about to get into?"

"Hypothetically, someone could access the Wi-fi and copy said footage." Jessi resumed tapping messages.

"You mean hack a private network, which is illegal. Making anything you find out useless in court and landing us in jail. Then there's the part about losing our agency license. I'd probably lose my social work license. Sure, blow up both our careers. It's not like babies are expensive." Charmaine's voice grew shriller with every sentence.

"Ok, ok. I said 'hypothetically'. Damn." Jessi clicked her tongue in annoyance.

"Thank you." Charmaine popped a milk ball in her mouth.

The next few days went by without major event. Jessi went to one of the last three homes Gina asked them to check. She found a ghost there but left her undisturbed. The energy was too weak to do more than cause a cold spot in the nineteenth century home on occasion. Jessi reported all clear to Gina. Then she got to work tracking down the valet from the party. She found him at his regular job working security at a luxury condo complex on Decatur Street. By Friday, both Jessi and Charmaine were more than ready for the weekend. That evening the guys were once again working late but a new couples' night was planned for Saturday. Charmaine had gratefully accepted a deep skillet filled with smothered okra with shrimp and sausage from their grandmother.

"Thanks so much, granny," Charmaine called out from her place on the sofa.

Charmaine had gone through the formality of insisting Mama Etta Ray didn't have to do anything. She knew the feisty sixty-eight-year-old would ignore her and take control. Etta Ray LaMotte was the one person she and Jessi let boss them around. She'd been there for them more than their mother. Her feet were propped on an ottoman, per Mama Etta Ray's command.

Mama Etta Ray had served Charmaine a plate, along with a side of coleslaw and her homemade hush puppies. She'd dusted after running a finger over several furniture surfaces. Now she was humming "He's An On Time God" with enthusiasm as she tidied up the kitchen.

Jessi rang the doorbell. She was visible through the drawn curtain over the kitchen door window. Seconds later Mama Etta Ray let her in. "Hey, Mama. Whew, it's cold out today. Don't let that sunshine fool ya."

"Probably would be warmer if you didn't wear them thin, skin-tight leggings. But hey, you're grown. I guess that's how young people are dressing these days." Mama Etta Ray gave her a sweet smile. A gospel ringtone came from her large purse sitting on a chair. "Let me get that. Might be your Aunt Dot."

Mama Etta had a younger sister Dorothy, nicknamed Dot, who lived in Baton Rouge. They had always been close. Mama Etta Ray bustled over, tossing aside the dishcloth in her hand onto the countertop.

"Thank God it's Friday, huh?" Charmaine sighed with contentment, a hand on her belly.

"Yeah. I see you're getting the pregnant princess treatment," Jessi teased.

"You know how Mama Etta Ray is, girl. Not like I had a choice," Charmaine replied.

"Oh, you're really suffering. You've been fed, got your feet up, and let me guess. She's cleaned house, too." Jessi glanced around as she spoke.

"Okay, so I didn't put up much resistance. I get so tired." Charmaine gave in to the urge and yawned widely. Then she burped. "Oops, excuse me. Lord, please don't let me be the gassy pregnant lady for the next seven months."

"I think that ship has sailed. I'm just glad it's not coming out the other end." Jessi ducked when Charmaine threw a small throw pillow at her head. She picked it up from the floor and put it back on the sofa.

"Well, that was Gracie from church. Y'all remember Miz Gracie, right?" Mama Etta Ray plunged ahead without waiting for an answer. "I swear, she's my good friend but being president of the Ushers Ministry has gone to her head. Now she wants us to get new uniforms. I keep telling her white tops and black skirts for the women and black suits for the men been fine for umpteen years."

"Ain't no drama like church drama," Jessi murmured.

"Cause church drama don't stop," Charmaine chimed in. They shared a grin.

"Anyway, those suits she showed us do look kinda nice. Guess you got to move with the times." Mama Etta Ray didn't seem to have heard them. Or if she did, chose to ignore their teasing. She let out a soft grunt as she sat in the stuffed chair next to the sofa.

"Yes, ma'am," the sisters said in obedient unison after exchanging a glance.

"What you two been up to? I love how y'all stay working hard. That's the way to make it in this world. Not that I approve of that voodoo stuff y'all be doin.'" Mama Etta Ray smoothed down the front of her track suit top. She wore silver hoops that compliment her mixed gray and white hair. She studied the sisters in turn as if waiting for answers.

"For the fiftieth time, we don't practice voodoo. And you know it," Charmaine said patiently.

Jessi, who had long ago given up arguing, merely smiled at Mama Etta Ray. "I'm going to get some food."

"All I'm sayin' is don't call on the devil and maybe he won't show up. I taught y'all from the Bible, so you know how I feel." Mama Etta Ray crossed her ankles and fanned her face with a paper towel.

"Yes, ma'am," Charmaine said.

"Spirits are all up in the Good Book. What we do is help the departed find some kind of peace. And send the ones that want to cause trouble on their way. Maybe to your hell." Jessi returned to the living room with a small plate. She sat on the opposite end of the sofa from Charmaine.

"I know you're good girls. You both got the gift of seeing. I don't know why, but the Lord has a plan. And I trust him. I just worry y'all getting close to sorcery and witchcraft. I keep y'all lifted in prayer though." Mama Etta Ray sighed and looked at Charmaine. "Don't you expose that baby to no spirits."

Jessi cocked an eyebrow. "She—"

"No, granny. I'll be careful," Charmaine said, cutting Jessi off.

"She's taking it pretty easy considering." Jessi smirked and avoided Charmaine's hot side-eye.

Mama Etta Ray frowned. "Considering what?"

"She means I'm working at the clinic and running a business. But Jessi and Scotty have taken on more to help," Charmaine said quickly.

"That's good. Speaking of Scotty, he got you a ring yet?" Mama Etta Ray spoke casually, but her steady gaze fixed on Charmaine.

"We're probably going to discuss marriage at some point. I'm not ready to rush things." Charmaine returned her grandmother's scrutiny with a determined expression.

"I'm not trying to tell grown folks how to live. I'm lookin' out for you. Marriage is more than a piece of paper," Mama Etta said. "Well, enough of that. I heard about Diamond from her aunt. That child got herself in a big mess."

"She didn't do it, of course," Jessi said.

"A fast life always leads to jail or the cemetery. Is what they said in the news right—about her dancing naked at a party?" Mama Etta Ray looked at Jessi.

Jessi hissed in annoyance. "Diamond was in a costume."

"I know the old saying is true. Believe half of what you see and none of what you hear. I also know you girls been in them streets." Mama Etta Ray looked from Jessi to Charmaine and back again.

"She wasn't naked and she didn't kill the guy," Jessi said in a firm tone.

"I never believed little Diamond did any such thing, so you don't have to convince me. Now, the police and the court system is another thing."

"They're building a case. Kennedy's family is out for blood. But we're investigating leads," Charmaine said.

"Well, there's another reason I came over. Gracie didn't just call about the usher ministry. When I saw the news, I remembered her saying Bernice's cousin cleans house. Y'all know Miz Bernice Glover. Tall, walks kind of bent over cause she got arthritis in her back real bad. Well, she used to but then they did an operation and gave her some injections. Bernice is like a new woman. Dyed her hair red, got a new boyfriend. I told her to be careful cause the devil stay busy trying to lead God's people astray."

"The other reason you visited," Jessi said. She glanced at Charmaine, her lips twitching.

"Yes, granny. You wanted something else?" Charmaine nodded to reinforce Jessi's point. They both knew Mama Etta Ray well. She was headed into what threatened to become a long-winded monologue on staying right with the Lord.

"I was getting to it. Young people always rushin'." Mama Etta Ray clicked her tongue but continued. "We was talkin' about how terrible it was after church last Sunday. Not that I'm one to gossip."

Jessi shook her head. "Not you."

Their grandmother was so into the story that she missed the note of sarcasm. "Bernice's first cousin cleans house. She has worked for the family for ten years now. They spent half the time fighting and the other half not speakin' to each other. He liked to party with women, the younger and wilder the better. Says he even gave the wife an STI. That's a—"

"Sexually transmitted infection," Charmaine broke in. "Oh my God."

"Bernice's cousin said that was ten years ago and she doesn't think his wife let him touch her since. And they fought over money, too. Ask me, the police should be looking at *her*." Mama Etta Ray folded her hands and sat back. "But you know who got the power in this world."

"Loreen Kennedy definitely doesn't like people poking into their life," Jessi said with a scowl. "Thanks for the info."

"I figured you girls would want to know. I got the cousin's name and phone number somewhere in my purse. I talked to her myself just to verify. Gracie don't always get a story straight. I didn't want to send y'all off on a wide goose chase. I remember that time she told everybody Deacon Bell had died. The man just passed out while cutting his grass. His wife said he wasn't drinkin' enough water in the heat." Mama Etta Ray chattered on as she bustled to her purse and rummaged around in the large faux leather satchel.

"You think Harrison will listen to us about Loreen Kennedy?" Jessi whispered as she leaned toward Charmaine

"Wrong question. Can he do anything about it? Harrison has closed a lot of cases and helped powerful people avoid public embarrassment—"

"With *our* help," Jessi broke in.

"But I'm not sure it's enough to fight against these particular heavy hitters," Charmaine said. She started to say more but stopped when their grandmother returned.

"Here ya go." Mama Etta Ray handed Charmaine a torn sheet of note.

"Thanks, granny." Charmaine read the note written on it in blue ink.

"Oh, and according to Arlene, that's Bernice's cousin, Bernard Kennedy's oldest son is going to run for congress one day. They don't want no kind of scandal messing up his future campaign." Mama Etta Ray stuffed items back into her large purse as she talked. She took out a small cosmetic mirror and gazed at herself.

"Memories will fade if they can get this scandalous episode over fast," Charmaine said.

"Yeah, which means throwing Diamond under the legal bus," Jessi agreed.

"Speaking of family, your mama is doing good. Y'all could give her a call more than once a year." Mama Etta Ray raised a palm at their twin frowns. "I know Monica made mistakes. Lord knows I made my own. You'll learn now that you're having one of your own." She raised an eyebrow at Charmaine.

"You didn't have men in and out of your house or put them before your kids," Jessi said in a flat tone.

"She's turned her life around. No, now listen." Mama Etta Ray plopped on the sofa, purse in her lap. "She's married to a preacher with a strong ministry. Monica is a different woman."

"Uh-huh. Thanks for the update," Jessi drawled.

"We know about Monica and her husband Reverend Ronnie Newsome. We're investigators after all," Charmaine said.

"Newsome is a shady prosperity preacher who left his first wife to marry Monica."

"Rev. Newsome and his wife were already separated," Mama Etta Ray protested. "And people do change. Look at you, Jessi. You're a professional woman now."

"I was a pro before," Jessi quipped with a sly giggle.

"You know what I mean. Judge not lest ye be judged." Mama Etta Ray shook a finger at them.

"We'll think about it and reach out," Charmaine rushed to say before Jessi could answer.

"Be kind to one another, tenderhearted, forgiving one another, as God in Christ forgave you." Mama Etta Ray gazed at Charmaine as she quoted Ephesians. "Now I know your pastor done told you about forgiveness, baby."

Charmaine squirmed. "Yes, ma'am."

Jessi squinted at Mama Etta Ray. "Serving up a big helping of guilt along with the food, huh?"

"A little bit of guilt keeps us from sinning, child. Anyway, I heard you was praying the other day. We gonna get you in church one of these days." Mama Etta Ray nodded.

"Me?" Jessi blinked at her and then looked at Charmaine.

"When we were at that property and the 'cat' came at us. You recited—"

"Words can shift energy and frequencies. Science. I wasn't praying to some imaginary daddy figure in the sky," Jessi snapped.

"All the same, you have to admit that religion and science aren't incompatible," Charmaine countered. She shrugged when Jessi scowled back.

Mama Etta Ray stood, her purse dangling from the crook of one elbow. "God made everything in the world, Jessi. The Bible says there is life and death in the tongue. One day you gonna have to admit it, child." She gave Jessi a maternal pat on the head like she was stubborn toddler. "Now I got to go to the church. We having a prayer breakfast Saturday. Y'all take care."

Charmaine struggled to her feet and kissed Mama Etta Ray's plump cheek. "We know you want the best for us."

"Listen, I ran the streets in my day. I could have done better raising Monica and her brothers. In a way their mistakes are mine, too. Think about that." Mama Etta Ray hugged Charmaine and then glanced at Jessi. She sighed when Jessi's hard expression didn't budge. "See y'all later."

"Bye, granny," Jessi called out.

"Bye, baby."

That was it. Jessi and Mama Etta Ray's stand-off on the subject of Monica continued. Their affectionate farewells signaled they were still on good terms despite the ongoing disagreement. When Charmaine returned from walking their grandmother out, Jessi held up a hand.

"Don't start. I'm not going to make nice with Monica. Y'all gonna find out when the truth comes out about him stealing money or sleeping with members of his congregation. Or both," Jessi said.

"A phone call isn't going to kill you. That's all I'm saying." Charmaine sat on the sofa with a sigh.

"Back to Loreen Kennedy," Jessi said, forcing a change of subject.

"Him being a trifling husband doesn't add up to proof she killed him. We need more."

"I hate to admit it, but Harrison is right. The prosecution's case is more solid with the texts. Anyway, I'm heading out, too. A few of us are going to take Diamond out for drinks to cheer her up." Jessi stood and walked to the kitchen. "Yay! Granny left bread pudding for dessert."

"Okay. She probably made enough for an army. Take some for Diamond and Indyah." Charmaine's eyes fluttered until they closed. Jessi's irritated tone shook her from sleepiness.

"I said no," Jessi said.

Charmaine left the sofa to join her in the kitchen. She looked around but saw nothing. "You talking to me?"

"Madame Laveau is back complaining that we won't sue the latest movie company for slandering her name. She says congratulations on your happy condition. Blessings on the baby," Jessi said around a mouthful of bread pudding.

"I can speak for myself," a disembodied whisper said.

"I heard that. Just barely. Bonsoir, Madame, et merci," Charmaine said with a smile.

"De rien," Madame Laveau replied in a softly accented voice. "I beg you to reconsider. My descendants should not have to suffer these lies. I was and remain a good catholique. I attended mass and—"

"Yes, yes. I know. I can't file a lawsuit on behalf of a ghost. The attorneys at my firm would laugh in my face and then fire me. And the statute of limitations ran out over 200 years ago on any property you lost," Jessi said.

"Not lost, stolen. My children should own valuable property in Le Vieux Carré," Madame shot back. Her voice grew stronger with outrage at the centuries old wrong done to her.

"And there's still nothing I can do. Besides, the Glapion family has done pretty well in New Orleans," Jessi said.

"They show the grit and intelligence of our line. Ah well, I must let the past be past it seems. Especially since you won't help me," Madame Laveau said.

"I missed that last part." Charmaine cocked her head to one side. The whispery words faded. Her ability to hear spirits was tenuous at best. Jessi explained her telepathy probably helped her tune in at times.

"More guilt from an elderly woman," Jessi quipped. "Okay, Madame. Did you just drop in to complain?"

"I have followed your latest cases. Quite interesting. Your friend is in a spot of trouble, mais oui." Madame Laveau clicked her tongue.

"Anything helpful would be appreciated," Jessi said.

"Non, but the other, Madame Chatelaine, I knew certain of her ancestors. Pfft, looked down their noses at me." Madame Laveau let loose a string of Creole French from centuries ago.

"I don't understand what you just said, but I'm pretty sure it wasn't very nice," Jessi said with a laugh.

"But quite true. I have something about your investigation, by the way," Madame said. "Secretive parties interested in the land you keep visiting. I do not know the details. Reconsider my request and I'll find out."

"What's she saying?" Charmaine looked around, straining to get in on the conversation.

"Blackmail. She'll tell us more if I consider taking up at least one of her pointless legal claims," Jessi retorted. She frowned at the spot directly in front of her.

"We accept," Charmaine said. The hum of ghostly laughter, a throaty contralto, floated on the air.

Chapter 8
Family Business

Monday morning dawned cold. February promised to bring a chill to the upcoming Mardi Gras parades, which wasn't unusual. Charmaine felt a burst of energy as she went through her morning appointments. She kept up a running text conversation with Jessi, who was collecting documents on both cases. The evidence against Diamond was still circumstantial. Even Harrison agreed. What they really needed, Jessi insisted, was reasonable doubt. But who would believe Mrs. Loreen Gladstone Kennedy, former debutante and Mardi Gras queen, would kill her less-than-beloved husband? By that evening, both were tired. They sat in Charmaine's home office. Both had their feet propped up.

"Tell you what, Loreen Kennedy must have hired a damn PR firm. I've read three stories about her and Bernard Kennedy's charity work. Two stories about his successful business ventures." Jessi pointed her chopsticks at Charmaine. A plump shrimp dangled between them. Then she popped it into her mouth.

"Yeah. I read one about her son and his wife. They belong to the Krewe of Poseidon. This year their theme is 'A Child's Imagination', and with fundraising for Children's Hospital," Charmaine replied. She pushed away her half-eaten bowl of wonton soup. She burped and waved away Jessi's silent offer of a pork eggroll. "Uh, I'm back to not wanting much to eat."

"You have to feed my niece. At least eat some vegetable fried rice since you can't stand the sight of meat." Jessi set about finishing off the soup Charmaine had left. She downed the wontons in the bowl.

"Ugh, I stuffed myself on Mama Etta Ray's cooking two days straight. I might sip soup for another week." Charmaine shifted in her desk chair to get more comfortable.

"I'm going to bribe her to make seafood gumbo. Going to the store for all the ingredients," Jessi said with a wink.

"I sent Monica a text. Told her you said hello." Charmaine shrugged when Jessi gave her a mean side-eye.

"She knows you lied. The trifling heffa is clear on what I think," Jessi retorted.

"That's a terrible way to talk about your mama. At least she's trying. Anyway, she said pretty much the same but to tell you she understands. She sounds different."

"Humph. Let's talk about something that *matters*. Fannie Wilkens is a beast in a courtroom," Jessi said.

"I'm not sure that will be helpful, Jess. She helped that gang leader running a major dope operation get off." Charmaine frowned thinking of the controversial lawyer.

"NOPD and the DA tried a smear campaign because she beat them at their own game," Jessi replied. "As for Dirty Bird D, everybody deserves the best defense."

"Bought with drug and hit man money." Charmaine shook her head.

"Whose side are you on anyway? Like the lawyers I work for say, it's the opposing counsel's job to prove their case. If Fannie outplayed the DA, that's their problem. The state has the cops collecting evidence and taxpayer money to go against the little guy. We need all the leverage we can get."

"I'm just thinking of how Mrs. Kennedy's team will spin the fact that Ms. Wilkens is representing Diamond. They've set up a good clean image for themselves," Charmaine said.

"Which is why we need to find dirt. Nothing more than rumors so far." Jessi wiped her hands on a napkin. She gathered up the remains of the Chinese food takeout containers and took them to the kitchen. "Let's see what we got."

"Not much I'm afraid. Gossip, juicy as it is, won't get very far in court. I don't need a law degree to know that much," Charmaine said.

Jessi opened her laptop on the tray table that had held her dinner. Her fingers moved over the keys for a few seconds. "You know what Uncle Nate always says—follow the smoke to find the fire."

"You mean where there's smoke, there's fire." Charmaine laughed. Their great-uncle had a habit of switching up old sayings.

"Uncle Nate knows exactly what he's saying. Fannie says we need credible info to offer an alternative theory of the crime. What do we know so far? For one thing, good old Buddy couldn't keep his clown pants up. From my experience, men with problems telling the truth at home probably do the same at work," Jessi said.

"We haven't found anything shady with his business though," Charmaine countered.

"Not yet. But I'm still looking." Jessi went back to searching the internet on her computer.

Meanwhile Charmaine, tired of sitting all day, went into the kitchen to clean up. As expected, Jessi had merely moved the empty food containers from the office to the island top. Charmaine threw all the paper boxes and cups away. Then she washed the ceramic bowl that had held her soup. She returned to the office to find Jessi still staring intently at her computer screen. With a sigh, Charmaine decided to turn her attention to Mrs. Chatelaine's case. She went through the stack of papers the elderly woman had given them. After twenty minutes and dry eyes from reading, Charmaine let out a sigh.

"More bad news. Mrs. Chatelaine didn't do a good job keeping up with her property. We need to meet with her about these loans she took out." Charmaine yawned. "Let's take a break for now."

"Okay." Jessi stood and stretched. "I've got a few leads on Bernard Kennedy's real estate deals I want to check. He acquired ten lots after Hurricanes Katrina and Rita. I want to know if he bought that land legally. He funded some of his projects based on their value."

"It's only seven now. I'll call Mrs. Chatelaine so we can talk to her tomorrow afternoon. Not only are there loans, but at least one boundary dispute with a business claiming she's wrong about how much property is hers. What a mess. I say we collect what we have and let her hire a good real estate attorney." Charmaine pulled up Mrs. Chatelaine's number in her cell phone.

"Well, I hope she's got enough cash. Lawyer fees can eat up the value of her estate. Developers like Gina Shaw and Buddy Kennedy hold all the cards. At least we can concentrate on clearing Diamond." Jessi tapped a few final keys before she closed her laptop.

"Yeah." Charmaine dialed the number and made the appointment.

Tuesday afternoon Jessi met Charmaine at Mrs. Chatelaine's home. The cottage had green, gold, and purple ribbon wrapped around the porch posts. An elaborate carnival mask hung on the front door. When Jessi pushed the button, the bell played a familiar carnival bluesy tune. Mrs. Chatelaine answered the door by flinging it wide.

"Hello, children. Welcome to the ball!" She held a wine glass in one hand.

"Hi." Charmaine looked past her. Several middle-aged women giggled in the background. "We're here to meet with you?"

"Oh, don't worry, hon. Our brunch is just wrapping up." Mrs. Chatelaine waved a hand at her guests. She beckoned them in and began introductions.

"Brunch time was over hours ago," Jessi murmured aside to Charmaine. "I want this kind of old age."

They nodded as Mrs. Chatelaine pointed to her friends. Six women dressed in bright colors, some wearing hats decorated with Mardi Gras beads, chattered away. They waved greetings to Jessi and Charmaine with a chorus of "Nice to meet you" before continuing to party. Trays were scattered on the tables of Mrs. Chatelaine's living room with the remains of finger sandwiches, cupcakes, cheese, and more.

"All right, ladies, I'm afraid the good times must end. I have business to take care of," Mrs. Chatelaine called out.

She playfully shooed her pals out one by one. Their tipsy farewells took another twenty minutes. Jessi took the time to feast on the food that was left. She munched on brie and crackers. Charmaine gave her a look.

"Hey, you should try some. These roast beef finger sandwiches are the best." Jessi continued to nibble on the delicacies without a hint of shame.

"Help yourselves. We have mimosas left, I believe. Oh wait, you shouldn't drink in your condition," Mrs. Chatelaine said aside to Charmaine. "I have juice for you."

"Thanks, but don't go to any trouble," Charmaine said with a smile.

"None at all. I've been in hostess mode all day." Mrs. Chatelaine bustled to the kitchen. She only swayed a little. She called out a few seconds later. "Afraid I'm all out of orange juice. My girls love their mimosas. But no worries. I had a bottle of apple juice in the fridge. Marlene loves her rum and apple juice cocktails."

Mrs. Chatelaine kept up a stream of chitter-chatter from the kitchen. Her voice faded in and out; they heard her open and close cabinets. Charmaine shrugged when Jessi looked at her in frustration and mouthed, "What the eff?" After ten minutes, Mrs. Chatelaine returned with chicken salad and mixed fruit.

"Um, thanks. But I didn't... You know what, it's fine. I had a lite lunch anyway." Charmaine smiled as she accepted the ornate porcelain plate decorated with pink roses.

Jessi sat across from them in a stuffed chair. "Mrs. Chatelaine—"

"Call me Lydia, dears. No need to stand on formalities. Besides, it makes me feel twenty again when young women use my first name." Mrs. Chatelaine sat down. She drained the last of a mimosa from a random glass on the cocktail table. Then she sighed.

"Lydia, we found letters from two companies with overdue notices. Property used as collateral complicates proving ownership. Redwood Consolidated of California has liens on two of your lots." Jessi spoke in a measured fashion as Mrs. Chatelaine gazed at her.

"Nonsense." Mrs. Chatelaine flipped the fingertips of one hand.

"No, it's not. RC could take your land because you didn't make timely payments." Jessi stopped when the older woman waved her hand again. She looked at Charmaine and murmured, "You try, Ms. Social Worker."

"You remember borrowing money and putting up some of your lots as collateral, right?" Charmaine said.

"I haven't taken out any loans. Period." Mrs. Chatelaine squinted at the document Jessi put on the table.

"Here is one agreement. Maybe you forgot about it. I mean, this was back in 2016. That's a long time ago," Jessi replied with a frown that said her patience was wearing thin.

"I didn't sign any such thing. I don't need to read it. More juice?" Mrs. Chatelaine smiled at Charmaine and held up a wine glass.

"You didn't bring the juice, Lydia. Maybe we should have this talk another day when you're not so... tired." Charmaine patted Mrs. Chatelaine's hand.

"Don't patronize me. I'm not tired or drunk. I did *not* take out loans. Why should I? My last husband left me a nice life insurance settlement. I own my house, and I have a comfortable retirement income. Does any of that sound like I need to borrow money? No!" Mrs. Chatelaine lifted her chin and raised both eyebrows at the sisters.

"Look closely anyway. Are you saying those aren't your signatures?" Jessi turned two pages to the last one. She pointed to a florid handwritten scrawl next to dates.

"Well, since you insist on interrogating me," Mrs. Chatelaine sniffed. She rose and went to a vintage small desk against one wall. She took out a pair of eyeglasses and returned. She studied the signed page. Then she flipped back to read first page. "Lies. I never agreed to this."

"But the question is, did you sign it?" Jessi pressed.

"I'm not senile or stupid," Mrs. Chatelaine clipped. She continued to read before shaking the papers in her hand. "Someone forged my signature."

Jessi shot a side glance at Charmaine before turning to Mrs. Chatelaine again. "Are you sure? Because—"

"I might forget minor details. But I've never entered any kind of legal agreement without fully understanding the whys and wherefores of every paragraph. My father, may he rest in heaven, taught us to never sign anything we didn't read thoroughly. Black Americans lost land or businesses because they were taken advantage of in previous generations. Why do you think our ancestors were so focused on literacy and education? Because signing papers you don't understand is one method used to steal from us. Especially after Reconstruction, we—"

"Yes, ma'am," Charmaine interrupted to stem the tide of a history lesson. "You mentioned a few hard times after Hurricane Katrina though. Trying to rebuild and move back from Atlanta where you moved to live with your great-niece."

"I didn't sign these papers. I've never heard of Redwood whatever. That property is mine. I'll sue anyone who says differently." Mrs. Chatelaine dropped the loan document onto the table.

"Hey, we're on *your* side, okay? If you say you didn't sign, then we'll get to the bottom of what's going on," Jessi replied.

Mrs. Chatelaine let out a long sigh. "I'm tired of having my mental capacity questioned. So what if I put my keys in the refrigerator a few times. Everyone misplaces things, even young people."

"Yes, ma'am." Charmaine gave Jessi a "what can I do?" shrug when Jessi glared at her.

"So here's what we're gonna do. I'm going to look into Redwood Consolidated, get background on them and the loan. We'll figure this out one way or another," Jessi gathered up the documents and put them back in her backpack.

"Yes. Find out who's spreading lies about me. Be sure you tell my nephew. Wait a minute. Did Andre and his sisters put you up to this?" Mrs. Chatelaine's light brown eyes narrowed to slits.

"Up to what?" Jessi glanced at Charmaine and then at Mrs. Chatelaine.

"Trying to prove that I'm losing my mind so they can get their hands on my assets. They always talk about how I'm physically healthy and will live forever. Can't wait for me to die and get their hands on my estate. No, they want to have me locked up so they can live high now." Mrs. Chatelaine's voice trembled. She pressed a soggy napkin to one eye and sniffled.

"Your nephew might have hooked us up, but we don't take orders from him. Or anybody else for that matter. You're the client," Jessi said and sat next to Mrs. Chatelaine on the sofa. She rubbed the older woman's shoulder.

"And we're not reporting to any of your relatives either. Unless you sign a release allowing us to do so," Charmaine said.

"Right. Even if they ask, the answer will be 'none of your business!'" Jessi added.

Mrs. Chatelaine dabbed at her eyes one last time. Mascara stained the napkin. "I'm being a silly, weepy old woman. Of course you're trying to help me. Let's have a toast!"

Charmaine and Jessi blinked at the sudden change of mood. They looked at each other over Mrs. Chatelaine's head and shook their heads in unison. When Mrs. Chatelaine reached for an almost empty bottle of Chardonnay, Charmaine gently pried it from her grip.

"I think you've toasted enough for one afternoon. Let us help you tidy up. Your lady friends seem so sweet." Charmaine stacked plates with remains of food on them as she talked.

She deftly distracted the tipsy Lydia by drawing out gossip about her social circle. Mrs. Chatelaine launched into spirited anecdotes about her pals. Some of them a bit less than discreet. Which made Mrs. Chatelaine chuckle harder at their expense. Scandals from the sixties and seventies mattered much. Charmaine enjoyed the decades-old tea being served up all the same. After another thirty minutes of making sure the older woman was settled, they left. Mrs. Chatelaine assured them she was fine. Her twice-weekly housecleaner would empty the dishwasher and put things away.

Charmaine followed Jessi to her two-bedroom bungalow since it was on her way home. Jessi put a large pan pizza in the oven. While they waited, Jessi called to check on Diamond.

Charmaine propped her feet up and watched the news. When the oven pinged the pizza was done, Charmaine took on the task of serving. She put slices on plates for them both, grabbed two bottles of root beer, and returned to the living room. Jessi took the tray from her.

"You look worn out. Maybe you should go on maternity early." Jessi put a pillow behind Charmaine as she sat on the sofa.

"Gee thanks for telling me I look like crap," Charmaine retorted as she plopped down. "Ugh, it does feel good to get off my feet though."

"I could get an assistant for these two cases. Then you can take it easy," Jessi replied.

"Like who?" Charmaine tore off a bit of pizza and ate it.

"One of the SUNO students from a talk I gave is interested in interning at a 'non-traditional' site. She's an African-American Studies major. I could give her a call."

"Bookmark the idea. I'm good for now." Charmaine blew out air and yawned before reaching for more pizza.

"If you say so." Jessi pursed her lips.

"I can empathize with Mrs. Chatelaine. It's annoying as hell having your competency questioned all the time." Charmaine glared at Jessi as she chewed on cheese and sausage layered on the crust.

"Okay, okay. Just don't start bitchin' to me when your back hurts or your feet swell. I'll be like, grab that jack and change your own tire, woman!"

"Ooo, you're so fun-ee." Charmaine rolled her eyes. Then she grew serious again. "We need to tell Lydia's niece about her behavior. Mood swings, lack of impulse control, and forgetfulness are signs of dementia."

"She looks good, but Mrs. Chatelaine is seventy-eight-years old." Jessi wiped her mouth and gulped root beer.

"People even younger, like in their fifties, can develop what's called early onset dementia. I'll send her niece an email tomorrow with information on doctors. I think she should see a neuropsychologist, personally."

"Well, do your thing. I'm going to contact Redwood. Maybe they took advantage of Lydia. Sometimes lenders market to older people. Like those reverse mortgages. Or they know who's behind on taxes and offer them loans," Jessi said.

"Scumbag move, but not illegal," Charmaine replied.

"Contracts can be deemed invalid because of a bad mental state. In the law it's called contractual capacity. I did research on a case last year for one of the lawyers. This man had his sick wife sign all kinds of stuff. Basically, he got his hands on her trust and was going to finance a life with his mistress. Or least he tried to. He was younger than the wife, and her estate would have gone to two adult kids from her first marriage."

"Now that you mention it... When I worked at Horizon Inpatient psych unit, social workers were trained not to allow anyone visiting a patient have them sign documents." Charmaine nodded.

"So, we need to prove Lydia's nuts and didn't understand what the hell she signed." Jessi tapped her temple with a forefinger.

Charmaine winced. "Cognitive impairment is the accurate phrase."

"Whatever. Dress it up all you want, but Lydia is going to be pissed. You saw how she acted when we implied that she was more than a little forgetful. I'll let you deal with her and the family on this one."

"I'll call Angela first and follow it up with an email."

"Good luck. I just hope the vultures don't start circling. I know they're acting all concerned now, but Mrs. C. has a lot of property. Relatives can get greedy." Jessi clicked her tongue.

"Then we'll have to protect her."

"Excuse me, but we're hired to make sure developers don't get their hands on her land. I'm not wading into a nasty estate battle," Jessi said, shaking her head no.

"As far as I'm concerned, we're supposed to make sure she doesn't lose assets to *anyone*," Charmaine insisted.

"Here you go in peak social worker style. We should stick to the original services contract," Jessi argued. "Get paid and get out."

"Not everything is about making the most dollars, Jessi."

"Says the woman with a serious addiction to designer handbags," Jessi tossed back with a smirk.

They continued to debate what the scope of their work for Mrs. Chatelaine should be. The discussion ended in a stalemate. Neither budged from their position. Charmaine finally left for home. The next few days passed in a routine way. As normal as New Orleans could be during carnival season. Tourists filled up the streets, restaurants, and historical sites. Jessi made the rounds of Mardi Gras pre-parade parties. By the end of the week, they regrouped to compare notes. Scotty sang along to popular R&B hits from Charmaine's playlist as he cooked dinner. Jessi arrived to Charmaine's house at seven that Friday night.

"Hey, something smells good but what is that howling sound in the kitchen?" Jessi joked after Charmaine let her in.

"Don't talk or you won't get fed," Charmaine teased back. "We're having gravy steaks, garlic mashed potatoes, and grilled asparagus."

"Yummy. Sounds like he's slaughtering the poor cow in there though." Jessi walked across the living room to the open kitchen.

"I was the star in our high school chorus group." Scotty let out a baritone rendition of an Usher hit song.

"Just kidding, bro-in-law. Keep doin' it." Jessi screwed up her face into a comic frown.

"Hater." Scotty went back to cooking.

"I've got news. Good, bad, and indifferent." Jessi leaned against the counter.

Charmaine paused in mixing salad greens with olive oil in a large bowl. "Bad news first."

"I haven't been able to find incriminating evidence on Loreen Kennedy or any of Bernard Kennedy's associates. He wasn't as widely liked as the way he's been portrayed by Loreen's publicity team, but nothing that could add up to a strong motive. Diamond's text messages with the guy don't look good." Jessi frowned. "I asked her aunt and cousin to check on her every day. She's depressed."

"With a murder charge hanging over her head, no wonder," Scotty called from the kitchen.

"What does her attorney say?" Charmaine frowned at the look of gloom on her sister's face.

"The DA has a solid circumstantial case." Jessi's scowl eased a bit. "The good news is Tranisha is willing to give a statement that might help. From Buddy's requests for other services, she can state that he liked to be 'disciplined,' including dirty talk and threats."

"That's good then," Charmaine replied.

"Yeah, kinda." Jessi's expression didn't reflect optimism.

"There's more to Loreen Kennedy than meets the eye. Something unpleasant just beneath the surface." Charmaine munched on a cucumber slice. "Wish I could come up with an excuse to meet her face-to-face. Maybe I'd learn something."

Scotty loaded a platter and placed bowls of food on the table. "You don't exactly hang in the same social circles."

Jessi snapped her fingers. "One of the female attorneys belongs to her Mardi Gras krewe, well one of two Loreen belongs to. The Steel Magnolias."

"Seriously? Talk about a southern belle cliché," Scotty said with a laugh.

"They're having a swanky to-do for the Crescent City Pantry. They serve free and discounted meals to folks who are struggling. You could show up at the luncheon where the Steel Magnolias are going to present CCP a fat check," Jessi said.

"I don't have an invitation, Jessi. Security will bounce my butt right on out the door," Charmaine said with a snort.

"I'll take care of that. The attorney gave one to an associate, who flaunted it under our noses. You know, bragging she's got an in with the bigwigs. Anyway, I can copy the design easy. You're in, sis!" Jessi grinned.

"They'll spot a fake when I show up," Charmaine said.

"Actually, I've done security for a few charity luncheons. Wave your invite in the general direction of whoever is working the door and act like you belong," Scotty put in.

"Mr. Follow-the-Rules is giving tips on committing shenanigans." Jessi mimicked a shocked face, hand on her throat. "My pearls are clutched."

"Yeah, well, this is for the cause of justice. Not for general use." Scotty jabbed a forefinger at Jessi.

They finished dinner discussing the local news in and around New Orleans. Scotty and Jessi insisted on doing kitchen duty. They ordered Charmaine to relax in the living room. Despite her grumbling, they set her up with her favorite dessert and insisted she prop her feet on the ottoman. Charmaine tried and failed to pout. She scooped chocolate pudding into her mouth and watched a replay of the news. After a few stories she started to doze. The words "fake signatures" and "land titles" made Charmaine's eyes pop open. She stared at the television, no longer sleepy.

"Ted Hemmings was shocked to learn that the house he and his wife had purchased had a lien on it."

A male reporter spoke into a microphone standing outside a house. The footage had obviously been shot during the daytime. Sunshine bathed the background. As the details unfolded, Charmaine's mouth dropped open wider.

"Jessi, get in here and look at this." Charmaine sat straight. She hissed when the story ended before Jessi got there. "Get your tablet or phone."

Jessi came in with a striped yellow hand towel over one shoulder. "Don't tell me you want more pudding. You ate two helpings of mashed potatoes."

Charmaine brushed past her. "Gotta look up something."

"Okay."

Jessi returned to the kitchen. Moments later Charmaine returned from her home office. She read the screen of her iPad as she walked. Scotty and Jessi exchanged puzzled glances. Scotty went back to loading the dishwasher after a shrug.

"Don't ask me what's going on," Scotty said over his shoulder. "Maybe she saw something on TV she wants to order for the nursery."

"Look at this. It's the same loan company." Charmaine held out the iPad to Jessi. "Redwood Consolidated of California."

"Huh?" Jessi scanned the line Charmaine pointed.

"The company that has a lien on Mrs. Chatelaine's lots. Now whose brain is fogged? This guy bought a house in Tremé." Charmaine pulled the tablet back and read on.

"Humph, gentrifier. Historically African-American neighborhoods are now mostly white hipsters. From out of state. Trying to find a house to buy or rent that doesn't cost a pile of cash is—"

"That's not what I'm talking about. Someone got title to his home. Except *it's not his signature on any of the documents.* They got a sixty-thousand-dollar home equity loan to make renovations that were never done." Charmaine waved the tablet for emphasis.

"Let me see." Jessi took the iPad and read. Then she started scrolling.

"What's going on now?" Scotty joined them. He peered over Jessi's shoulder at the iPad.

"Our case just took an interesting turn, that's what," Jessi murmured.

"Good for your client?" Scotty went to the living room and switched to a sports channel. He sat on the sofa, remote control in one hand.

"Could be," Charmaine called back.

"I'll call the handwriting expert the attorney used in that case. She'll need the loan contract and documents with Mrs.

Chatelaine's signature around the same time. Preferable the same year," Jessi said.

"Why?" Charmaine asked.

"According to the expert, our handwriting changes over time. So, for an accurate examination she wants to see her signature at that time on other papers. Fascinating stuff." Jessi went to her purse and took out her smart phone. "I'm going to send her a text."

"How long will it take?"

"Could be awhile. Kayla's the only certified forensic document examiner in south Louisiana. She's got lots of assignments."

"Mrs. Chatelaine's niece called me at work this morning. It took her two days to convince Mrs. Chatelaine to go to the doctor's appointment. And she'll only go to her primary care doc. Just the word psychologist set her off." Charmaine shook her head. "I'm not surprised, but it's something. She trusts her doc, so maybe if she finds the need for a referral Mrs. Chatelaine will listen. They're going next Wednesday."

"She's already mad at us. Mrs. Chatelaine will probably cuss us out if we ask for any more paperwork." Jessi pursed her lips.

"We shouldn't have to. She gave us a file folder full of documents, papers to prove she owns all of her land."

"Great. Maybe Kayla will do me a favor and give us an opinion fast."

"Okay. Now if we could find anything to help Diamond. I tried calling Harrison but his assistant said he was busy. I think he's avoiding us," Charmaine said. "I suppose he's in a tough spot."

"Oh boo-hoo for him," Jessi retorted. "He should grow a backbone and stand up to his boss. Harrison is too concerned about that political BS."

"C'mon. He has to step lightly sometimes. His job could be on the line." Charmaine squinted at Jessi's hiss of contempt. "And if we lose him, I can't think of another NOPD cop that will give us the time of day, let alone a *district commander*."

"We have Ricky," Jessi replied, referring to her romantic interest Detective Richard Ward.

"Ricky doesn't have Harrison's rank, seniority or network in NOPD and the Orleans Parish Sheriff's Department. Not to mention contacts with the local FBI and—"

"I get it. He's the best we got," Jessi cut in. "Anyway, Harrison playing hard to get might not matter. Diamond's attorney is waiting for the DA to respond to her discovery request. We don't want any surprises."

Scotty left the sofa and walked past them to the fridge. He opened it and took out another bottle of root beer. "Like damn, I should be pulling for the Pelicans, but Milwaukee is my team. And they're looking good this year."

"Don't be a traitor just because you were born there," Charmaine quipped. "Your mother is from New Orleans. Y'all moved back home when you were in diapers." She playfully punched his thick bicep.

"I'm just sayin'," Scotty replied with a laugh. "What do you think, Jess?"

"Huh, yeah. Guess so." Jessi looked past him and blinked hard.

"Oh right. You don't care about basketball. Gymnastics are your thing." Scotty glanced behind him and back to Jessi. "What, something going left with one of the cases?"

"Uh, no. I'm just thinking hard. Mind going in all different directions. Oh, what are they saying about the NBA rankings having a shake-up?" Jessi craned her neck to look at the fifty-five-inch television."

"It's early in the season. Things could still change." Scotty strode back to the living room. He stood before the wide screen with his arms folded.

"Guess you got a point," Jessi replied.

"Like you know or care about basketball," Scotty teased, his gaze still glued to the team of commentators holding forth.

"A bunch of guys chasing a big orange ball. Not really." Jessi tugged Charmaine by the arm. "C'mon sis. Let me show you something."

"Wha—"

"I got an idea for the baby's room." Jessi jerked her head for Charmaine to follow. She mouthed something.

Charmaine blinked at her. "Uh, oo-kay."

Jessi shushed at her when Charmaine started to say more. Jessi pulled her along to the extra bedroom Scotty had started decorating. Then she closed the door. "Madame is here."

"He's going to wonder why we disappeared," Charmaine whispered.

"Scotty's feeding his sports news addiction. He won't notice. Okay, Madame. What you got for us?" Jessi looked at a spot on the wall. Scotty had applied wallpaper with cute baby animals against a yellow backdrop.

"You may find it strange that Le Cercle Harmonique is keenly interested in homes around New Orleans," a disembodied soft accented voice breathed.

"I heard you again!" Charmaine blurted.

"Don't announce it to the world," Jessi hissed.

"Oh, right," Charmaine said, dropping her voice low again. "Who or what is Le Cercle Harmonique?"

"A collection of like-minded spiritualists who held séances for twenty years starting in the 1850s. Free born Creoles, like moi," Madame Laveau said, her voice a velvety hiss. "Francois 'Petit' Dubuclet and Victor Lavigne were the main mediums. Always the number of participants was seven."

"Seven is considered spiritually significant, symbolizing completion, perfection, and even divinity," Jessi put in.

"Pfft, I never crossed paths with their members. Held themselves apart as better than us common folk," Madame Laveau replied. "They rarely allowed women into their precious Harmonic Circle."

"I don't get it. You said they met for twenty years. That means the séances stopped in the 1870s." Jessi frowned at the space Madame Laveau apparently occupied.

"1877 justeuman," came the terse reply in Louisiana Creole, meaning "precisely."

"So, they're all long dead and the circle hasn't existed for almost 150 years." Charmaine blinked at the empty space as if she could see Madame Laveau.

"A modern version revived le cercle in the 1950s. Now they searching for treasures in old houses. Ask this woman... this Gina Shaw." Madame Laveau chuckled at the astonished expressions the sisters wore.

Chapter 9
Real Estates

"This is the last one." Jessi said. She stepped forward and the original hardwood floor creaked beneath her feet. The sound echoed in a weird fashion through the house.

Monday night brought them to a two-story Victorian mansion on Prytania. Jessi and Charmaine both carried flashlights. They'd arrived just after seven o'clock, well after nightfall. Twin beams swept the interior of the room they were in. The first of two parlors was empty of furniture since it had not been staged yet for sale. A fireplace with the original ornate mantel sat in the south wall to their right.

"Find a switch so we can turn on the chandelier. Somebody will call the police to report us as burglars," Charmaine mumbled.

"No, I need it dark. Some spirits won't appear in white light. The spectrum drives them away," Jessi said.

"Isn't that what we want?" Charmaine gazed at the wallpaper pattern. "Ugh, I don't get the obsession with cabbage roses."

"According to Gina, they're still making design changes. This house was built in 1900 on land originally owned by a member of the Glapion family." Jessi found a small lamp sitting on the floor against one wall. She turned it on and soft yellow light spilled from beneath the creamy shade. "That's not too bad."

"Listen, I don't know why you're letting Madame Laveau—"

"Madame Glapion, to be accurate. Jean Louis Christophe Duminy de Glapion was her last husband," Jessi corrected.

"Wow, what a mouthful. He probably collapsed under the weight of that name." Charmaine giggled at her own joke. "Anyway, I'm not a lawyer but even I know you can't sue to reclaim land lost over two hundred years ago. Aside from the statute of limitations, tracing ownership documents will be next to impossible. Records have been lost in floods, fires, and just misplaced over the decades."

"We'll see," was Jessi's soft reply. She walked in a circle, staring up at the plaster medallion on the ceiling.

"You getting anything yet? My EMF meter hasn't said 'boo' since we got here. I think Gina is imagining things at this point. She's spooked by the other two encounters" Charmaine shook the device and it let out a sharp beep. "False alarm. I touched the test button."

"There's something funny about this one." Jessi glanced at her anemometer in her hand. "You feel it? The air is heavy."

"Stuffy, you mean. I'm going to check out the dining room. Bet the same busy wallpaper is in there, too." Charmaine started to walk toward the archway.

Jessi blocked her path. "I don't think we should split up."

"Girl, not even the dust is stirring in here. My ankles are starting to hurt. Go upstairs while I finish going through the rooms down here." Charmaine went around Jessi and pressed a wall switch. "Huh, that's weird. Must be a short in the wires."

Both looked up at the chandelier with faux candle sticks. The bulbs glowed dim and then pulsated. A shadow spread across the ceiling like a stain. Loud clacks like they were inside a giant popcorn machine reverberated through the room. Charmaine dropped the EMF meter and clapped both palms over her ears. She shrieked when the bulbs shattered one by one. Jessi sprinted for her duffle bag.

"Go to the hall! Run!" Jessi yelled over the noise.

Charmaine went to the archway but didn't leave. "Don't stay in here. The disturbance seems to be centered in this room."

Before Charmaine could say more, she yelped at being pulled by the back of her jacket. A large invisible hand seemed determined to drag Charmaine across the parquet floor of the entryway. Charmaine was gently pressed into a closet set in the curved stairway. She heard Jessi swearing in the other room. The walls lit up as if lightning flashed around them. Charmaine felt a cold wave and then warmth. She stayed put. Seconds later the popping stopped. Noise seemed to be sucked away as if by a giant vacuum cleaner. Then the house became still. After all the chaos, the quiet felt unearthly. A hallow bass voice rang clear.

"Get out," it rumbled. Then overhead fixtures spread light.

"Jessi, you okay?" Charmaine stuck her head and peered around the entrance hallway. "Say something."

"I'm here." Jessi strode over to the closet and stuck a hand in.

"All hell broke loose before we could blink!" Charmaine grabbed on and let Jessi pull her out.

"You're not hurt?" Jessi looked at her from head to toe.

"No, but I'm damn sure shook up. Whatever it was, it's over." Charmaine blew out a slow breath. "

"Yeah, the meters are quiet."

Charmaine frowned. "They were quiet before. Maybe they malfunctioned?"

"Both have full charges. Freakin' strange that we didn't have warning. And how did you end up in that closet?" Jessi closed the door. "Look, the molding blends in so it looks like solid wall."

"It wasn't open when we came in either. Somebody shoved me in. Well, not a *body*, more like a force," Charmaine said.

"Come see."

Jessi jerked a thumb toward the living room they'd been in, and Charmaine followed her. Jessi pointed up. Charmaine's gaze followed Jessi's raised arm. The bulbs in the chandelier glowed softly, all of them intact.

"A ghost with magic tricks. Nice," Charmaine said with a grunt.

Jessi nodded to the wall at Charmaine's back. Charmaine turned around to look. The wallpaper had four long slanted slashes in it. Yet the rest of the room was undamaged.

"A giant claw ripped into it?" Charmaine peered at the ominous aftermath of a supernatural entity.

"Don't go closer. Let me test it first." Jess pulled her curious sister away from the wall. "We don't know how any residue of AEBE might affect the baby. Research is limited. Which is why I tried to make you stay home."

"Two paranormal investigators in the UK kept working through their pregnancies. I looked it up. They had no problems," Charmaine replied. Still, she let Jessi take the lead.

"Whatever, but let me handle the inspection of..."

Jessi waved at the wall and went to it. She stood until her the tip of her nose was only inches away. She sniffed a few times. Then she took out a giant pair of tweezers from an inside pocket of her jacket. After taking a ragged sample of paper, Jessi placed it into a handheld device. A series of blue, green, and then violet lit up the screen.

"Humph. Not all that strong. A warning instead of an attack. Whatever showed up obviously had the power to kick our asses if it wanted to. Maybe our devices are outdated. Wonder if some AEBE's are on a higher spectrum than these can detect. Although, most believe all spirits operate on lower frequencies. And I know what you're about to say. These can be upgraded for a reasonable cost. What? No sarcasm? Jessi glanced up to find Charmaine staring with wide eyes and an open mouth.

"She's here."

Charmaine stabbed a forefinger at the faint outline before her. Madame Laveau wore a dark lavender blouson tucked into a floor-length floral skirt. A shawl with delicate fringe draped her shoulders. Dark tendrils of hair fell from her tignon. The fabric of her head scarf matched the skirt.

Madame Laveau sniffed in disapproval. "Did not your elders teach you how rude it is to point. Of course I'm here."

"You look... lovely." Charmaine dropped her hand.

"Hmm." Madame Laveau seemed to accept her compliment as an obvious fact. "So, once again you disturb the peace of spirits."

"They disturbed the hell out of us," Jessi shot back. She pointed to the wall.

"Ah well. Tell me about progress removing thieves from my property." Madame Laveau gazed at Jessi.

"I've explained the challenges. Maybe if your great-great nephew hadn't had a little gambling problem." Jessi shrugged.

"Etienne had his faults, but he wasn't a fool. The corrupt government used immoral means to take advantage of him," Madame Laveau clipped.

"He fell behind on tax payments. Then there is the issue of limitations on filing claims." Jessi clamped her mouth shut at the heated look her words inspired.

"Excuses. If you're afraid to take on the authorities just say so." Madame Laveau tossed her head, making the twin thick curls on either side of her face bounce.

"Don't start with me. I know what you're trying to do," Jessi replied.

"My dear grandmother Catherine was given this land by Henri Roche Belaire. The scoundrel. It was the least he could do after denying her mother freedom for so long. Imagine having to *pay* for your own body. The lot was stolen. I want it back."

"Yeah. Let's have this discussion somewhere quieter. You know, away from giant ghost hands." Charmaine glanced around as she spoke.

"I managed to guide you away from Obadiah Gladstone. You're welcome." Madame Laveau strode around in a small arc examining the room. "Gauche. These people lack bon goût."

"Who?" Jessi followed a few steps behind Madame Laveau.

"He purchased the land in 1897 I believe. This house was completed in 1900. His wife had even less style, if you can imagine. He died ten years later. In one of the bedrooms." Madame Laveau pointed to the ceiling as if they could see the second floor. "Mostly he stays up there. He's a bit intimidated by the loup garou that occupies the attic."

"Wait, are you saying a werewolf lives here?" Charmaine gaped at her and then whirled to face Jessi. "We need to increase our rate significantly or Gina Shaw can hire somebody else!"

"Calm down, cherie. I found Augustin a new home. He prefers the bayous and prairies of Pointe à la Hache anyway. He simply lost his way." Madame Laveau waved a hand, dismissing Charmaine horrified reaction.

"A werewolf has been preying on people in the city and nobody has noticed? Charmaine felt a flutter in her belly as if the baby was interested in hearing the answer, too.

"Augustin is a spirit. He died in 1877. Now there's an interesting story. You see—"

"Madame, let's save story time for later. If you knew all this, why didn't you warn us before we showed up?" Jessi squinted at her.

"I know you'll find this hard to believe, but I have my own affairs. I happened to attend a rather lively function over at Number 3," Madame Laveau said, referring to historic St. Louis Cemetery No. 3. With expansive avenues, it housed the graves of famous musicians and other New Orleans notables from the nineteenth century.

"You stopped at a party before coming over to tell us a crazy poltergeist and wolf beast would be waiting. Really?" Jessi threw both hands in the air.

"Pardon moi?" Madame Laveau placed a palm over her heart. She batted long eyelashes in a feigned wide-eyed look of innocence.

"I've pulled your fat out of the fire a few times," Jessi said, her eyes flashing.

"Hmm, let me think. I seem to recall only once you came to my aid. While I've helped you in six investigations, seven including tonight. And what do I have to show for all my efforts, eh? You put me off with talk of limitations and silly rules. Pfft!"

"She has helped us out a lot. But that doesn't mean we can work a miracle for you," Charmaine added when Madame Laveau turned to her. "The land has changed hands several times over two hundred years. Your descendants haven't pressed a claim since the 1870s. And the city won."

"Corrupt carpetbaggers," Madame Laveau hissed. She let out a stream of Caribbean and nineteenth-century New Orleans Creole insults.

"Listen, a recent case in another state has given me an idea. But no promises. It's still a very long shot," Jessi said.

Madame Laveau stopped cursing in French and smiled. "A shot, you say? Ah, you're going to dispatch my adversaries. I approve, though you must plan carefully to avoid being imprisoned. I have a few ideas."

"We're not talking about killing anybody," Charmaine said.

"It might move things along." Jessi grinned when Charmaine became incoherent with outrage.

"You know Madame takes things literally. No more graveyard humor. Pun intended."

"A family recently had their property returned after it was taken by the state using eminent domain. But Louisiana is *not* California," Jessi said to Madame Laveau, referring to the state's ultra conservative politics.

"I have faith in you, clever girl. You must study to become a lawyer. None of those others have your brains and initiative." Madame Laveau transformed from angry spirit to a proud auntie. She beamed at Jessi and Charmaine. "Mais attendez, let me tell you how I came to be here."

"Please." Charmaine leaned against the wall. "My feet are aching, but I'm not about to look around for a chair."

"I turned on the neutralizer. Even if Madame Laveau hadn't shown up, at the very least Obadiah would be gone." Jessi disappeared through an archway leading deeper into the house. She yelled back though out of sight. "Not sure if it would have worked on Augustin. Haven't tried it on a loup garou. I didn't think they were real."

"Their existence has been debated for centuries, oui," Madame Laveau agreed. "The condition is rare."

"Oh really." Charmaine yawned. Not even the bizarre conversation with a long-dead voodoo priestess could defeat her exhaustion.

"Yes. Doctors even before my time debated the condition. Jessi is correct. Many things seen as magical, even demonic, in ages past have been explained by science."

"Um. Sure." Charmaine's eyes drifted shut. She opened them to find Jessi shaking her arm.

"Sit before you slide down to the floor." Jessi placed a folding chair next to Charmaine.

"I'm a little tired." Charmaine sank onto the cushioned seat with a noisy sigh.

"From now on you'll stay home," Jessi said in a firm tone.

"You need me," Charmaine protested.

"Yeah, you were a big help from the closet." Jessi faced Madame Laveau. "Okay, so you were telling us about the house and Augustin."

"He and Obadiah have been dealt with and are of no consequence now. My dears, you need to know what I learned at the Number 3 fête. I have la dite. As you say, the tea!" Madame Laveau became animated, which looked odd for a semi-transparent essence.

Jessi's eyes lit up. "Well, fill up our cups."

"So, the spirits were sent to dispatch you and—"

"Someone sent ghost hitmen after us?" Charmaine scanned their surroundings.

"Again, they've been sent packing. Here's the fascinating part," Madame Laveau replied.

"I'm more interested in who's trying to kill me," Charmaine retorted.

"Be patient, ma petite." Madame Laveau hissed a sigh to indicate her own patience was being tested.

Jessi put a hand on Charmaine's arm to prevent a tart reply. "Let Madame tell it in her own way."

"The original Le Cercle Harmonique did indeed disband in 1877. However, it was revived in 1946 by two men, one a descendant of J. B. Valmour. They later were joined by a direct descendant of Henri Louis Rey, the founder the first circle. Four more who fancied themselves in touch with the unseen joined them. Eventually, they created a society of over forty members. But all séances were conducted with seven, as was the earlier custom." Madame Laveau paused for effect. "They continue today."

"Thanks for the history lesson," Charmaine mumbled.

Madame Laveau seemed too pleased with herself to notice. "They've added a less admirable mission to their society. At least a small clique has. Until recently largely unknown to the majority. They contact the spirit world to find valuables long lost in properties around New Orleans. Then they either buy the land or houses themselves or pass the information on to... what do you call them? Land speculators. After the War Between the States, carpetbaggers arrived to lie and thieve their way into fortunes."

"We call them property developers, real estate agents, and gentrifiers these days," Jessi said, her lips curled in distain.

"Gina Shaw is working with this circle and set us up? But that doesn't make sense. Gina looked genuinely terrified back at the first house we had to clear. If it was an act, then she deserves an Oscar. Plus, she could just fire us. No need to risk a possible murder charge." Charmaine turned to Jessi.

"You should be happy I attended the party. It was there that I learned about the sinister plot. Gossipers at the fête were abuzz with the news of *move vivan* going after two young spiritualists," Madame Laveau said, using the Louisiana Creole French phrase for evil spirits who haunt houses. "I thought of you when they mentioned these women were in for a nasty surprise."

"You wait until I see Gina again," Charmaine snapped.

"I recruited Lucas to confirm. He found their usual haunt but was too frightened to come with me. You know how skittish he is around violent spirits." Madame Laveau shook her in with a look of maternal disappointment.

"Yeah, Lucas likes to avoid a fight," Jessi replied.

Lucas Dias belonged to Jessi's cadre of spirit informants called the Shadow Squad. Born free in 1844, he died at the tender age of twenty-two from tuberculosis. Of slight build and a poetic nature, Lucas was as averse to violence in death as he had been in life.

"I lingered to get the most details possible after Lucas left. I knew you ladies could handle yourselves, at least until my arrival. But then I hurried when I heard Augustin had been enlisted. He has a particularly nasty temper. Sadly, a silver bullet to the heart ended his days before Augustin could be freed from the curse of loup garou."

"Yeah, poor guy." Charmaine snorted to emphasize her lack of sympathy.

"His circumstances are no excuse for such uncouth behavior," Madam Laveau agreed. "We're trying to find a way to transform him so he'll be less angry all the time. Then he will truly rest in peace."

"Back to this Harmonic Circle," Jessi said. "What else did you find out?"

"Ah well, now we come to their less savory activities. Spirits provide all kinds of information at the séances. Including descriptions of concealed family heirlooms or stashed valuables. For example, one home had hidden documents that fetched a nice sum at auction. Speculators who bought it found letters signed by Bienville, the first governor of Louisiana and the founder of Nouvelle Orleans. With information provided by members of Le Cercle Harmonique."

"Hmmm. So, Gina is not only snapping up valuable properties to sell, she's finding treasures, too. Still doesn't explain why she'd hire us though. Seems like she'd be afraid we'd screw up her game." Jessi frowned and crossed her arms.

"Spiteful spirits are a problem not just for home sales. Once we clear them out, Gina and friends can safely search for hidden treasure," Charmaine explained.

"Good point," Jessi replied. "If what Madame says is true, having us involved is worth the risk."

"The first circle contacted martyrs and benevolent spirits who worked for social justice while they lived. They claimed to have received counsel from Confucious, Frederick Douglass, and Bishop Jeanmard to name a few. This search for loot is a corruption of their noble pursuit," Madame Laveau said.

Jessi shrugged. "Money changes everything."

"Bernard Kennedy and Gina were partners. Could his murder have something to with the treasure hunt scheme?" Charmaine stared at Jessi.

"How'd you make that leap?"

"I don't know... everything about his death seems off." Charmaine's face screwed up as she considered the disparate facts they knew so far.

"Girl, I'm sure Buddy thinks being clipped in a clown suit is more than a little 'off'." Jessi barked a laugh as she made air quotes.

"You know what I mean." Charmaine's expression cleared as she glanced around. "I've had about enough of this place for one night. Let's get out of here."

"Hold on. Me and Madame will sweep the top floors just in case." Jessi waved the EMF meter she held.

"You no longer require my assistance," Madame Laveau declared.

"A final check won't take long. Ten minutes, twenty tops." Jessi waved for Madame Leveau to follow.

"I have complete confidence in your abilities. You children are quite capable of any lingering spectral presences." Madame Laveau faded into a wispy outline as she spoke.

"Maybe we'll find something priceless hidden in a wall," Jessi replied. "Like a hidden trunk of two-hundred-year-old deeds to prove your case."

"Ha! If such existed, I would know. Besides, I have talked to ten spirits of former owners and even descendants. Nothing is here." Madame Laveau fluffed the curls on either side of her face. "Now, I will go. The fête is still in full swing. Louis Armstrong will grace us with a performance. Bonne nuit."

"Maybe just a minute or two of your time..." Charmaine turned to smile at her but blinked hard at air. "Wow. She's just going to leave us hanging?"

Jessi took the most powerful EMF meter she owned from the duffle bag. The black box measured three feet across. At three pounds it was easy to transport. After Jessi flipped a switch to activate it nothing happened.

"Obviously. But she's right. This has a range of up to eleven hundred square feet. We're good," Jessi announced. "Hey, it's only eight-fifteen. Let's get something to eat. I only had time for a sandwich before I picked you up. A small one at that."

"You're kidding. Feels like we've been here for hours and hours," Charmaine said. She put a hand on the swell of her tummy. "I don't know if I can stomach anything after all this commotion."

"Fine—you can watch me eat. Let's go."

"Look!" Charmaine pointed to where slashes had appeared earlier. The wallpaper was intact.

"Maybe Madame Leveau made ol' Augustin and Obadiah fix it before they left. They might consider themselves tough, but Madame is an original badass." Jessi laughed and packed up their equipment.

Despite her assertion, Jessi did one final sweep of the historic mansion before they left. Nothing significant registered, only lingering residue. Jessi liked to call it spirit leftovers. New owners wouldn't notice anything except a few extra odd knocks or pings. They'd attribute the noises to an old house settling.

Jessi drove them back to Charmaine's house and parked on the street. Once inside, Charmaine ordered fried chicken from a local soul food café. She ignored Jessi's raised eyebrows at the number of side dishes added.

"Well, that was quite the adventure." Jessi settled at the kitchen counter with a bottle of water before her.

"I just texted Scotty to let him know we're back safe and sound." Charmaine perched on the bar stool next to her with a sigh.

"Uh-huh. How much did you tell him?"

"Enough to reassure him. I didn't lie," Charmaine added when Jessi pursed her lips.

"Okay."

"I told him we did have to neutralize an entity, but we got it done."

"Not the truth, the whole truth, and nothing but the truth."

Charmaine let out a longer sigh. "He's sweet to worry about me. It's irritating, too. Is this what being part of a couple is like?"

"Girl, who you askin'?" Jessi laughed. "Ricky is the longest steady man I've had since... Hell, this might be the longest relationship I've ever had."

"I'm surprised you haven't found a reason to break up with him. Not that I'm judging."

"You can't help being a therapist, can ya?" Jessi rolled her eyes. "Mind your business."

"I'm just saying, don't run from a real one. You and Ricky are good together. Subject closed." Charmaine mimed zipping her lips shut.

"If only," Jessi snipped and grinned at Charmaine. "So, Le Cercle Harmonique and hidden treasure. Didn't see that shit comin.'"

"How exactly do we follow up on it though?" Charmaine snapped her fingers. "I know. Everybody has a website or social media page." She left the stool and retrieved her iPad.

"Good luck." Jessi tapped her finger on the counter. "Where's the food? My stomach is complaining."

"Patience is a virtue, greedy girl. Text says it should arrive in twenty minutes." Charmaine continued to scroll through pages.

"I need a snack then." Jessi found a bag of peanuts and poured a handful before she sat again. "Anything?"

Charmaine frowned at the screen. "No. Everyone has a digital footprint. What kind of backward heathens are they?"

"If they have social media accounts, I'm sure they're set to private. I'll get the Shadow Squad on it."

"Madame said she'd tell us more."

"Yeah, well I won't count on her alone. You know how moody she can be. Lucas is eager to help after his no-show act tonight."

"I'll bet he wants do it for you. Big time crush. He's kinda cute, too." Charmaine giggled at the grunt Jessi let out.

"You've never seen Lucas," Jessi shot back.

"One time. I admit it wasn't a clear sighting. It's adorable how devoted he is to you. Is he jealous of Ricky?" Charmaine leaned forward.

"Ricky complained a few times about stuff going missing at his house. The 1967 Camaro he's restoring mysteriously had scratches on its new paint job a few months ago. He didn't think much of it. I set Lucas straight."

"Must be nice having two hot guys after you." Charmaine giggled harder when Jessi scowled at her.

"Are we back in high school? Focus," Jessi snapped. "I have an idea. Let's talk to local mediums, express an interest in attending a séance."

"Good idea. Oh, and say hello to Lucas for me." Charmaine smirked at the heated look Jessi gave her.

The next two days went by without any excitement. Charmaine ended her last appointment at two thirty in the afternoon on Wednesday. She decided to leave work early. She planned to finish her clinic notes from home. After a four o'clock virtual clinical team meeting, Charmaine settled on her sofa for a quick nap. Jessi ended that plan. She let herself into Charmaine's house using her key.

"Hey, I thought you're supposed to ring the bell and stop barging in like you own the place." Charmaine yawned.

"This is an emergency. Diamond is gone. Like vanished. We put up her bond." Jessi waved her arms in a pinwheel.

Charmaine swung her feet from the ottoman, sleepiness gone. "What do you mean 'we put up her bond'? Her bail was $150,000. Damn it, Jessi. Are you telling me you used the company credit card?"

"Only five thousand. And I did a home equity loan on my house." Jessi paced as she talked.

Charmaine rubbed her forehead. "We already had a big balance. The interest rate on that card is eighteen percent. And now she's gone. You'll lose your house!"

"She panicked, but once she calms down and realizes..." Jessi dropped her bag onto the chair. She went back to pacing.

"Okay, okay. Maybe she's taking a break to breathe. Call her cousins. She doesn't get along with her sisters, but maybe she went to one of them?" Charmaine looked at Jessi.

"I tried calling them already. One hung up on me. Her middle sister is back in jail in Atlanta. Identity theft. Again. The younger sister hasn't heard from her. I went to Diamond's house. She packed clothes for her and Indyah," Jessi replied.

"Then her cousin Keisha."

Jessi shook her head. She was about to speak when her cell phone went off. "Hey, Mama Etta, can't talk right now. We have to find Diamond and—"

"What?" Charmaine asked when Jessi's mouth dropped open.

"I'm putting you on speaker. Say it again." Jessi held out her phone.

"Diamond wanted to take a vacation. Her job gave her time off, so I lent her some money to take Indyah to Safari Quest in Hammond. They booked a guesthouse. My friend Anna's daughter rents out the addition on her house. You know, with one of them Airbnb companies or something like that. Anna says she makes good money. They cut us a deal and I paid for a long weekend. That poor child has been through enough and—"

"Mama," Charmaine yelled. She took a deep breath to steady her tone. "Diamond is out on bail. She shouldn't be traveling."

"Hammond ain't far, and she's still in Louisiana. Her lawyer said it was fine. Her and the baby deserve a little bit of fun," Mama Etta Ray said.

Jessi shook her head no when Charmaine glanced at her. "You talked to her?"

"Not since a couple of days ago. If something happened with her case, call her," Mama Etta Ray replied.

"She's not answering." Jessi huffed.

"They're probably busy having fun. Poor thing. She was a nervous wreck when she asked me to help her get away for a few days. Police know how to pluck poor folks off the street, but rich people get away with everything." Mama Etta Ray went on a rant about the criminal justice system.

"Diamond wouldn't run and let you lose your home. You're overreacting maybe," Charmaine whispered.

"I'm on mute," Jessi replied as Mama Etta Ray's voice droned on. "I'll bet Diamond took the money but didn't go to Hammond."

"Take it off mute," Charmaine said. After Jessi tapped the screen, Charmaine stood. "Mama Etta Ray, give us the number for where she's staying. The host I mean."

"I got it right here on a notepad. I had it right here on the side table. Doggone it. If I didn't live alone, I'd swear somebody be movin' my things around. Maybe your grandaddy's ghost is over here having fun. Y'all should come check out my house." Mama Etta Ray let out a hearty laugh.

Jessi blew out a air. "Mama—"

"I'm just messing with y'all. I'm a good Christian woman. When the good Lord calls the righteous home, that's it. No hanging around. Your grandfather wasn't no saint, but he made it to heaven. I'm sure of that. Oh, here it is." Mama Etta Ray read off the phone number and name.

"Thanks. We'll talk to you later," Jessi said.

"Is something wrong, baby?" Mama Etta Ray's worried tone came through the speaker.

"Umm, her lawyer has a question or two. That's all," Jessi said.

"Oh, okay. Bye. I gotta get this other call."

Jessi put in a call to the short-term rental host. "Hi, I'm trying to get in touch with my friend. She checked in with you today, I think. Diamond Phillips and her little girl. Okay, thanks."

Charmaine knew what Jessi was about to say by her scowl. "She's not there."

"She cancelled three days ago saying she had other plans. Shit." Jessi paced again.

"We better call her lawyer and then Harrison." Charmaine stood and joined Jessi in pacing.

"No," Jessi blurted out. "We can't or the bail will be forfeited."

"And you'll lose your house." Charmaine clapped a palm to her forehead. "And we'll be paying off that huge credit card balance for a long time."

We gotta get her ass back before anyone finds out."

"Right, right." Charmaine stared at Jessi. "Any idea how?"

"A few. You won't like any of them."

Chapter 10
Distressed Property

Jessi knew Charmaine the rule follower well. She had to keep repeating the amount of money they had on the line. They had to act fast to keep the authorities from finding out Diamond was on the run. Diamond's lawyer had a duty to report her missing.

"Skipping bail is a crime. Fannie is an officer of the court, so she can't keep quiet," Jessi explained as she drove them to Scotty's office.

"I thought that would be under attorney-client privilege thing," Charmaine said.

"Seriously?"

"Okay, I was grasping at any straw," Charmaine admitted with a deep sigh. "Well, we could try skip tracing?"

"Diamond has seen us work enough to know we'll think of that." Jessi chewed on a thumbnail then grimaced. She glanced at the purple finish set with green rhinestones. "Damn it, I paid too much for these soft gels."

"Okay, only the police have the authority to track bus tickets or plane tickets. So, we have to call them." Charmaine reached for her cell phone on the coffee table.

"Two words; bond forfeiture. But you're right. We need a cop." Jessi dialed and had a contentious but short conversation with Ricky. She walked away speaking low into the phone. Minutes later she returned. She blew out a harsh sigh after ending the call.

"You didn't call Ricky." Charmaine's eyes went wide when Jessi nodded. "Well?"

"He agreed."

"Jessi, this could cost him his career."

"I know, alright? It wasn't an easy ask for me. We should have to make sure once he tracks her that we get Diamond back in New Orleans fast," Jessi said.

"And keep Ricky's name out of it." Charmaine dialed Scotty's number, gave him a quick summary of the situation, and hung up. "He's going to do what he can. If we get information, Scotty will follow it up."

"Ricky can send me a message over Signal on his personal phone. His texts and voice messages self-destruct after." Jessi tapped the screen of her cell phone as she talked.

"Hmm, what is he up to?" Charmaine raised both eyebrows.

Jessi finished her message. "Don't look at me. I haven't pulled him into anything shady. He's considering a career change and doesn't want NOPD to know."

"Really?"

"He's taken a few law courses. Plus, he's had cybersecurity workshops offered to local police by the DOJ."

"Good for him. But then he might move away." Charmaine stared at Jessi.

"Who knows?" Jessi shrugged off the possibility, her expression neutral. "Anyway, let's hope Diamond hasn't gotten far."

"Yeah."

"In the meantime, here." Jessi went to her bag and pulled out a square envelope. "Your invitation to the luncheon where Loreen Kennedy will be Friday."

"If I can concentrate. What the hell is Diamond thinking?" Charmaine leaned against the sofa back.

"All she can see is prison time and Indyah going into the foster care system. You know she's not close to her sisters. Not that she'd want Indyah going to them anyway. Her cousin has five kids." Jessi sat down hard.

"Between Ricky and Scotty, we'll get her back." Charmaine forced as much confidence into her voice as she could.

"We have to or you and Scotty will have a roommate. Me," Jessi said with a grim expression.

Charmaine made her way through the elite crowd at the Monteleone Hotel's small ballroom. She nibbled on olives, cucumber slices, and other veggies on a porcelain saucer. Wait staff circled the room with trays and drinks. One waitress had served her a virgin cocktail. She had to admit hanging out in such a swanky atmosphere was a welcome distraction. Jessi texted her updates on efforts to find Diamond. Along with reminders that she needed to focus on Loreen Kennedy. The target stood across the room at what seemed an impossible distance. Mrs. Kennedy was dressed in a gray boucle jacket and a matching skirt. Black Tahitian pearls around her neck and button earrings completed the elegant outfit.

"So glad you could come," a female voice behind Charmaine said.

Charmaine braced to defend her presence. She turned to face the speaker and gasped. The CEO of the clinic where she worked smiled at her. She coughed when a bit of cheese when down the wrong way. Then managed to stammer out, "Thank you."

"Oh, goodness. I didn't mean to startle you. Here, let's get you water." Pamela Wainwright waved to a waiter, who arrived seconds later with a glass of water. "There you are. We can't have the new mother in distress."

"I'm fine. Really." Charmaine cleared her throat as her thoughts raced. "So, you're a Steel Magnolia?"

"No, my mother is a member. Their fundraising this year has been such a success." Mrs. Wainwright went on about the charitable work.

Charmaine nodded and made the appropriate responses she hoped at the right times. Finally, Mrs. Wainwright wound down after a minute of talking. "How wonderful considering the challenging economy."

"Yes, I suppose you have a point. Come over to my table and I'll introduce you to mother." Mrs. Wainwright beamed at her as if sure Charmaine would be happy to follow.

"How lovely," Charmaine murmured.

She trailed after her like a small boat in the wake of a yacht. They arrived at the table where two ladies and a man with white hair were seated. Charmaine guessed none of them were under the age of sixty-five. All looked equally prosperous. Their polished manners didn't hide their surprise to find Charmaine in their midst. Introductions were made all around. Mrs. Wainwright's mother insisted Charmaine sit in the empty chair.

"You shouldn't be on your feet the whole time in your condition," she said.

"Indeed. Sit right here." The older gentleman wore a wide smile as he waved to the cream-colored cushion.

"Thanks. I was feeling a little tired." Charmaine glanced at the other women. They wore matching chilly smiles as they gazed at her.

"March Preston, and this is my wife, Marjorie. March and Marjorie. Sounds like a vaudeville act, doesn't it?" March chuckled at his own joke and sipped from his martini glass. He went on for a bit talking about himself and his business.

"Hmm." Charmaine tilted her head to one side as she listened, feigning interest. She made a note to look up what vaudeville meant.

March leaned closer to Charmaine. "The two speakers went on a bit too long. And now we have to chat up the big corporate donors. You know, show our appreciation. Make them think they're part of us."

"It's for such a good cause," Charmaine replied.

"The parties and Mardi Gras balls are more fun, but it's all part of the game I suppose. Show people we're not just about lounging at the country club. Tiresome but such is life." March grinned at her.

"Well, we all go through difficulties." Charmaine spotted Loreen Kennedy a few feet away. "Like poor Mrs. Kennedy. Not that I know her personally. But so sad about her husband. I mean, based on the news reports."

"Hmm, Buddy had a bad end. Loreen is holding up well, though. She's a fighter. Here, I'll introduce her." March winked and helped her up. He seemed not to notice or care about his wife's sour expression.

"That's kind but don't go to any trouble." Charmaine stood despite her words and the look Mrs. Preston gave her.

"Don't you worry, Mrs. ..." March raised a greying blond eyebrow at Charmaine as a prompt.

"Ms. Joliet, but really, you don't have to." Charmaine protested for show only. Busybody March was a gift.

"Of course I must. The whole point of being at these things is to mix and mingle. Besides, we might get juicy tidbits firsthand. You're hardly alone. Behind the polite smiles, everyone here is dying to hear salacious details from the horse's mouth."

"Maybe I could refresh my drink. My throat is a little dry." Charmaine pretended to be a bit out of breath. She wanted to slow March down to pump him for gossip. It worked.

"Ha, great idea. I could use a top up myself. I've escaped the voice of reason telling me I've had enough wine. As if there's such a thing."

March proved an expert at weaving through the crowd while greeting others. He kept them moving to the bar in a corner of the room. Once there, he got himself another drink and more fruit juice for Charmaine. They stood to one side as another couple approached.

"Mrs. Kennedy seems to be presenting a brave front considering... you know." Charmaine spoke aside to him in a casual yet confidential tone.

March sipped from his wine goblet and hummed in appreciation. "Loreen comes from sturdy stock. Both her grandfather and father were hard-nosed businessmen. Few people who crossed them left without bruises. Literally."

"Oh, my goodness." Charmaine blinked at him with eyes wide as if scandalized.

"They got it honest, as the old saying goes. Her great-grandfather worked on the docks before he started a general store. New Orleans business has always been rough and tumble. Not much has changed. I guess that's why she found Buddy attractive. Growing up with hard-hitting, no-holds-barred men, you see." March drank more wine and looked around the room. He raised the glass to a man who smiled in return as he strolled by.

"Still, it has to be devastating. It's one thing to lose a husband to illness, but murder," Charmaine replied.

"I guess you know he was at a wild shindig." March's eyes twinkled when he gazed at Charmaine.

Charmaine lifted an eyebrow at him. She sidled a bit closer to him to urge March on. "The papers made it seem like a pretty sedate event."

"The media didn't want to hear from Loreen's high-powered lawyer. A pretty young 'escort' has been charged. The police have managed to keep a tight lid on details. Rumor is Buddy had been her regular customer. Drugs were also involved. But you didn't hear it from me." March tapped his lips, winked, and downed more wine.

"How awful for the poor woman."

"Don't let the charm school fool you. She's got steel in her spine. Come on, let's go say hello."

His refreshment mission accomplished, he resumed their beeline to Loreen Kennedy. He guided Charmaine along with gentlemanly decorum, one hand on her elbow. Mrs. Kennedy stood in the center of a small knot of similarly well-dressed women in their forties to fifties.

"Hello, ladies. Loreen, you look lovely as ever," March boomed when they were a few feet away. The other women gave him tight polite smiles as he addressed each by name in a boisterous manner. They looked at Charmaine. Seconds later they drifted off in different directions to chat with others. He let go of his hold on Charmaine's arm to give Loreen a brief hug. "How are you holding up, duchess?"

"Hello, March. I'm fine. I assume you've already written a nice check." Mrs. Kennedy smiled at him.

"Naturally. Marjorie wouldn't let any of the ladies in our country club upstage her." March winced as if remembering the dollar amount.

"Your wonderful wife can always be counted on." Mrs. Kennedy stared at Charmaine.

"Forgive me. My charming young companion is here to support helping the less fortunate," March said with a smile.

"Wonderful event, Mrs. Kennedy." Charmaine spoke up before March could say her name.

"Thank you. The committee comes through every year. Have we met?" Mrs. Kennedy's cool gaze did a swift head-to-toe appraisal of Charmaine.

"I work at a non-profit. We've benefited from your fundraising in the past. We were given a limited number of invitations." Charmaine kept her explanation simple and close to the truth. Thanks to Jessi's homework, she knew employees from local charities were in attendance.

Mrs. Kennedy nodded. "Really, what—"

"Awful business about Buddy. We weren't always on the same page, but I respected the old bugger." March's sloppy compliment came out a bit slurred.

"Thank you." Mrs. Kennedy's frozen smile seemed close to cracking her face as March prattled on.

Charmaine affected a tolerant expression. She darted quick glances at the older man as he went on as if listening to him. Mrs. Kennedy's lips pursed after a few moments. March made indiscreet comments about how much Bernard Kennedy enjoyed a good time. Then he moved on to her son's political goals; and how the manner of his father's death shouldn't derail his future campaign. For her part, Charmaine concentrated on reading Mrs. Kennedy. A few profane names for March came through clearly. Then Loreen's thoughts turned to how much March resembled her late husband. And not in positive ways. Charmaine caught fleeting phrases of bitterness. Mrs. Kennedy despised being left to clean up her husband's sordid mess. Again. Then Loreen's thought turned to the family businesses. Something about another investigation? Charmaine's eyes narrowed as she pushed through to follow the lead. She blinked when March tapped her on the shoulder.

"Excuse me. I'm going to get a small last taste before Marjorie hunts me down. What can I get you ladies?" March looked from Loreen to Charmaine.

"I'm good." Charmaine put her empty glass on the tray of a passing waitress.

"Nothing for me. I suggest nothing stronger than water for you, March." Mrs. Kennedy looked down her nose at him.

March, unaffected by her disapproval, gave a dismissive wave with one hand. "No worries. One, I've barely had enough to get tipsy. Trust me, I can hold my own in the drinking department. And two, we hired a car service so I'm not driving."

"Mr. Preston seems like a sweet person." Charmaine put on a restrained smile while watching March stroll away. Despite the wine, he didn't seem unsteady on his feet.

"He's a tactless loud mouth, but he's a rich one from an old family." Mrs. Kennedy fixed Charmaine with a granite expression.

"Well, um—"

"Your explanation for being here is tissue thin and easy to see through. You've been watching me."

"No, I... You've been through a terrible ordeal. I understand how trying a first public social event must be. With all of the intense media attention, I mean." Charmaine started to go on but stopped when Mrs. Kennedy stepped closer.

"I'm not a fool, Ms. Joliet. My personal assistant discreetly took your photo and did a reverse image search. You're friends with that woman suspected of killing Bernard." Mrs. Kennedy's eyes took on a feral gleam.

Charmaine moved away a few inches. Acid from the fruit juice bubbled at the back of her throat. "How did you..."

"I've researched Ms. Phillips, her background, and her *associates*. Despite the crowd, I'm familiar with most of the people here. You stood out as one of the few people neither I nor my assistant could readily identify."

"Well..." Charmaine shrugged and decided on another strategy. Anything to stay close to Loreen before she got tossed out on her butt. "Fine. I wanted a chance to explain why the police have it all wrong."

"Ms. Phillips is a hooker who provided illegal party drugs. She played on my late husband's weaknesses, no doubt for money. And she took her 'entertainment' too far. I'd say the police have it all *right*. The district attorney agrees with them."

Her words pushed aside Charmaine's anxiety making room for anger. "Diamond didn't murder your husband. Rushing the wrong person to prison isn't justice," Charmaine said.

"You would say that. I suggest you spend time raising money to pay for a good lawyer," Mrs. Kennedy said with a caustic laugh.

"And the real killer could still be a danger to someone in your family," Charmaine clipped.

Mrs. Kennedy's eyes narrowed to slits. "Is that a threat?"

Charmaine gasped and blinked hard at her. "No, of course not. I only meant—"

"I don't respond well to intimidation tactics. I may not come from a grimy housing project, but I know how to fight back. Stay away from my family." Mrs. Kennedy's voice cut through the inches between them with the sharpness of a switchblade.

March, another glass in his hand, returned wearing a smile of good humor. "Well, for once I'm enjoying myself. Don't know why Marjorie keeps giving me looks that could kill. She should loosen up. After all, she drags me to these things. You two getting acquainted?"

"Oh, I think we understand each other very well." Mrs. Kennedy wore a smile that could drip icicles.

"Excellent. Everybody is having a grand time." March went on talking, totally unable to read the room.

"Thank you so much for the hospitality. It's been a wonderful event but I should be going." Charmaine smiled to maintain his cordial façade.

"Nice meeting you indeed. Such a lovely young woman. You certainly brightened up the place." March raised the glass in a toast to Charmaine and then gulped wine.

Mrs. Kennedy cut side-eye of scorn at him before she turned a stony gaze to Charmaine. March's wife joined them. Mrs. Preston greeted Mrs. Kennedy with warmth. Her good humor evaporated when she looked at her husband. Charmaine made a wide berth of the room to avoid the clinic CEO. She bumped into a young white woman with dark brown hair.

"Excuse me." Charmaine continued toward the exit.

The brunette matched Charmaine's pace, walking beside her. "I'm Mrs. Kennedy's PA, Ms. Joliet. I'm sure District Commander Harrison will be interested to know you're harassing a murder victim's grieving widow."

Charmaine stopped and faced the woman. "Excuse me, but this is a public function and I have an invitation."

"Enjoy the rest of your day—while you can." The woman left without looking back at Charmaine.

Later that evening, Charmaine and Scotty sat at their friend's soul food café. Scotty had Jamaican oxtails, rice with beans, and sweet potatoes. Charmaine had ordered her favorite, fried catfish with a side of hush puppies and collard greens. There was a constant hum of conversation from the full restaurant. Tourists in town for Mardi Gras and locals made a lively mix. Kat's Fleur de Lis Café benefited from positive reviews on a popular travel vlog. Kat strolled over to their table. She wore a full black apron with a gold fleur de lis embroidered on the left chest. Her shoulder-length locs were tied into a ponytail.

"Look, I work too hard on these delicacies to have y'all picking at it like that." Kat stood with one hand on her hip.

"Your food is delicious as always. We're distracted." Scotty patted his lips with a napkin. To prove his assertion, he ate a portion of the fall-off-the-bone meat.

"Absolutely, Kat. It's not you. It's me." Charmaine smiled up at their friend.

Kat took a seat at their table. "Any news on Diamond?"

"Jessi somehow convinced Diamond's cousins to tell her where she is and—"

"Translation, she terrorized them until they spilled the deets. If you know, you know," Scotty drawled.

Kat nodded agreement. "For real, she don't play."

"Why does everyone think we go around threatening people?" Charmaine huffed at the look Kat exchanged with Scotty. "Anyway, Jessi is in Houston. I hope she gets to Diamond before she boards that flight to the Dominican Republic."

"She's leaving the country? Wow," Kat replied.

"Diamond has family in Trinidad on her father's side. I'm guessing she thought Jessi would look at flights there first. So, take a flight to the DR first and then on to Trinidad." Scotty ate more of his food. He smacked his lips in appreciation and gave Kat a thumbs up sign.

"Okay. So, she's been found before the cops or the DA knew she was even gone. Why are you still gloomy?" Kat said to Charmaine.

"We don't know if Jessi got to her yet. Besides, they still don't have a solid alternative suspect to give Harrison," Scotty put in.

Charmaine snatched up her phone when a text notification sounded. Kat and Scotty stared hard at her expression in anticipation. "Jessi caught up with her before she checked in. There was a long line and… crap. Diamond made a scene. Security and TSA got involved. Jessi managed to smooth it over."

"That's good, right?" Kat looked from Scotty to Charmaine again.

"I wish I could have a strong drink right now." Charmaine let out a slow groan as she fell against the chair back.

Scotty rubbed the small of her back. "But you have southern fried catfish, honey."

"You're right. All of a sudden, I'm hungry. And it's still warm. Thank you, Lord!" Charmaine blurted out. She devoured half of the filet. "

"I've got something even better than alcohol for the expectant mama." Kat grinned at Charmaine and left the table.

Scotty watched Charmaine savor her food and he finished his plate as well. After a few moments he said, "When will they get home?"

"Hmm." Charmaine wiped her hands on a napkin and drank sweet tea. "Jessi already booked a Monday morning flight."

"She planned ahead."

"You know Jessi. When she's on a mission nothing is left to chance. I just hope they'll be okay during the weekend." Charmaine frowned.

"Harrison and the DA don't know Diamond went anywhere. I'm guessing a couple of more days won't cause a problem," Scotty said.

"I'm not worried about Harrison. Besides, even if he does somehow find out, I'll just tell him exactly where she is and that she went to visit a relative. Her lawyer said her travel restrictions just said she couldn't leave the country."

"Which she was about to do," Scotty mumbled low. "But wait, didn't the court make Diamond surrender her passport?"

"She did. Her *American* passport. She has one from Jamaica. Her maternal grandparents emigrated from there, which means she qualified for dual citizenship."

"And naturally they didn't mention her having to give up Indyah's passport. Kind of genius planning when you think about it." Scotty wore a sideways grin.

"Yeah, a plan that was going to put her friends in bankruptcy," Charmaine snapped. "I know facing a murder trial is scary, but when I think what we could have lost..."

"Jessi came up with an equally devious way of finding her. You have one less thing to worry about. Think of little Marquis Elliot Minor. He needs your nerves settled." Scotty pointed to Charmaine's round tummy. He leaned over and pecked her cheek.

"First, we don't know it's a boy. And second, where the hell did you come up with that name? No way is any kid of mine going to be called Marquis," Charmaine said with force.

Scotty laughed. "My mama and Aunt Ida floated the idea. Believe it or not Marquis was their dad's name and Elliot was their favorite paternal uncle. And yes, they were dead serious." He laughed harder at the look of horror on Charmaine's face.

"I love your mama; really, I do. But I draw the line at the name suggestion. We have figure out a way not to hurt their feelings," Charmaine said.

"I already handled it. Mama is fine with the new mother picking out a name. Aunt Ida is a kinda sulking, but she'll get over it."

"She's gonna have to," Charmaine tossed back. "Let's have a quiet weekend. Who knows what will hit the fan next week."

"Poor baby. I'll take care of you for the next few days." Scotty kissed her on the forehead.

"Here ya go, mommy!" Kat returned carrying two sundae dishes. "Made this morning."

"Her favorite." Scotty grinned when Charmaine's face lit up with delight.

Charmaine clapped her hand at the sight. Vanilla wafers layered the sides of the creamy yellow pudding. Banana slices graced the whipped cream topping. "I have the best family."

The weekend didn't turn out to be quite uneventful. Gina Shaw called Saturday to ask if Jessi could make a quick pass at one last property. An open house event would be held Sunday starting at noon. Charmaine's diplomacy skills were put to the test. Gina first tried to sweet-talk Charmaine into agreeing. Then she turned on the pressure with talk about their contract. Scotty came close to interrupting but Charmaine stood firm. Gina accepted neither of the sisters would show up but made her annoyance known. Thankfully, Sunday went by with no hysterical call from Gina about ghosts or goblins.

Monday morning at the clinic proved to be a busy one. Charmaine welcomed the distraction of a full schedule. Her last one before lunch turned out to be Andre, Mrs. Chatelaine's nephew.

"How is the med change?" Charmaine asked

"It's okay. Wish I could get off these drugs though." Andre puckered his lips in distaste.

"We talked about the importance of compliance," Charmaine said.

"I'm not saying I won't take the stuff. I guess it'll help me deal with all the damn drama."

Charmaine leaned back and gazed at him. He didn't seem agitated. No pressured speech or fidgeting. "What's going on?"

"My lady friend, Allison, gave me the 'where are we going with this' speech. I mean, we'd had a nice Saturday. We went to two parades. Had a nice dinner, and that was probably my mistake. Things always get tricky when you spend the night."

"You've been seeing each other for quite a while now," Charmaine prompted when he seemed lost in thought.

"Almost six months. Anyway, Sunday morning I'm spooning blueberries on top her pancakes and bam! Uncomfortable conversation to spoil things." Andre hissed his displeasure at being caught off guard.

"Oh, I see."

"Right?" Andre blurted out as if Charmaine's neutral response was agreement. "A perfectly good weekend went left. Allison says she needs a break to think."

"You've been divorced for three years. You mentioned how much you liked being in a relationship. Some of your most stable years were during your two marriages."

"Yeah. I don't know. The last divorce busted me up. Sharlena and I were so good. Until we weren't. And the legal fees." Andre pulled a large hand over his face.

"You had two affairs and gambled a lot," Charmaine said in a level voice.

"Hmm. I know what you're going to say. I stopped seeing my psychiatrist and started self-medicating. I'm clean now though. But I'm still gun shy about making a commitment."

"Feeling pressure is also a trigger for you. Let's go over the coping strategies in your recovery plan."

For the next twenty minutes, Charmaine guided him through two exercises. Andre had chosen those that appealed to him. He ended with a calming routine that included measured deep breathing.

"Those always help me feel better. I'll call Allison tonight and ask her to meet me for a talk. I don't want to lose her," Andre said once they'd finished.

"It might be a good idea to practice what you'll say. Don't make a decision you really don't feel right about, Andre. Be honest with her and yourself," Charmaine replied.

"I hear you, Ms. Joliet. Thanks." Andre heaved a sigh. His draw eyebrows pulled together. "Wish dealing with the family mess was as simple."

"More conflict with your children?" Charmaine asked. Andre had two adult children from his first marriage and a teenaged daughter from his second one. His erratic behavior meant he'd been inconsistent in their lives.

"No, no. For once I'm getting along with all three of them. I'm talking about the uproar with my cousin trying to get Aunt Lydia to the doctor." Andre shook his head in dismay.

"Did she go?"

"Yeah, but let me tell you she wasn't happy about it. Then Auntie starts accusing us of forging her name to get our hands on her property. Aunt Lydia went in on everybody. Saying we're trying to come up with an excuse to lock her up in a dementia unit."

"I'm sorry she's upset. Maybe you should give her some space. Your cousins and sister seem able to talk to her."

Charmaine glanced at the time display on her computer monitor. "Well, that's all for today. If you need to talk before our next appointment call or text."

"Thanks again. I'll let you know how it goes with Allison." Andre stood. "Please help Aunt Lydia. I know she didn't mean the things she said. Maybe she does have some kind of health issue affecting her."

Charmaine stood with him. "We're working on it is all I can say."

"Auntie is eccentric. It runs in the family," Andre said with a shrug. "But borrowing money and not remembering… it's not like her at all."

"We'll make sure she's okay."

Once he was gone, Charmaine checked her text messages. Nothing from Jessi, but then they were probably boarding their connection. Jessi, Diamond, and Indyah's flight would arrive at the Louis Armstrong International Airport by five o'clock. The hours dragged on as Jessi sent cryptic updates via text. She and Diamond were barely speaking. Diamond had lapsed into silent, seething submission. The intervention of Houston airport security about their loud argument had done the trick. Jessi's threat to call NOPD also helped. By nine o'clock Monday night Jessi was at Charmaine's house. She collapsed onto the sofa with a groan. Jessi pulled off her leather boots. Her head fell back onto the sofa cushion.

"What a crazy last few days. You don't know how many times I wanted to scream."

"I got you some dinner. Figured you wouldn't eat with Diamond." Charmaine placed a takeout plate of food on the coffee table. "Kat cooked meatloaf, gravy, green beans, and rice."

"Thank you. Finally, someone appreciates what I've gone through." Jessi padded down the short hallway to wash her hands in the bathroom. She yelled back over running water. "Diamond had the audacity to be pissed at me. I'm the only reason her ass isn't sitting in a jail cell right now."

"She's terrified, Jessi. Not that it's an excuse for almost making you lose your house,"

"Damn right it's not. I told her so, too. Had Indyah confused and scared as hell. I almost got a migraine from the effort not to read Diamond for filth in front of that baby." Jessi dropped onto the sofa again and opened the box of food.

Charmaine let her eat without peppering her with questions. Instead, she turned on the news. When reports of shootings and a robbery made for grim listening, Charmaine turned to a classic movie channel. A black and white western played as muted background noise. Jessi focused on her dinner. Charmaine watched the television without paying attention.

"Your friendship doesn't have to be over you know." Charmaine hit the mute button on the already low volume.

"We've been through worse. One time we got into a fight, I mean hands thrown for real, for real, at the club we were dancing at. She kept flirting with my customer." Jessi sliced a chunk of meatloaf and popped it into her mouth.

"I can't believe you fought over a *man*." Charmaine pretended to clutch imaginary pearls.

"Girl, not him. The twenties he kept stuffing in my thong. Don't play with me about my money."

"There's the Jessi I know," Charmaine quipped. Then she grew serious. "But what's happened between you two is on a different level."

Jessi put down her fork and sighed. "Yeah. We gonna work it out though."

"I hope so because…" Charmaine stopped and picked up her ringing cell phone. She held it out so Jessi could see.

"Gina Shaw. Huh." Jessi's eyes narrowed. Then she nodded.

Charmaine hit the "accept call" icon. "Hi Gina. Okay. I can do that. Bye."

"Well?"

"I told you Gina tried adding another property to the list we originally agreed to. Seems the open house Sunday had a few *worrying incidents*." Charmaine made air quotes with her fingers.

"And?"

"She is willing to pay us for one more spirit sweep. I'm to send an amendment to our contract to include it." Charmaine looked at her sister.

Jessi gazed back at Charmaine for a few beats. "Let's go find out what kind of trap has been set for us. This time, we'll be ready."

Chapter 11
Pros and Cons

Their next field visit to a Shaw Realty property was scheduled for late Thursday afternoon. Gina decided to hold off showings until then. The house was still being renovated but major renovations had been done. Still, Gina was antsy about being able to get it sold quickly. Which made Jessi and Charmaine wonder if her business was on shaky ground. In the meantime, Charmaine tried to play peacemaker between Diamond and Jessi. Pouring oil on those particular troubled waters proved challenging. At least Diamond responded to her text. Charmaine started out by asking pregnancy and new mom questions. When she brought up Jessi being an aunt, Diamond changed the subject. More work had to be done, but Charmaine would keep at it.

In the meantime, they had a Tuesday meeting set up with Mrs. Chatelaine and her niece Angela Patin. Jessi picked up Charmaine at her house and they headed to Vallette Street. The Mardi Gras fringed banner attached to the fascia of her cottage fluttered in the cold wind. With Mardi Gras Day being the next Tuesday, traffic from tourist buses and rental cars clogged the streets. Parades leading up to the main raucous celebration proved just as big a draw.

"Brace yourself. We might not get a warm reception," Charmaine said as she released her seat belt.

"Use your therapy skills on her." Jessi tapped the screen of her cell phone. "I just sent another begging message to the fingerprint expert. Kayla's in court but will get back to me."

"Okay. No use putting this off. Let's face the wrath of Lady Lydia."

Charmaine got out of Jessi's Jeep and followed her to Mrs. Chatelaine's front door. A tall woman with tawny skin and thick shoulder-length curls answered the bell. She greeted then with an encouraging smile.

"Hi, I'm Angela Patin. We emailed but you spoke to my cousin on the phone the other day. Thanks so much for all the documents you've researched." Angela led them into the living room. "Aunt Lydia will be here in a minute. She 'visited the powder room'. I think she's one of the few people who still use such phrases."

Angela let out a musical laugh of affection. She served them hot tea and butter pecan cookies. Jessi, never one to turn down a treat, ate two in no time. Angela entertained them with fond anecdotes about her aunt and other New Orleans Creole relatives. When Mrs. Chatelaine joined them, she seemed calm enough. Dressed in a sweater with floral embroidery and a coordinating skirt, she looked the picture of mature casual elegance. Jessi exchanged a hopeful glance with Charmaine.

"Those are an old family recipe." Mrs. Chatelaine pointed to the tray of cookies. She sat down on the sofa next to her niece. She didn't appear hostile, but then the regal older woman didn't radiate friendliness either.

"They're so melt-in-your-mouth good." Jessi eyed the tray as if considering a third helping.

"My cousin Nicholas and his wife have a baking company in Atlanta. Very successful," Angela put in.

"Not surprising. They're bestsellers from the private cookbook of my great-grandfather." Mrs. Chatelaine lifted her chin.

"They even smell delicious," Charmaine said. Indeed, the home still held the scent of vanilla in the air.

"Hmm, and trademarked, so don't ask me to share it," Mrs. Chatelaine replied in a clipped tone.

"Auntie!" Angela let out short nervous laugh.

"Nicholas' business is built on these cookies. They're his second most popular product." Mrs. Chatelaine appeared unaffected by her niece's gentle scolding.

"I definitely understand protecting a brand from a legal standpoint," Jessi said to Mrs. Chatelaine. "Recipes are covered under trade secrets law."

"Really?" Angela's shapely eyebrows rose.

"Oh, yeah. They're a form of intellectual property. I can see why you'd want to hold onto these goodies." Jessi helped herself to another cookie.

Mrs. Chatelaine glanced at her niece and then at the sisters. "Speaking of property, let's get down to business. Despite the tea and cookies, this isn't a social call."

"Aunt Lydia, really. Jessi and Charmaine have been nothing but supportive. They're working for you," Angela put in before Jessi or Charmaine could reply. She frowned a warning to her aunt.

"Are they? Making me out to be a senile old woman who's running amok doesn't seem loyal. Not to me anyway." Mrs. Chatelaine pressed her lips together in a hard line.

"Memory issues are normal as we age, Mrs. Chatelaine," Charmaine put in. She flinched when Mrs. Chatelaine glared at her.

"We never accused you of 'running amok. You're way too classy," Jessi said. "Drink some tea and calm your nerves. We're on your side, Lydia."

"Don't patronize me. And it's Mrs. Chatelaine to you." Mrs. Chatelaine stared ahead, not looking at Jessi or Charmaine.

"Aunt Lydia, really..." Angela faced Charmaine with a tentative smile.

When Jessi's phone buzzed, she stood. Jessi left the chair to huddle in a corner of the room. "I need to take this."

Charmaine watched Jessi go. She turned back to find Mrs. Chatelaine's stony gaze fixed on her. "We have a lot going on. So..."

"Oh, don't let my little case get in the way of more *important* matters," Mrs. Chatelaine retorted.

"This rudeness isn't like you at all," Angela snapped.

"Aha, now you're making the case that I'm not myself. Off my rocker, I suppose. Building up evidence to have me declared incompetent. Maybe you and Andre cooked up this scheme. Which is why he sent them here in the first place." Mrs. Chatelaine's voice became shriller with each word. Her eyes grew glassy with unshed tears.

Angela swallowed hard as if controlling her temper. She placed a hand on Mrs. Chatelaine's shoulder. "We love you to the moon and back. Nobody is going to take anything from you. Not your home or your autonomy."

"I just don't understand what's happening. If Gerald was still alive..." Mrs. Chatelaine shook her head and covered her face with both hands.

Charmaine stayed quiet for a few minutes as Angela consoled her aunt. She decided a close family member offering assurance would mean more. Angela nodded to Charmaine as she led Mrs. Chatelaine to her bedroom. Moments later, Angela returned alone.

"She's going to fix her makeup. Even upset, Auntie Lydia wants to look her best," Angela said with a soft smile of fondness. "I want her to live out the rest of her days in dignity. And security."

"Your family is blessed, Angela. Your aunt has resources," Charmaine said.

Angela dabbed her eyes with a tissue. "Not if her property is taken away. I should have noticed she wasn't herself sooner."

"Don't blame yourself. The cognitive changes can be so slight they're easy to miss."

"She's always been independent and headstrong. She traveled alone to Europe when she was twenty. Family gossip says she had a fling with a duke in France. Or maybe Scotland. I never got up the nerve to ask her. I don't want her to lose memories of all the adventures."

"There have been a lot of advances in treatment. What did the doctor say?"

"He's scheduled a CAT scan and other tests. She has an appointment with the neuropsychologist Thursday morning."

Angela put on a smile when Mrs. Chatelaine returned. "Feeling better?"

"Well, if I'm losing my marbles, I might as well look decent doing it. I've still got life left in me. I'm going to party right up until you put me in a nursing home!" Mrs. Chatelaine patted her niece's hand.

Angela put an arm around Mrs. Chatelaine's shoulders. "Oh, Auntie, we're a long way from making any decisions."

"Better wait to see what all those tests say. Still, no gloomy faces for now. It's Mardi Gras. I've got an outfit picked out for the Queen Sheba Krewe ball Saturday." Mrs. Chatelaine winked and scurried off again. She returned with a deep green sequined evening gown.

"Gorgeous!" Charmaine rose to examine the dress closely.

"My friend dyed pumps this same shade. I bought a purple faux fur wrap to go with. It's so dark it almost looks black. Maybe I'll finish it off with a tasteful gold tiara or a feathered fascinator headband! My friend Zelda and I have one last shopping run before the big day." Mrs. Chatelaine's light brown eyes sparkled with excitement. Her earlier despondent mood seemed to have been forgotten.

"Sounds like you're going to party until dawn." Charmaine grinned at her.

"The days of staying up all night are far behind me. But I'll shake what my mama gave me until well after midnight for sure. "

Angela chuckled as she watched her leave again to put the dress away. "Aunt Lydia has had an ongoing feud with Mrs. Auzenne for *years*. All smiles when they meet, but the shade that gets thrown."

"I feel better already. Oh, and I have a date. Hazel Auzenne and her witch's coven are Mardi Gras green with envy," Mrs. Chatelaine declared when she returned again.

"Who, Auntie?" Angela's eyes were wide with curiosity.

"Randall Thierry." Mrs. Chatelaine nodded when Angela gasped. She turned to Charmaine. "Randall's wife died last year. He's a retired pharmacist. He could barely get home from the funeral before Hazel started campaigning to be the next Mrs."

Angela and Mrs. Chatelaine dove into a gossipy exchange as Charmaine lapped it up. Backstories about Mrs. Chatelaine's sparring matches with Hazel were juicy and amusing. Charmaine was delighted to peek into the lives of New Orleans' Black social elite. Jessi joined them in the middle of an account about a particularly nasty family fight over an inheritance.

"Mama always said, you find out how people really feel once someone dies." Mrs. Chatelaine looked at Angela. "I'm going to make sure my affairs are in."

Jessi joined them still holding her cell phone. "Well, seems we've got a lot more work to do for you, Mrs. C."

"Oh?" Mrs. Chatelaine raised both eyebrows at her.

"That Kayla Prentiss, the handwriting expert. Those signatures on those deeds were forged. And get this, whoever did it obtained loans based on the property values."

"But how is that possible?" Angela blurted. "Aunt Lydia is on record as the owner. She has been for years."

"Deed and title fraud have become more and more common. It's identity theft taken to a whole new level. Instead of stealing credit cards, folks just forge a deed. Some go to the assessor's office and present phony sales papers and get the titles transferred to their name," Jessi explained.

Mrs. Chatelaine slapped a palm on the sofa cushion. "I just knew it! I may be old, but I haven't totally lost it yet."

"I can't believe someone can just walk in with fake papers and walk out with someone else's land." Angela stared at them with her mouth open.

"Louisiana is like most states, playing catch-up when it comes to this stuff. Right now, staff at the assessor's offices don't have procedures in place to verify identity or notify owners if someone shows up to change a title," Jessi replied.

"I'm ready to fight," Mrs. Chatelaine said. "What's next."

"After I talked to Kayla, I called another friend. She's a paralegal who works with real estate attorneys. We've got to create a paper trail to prove ownership. Kayla will send a written report about the forgery. Do you have a lawyer?" Jessi looked from Mrs. Chatelaine to Angela.

"I know several," Mrs. Chatelaine said before Angela could reply. "Lanessa Marchand took over their father's firm when he and her uncle retired."

For the next hour Jessi led them through the first steps needed. Mrs. Chatelaine and Angela were able to get the attorney on the phone. They arranged a video conference in a few days. Jessi would send her documents. Mrs. Chatelaine seemed energized at the notion of a battle. By the time Charmaine and Jessi left, they had a solid plan.

"I can't believe this," Charmaine said as Jessi drove to drop her off at home. "Like Angela said, some scrub can take your house and make it official."

"Yeah. Mrs. Chatelaine will likely end up in court. But there is a little bit of hope. My friend did a lien search. She hasn't found any so far."

"Okay, but losing ownership is still bad."

"Yeah, but it's weird because my friend says in most cases scammers borrow money and then don't pay up. Which means the lenders foreclose. Mrs. Chatelaine swears she hasn't gotten any final notice letters or strange mail related to her property. Angela is going to check her credit reports."

"What's next?" Charmaine yawned, a hand on her swelling tummy.

"Go home and put your feet up is all that's next for you. I'm going to do more research since I have time on my hands." Jessi frowned as she pulled up to a stop light.

"Meaning?" Charmaine heard the note of sadness beneath the words.

"I won't be hanging out with my best friend for a while. Or should I say my ex-bestie. And things are tense with Ricky, so no romantic dinners or dates for a while."

"He's helped you out but wasn't happy about it," Charmaine said.

"No, he wasn't. Oh well, what's the old saying? Men are like buses. Another one will come along." Jessi shrugged.

They arrived at Charmaine's house after twenty minutes of maneuvering through clogged streets. Charmaine had a weird nervous energy. Despite weak objections from Jessi, she started dinner. First, she seasoned chicken wings and put them in the tabletop air fryer. Then she whipped up a large salad green salad. Charmaine knew very well that Jessi didn't want to go home alone.

"I'm not tired after all. Go to my office and work your private eye magic." Charmaine pushed her out of the kitchen.

An hour later they sat at the kitchen island drinking root beer. They left twin piles of chicken bones piled on their respective plates. Charmaine savored the last corner of French bread smeared with garlic butter. She sighed with satisfaction.

"Cajun wings and root beer almost make everything right with the world." Charmaine closed her eyes and opened them again.

"Almost. So, you learn anything useful at the luncheon?" Jessi removed the dishes and tossed the scraps away. Then she loaded the dishwasher.

"Well, Loreen's definitely not grieving her husband. I did get that he's not going to be a problem now that he's gone." Charmaine frowned as she sorted through the bits of thought she'd picked up telepathically.

"Which means she's got motive. A cheating husband who got high and reckless. Buddy made a hobby out of embarrassing the family. Reputation means a lot to those types."

"No, it's more. Find out what you can about their finances. But don't do anything illegal." Charmaine gave her a pointed stare.

"Girl, we got a murder to solve so Diamond doesn't go to prison. Oh yeah, and my house is on the line. I don't give two shits about no damn rules," Jessi replied with a snort.

"We don't need Harrison and NOPD on our tails, Jessi. And Ricky—"

"Harrison always has a bug up his ass. And Ricky... well, he's on his way out the door anyway." Jessi frowned at the mention of her lover, a sign she cared more than she let on.

"Okay, I tried. At least don't get caught." Charmaine got up, stretched, and rubbed her lower back.

Jessi shook her head as if clearing thoughts of the handsome redhead. "Nah, we gotta at least find reasonable doubt if not the real killer."

"Agreed."

"I..." Jessi paused when the doorbell rang. She rose and walked to a side window to look out. "I thought Scotty was working tonight."

"He is. I got a text from him before dinner. Maybe it's Mama Etta Ray with more bread pudding." Charmaine licked her lips.

"You know Mama stopped driving at night. What the hell..."

"We need to talk." Diamond wore a grim expression.

She brushed past her after Jessi unlocked the storm door. She had both arms tightly crossed as if cold. Charmaine coaxed her into shedding the blood red wool jacket she wore against the chilly evening. While Charmaine put water on for hot tea, she darted nervous glances from Jessi to Diamond. They circled each other like female wrestlers sizing each other up. She stood between the women making pregnancy small talk. The kettle whistled; Charmaine steeped tea and poured three cups.

"Let's sit in the living room," Charmaine announced when Jessi started to speak. She read the angry speech building up in her sister's mind. Carrying a tray with the cups and a sugar bowl, she smiled. "Lemon balm with honey. To settle our nerves. Keep things low key."

"Humph." Jessi stomped to one of the two chairs that matched Charmaine's sofa and dropped onto it.

Charmaine tried to give her sister a look of caution, but Jessi didn't return her gaze. "So, Dee. You wanted to talk to us."

"Yeah. Start with explaining how you was willing to throw us under the fucking bus!" Jessi's words shot out as if a pressure cooker blew out steam. "We put everything we own on the line for you and—"

"I know. Okay? I'm sorry, but after I got that message about Indyah, I couldn't take no more. If it was just about me..." Diamond burst into tearful incoherence. It took several minutes for her to calm down.

"A message from who?" Charmaine asked in her most soothing therapist voice.

Diamond blew her nose into a napkin Charmaine provided. "I don't know. I got a text message. How did they get my number?" She looked close to dissolving into hysteria one more.

"We'll figure that out." Charmaine inched close to Diamond on the sofa and hugged her. "Scotty and Jessi have resources on the street. But you need to focus. We dodged a bullet on the bail situation."

"I didn't mean to hurt y'all. I just freaked out. They know about our schedules. When I work at the hotel. What time the bus drops her off at my cousin's house three days a week. Then that she goes to my aunt's place on Thursdays and Fridays. Cause Keisha works Saturday to Wednesday and—"

"Okay, slow down. Deep breaths." Charmaine counted to five as a guide while Diamond inhaled and exhaled.

"Give me your phone." Jessi held out a hand with an impatient frown. She ignored the scowl of condemnation on Charmaine's face.

"She's been through a lot," Charmaine snapped.

Diamond sniffled as she dug the iPhone out of her purse. "I, uh, deleted it. Just knowing it was on there gave me the creeps."

"Real smart." Jessi took the cell phone from her hand.

"Jessi!" Charmaine continued to rubbed Diamond's shoulders to console her. "Being mean to Diamond isn't helping."

"She's right though. I should have stopped to think but I couldn't. All I could see was somebody snatching my baby and..." Diamond's sobs were muffled by the napkins pressed to her face.

"Will you just stop?" Charmaine hissed at her sister over Diamond's head. She rose, went to her bathroom, and returned with a large box of facial tissues.

"I packed two bags for us. Then I called my aunt in Jamaica. She was happy we were coming to visit," Diamond said when she recovered one again.

"I know how to find deleted messages," Jessi muttered as she swiped the phone's touch screen.

"Like I said, they were from marked 'unknown' on the caller ID." Diamond glanced at Jessi.

"Probably bought the phone at a discount store and then threw it away. Unless we're really lucky and can figure out where they bought it, get security camera footage, and..." Jessi huffed out air in frustration.

"I doubt we'll be that lucky, unless they're stupid." Charmaine stood and looked over Jessi's shoulder.

"They set her up for murder pretty good. They're no dummies for sure," Jessi replied.

"Oh my God. You think a killer is watching my baby?" Diamond started to hyperventilate.

Charmaine concentrated on getting Diamond under control for a third time. She poured out the neglected cold tea Diamond hadn't touched. Jessi seemed oblivious to the havoc she kept causing. Instead, she grimaced in concentration while tapping texts on her own phone. Diamond managed to take a few sips from the second cup of tea. She stammered out that Indyah should be safe.

"She's with my other aunt. Her son LeDarius is home from jail. Aunt Dree keeps a loaded gun handy and LeDarius, well…"

"A gun around young children is a terrible idea." Chamaine looked at Jessi in alarm. Diamond's Aunt Shandricka and her son had both faced charges of assault in the past. They'd also taken turns serving jail time for drug dealing.

"Aunt Dree is good with gun safety around her grandkids," Diamond responded with a nod of assurance.

"We need street soldiers sometimes." Jessi sat in a chair. She continued to glance between her phone and Diamond's. "You got a second message."

"Something about…" Diamond gave a visible shudder.

"That the charge will be reduced to involuntary manslaughter. If she doesn't fight it, calls off her 'witch pals', then her sentence wouldn't be long." Jessi put Diamond's phone on the coffee table. Her eyes narrowed as she stared at nothing.

"What?" Charmaine picked up Diamond's phone and read the anonymous text.

"This had to be sent by somebody with an inside at the DA's office." Jessi looked at Charmaine.

"The Kennedy family," Charmaine replied. "If Diamond doesn't play their game, things will be worse for her."

"Wait a minute. How did Harrison get the DMs between Diamond and Buddy Kennedy?" Jessi turned to Diamond, who shrugged and drank more tea.

"I'll call Fannie and find out. She'll have the details in discovery. In the meantime, no more running off. Have some faith in us and your lawyer," Jessi said to her friend.

"Running off was stupid. At least I didn't get y'all in trouble. Guess the Lord is gonna make me pay for living the fast life." Diamond rocked back and forth, misery stamped on her pretty face.

"No," Charmaine replied with force. "God doesn't work like that at all. He's all about grace and forgiveness. I—"

"Let me interrupt your 'Sermon on the Bayou', Bishop Joliet. What's happening is all down to trash human beings. You ain't gettin' payback from the imaginary Big Daddy in the Sky. Sheesh." Jessi rolled her eyes. A musical ping sounded from her phone. She went back to reading the screen.

"Don't listen to her. You and Indyah can attend services with me anytime. I think you'll enjoy it. And they have great programs for kids." Charmaine patted her hand.

"Thanks." Diamond sniffed and finished the rest of her tea.

"I messaged my friend Logan, geek skills like crazy. He just confirmed what we suspected. No way to trace the messages. But we do know the main person who has the most to lose. And I've got a feeling it ties back to good old Buddy and what he's been up to," Jessi said.

"Don't forget he did business with Gina Shaw. Coincidence she showed up to hire us after he died?" Charmaine gazed at her sister.

"Or a way to keep an eye on *us* for Loreen?" Jessi sat in thought for a few moments before she shook her head. "But I haven't found any evidence they've been friendly or in touch. Aside from Gina sending a floral to Kennedy's memorial service."

"There's something those two women don't want us to find out. Might not be a connection, but... I have a gut feeling," Charmaine said.

"I have to pick up Indyah." Diamond gave Charmaine a quick hug and stood. Then she turned to Jessi. "Thanks for not beating my ass after what I did."

Jessi stood to face her. "Yeah, well. Don't get too grateful. It could still happen."

Diamond and Jessi grinned at each other and embraced tightly for several moments. Charmaine joined them for a group hug. Once she was gone, Charmaine let out a long slow breath.

"Whew. These cases are getting *busy*."

Jessi nodded. "And we have one last spirit cleaning session with Gina. I checked out the place. Another big house with loads of 'historic character' according to the online listing."

"Meaning some kind of paranormal activity is likely. Nothing a buyer would find quirky and charming," Charmaine said with a chuckle.

"And a set up. You shouldn't come along. Maybe the intern..."

"No way. I've got the most experience and we're a team. Spirits can scare us but not act on the living physically. We'll go in prepared," Charmaine replied in a firm tone.

"Scotty is going to turn me inside out if anything happens to you."

"He trusts me to take care of business. I wouldn't go if the baby might be affected. We're all good over here. Right, baby?" Charmaine's eyes widened and she placed a palm on her tummy. "I think that flutter was an answer! Baby agrees."

"Girl, please." Jessi snorted to show skepticism. "Madame Laveau is going to provide us intel from the great beyond. I've got my best guns locked and loaded. Three containment tools and two EMF disrupters. I checked the NERA devices to make sure they're safe for you to use."

"Huh?"

"Negative Energy Repellant Agent filled with sage and frankincense. Negative spirits hate the stuff. But some species of sage can be toxic. I had Logan double check." Jessi pulled up a photo on her phone and showed it to her.

"Oh, those water pistols. Yeah." Charmaine blinked at the images. "I can't keep up with your gizmos."

"They're not toys, Charmaine. The trigger is battery operated so you don't have to pump. That means a continuous spray. Plus, increased target accuracy."

"Okay, cool. Where's the house again?" Charmaine took the tray of empty cups into the kitchen with Jessi following her.

"On Chartres. Not far from the LaLaurie mansion."

Charmaine put the tray down hard and spun to face her. "You mean..."

Jessi nodded slowly. "Yep. One of the most haunted parts of the French Quarter. Loads of bloody history on that street."

They stood outside the three-story house Thursday evening. Gina had put them off all day about showing up. Jessi suspected she wanted them to arrive after sunset. Floor to ceiling windows and balconies faced Chartres Street on all levels. Each held hanging baskets of ferns. Wall sconces held bulbs that flickered like antique gas lamps. The street seemed eerily quiet. Following

Gina's instructions, Jessi had parked her jeep behind the house in a narrow alley.

"You think she cleared the neighborhood for no witnesses?" Charmaine looked up and down the narrow street.

"The house to the west is vacant. The owners of the other house are in Mexico to get away from Mardi Gras crowds." Jessi nodded when Charmaine looked at her.

"She's really out to get us." Charmaine spoke in a low tone.

"Why are you whispering? Any spirits around already know we're here." Jessi laughed when Charmaine made a face.

"I'm not your intern," Charmaine tossed back. "You don't feel like it."

Jessi's gaze swept the entrance level. "Yeah. We got us a special welcoming committee."

"What did Madame say?" Charmaine carried the smaller bag with lightweight disrupters.

"A particularly nasty poltergeist from a fifty-year-old unsolved murder is stirred up." Jessi pulled a wheeled duffle bag behind her.

"Crap. My least favorite kind. They're so dang noisy," Charmaine grumbled.

"The spirit community is still talking about how we kicked ass the other day." Jessi stopped at the door. "I advised her to stay clear while we're working. Don't want her to feel the effects of my tools."

"It's you and me then." Charmaine pressed the doorbell. "Let's get this party started then."

A series of chimes played, muted by the closed door. The silhouette of a figure appeared briefly on the other side of drawn draperies of one window. Gina opened the paneled entry wearing a stiff smile. She waved them inside and shut the door.

"Thanks so much for taking on the extra property. I suppose I saved the best for last. I didn't mention it, but this was where poor Buddy's listing died. I rarely have Vieux Carré properties. His son asked my business partner and I to take it over." Gina spoke in a rapid-fire nervous manner, rattling off more facts. She stopped finally, panting as if she was out of breath.

Jessi exchanged a look with Charmaine before turning to Gina. "You okay?"

"I'm fine," Gina squeaked. She cleared her throat and her voice dropped an octave. "Long day. I tend to ramble when I'm tired."

Charmaine stepped closer to Gina. "You're here all alone, after dark?"

"Just me. I can't keep paying subcontractors for overtime." Gina forced a strained smile.

"Brave of you to stay by yourself." Jessi raised an eyebrow at her and then glanced around the foyer they stood in. Then she faced Gina again.

"I got here less than five minutes before you. I figured you weren't far away and would be on time. You've always been so... efficient." Gina swallowed hard as she blinked rapidly. "Let's get started. I have two buyers lined up. As you can see, we're starting to stage the lower floors."

Jessi and Charmaine followed Gina to the first living room and then the formal dining room. A kitchen and long, narrow butler's pantry were also on the ground floor. Gina gave them a tour, her descriptions delivered in a high-pitched, tense tone.

Charmaine looked at Jessi until her sister turned around. Then Charmaine pulled her close.

"She's on edge," Charmaine whispered close to her ear.

"Umm." Jessi gave a slight nod. She smiled when Gina glanced back at them. "This is a whole lot of house. Remind me when it was built."

"In 1830," Gina said. She started up the circular staircase. "An elevator was installed in 2011. You noticed the spacious carriageway already.

They continued on to the second floor and another living room. This one had a fireplace like the one below. Across the hall from it was one of the two primary suites. Gina kept up her jittery chatter as she described all the special features.

"Let's go to the third level. If anything pops off, it's generally near the top floor. Right, sis?" Jessi turned to Charmaine and tilted her head to one side.

Charmaine took her cue. "Yes."

"You sure everyone else left? I heard a knocking sound like somebody might still be working." Jessi craned her neck to look up the stairs.

Gina backed up as she answered. "I didn't hear anything. Since you don't need me, I'll get going. Use the lock box when you're done."

"We didn't mean you couldn't stick around. Jessi and I will make sure you're safe." Charmaine moved behind her. Gina turned to leave and let out a gasp when she realized her escape route was blocked.

"I don't want to be in the way." Gina slid through the small space between Charmaine and the wall. "Like you said, you can handle it like the last house."

Jessi squinted at Gina. "Yeah. The house on Prytania was a real experience. Wasn't it, Charmaine?"

"Unique. Why don't you stick around so we can tell you about it," Charmaine said to Gina.

"Your report was very thorough. No need. I'll get my things and..." Gina jumped when Jessi crossed to her quickly and closed hand around her forearm.

"You're going to stay." Jessi pulled Gina away from the top step and back onto the second-floor landing.

"I'm not picking up any strong readings so far." Charmaine spoke in a matter-of-fact fashion as she looked at her small EMF meter. Then she glanced at Gina. "We should be fine."

"Yep, everybody should survive," Jessi added.

"Oh, I don't think—"

"The history you sent didn't say anything particularly tragic happened here," Charmaine said. She brought of the rear as Jessi not so gently guided Gina to the second flight of steps.

"I'm assuming the info was complete. Right Gina?" Jessi looked at the now pale real estate agent.

"I really have to go. I- I have to pick up my... youngest from soccer practice." Gina gulped air and tried to twist out of Jessi's grip.

"No, you don't," Jessi said flatly.

Gina stared back at Jessi. With a determined glare, she jerked free. "You're the experts. Do what you've been hired to do."

"Ah, we're the help being ordered to do our job," Jessi said to Charmaine with a smirk.

"I've paid your fee, which is above the going rate for most other ghostbusters around town. Take care of anything that might cause a problem and send a report. Like the last time."

Gina looked down her nose at the sisters with a haughty glare. A nervous twitch at the corner of her mouth weakened her attempt at upper crust disdain.

Jessi advanced on her with a scowl. "You ain't goin' nowhere."

"You can't—" Gina stopped as her eyes went wide.

A loud thump made the house vibrate. Noise like the sound of a giant tuning fork rose from the hardwood floor beneath their feet.

Jessi grinned at Gina as she opened her duffle bag. "Too late, babe. You're in it."

"Please, let me go." Gina clutched her designer leather purse against her chest.

"No telling what is waiting for you down there." Charmaine jerked a thumb to indicate the ground floor.

"Whatever happens to us, happens to you. So, you better hope we're worth what you paid," Jessi said in a cheerful voice.

Chapter 12
A Booming Market

Gina pressed her body flat against the wall. "It wasn't my idea. I swear."

Jessi grabbed a fistful of Gina's blouse. She jerked her across the floor to the stairs. "Tell me more, Ms. Gentrifying Gina."

"Maybe we should let her go." Charmaine flinched when a shriek rang through the house. "Things could go sideways and she'll make our work harder."

"Listen to her. Listen to—" Gina clamped her lips together when Jessi looked at her.

"You lured us here knowing my sister is pregnant. You don't get to skip off into the sunset. C'mon." Jessi place a round device on the floor. Green and blue lights flickered on its surface when it whirred to life. "Charmaine, stay here. Buster will keep you safe."

"A robot vacuum cleaner? What's it going to do, sweep up what's left of me?" Charmaine gaped at the thing and then at Jessi.

"Logan and I modified it. Buster is an EMF disrupter plus a little something extra. I synced it via Bluetooth to the anemometer in your hand," Jessi explained, raising her voice to be heard over another unnatural scream.

"When a cold spot pinpoints an entity is detected, this little bot will take it down."

"Pretty genius. Wait, how much did you spend to—"

"Not now, Char." Jessi looked up at the ceiling. Four hard thumps sounded like giant footsteps.

"Right, budget talk later." Charmaine's gaze traveled up to where Jessi still stared. "You really going to take her with you?"

Gina shook her head hard until her brunette hair whipped across her face. She whimpered when Jessi affected a mean grin. The thudding overhead intensified. Charmaine muttered a curse word. She danced from one foot to the other.

Jessi glanced at Charmaine with concern. "What's wrong?"

"Baby is pressing on my damn bladder. I gotta go." Charmaine blew out air.

"Is the plumbing connected?" Jessi shook Gina hard.

"Ye-yes."

"I'll be there in a minute." Charmaine turned in the direction of the luxurious en-suite bathroom they toured. Buster the robot glided behind her like a puppy following its master.

"No, you stay here. I got this. Like I told you," Jessi yelled as she dragged Gina along beside her. "I came prepared."

Charmaine didn't pause to ask what Jessi meant. Instead, she hopped to the water closet in the spacious bathroom. She dropped the anemometer and the small bag she carried. Then she yanked down her clothes in one quick move. Five minutes later, she blew out a sigh of relief with her eyes closed. Still seated, she opened them to find "Buster" hovering patiently about three feet away.

"At least you respect boundaries." Charmaine grabbed a fistful of toilet paper. "Thank goodness for the house stager's attention to detail."

Moments later Charmaine had washed her hands. She sat on the unmade king-sized bed. Linens were folded, waiting to be put on it. Charmaine contemplated going to the third floor. Before she could decide, Jessi's voice crackled from the bag. She searched through it and found a two-way radio.

Jessi panted softly through the handset's speaker. "Charmaine. Check in."

"I'm okay. What's happening?" Charmaine sprang to her feet. A creepy piercing voice echoed through the house.

Jessi replied, "Banshee. Plus, two other dumbass spirits. Nothing major, but she..." The whish of static cut off the rest of Jessi's sentence.

"I can't hear you."

Charmaine turned the volume dial on the radio. She saw something move in the hallway. An object that looked solid since Charmaine rarely saw spirits. She looked around for something to use as a weapon. A thought came through to her; the sharp sense of her sister sending a message. Or trying to. Charmaine looked in the compact bag again and found a baton; the type police use. Then she heard what sounded like a smoke detector going off. She followed the sound to find a lanky figure being terrorized by...

"Buster?" Charmaine yelped.

The robot made an arc in front of a figure dressed in black. The intruder darted and dodged red laser beams Buster shot out. Pinpricks of red dotted the expensive wallpaper. Buster moved back and forth when the figure tried to go one way or the other.

Charmaine pressed a button on the baton and it telescoped to full length. So distracted by the noises on the third floor and Buster, the intruder seemed not to notice Charmaine. She swung the baton and struck one shoulder hard. A male voice howled with pain. He turned to run away. Charmaine whacked the back of his knees with all the force she could. The man went down with an agonized groan. Spit flew from his mouth. A mask covered most of his face. Jessi ran down the stairs, dragging an almost limp Gina behind. One of Gina's kitten heel pumps came off and bounced across the floor. Jessi propped Gina against a wall to free her hands. Gina slid to the floor; eyes stretched wide.

"Let's see who decided to join our little party." Jessi stuffed her own EMF meter into a pocket. Then she crossed to the still groaning intruder and yanked the mask off.

Charmaine gaped at him and pointed. "Harold!"

"You know him?" Jessi tussled with him as Harold tried to pull the mask back down. "Aht, aht. My sister will pop you again."

"He's the wallpaper guy. The carpenter I met at the first house we cleared for Gina. Why is he dressed like a cat burglar?" Charmaine let out a grunt in frustration. "I have to go again but I can't leave you alone with these two."

"Madame Laveau has arrived. Between her and Buster I've got plenty of help," Jessi replied and waved her toward the bathroom.

Harold stopped squirming in pain. His mouth worked like a fish out of water for few seconds. He finally managed lucid speech. "Did you say Madame Laveau? Marie Laveau? Here?"

Charmaine extended the baton to Jessi. "Just in case."

Jessi took it and turned to Harold with a wicked grin. He pushed his back to the wall as if trying to disappear. Buster emitted a series of beeps as if reminding the man of its presence. Charmaine trotted to the toilet again, used it, and returned. She heard a gaggle of frantic voices as she went to the landing. Harold and Gina talked at once in a loud competition to be heard. Jessi glanced from one to the other of them with a bland expression.

Gina shook her head. "I didn't know he would—"

"I stayed late checking if the paint was dry and—" Harold yelled over Gina.

Jessi and Charmaine allowed the battle to provide excuses to drag on for a few minutes. They exchanged amused glances as the babble droned on. After a while both wound down like toys with low batteries.

Jessi turned to what looked like empty space. "Madame, what were you saying about Harold?"

"I don't believe you're communicating with the other side," Harold said. Still, his eyes darted from Jessi to the space.

"You belong to the Cercle Harmonique. Y'all have been trying to reach her for years. She's been ignoring you. Says she doesn't talk to fools and thieves," Jessi said with a laugh.

"You're bluffing." Harold straightened his shoulders.

"Hmm." Jessi looked away from him and was silent for a few moments. The room temperature grew chilly. "She says at your last session, you contacted a cabinet maker who died May 4, 1842. He told you where to find a jewelry box in an old attic. The house is at 1605 Magazine Street."

Harold blinked at Jessi. "You can't..."

"It had been hidden in the wall since 1805. You sold a pearl and turquoise antique necklace set in gold. Then split the money with the other two people who attended the séance," Jessi went on.

"No. No." Harold shook his head hard. The half on, half off ski mask bounced crazily.

"You liar! I thought you didn't find any—" Gina clamped her mouth shut when Jessi looked at her.

"Should I tell you how much y'all made and about the other pieces you haven't sold yet? The cabinet maker is pissed by the way. You promised to use the money for charity. He doesn't have any living descendants.

"Two ghosts who don't like you, Harold. Not good. Maybe we'll leave you both, locked up in here with them for the night." Charmaine turned to Jessi.

"Or you could tell us what we want to know. Then we'll decide if we'll let you go." Jessi shrugged.

Harold struggled to his feet with a wince of pain. "I could press charges against you two. I was here doing my job when you attacked me." He glanced at Gina.

"Is there really a voodoo ghost here?" Gina shuddered and looked around with wild eyes.

"How are you going to explain wearing a mask to do carpentry work? And I don't see any tools." Jessi swept a hand out.

"I think the police will believe me over you." Harold stuck his chest out. Then he gasped and started to shake.

"Oh-oh, he's having a fit of some kind. We might have to call 911." Charmaine blinked at him in concern.

"He'll be okay. Madame is introducing herself." Jessi strode to the large EMF meter and adjusted dials. "I turned off the neutralizer setting so Madame Laveau and friends won't be disturbed."

"How many are there?" Gina covered her face with both hands.

"Enough. More arriving by the second." Jessi smiled when Gina whimpered.

"What do you want?" Harold gulped.

"The full story," Charmaine said. "Look, we don't intend for anyone to get hurt."

"Speak for yourself, sis. Madame and me are good with giving them a spanking," Jessi put in.

Charmaine chided Jessi with a head shake. Then she turned to Harold and Gina. "You've made poor choices but there's a way to make things right."

Gina looked from Jessi to Charmaine, to Harold. She stood and crossed to stand next to him. When he nodded at her, Gina reached into the purse she'd managed to hold onto. "I'll call the police. Let them sort it out."

"Okay, cool. Then you can explain the deed theft, fraudulent loans, and how it's all connected to a murder," Jessi said in a level tone.

"She doesn't know anything. It's a desperate bluff. I have a lot of influential friends. Several of them know higher-ups in NOPD." Gina looked at Harold. "Like you said, they'll believe us over them."

"You're trying to take a lot owned by Lydia Fisher Chatelaine. I've already found at least one loan document with her forged signature," Jessi said.

"Maybe Buddy Kennedy double-crossed you and got in the way, Gina." Charmaine raised both eyebrows.

"I help them find valuables in properties or buried in land around New Orleans. They use the money from auctioning off the stuff to finance development," Harold blurted. He flinched when Gina jabbed him with her elbow.

"Shut up. She's fishing," Gina hissed at him. Then she turned to Jessi. "I don't know anything about loans or Bernard's murder. Besides, your friend has been arrested. I hear the evidence against her is strong."

"I didn't say who was murdered," Jessi said.

"Right. Since he's willing to take orders and get rid of problem people for her," Charmaine added.

"No, no. no. I didn't sign up for no murder case. Look, you can ask my friends in Cercle Harmonique. They know about our arrangement. Gina's fights with her business partners had nothing to do with us." Harold hunched his shoulders and trembled again. "Please, ask Madame Glapion to leave me alone."

"I will—after we have a chat with plenty of details," Jessi said.

Charmaine looked at Gina. "We know about the loans. It won't take us long to follow the trail back to your company. Redwood Consolidated."

"Wire fraud, maybe even a RICO charge." Jessi grinned when Harold put space between himself and Gina.

"What is she talking about?" Harold blinked at Gina.

"Racketeering Influencing and Corruption Organizations. It's a federal act used to prosecute crimes found to be part of an ongoing criminal organization. You know, like companies working together to steal valuables from property owners," Jessi explained.

"Or forge title documents to obtain loans. File fake deeds to steal valuable real estate, gentrify whole neighborhoods, and rake in big-time profits," Charmaine added.

Gina's frightened expression faded into one of defiance. "You don't have proof."

"You mean, you covered your tracks well." Jessi stared her down.

"I mean there's no proof because I didn't do any of those things. My father is the main investor in my business." Gina limped over to her mislaid shoe and slipped it on. She turned to Harold. "I'm leaving. If you have any sense, you'll be right behind me. They're the ones in the wrong."

"Harold, Madame Laveau has promised to visit you if you don't cooperate. One of the properties they're trying to steal belongs to her descendants," Jessi said to him.

"They're fakes. They set up gadgets to make noises and then pretend to get rid of ghosts," Gina said with force.

Harold looked from Gina to Jessi. Then he swallowed hard. "I was here doing last-minute touchups."

Charmaine and Jessi watched them walk across the landing to the flight of stairs. Gina strode with as much dignity as possible. Her gait was lopsided since one heel had broken. Harold back away as though afraid to take his gaze off the sisters. They disappeared down the steps. Moments later the door slammed.

Charmaine sighed and sat down on a carpeted tread leading to the third floor. "She's right. We've got jack on her."

"We can track down the pawnshops and auction companies. Show Harold and friends have been selling valuables. There's gotta be a paper trail." Jessi scowled at the empty space Gina and Harold had occupied.

"So what? A lot of those properties are a hundred years old, maybe older. Ownership to anything they found could be disputed. Gina can say she bought those houses, including any contents. Harold can say he scavenged abandoned properties while scouting development locations for her." Charmaine stood as she rubbed the small of her back.

"Shit." Jessi picked up her equipment, including the baton, and stuffed them in her duffle.

Charmaine shrugged. She went to the main suite bathroom to retrieve the tools she'd dropped in there and returned. "RICO? You just pulled that one out of the hat."

"It's possible," Jessi accepted the smaller devices Charmaine and shoved them into her bag.

"Let's get out of here. I'm hungry. Again." Charmaine patted Jessi's shoulder to encourage her as she walked past.

Charmaine set the locks on the door to the luxury property when they left. Twenty minutes later they were at Charmaine's house. They'd picked up a chicken salad sandwich for Charmaine. Jessi ordered her to get comfortable. After a warm shower and getting into a soft knit lounge set, Charmaine had to admit she felt better. Jessi sat on a beige and green pouf, her computer on the coffee table.

"Here. You can have this. I'm not hungry anymore. I guess the baby is giving me a break." Charmaine's sandwich was still wrapped in paper on the table. She sank onto the sofa and propped her feet on the ottoman.

"Humph," was Jessi's vague reply.

"I don't know what our next move is. I'd like to knock that smug look off Gina's face for sure. But I gotta admit she's played her game well." Charmaine massaged her stomach. She gazed at her silent sister. "Hey, are you listening to me?"

"Uh-huh." Jessi continued to swipe the touchscreen of her laptop.

"You mean serious business when you get out the computer," Charmaine teased.

"Bigger screen. Better to navigate the databases." Jessi's gaze remained on the results of her searches.

Charmaine craned her neck to get a glimpse of what had Jessi so absorbed. "What are you looking at?"

"Pulled out the big guns. LexisNexis." Jessi huffed a sigh. "I can't let Gina win. I don't think she's that smart. And there's a reason Buddy Kennedy ended up dead."

"Go home and get some rest." Charmaine let loose a big yawn. She blinked when her cell phone rang. "Hello. Yes, but let me explain."

Jessi had gone back to working her digital sources. Without glancing at Charmaine, her fingers drummed the keypad. "Scotty upset you did field work, huh? I don't know why you insist on telling him *everything*."

"That was Detective Harrison. Gina filed a complaint about us. We've been summoned to his office. Tomorrow at two o'clock. No excuses." Charmaine's head plopped against the stuffed pillowback of her sofa.

"So much for bedtime. I'm going to get the goods on those two or else," Jessi snapped.

The next day Harrison made them wait almost twenty minutes. When his administrative assistant led them into his office, he didn't glance up from his computer. He spoke into a Bluetooth headset. The young woman gestured for them to take a seat and left. Another five minutes went by before he ended his conversation. Harrison tapped the earpiece but still didn't look at them. Finally, he sat straight with a deep sigh.

"You came this close to catching a case." Harrison pinched his forefinger and thumb almost together. "I don't know what the hell..." He broke off and rubbed his closed eyes for a few seconds.

"Whatever she told you is a damn lie," Jessi said. She stuck her nose in the air when Harrison shot a heated glance at her.

"Ms. Shaw alleges that you became overly aggressive when she refused to pay an additional excessive fee for your, and I quote, questionable services." Harrison read notes on his computer screen.

"Like I said. Lies. Did she mention coming to us for said services? Huh?" Jessi leaned forward and spat the words like bullets.

Charmaine placed a hand on Jessi's arm. "I have text messages from Gina requesting we tour the home. I also have an amended contract adding it to our original assignment."

"Yeah, and more receipts. She came to us. We didn't know her from a can of paint." Jessi started to say more but stopped.

Harrison held up one wide palm like a school crossing guard stopping traffic. He looked from Jessi to Charmaine. "You seem to be the more reasonable one. Let's talk. Ms. Shaw says she asked you to research any possible legal claims on certain historic properties. There's been a lot of accusations from New Orleans natives about developers taking advantage of them. In the process of your work for her, you claimed there were supernatural beings in the houses. And—"

"Are you effing joking right now?" Jessi blurted out. "*She* was the one who complained of paranormal activity. Ask the carpenters or plumbers she hired. They were scared to work after dark."

"I looked over your agreement. It says you'll look at the history of the house, perform a thorough search of records, and walk throughs. Services list included clearance and consultation on readying the homes for occupation," Harrison replied in a calm voice. "Nothing about ghosts."

Charmaine squeezed Jessis forearm tighter as she spoke up. "As you know, our *special* investigative services are discreet for good reasons. Many of our clients don't want the ridicule of believing in spirits. They're concerned about their business reputation. That's true especially if they're selling a residential property. We've worked with other sellers and a few buyers. They don't want unwanted attention that might jeopardize a sale."

"Okay." Harrison didn't seem quite convince as he gazed back at her. Still, he nodded for her to go on.

"We also have our reasons for keeping our *special* services low key. We're a general private investigative agency doing other work as well. We don't want that side of the business to be affected. If you know what I mean. Plus, it helps us to assist official agencies who don't want it known they consult... us." Charmaine tilted her head to one side.

Jessi added, "Pros who understand alternative forms of electromagnetic energy with biological origins. Aka ghosts, goblins, gremlins—"

"I get it, I get it," Harrison cut her off with a grimace. "All I'm saying is the lack of... specificity doesn't help your defense."

"Are we being charged?" Charmaine squinted at him.

"No, not with a criminal offense. A business deal gone sour is a civil matter," Harrison replied.

"Well, I'll tell you what's criminal. Gina and Harold Green attacked us. They planned it because of what we're uncovering. Which is also something against the law. Fraud. And—" Jessi stopped again when Harrison raised his palm a second time. She glared at him in frustration but waited.

"Ms. Shaw and Mr. Green have filed for a no civil contact order naming you two. She says not only doesn't she require your services, but she's concerned for her safety." Harrison wore a solemn face. "I hope you got paid. Ms. Shaw might file a lawsuit to get her money back. From what I hear, she was pretty angry."

"No, she won't. She's hoping we're too scared to keep scrutinizing her business." Charmaine gazed out of Harrison's office window.

"Let me guess. Some spirit from the great beyond told you that." Harrison shook his head as he looked at Charmaine.

"Common sense. She has something serious to hide. Bad enough for her to risk making life hard for us," Charmaine replied.

"I'm doing y'all a favor, okay? A friend in the superintendent's office told me they got a call. Back off this lady. She's got connections." Harrison pointed a forefinger at Jessi.

"Did we mention Gina Shaw did some development deals with Buddy Kennedy? This is all tied up," Jessi countered.

"Are you saying his murder has something to do with real estate?" Harrison looked from Jessi to Charmaine for an answer.

Jessi stood and looped the crossbody bag strap over her head. "We don't know yet. But we're damn sure gonna find out."

Harrison rubbed his jaw hard as he frowned at them. "Look, that's a real stretch. I know you want to help your girlfriend. But like my grandfather used to say, that dog won't hunt."

"Loreen Kennedy has something to hide," Charmaine blurted. She still focused on the view outside his window.

"You know this because you accosted her at a charity luncheon? Yeah, I heard about that, too. You two are making a career out of messing with powerful people in this city. Things will get bad for you if—"

"We keep quiet and let our innocent friend go to prison. Hell no." Jessi crossed her arms and looked back at him.

"It's not up to you," Harrison said.

"The DA has to prove his case beyond a reasonable doubt. We're not going to make his job easy. I don't care whose shiny reputation gets ruined. I'm going to throw every bit of dirt at them that I find. And believe me, I know how to find plenty." Jessi wore a determined smile that burned with ill will.

Harrison wore a somber expression. "You might want to sit down for the next bit of news."

Jessi remained standing. "Well?"

"Ms. Phillips' attorney has started discussions with the assistant district attorney about a plea deal." Harrison sat back as if anticipating blowback.

"No way. Diamond would have told me. She knows we're close to finding out who killed Kennedy." Jessi breathed hard as she stared down Harrison. "You got it wrong."

"Jessi, we're the investigating office. The ADA keeps us informed. We're still gathering facts, but if she accepts the offer..." Harrison spread his arms.

"Why?" Charmaine asked.

"The text messages are pretty damaging. Yes, it could be BDSM banter, but she was at the party. He tried to force his hand under her costume according to a witness. Ms. Phillips expressed a desire to be rid of him even though he paid well, according to the same witness. And..." Harrison wore a look a sympathy at Jessi's stricken expression. "Kennedy threatened to call her boss at the hotel where she works if she didn't keep servicing him."

"Shit." Jessi dropped onto the chair.

"Look, it's entirely possible Ms. Phillips will get minimal time. We got the hosts to admit that they supplied the party drugs. She didn't force him to take it. There's a lot of evidence the guy has used in the past. And drank heavily. Loreen Kennedy won't be able to keep that from coming out." Harrison sighed. "Taking a deal is your friend's decision."

"It's a damn stupid one. She's letting these rich white folks run over her." Jessi stood again. "Fuck it. We're going to keep looking. Come on, Charmaine."

"Anything else about us and Gina Shaw? Like do we have to pay a fine or something?" Charmaine said to Harrison.

"Well, it's their word against yours about whatever conflict you had the other night. Like I said, it appears to be a civil matter," Harrison replied.

"Nothing about us assaulting them?" Charmaine flinched at the sharp look Harrison gave her.

Harrison studied to the sisters in turn in silence for a few beats. "Neither one of them mentioned physical contact. Be careful about what you say next."

"If there was, it was self-defense. But there wasn't," Jessi spoke up before Charmaine answered.

"So, Ms. Shaw and Mr. Green left out information. I'm wondering why." Harrison rubbed his jaw again. Then he puffed out a gruff sigh. "Nothing is simple when you two are involved. Stay away from them. I don't want to know anything else you might do."

"Got it," Jessi said after a few seconds.

"Thanks for letting us know." Charmaine rose and followed Jessi out of the office.

"One more thing. Make sure Ms. Phillips doesn't travel and keep Ricky out of your antics. He's got a great career on the line." Harrison's baritone voice was heavy with warning.

Charmaine and Jessi nodded in unison. They left the building without speaking. Once at their SUVs parked side by side, Jessi exhaled like a deflating balloon. Charmaine clicked her tongue in dismay. They both leaned against Jessi's jeep as if they needed physical support.

"Diamond knew how you'd react. Which is why she didn't tell you. She's a got a right to consider all options." Charmaine read Jessi's thoughts. Her sister's worries appeared like captions beneath Jessi's dejected face.

Jessi slapped a palm on the Jeep's hood. "She should have trusted us, damn it."

"She's thinking about what's best for Indyah. As a mother, I'm not sure if I wouldn't do the same in her position," Charmaine replied.

"First, she almost costs us everything we own. Now she's going to accept a bullshit plea deal. I'm tempted to let her rot in jail." Jessi took tortoise shell sunglasses from her purse and put them on. Bright sunlight helped warm the still chilly day.

"You don't mean it."

"No," Jessi said after a few moments. "But only for Indyah's sake."

"You heard Harrison. The circumstantial evidence looks bad. And we haven't turned up anything pointing to another suspect. Don't be so hard on her, Jess." Charmaine nudged her sister's shoulder with her own.

Jessi looked off into the distance. "Yeah. Whatever. I'm going to get lunch before I go back to the office. What about you?"

"Not much going on at the clinic. We closed early. Mardi Gras madness is taking over the weekend. We're closed Monday, too." Charmaine squinted in the bright sunshine and put on sunglasses as well. "You got plans for the weekend?"

"Yeah. Turning over rocks to uncover slimy bitches and snatching skeletons outta closets."

The weekend revelry of Carnival in New Orleans went by with the usual joyful mayhem. Jessi understood why some longtime New Orleanians chose to take vacations elsewhere. Jessi decided to take a break from her intense search to attend at least two parades. She joined in the street dancing as bands played. She sent Charmaine photos and videos of her working hard to have a good time. Saturday was all fun. Sunday, Jessi went back to work. Since Scotty had security jobs lined up in three parts of the city, Charmaine decided to nest. After the excitement they'd faced in the past few days, quiet time appealed to her. Sunday afternoon, Jessi maneuvered around parades and traffic like a true native. Once she arrived, Jessi made a fuss over Charmaine. They bickered over Charmaine's burst of activity around the house. She'd cleaned out closets. Bags full of clothing to donate or recycle sat in a corner of the kitchen. Then Charmaine had tackled the storage shed in her backyard. More household items she no longer used or wanted were set aside.

"You're not going to have a yard sale, Char. Get somewhere and sit down." Jessi huffed in exasperation. "Aren't you Christians supposed to use Sunday as a day of rest?"

"Speaking of which, the worship service today was really inspirational. Diamond seemed calmer, more at peace. And Indyah loved the children's church." Charmaine smiled as she sat on the recliner. She pressed a button and the footrest came up.

"Great. You've got my friend in your cult," Jessi grumbled.

Charmaine stared at Jessi for a few moments. The muted television show provided background noise. One of many black and white monster movies from the 1960s played. Godzilla stomped his way across one more city.

"Diamond is going through a lot. I mean, yeah, you both have faced the criminal justice system before. But nothing that could end in decades behind bars." Charmaine stared at the action on television without paying attention.

"Humph."

After another few moments, Charmaine struggled to get out of the recliner. "Mama Etta Ray brought me a gallon jug of her strawberry sweet tea. I've been craving it for two days."

Jessi tapped a final keystroke and stood. "I'll get it. Stay put."

Charmaine accepted the glass when Jessi returned. "I don't why I keep sucking this down. I'm going to pee every two minutes. One this early won't be so bad though."

"Maybe the baby wants it." Jessi flashed a brief grin and then went back to researching.

"Could be. I look at everything different now. I guess it's motherhood hormones or something," Charmaine said with a chuckle.

"Nope. Pregnancy doesn't magically make all women become good mothers. Monica is one of many examples." Jessi grunted at her rare mention of their mother.

"She did the best she knew how at the time. I think she's changed. Having a baby is tough physically and emotionally. And when your child is threatened..." Charmaine studied Jessi, who didn't look up from her laptop touch screen. "You should talk to her, Jessi. Not just talk, *listen*."

"I'm not calling Monica. Our last convo didn't go well," Jessi said in a flat one.

"Understatement of the decade. You called her a gray-haired thot. Among other names."

"She started it, bringing up my past. She had the nerve to preach at me." Jessi rolled her eyes and snorted. "With her rap sheet."

"I meant you should talk to Diamond," Charmaine said. Seconds ticked by with no reaction from Jessi. "Well?"

"We talked. The other night. Another discussion that went to shit." Jessi sighed. She stopped hitting the keys. "I was still angry."

Charmaine studied her for a few moments. Waves of emotion came to her instead of thoughts. Jessi's last statement rang with an admission that she was wrong. "So, apologize. A *real* one. Not 'I'm sorry, but...'"

"I did. It went... well, it went. At least we didn't cuss each other out. I'm gonna need time to get over the bail-jumping thing," Jessi admitted.

"Yeah. I can imagine Diamond will need time to get over being called a backstabbing, selfish bitch."

"How did—" Jessi let out a sharp laugh. "Right."

Charmaine finished her glass of tea. "You'll both get past this bump in the road."

"More like a giant sinkhole. Oh well, such is life."

Jessi went back to looking through her research results. She frowned at the screen. Charmaine watched the tiny humans defeat Godzilla. Or least the gigantic lizard retreated into the sea. With Jessi absorbed, Charmaine got up again to get herself a snack. When she returned, she decided to lie on the sofa. Seconds after her bottom hit the cushion, Jessi startled her when she let out a ringing whoop. Charmaine spilled seasoned popcorn from the bag she held. She picked up kernels from the seat and blew on them before eating a few.

"Damn it, girl. You almost gave me a heart attack."

"Not you cussing on the Lord's day," Jessi teased without taking her eyes from the screen.

"He knows my heart." Charmaine murmured a short prayer asking for forgiveness.

Jessi's fingers moved fast across the keypad. Quiet clicks went on for a few more minutes. "I gotcha! Finally. Something that starts to make sense."

"Hmpf?" Charmaine tried and failed to talk around a mouthful of popcorn. She chewed and sipped tea.

"Okay, follow the thread. Lydia Chatelaine is a bit forgetful, so she neglects taking care of business. By that I mean, she missed a few property tax payments. She's not paying attention to mail that arrives." Jessi rubbed her hands together as if she was just getting warmed up.

"Okay." Charmaine put down her snack and tea on the coffee table.

"She's not alone. Over the years since Hurricanes Katrina and Rita, a lot of displaced residents had survival on their minds. Their family property kind of went neglected. Not kind of, but actually. Anyway, the city was in shambles after Katrina. People were given a little grace on tax collections, but the city needed that money."

"Why are we talking about taxes? I know Mrs. Chatelaine's case is important, but Diamond's problem is priority. You know, a murder rap?" Charmaine said.

"Be patient," Jessi clipped. "What happens when you don't pay your property taxes?"

"Um, the city slaps a lien on your house, or lot." Charmaine shrugged.

"Or anyone can step up and pay the taxes. After a certain number of payments, they can then become the owner. Basically, the property is considered abandoned. Sort of." Jessi waved a hand. She started typing again as she spoke. "Anyway, that's how a lot of outsiders ended up owning New Orleans property in the years following Katrina. But the city and state started giving local residents more assistance. And as more people returned, they got their business straight. More than a few got their property back."

"Mrs. Chatelaine calls them carpetbaggers. I had to look up what it meant," Charmaine laughed and then grew serious again. "Are we closer to the finish line on how this relates to... *anything*?"

"So, local and outside developers—"

"Wait, I gotta pee."

Charmaine scurried out of the room. Distant flushing sounded. Jessi chuckled and shook her head. Her attention stayed on the computer. She switched back to using the touch screen feature. She stopped when Charmaine settled on the sofa again.

"As I was about to say, real estate investors or realtors started making people offers. Some had to accept because they were broke. They couldn't afford to rebuild," Jessi said.

"Prices for building materials went up. Contractors decided to cash in on demand."

"Right. Which meant that even people who tried to fix their homes or build new ones couldn't pay taxes and for construction. Again, a lot simply gave up while they scrambled to make ends meet. Perfect storm. Toss in deed and title theft and bam!" Jessi said.

"I would say I see, but I don't." Charmaine frowned at her.

"Okay, I may have gotten sidetracked. Gina and Buddy Kennedy both made money in real estate. They did deals together. They borrowed money using pieces of property as collateral. But here's the kicker, and I gotta tell ya, this is pretty damn slick. They pay back the loans." Jessi sat back with a pleased expression.

"I thought the whole point is to take the money and run. Disappear and leave somebody else holding the bag." Charmaine blinked at her in confusion.

"Not if you're still doing business 'legitimately' and don't want smoke. As in a jail sentence. I think old Buddy got to partying and let things slip. Like making payments on the loans."

"And he was murdered because of deed fraud? Sounds thin," Charmaine said.

"People have been whacked for less. Gentrifying is pretty lucrative. I'll bet they had a falling out. Once again, Joliet Investigations solves a case before NOPD. I can't wait to see Harrison's face when we tell him." Jessi laughed.

"I can. I can definitely wait." Charmaine went back to munching on popcorn with a scowl of dread.

Jessi started to reply when her mobile phone played a Beyoncé tune. She looked at the screen. Then she held it up for Charmaine to see. "We've been invited to meet with members of Le Cercle Harmonique."

Charmaine stared at the message. It ended with an address in the Tremé. "The plot thickens."

Chapter 13
Cul-De-Sac

Lundi Gras and Fat Tuesday meant regular business took a back seat for most of New Orleans. Music, laughter, and dancing went on all around the city. If the major krewe floats weren't rolling, neighborhood unofficial foot parades carried on the party. Yet the buzz from the festivities seemed far away. They arrived at the home on Ursulines Avenue at eight o'clock on the dot Monday night. A tall woman greeted them at the doorway. She swept an arm as a gesture for them to enter after a brief welcome.

"I'm Madeline," the woman purred, pronouncing her name in the French style. "Please follow me."

Jessi and Charmaine exchanged a glance before they complied. She led them down a narrow hall. The shotgun-styled house had rooms on either side. The doors were closed, so they didn't get a glimpse of what lay beyond them. However, the walls were lined with paintings, giving the place a museum or gallery feel. A staircase toward the rear led to a second story. More paintings, these mostly portraits, hung on the walls. Jessi and Charmaine studied various shades of brown faces as they climbed. The second-floor landing looked surprisingly spacious. Antique and modern furniture blended well. Amber light came from lamps on a five-foot-long cherry wood credenza. They arrived at an ornate door at the end of the hall.

"You are welcome to the circle," Madeline announced as she turned the knob and pushed it open. She smiled, turned, and went back the way they'd come. Seconds later she'd disappeared down the stairs, her footsteps muffled.

"They like drama," Jessi whispered aside to Charmaine.

Seven people sat around an oval antique English walnut table. Their murmured conversation petered out as each turned to study the sisters. Some wore impassive, but alert expressions. One, a woman who seemed to be in her thirties, wore a faint smile. Jessi looked at Charmaine.

"Well?" Jessi whispered.

"They're curious about us. Even excited," Charmaine murmured.

The woman stood. "Please come in. We won't bite. I promise."

Several of her older companions wore faint frowns of disapproval at the woman's playful demeanor. Yet they remained silent. Charmaine went past Jessi across the threshold first. She surveyed their surroundings as she walked. The wide room probably would otherwise function as a bedroom. Instead, it was obvious where meetings were held. A tall man stood.

"I'm Mathias. Thank you for coming."

His somber basso voice implied their presence was momentous. He proceeded to introduce the other people around the table by first name only. The older woman was Beatrice. The other men were James, Charles, Elias, and Nathaniel. Each nodded in turn with a murmured welcome. The younger woman spoke up on her own when he got around to her. His tight expression in reaction was the only hint of annoyance.

"I'm Alyssa Arámburo. My *real* name, by the way. Le Cercle Harmonique greets you in the spirit of camaraderie as fellow seekers who wish to make the unknown known." Alyssa finished with a flourish, using both hands.

"As usual, Alli goes from comical to dramatic in the blink of an eye." The only other female member laughed softly with a look of amused tolerance.

"I don't see the need for secrecy. After all, they have uncommon gifts. Abilities we've dreamed of having," Alyssa replied. She turned to examined Jessi and Charmaine with interest. "And they're very good at investigating. They'll find our government names fast. If they haven't already."

"Y'all are pretty good at hiding. No social media footprint. No website." Jessi walked farther into the room. She turned in a circle, taking it in. "Not surprising since most of your membership is Gen X and older."

"True. We have our professional reputations to consider," Mathias replied.

Alyssa chuckled. "No one wants a doctor who talks to phantoms. Or the head of a university department head who—"

"Enough, Alli. The point is made," Beatrice cut in. Her eyes narrowed in warning as she stared at Alyssa. Then she turned her attention back to the sisters. "We're also not stupid enough to draw unwanted attention."

"Which brings us to our first question. How do you know about us?" Mathias said.

"How do you know about *us*," Jessi tossed back.

"At least offer them something to drink and a seat before you grill them, Matty." Alyssa feigned a look of reproach. A mischievous smile broke through to spoil the effect.

"Ahem, sorry. Of course." Mathias's face flushed as he waved to two empty chairs. He nodded to another man who rose and went to the bar in the corner.

"Water for me," Charmaine called out.

"We have chilled peach juice mixed with beetroot. Both are good for expectants mothers," the older woman said with a motherly smile at Charmaine.

"Um, thanks." Charmaine accepted one of the two clear glass goblets when the man returned. She looked at the dark red liquid.

Jessi took her goblet, held it up to the light, and took a sip. "A pretty fine cabernet sauvignon. My kind of juice."

Charmaine sat down but didn't drink. She waited until Jessi was in the other chair and put the glass on the table. "We did our research as part of a case and—"

"Madame Glapion, aka Widow Paris, aka Marie Laveau, told us," Jessi broke in. She smirked at the gasps the response brought.

"So, it's true. You're not one of those fake ghost chasers. And to think you all argued against meeting them." Alyssa laughed in delight.

"You conduct séances?" James asked.

"Use a pendulum, altar? Perhaps a Ouija board. Seems to be foolishly popular with young people," Nathan said with a sour expression. With iron-gray hair, he looked to be the oldest of the group. "Causes no end of problems. Any spirit, including the bad kind, can show up."

"She speaks directly to us," Jessi said.

"Sometimes when we wish she wouldn't," Charmaine muttered. She pointed to Jessi. "Mostly to her."

The man who asked about séances leaned forward. "Did you summon her tonight?"

Jessi barked a laugh. "Madame Laveau doesn't show up unless she wants to, or wants something."

Four of the seven turned to each other in whispered conversations. One man, with skin the color of aged parchment and green eyes, bent his head to Mathias. They murmured low in what seemed a debate. After a few seconds Mathias rapped the table with his knuckles. Alyssa alone sat silent. Her gaze never left Jessi.

"You're saying the spirit of Marie Laveau visits you regularly and speaks to you," Mathias said.

"Yep. I can see her at times, too. My sister? She reads minds." Jessi grinned at the stunned expressions on their faces. Even Alyssa lost her blasé attitude.

"Good Lord." The older woman put a hand on her chest.

Jessi drained her glass and put it the table. "Okay, this has been fun, and thanks for the wine. Now tell us why we're here."

Mathias nodded again to Charles, a muscular man of somewhere south of forty. He rose and went through a side door. He and yet another man marched in with Harold Green between them. The new man gave Harold a sneer. Harold flinched at what seemed an unspoken threat. Still, Harold did have visible bruises.

"We have a total of twenty-one members. Circles of seven hold sessions at various times during the year," Beatrice explained.

"Harold was a member of one. Until recently." Alyssa tsk-tsked at him.

"He's going to tell you what he knows." Mathias fixed Harold with a cold look of contempt.

"Part of his punishment. Like the original circle members, we contact spirits to get guidance that will benefit our community. Not to become grave robbers," Charles barked.

Harold looked at the floor to avoid returning their gazes and said nothing. He stood with both hands folded in front of him; almost as though he wore handcuffs. Jessi's eyebrows arched as she glanced over at Charmaine.

"Alrighty, Harold. Let's hear it," Jessi said.

Charmaine put a hand on Jessi's arm. "Hold on. You said 'part' of his punishment. We won't be complicit in any kind of violence or harmful treatment."

"Speak for yourself," Jessi mumbled. She ignored her sister's look of reproach.

"We're not going to beat him up. Harold has been banned from circle activities. He has to complete what we call acts of contrition. Only then will a council consider restoring his membership," Mathias said.

"And even if his request is granted, he'll be on probation for a set number of *years*," Beatrice added.

"Okay," Charmaine said after a few beats.

Jessi looked at Harold. "Go on. Fill in the blanks for us."

Harold opened his mouth but no sound came out. He flinched when Charles jabbed him with a beefy elbow. "I have my own business doing carpentry, painting, hanging drywall, and wallpaper. My great-grandfather did most of the fine carpentry work around New Orleans in the early 1800s and—"

"Skip the family history," Jessi said.

"Ahem, just providing context. We've had an excellent reputation for over one-hundred years," Harold explained.

"Yes, *had*. Past tense." Alyssa shook her head and sipped from the goblet she held.

"My brothers had nothing to do with that part of it," Harold said. "They don't even believe in the work we do. The circles, I mean. Say it's a bunch of superstitious nonsense. Don't ruin Green Contracting because of me. Please."

"We'll discuss it later," Mathias replied.

"He's telling the truth. His brothers Thomas and Robert don't know anything about his side hustle," Charmaine said. She turned to Mathias. He inclined his head to her as if accepting her judgement.

"Thank you. They don't deserve to have what they've built destroyed because of me." Harold looked around at the circle members.

"Keep going," Jessi said.

"I had been working for Gina for about a year when one day we found a silver serving tray under floorboards in a house. I mentioned it to Roger. We joked about getting spirits to tell us where they hid things. After a while it wasn't a joke anymore."

"Roger is another circle member," Alyssa explained to Jessi and Charmaine.

"So, we formed our own circle." Harold swallowed hard.

"They needed five more to make seven, the number of completion and of finding answers in the spiritual world," Beatrice said.

"Just as the number three is a symbol of communication. Three can hold a session, but seven is more powerful," James added.

"We've never been much into numerology," Charmaine replied with a glance at Jessi.

"She's a church lady," Jessi quipped.

Alyssa smiled at Jessi. "But not you."

"Religion is no different than the magic our ancestors used to believe in. Magic is what science hasn't explained yet," Jessi said.

"We can debate God and intelligent design later," James said. He jerked a nod for Harold to keep talking.

"I didn't want to risk getting arrested for burglary. Searching mansions or even vacant property takes time and sometimes equipment. I overheard Gina talking about cash flow problems. Same for Bernard Kennedy. He was taking money from his business to party. I went to Gina with my idea because we got on pretty good. She laughed in my face. Then I showed her a picture of the silver tray and auction house receipt. It sold for just over two thousand dollars. Gina's friend handles vintage and antique pieces. She figured we could cut out the fees. But she was still skeptical. We had another séance and learned about letters between Bernardo de Gálvez and relatives in Spain."

"*The* Galvez, one of the most prominent Spanish governors of Louisiana?" Charmaine gaped at him.

Harold's eyes lit up with greed. "Yes. You can imagine how fast Gina became a believer once I found them. A private collector in Europe paid big time."

"The same amount you're going to donate to charity," Mathias snapped.

"Yes. Of course." Harold became solemn again. "Finding valuables became a regular thing for us. Gina and Bernard Kennedy looked for historic houses or lots to buy. Me showing up as their contractor to tear into walls, floors, or dig in the ground didn't look suspicious."

Jessi rose and walked over to Harold. "Gina and Bernard Kennedy used the money to prop up their businesses financially."

"I needed extra money for mama. She's been really sick and..." Harold's voice died away at a sharp look from Beatrice.

"More lies," Beatrice hissed. "Your mother is as mean and healthy as ever. Did you really think we wouldn't find out the truth?"

"So, what happened? Did Kennedy get scared, wanted to back out, and he had to go?" Jessi asked.

Harold stared at her with a wild-eyed look of alarm. "I took and sold antiques. Nothing else."

"My grandmother used to say a liar will steal, a thief will kill." Alyssa drawled. She didn't look at Harold but examined her perfectly manicured fingernails.

"No way! You all *know* me. I wouldn't... I couldn't." Harold's chin quivered and he looked close to tears. He sent a pleading look around at the other circle members.

"We thought we knew you, Harold," Beatrice said.

"You attacked us. Twice," Jessi hissed at him.

"That first time wasn't me. The second time I was just trying to scare you off. At first Gina didn't say why you two were there. Then I overheard y'all talking. I thought you were fakes like a lot of paranormal investigators. But then I got to thinking. You could somehow find out about me and..."

"And maybe you didn't want Bernard Kennedy to mess up your scam either. We know you're capable of violence." Charmaine scrutinized his non-verbal cues.

"I never dealt directly with Kennedy. Gina was his pal and business partner," Harold said.

"You're saying Gina killed him?" Charmaine frowned at him.

"I'm saying I don't know who killed him. Don't tell Gina I accused her, please. She has a lot of pull with other companies and our business..." Harold rubbed his face with a shaky hand. "Look, from what I heard, Kennedy had plenty of people who hated his guts. He wasn't exactly Mr. Nice Guy."

"Names and details," Jessi barked.

James sent Harold a scathing look as he pushed back his chair to stand. He crossed to a desk set against another wall. When he returned, he placed a laptop on the table. He pointed to the chair. Harold sat down, wiping his eyes with the back of one hand and swallowed hard. He looked around as if seeking sympathy. Finding only cold expressions, Harold typed.

"You believe that's all he knows?" Jessi said to Charmaine.

Charmaine stared at Harold for a few moments as everyone watched her. "Not sure. His mind is jumbled by fear."

"Thank you," Harold said in a strained voice. His shoulders sagged as he huffed a sigh of relief.

"I did get something though. He left out two other hauls he got. Make him tell you about those," Charmaine said.

"Madame Laveau will provide the details if he doesn't." Jessi clamped a hand on his shoulder. "You really don't want to get on her bad side any more than you have already."

Harold shivered so hard that he dropped the ink pen. He jerked around to look at Mathias. "I was going to tell you, I swear!"

"Write," James snapped.

Harold used the keypad for several minutes as the other watched him in silence. Mathias whispered instructions to James, who nodded assent. Then Mathias gestured for the others to follow him. They retreated to an adjoining room. Chairs and stuffed benches provided comfortable seating for at least thirty people. A podium was positioned to face them. Madeline entered carrying a tray with more filled glasses. Mathias gestured for them to sit. He waited until Madeline left as quietly as she'd appeared.

"Harold is sufficiently motivated to give a complete report. James will make sure of it," Mathias said in a matter-of-fact tone. "No point in intimidating him with our presence."

Alyssa leaned forward with an intense expression. She looked from Charmaine to Jessi and back again. "I honestly didn't believe you two were real. I've met so many talented phonies."

"We've been called worse," Jessi said with a crooked grin.

"What's next?" Charmaine asked Mathias since he seemed to be in charge.

"James will text or email you a copy of Harold's statement," Mathias said.

"Text is fine." Charmaine dug a business card out of her purse and handed it to Alyssa.

"Interesting." Alyssa looked at the card with both eyebrows arched. "I coordinate events for the circle. Invitation only to non-members. Would you and Jessi be open to being guest speakers?"

"Nope, no way." Jessi said as she shook her head. Her braids bounced.

"Discretion is a big part of our business," Charmaine said in a more genial tone. She gave Jessi a sharp side-eye. "New Orleans isn't so big that folks couldn't easily identify players in our cases."

Alyssa started to press her case but stopped when Mathias raised a palm. "Understood," he said. "We feel the same way. People who submit requests to us can expect confidentiality."

"Though we don't get many," Beatrice put in. "We purposely keep our profile low and our membership limited."

"Sessions are typically only held once per quarter," Mathias added.

"I'd think you would be calling the spirits for answers more often," Jessi said.

"The Circle is concerned with big questions. Learning from the wisdom of our ancestors guides our social activism. One of our most exciting séances was the one with Dr. Dubois." Mathias wore a satisfied smile. "Extraordinary."

"When the spirits speak it's a true gift. We don't want to intrude on them with petty concerns," Beatrice said.

"Which is why we're absolutely amazed that you're in regular contact. And you say they actually come to you?" Alyssa looked from Charmaine to Jessi.

"Yeah. Sometimes when it ain't convenient," Jessi quipped.

"Your work helped us uncover Harold's dirty little side business," Alyssa said with a crooked grin.

"How?" Charmaine asked.

"He was terrified after the last encounter. He doesn't have your level of perception, but he is a 'sensitive'. Harold was afraid his thefts had led to angry spirits being bound to him. So, he came to us for help," Beatrice explained.

"James isn't psychic, but he is an empath. He knew Harold wasn't telling us the whole truth and nothing but the truth. He and Charles made him sweat until he talked." Alyssa giggled. "That was one hell of a meeting."

"The kind that we don't wish to repeat." Beatrice squinted disapproved at the younger woman.

"Fortunately, we can replace Harold and his partner in crime from our waiting list." Mathias frowned as if thinking about administrative details. Then his face relaxed as he turned to Charmaine. "If the Circle can help you in any way, let us know."

"Actually, I think you can," Jessi spoke up with a wide smile.

An hour later they'd managed to make their way to Jessi's house through the craziness of Mardi Gras. Scotty met them there and would drive Charmaine home. He brought in containers of soul food from Kat's café. He had extra portions to provide leftovers, too. Charmaine had a fried crawfish salad with Kat's signature remoulade sauce. Jessi applauded when he put an order of fried catfish, coleslaw, and hush puppies in front of her.

"You passed up all of Kat's fabulous seafood for grilled fish?" Jessi pointed to the takeout plate in front of Scotty.

Scotty shrugged. "I got to keep fit. Besides, I can't be weighed down. I'll be on extra family duty soon. Cleaning, laundry, errands."

"You eat like that most of the time." Charmaine sighed. "He's been a good influence on me until now. I crave fried seafood and bread pudding the most."

"My niece is a Louisiana girl," Jessi grinned and stuffed her mouth with a piece of fish.

"Nephew," Scotty shot back.

"Accept the fact that you're getting a girl. You're about to be outnumbered," Jessi teased.

Scotty and Jessi got into a good-natured argument about the gender of the baby. They exchanged pokes at each other while Charmaine dug into her food. They must not have heard the doorbell over music and their own voices. Charmaine laughed at their antics as she went to the door. She expected to see Diamond. Instead, Charmaine blinked in surprise to see Detective Harrison. Dark circles accentuated the weary look on his brown face.

"Sorry about the unannounced visit. But we need to talk." Detective Harrison gestured toward the house's interior.

Ricky walked up to stand beside him. "Hi, Charmaine."

"Hey, uh. Yeah, come on in." Charmaine stared at them hard.

She stood aside as they strode in. Both their expressions looked so grave. She tried to at least catch a hint of what was on their minds. Nothing. After a few seconds of greetings, the two policemen sat down. They politely turned down offers of food. Ricky and Jessi only shared a brief gaze before both looked away.

"I thought you'd want to know. Loreen Kennedy is pressuring the DA not to offer a plea deal," Harrison said.

"I thought she wanted the case to wrap up fast; avoid more of their dirty family laundry flapping in the wind," Jessi said.

"I thought so, too. Seems she wants Diamond to get a long prison sentence even more. The ADA handling the case gave me a heads up. She thinks it's total BS, but if her boss hands down orders..." Harrison rubbed his eyes and shook his head. "Early retirement is looking real good right now."

Ricky looked at his commanding officer with sympathy. The others didn't have to ask Harrison what he meant. A string of corruption scandals, political gamesmanship, and out-of-control homicide rate explained his mood. Scotty went to Jessi's kitchen. He returned with two beers. Harrison refused with a waved of one hand.

"I'm off duty." Ricky accepted the amber bottle. He took a pull.

Charmaine leaned forward. "But the decision to withdraw the offer hasn't been made yet."

"The ADA pushed back. At least there are some of us in the system willing to do right," Harrison with a grunt.

"What can we do to help her then?" Jessi stood as if ready for battle.

Harrison seemed to recover a bit of his usual energy. His dark eyebrows pulled together. He pointed a forefinger at her. "You didn't get this from me."

Jessi studied him for a few seconds. She sat across from him again. "You know we can keep shit quiet."

"Right, and sometimes things you *should* tell me," Harrison replied. "I can't believe I'm about to say this..."

"It's not illegal, boss," Ricky said.

"The ADA has facts on her side, which buys some time. Buddy Kennedy's previous use of drugs and over drinking is well document. Add to that, he obviously was a willing customer. He enjoyed being a submissive."

"Also proved by text messages and files from his digital devices." Ricky nodded. "No wonder his family didn't want to hand them over at first."

"Another illustrious former public servant exposed," Harrison said with a snort.

"NOPD leadership can't blame the Kennedy family's embarrassing publicity on you. Things come out in every investigation," Charmaine said.

"Except the last three cases that resulted in disgraced prominent figures were *mine*. The deputy superintendent even hinted I was intentionally going for big targets, maybe motivated by my own political ambitions." Harrison clenched his jaw tight for a few seconds. "Punching him dead in the face crossed my mind."

"Please make sure someone gets it on video if you do," Jessi quipped.

Harrison barked a laugh. "You would say that. Anyway, Mrs. Kennedy started her pressure tactics this morning. The DA didn't fold. If news sources got hold of more details about Buddy Kennedy's sleazy hobbies..." Harrison looked from Jessi to Charmaine.

"Which will make the ADA's arguments about his behavior even stronger," Scotty said.

"And point to additional possible suspects and motives. I'm willing to bet Mrs. Kennedy will get busy doing damage control." Ricky looked around at them all.

"Buddy Kennedy used deed fraud to claim ownership to properties. He started back in mid-2007. But he put a new spin on it. He'd take out loans using the property as collateral. Use the money to develop properties he actually owned and pay the money back. Then he'd go back to the assessor's office and transfer it back," Jessi said to Harrison.

"Okay, but he didn't default. Then he, or somebody else, changed the titles back. I don't see a motive for murder. Matter of fact, I doubt the DA would bother to follow-up even if the guy was alive," Harrison replied.

"I know, but it's a start. Let's yank on that loose end until the whole story unravels," Jessi said.

"Ah, now I get it. You want me to use department resources to go after Loreen Kennedy and pals. Uh-uh. Paper thin," Harrison said with force.

"Part of any murder investigation is to find out as much as possible about the victim. Right? All I'm saying is look into his business dealings with a microscope," Jessi said with equal energy.

"So, now she's telling me how to be a homicide cop," Harrison clipped. He looked at Jessi, his brow creased.

Jessi glanced at Ricky. "Well?"

Ricky wore an impassive face as he returned her gaze. "We did take our foot off the gas with the evidence on Ms. Phillips. Kennedy's financials could stand a closer look based on what they've found."

Harrison stood. "No promises."

"Thank you so much, Detective Harrison. Ricky, you're a keeper." Charmaine smiled at Harrison and then hugged Ricky.

Harrison jabbed a thick forefinger at Jessi and then Charmaine. "Stay away from Gina Shaw and Loreen Kennedy."

"Yes, sir." Jessi stood and gave him a sharp military style salute.

"Jesus be a fence." Harrison waved goodbye and headed to the door.

"Good work you two," Ricky murmured. When he looked at Jessi, he seemed about to speak. Instead, he followed his boss.

"Call me when things get less busy," Jessi blurted as she watched him leave.

He turned back with a smile. "I will."

Moments later Scotty had a short exchange with the two policemen as he let them out. He locked the door and faced the sisters. "Well, that wasn't all bad news. Are you going to tell Diamond?"

"Hell no," Jessi said fast. "She's on the edge as it is. We've got breathing space to find out more about Buddy's slimy secret life."

"One of my old college classmates has a true crime vlog and fifty thousand followers. He loves stories about injustice in the system. Plus, Kennedy's murder has the kind of juicy elements influencers love," Charmaine said.

"Rich people into kinks, fraud, and murder. They'll eat it up," Scotty added.

Jessi took out her cell phone. "Yeah, and I know one brave reporter who wouldn't mind added spice to their updates on the case. They live to expose one percenters."

"What about the title fraud?" Scotty looked from Charmaine to Jessi.

"Before I'm through, I'll know more of Buddy's business than he ever did." Jessi wore an evil grin.

Wednesday dawned. The first day of the Lent when the excesses of carnival were put aside by the faithful. Catholics attended services all over New Orleans and Louisiana throughout the day. Gray lines of ash marked the foreheads of many. The season to commemorate the forty days Jesus spent in the desert fasting and resisting temptation had begun. People discussed what they'd given up, their own symbols of sacrifice. Charmaine took the day off from the clinic. She didn't have appointments anyway. She used the early hours to catch up on paperwork; therapy notes and details for the business office to file insurance claims. Jessi used the day for remote work. Most of the morning, she'd been at her house. Close to lunchtime, she arrived at Charmaine's place. She let herself in with the key Charmaine had given her. They dined on chicken salad sandwiches, chips, and Barq's crème sodas.

"You're not Catholic." Jessi looked at the cross on Charmaine's forehead.

"Protestants take part in the tradition of Ash Wednesday, too. My church follows the Nazarene tradition," Charmaine tossed back. "You'd know that if you weren't a backslider."

"I was never *in* church, so I haven't backslid into anything. I been wallowing in pleasures of the flesh all along," Jessi quipped.

Charmaine clicked her tongue. "And proud about it, too. I'm gonna keep lifting you up in prayer. If mama can turn it around you can, too."

"Ha! You think her hooking up with a wannabe megachurch pastor is genuine? They're both in it for big stacks. Just take a look at their YouTube channel. Between every scripture they quote is a request for cash."

"Ministries do a lot of work to help their communities. It takes money," Charmaine argued.

"Yeah. Okay." Jessi let out snort. She headed to Charmaine's home office.

Charmaine followed her after a few minutes, a bowl of grapes in one hand. "Take my church. We serve free lunches to anyone who shows up once a week and free breakfasts on Sunday mornings. St. Mark Baptist has a thrift store that finances their ministries. Trinity AME operates a daycare center for single mothers with low income. Christ the King has—"

"I get it. Some do good. Not all." Jessi sat at Charmaine's desk. She removed her laptop from her bag.

"We have the same human flaws as the rest of the world. But we try. You know, like the song says, we fall down, but we get up." Charmaine walked to the window and looked out before she faced Jessi again. "Nice and quiet. I like the calm after the storm."

"Everybody sleeping it off. Including the good church folks who ate, drank, and screwed themselves into a coma." Jessi giggled at the severe look Charmaine gave her.

"Yeah, well. Like I said, we don't claim to be perfect."

"Speaking of sinners, I've got more tea on the Kennedy family. The tradition of getting rich by exploiting other people runs deep on both sides. Partying, too. Buddy got his hard drinking honest from his daddy. But old man Kennedy knew how to wheel and deal. He set all three of his sons up in business. Buddy was the least successful until the early 2000s." Jessi signed into her laptop.

"Is that when he started the title transfer scam?" Charmaine sat in one of two chairs facing her desk.

"Not sure. A lot of records were damaged when Hurricane Katrina hit in 2005. Flooding. I found two instances in 2007, when he and Loreen came back to New Orleans. They evacuated to Austin, Texas, before Katrina hit."

"Interesting, but Harrison has a point. Buddy's scheme made him even wealthier. Which would please Loreen to no end. Same for Gina. No motive to cut off money supply." Charmaine ate five red seedless grapes in quick succession.

Jessi glanced up from the computer screen. "By the way, what did you give up for Lent?"

"Mama Etta Ray's praline bread pudding."

"Ouch." Jessi grinned. She switched her attention back to the computer.

"Let's not talk about it, please. Or my craving will kick in and kick my butt." Charmaine said with a deep sigh. She ate another grape.

Jessi laughed but grew serious again. "I hate when Harrison is right.

The next hour or so, Jessi continued to read while Charmaine answered emails. Jessi spent time sending and receiving texts. Charmaine sensed they were related to their cases, but didn't pry. She had a feeling Jessi's methods weren't quite legal. Something that would send Harrison into a fit if he found out. Charmaine decided to maintain plausible deniability just in case. Not that the sharp-eyed cop would believe she wasn't complicit.

Jessi stood, stretched, and rolled her shoulders. "Kennedy stopped his deed tricks abruptly almost a year ago."

"So, he made enough money and decided to stop risk getting caught." Charmaine spoke around chewing two large grapes.

"Buddy doesn't strike me as the kind of guy who had much self-control. Not when it came to making bank. I don't think he'd give up a sweet system.," Jessi replied.

"Maybe Loreen caught wind of what he was doing and made him stop?" Charmaine squinted as if trying to see if her theory made sense.

"You seriously think Loreen has a moral compass Buddy didn't have?"

Charmaine thought back to her encounter with Mrs. Kennedy at the luncheon. "Not really. But if she thought it could mess up her son's political future... She might have convinced Buddy to cut it out."

"Nah, she's privileged. Entitled. They'd figure out a way to bury the evidence and keep going. I think it's more likely he had a bigger reason to—"

Jessi broke off when chimes echoed through the house. She went to the side door leading from the kitchen to Charmaine's covered carport. Ricky stood on the other side of the door with an eager expression. Charmaine beamed at him and waved for him to enter. She could read his emotions. The handsome redhead wasn't sure Charmaine would welcome him alone. Not since he and Jessi had a bit of a romantic beef going.

"Hey, Ricky. We got my famous chicken salad if you haven't had lunch," Charmaine said. She crossed to Ricky and gave him a quick hug.

"No thanks. I grabbed something earlier. Listen, I had to come over and tell you the latest. But you didn't hear it from me."

"Ahem, I thought you were through breaking the rules for us." Jessi raised an eyebrow at him.

"This is kind of bending them a little bit," Ricky grinned. "Anyway, all you gotta do is wait a few more days. Act surprised when the news hits."

"You mean that Buddy was being investigated for fraud by the feds, or maybe the attorney general?" Jessi chuckled when his blue-gray eyes popped wide.

Chapter 14
Closing Costs

Friday evening the sisters went to Mrs. Chatelaine's after busy days at work for both. Charmaine had gone to the clinic. Jessi had worked at home so Charmaine swung by her house to pick her up. Traffic had somewhat returned to the usual pace. Most tourists had either gone home or were still resting after days of partying.

Angela, Mrs. Chatelaine's niece, let them in. After the customary round of Southern chit-chat while sipping raspberry lemonade, they'd gotten down to business. Jessi took the lead in providing a succinct update. The two women became emotional at the good news.

Mrs. Chatelaine dabbed tears from her light brown cheeks with a tissue in one hand. The other clutched the hand of her niece. "I knew you'd come through for us."

Angela put an arm around Mrs. Chatelaine's shoulders. "I told you things would turn out right."

"Oh, I never doubted them for a minute."

"Now Mrs. C." Jessi eyeballed her. "You pretty much called us incompetent and crooks."

"Me? Why I don't remember any such thing." Mrs. Chatelaine assumed a dramatic look of innocence.

"Convenient how the memory loss kicks in right when you need it," Jessi wisecracked.

"I have a medical condition. My doctor proved it." Mrs. Chatelaine turned to her niece. "What is it again, Angela?"

"Polypharmacy related cognitive impairment." Angela turned to Charmaine and Jessi as she spoke. "Basically, Auntie had a combination of prescription medications that made her confused, forgetful, and even more eccentric than usual."

"I beg your pardon! Sounds like a nice way of saying I'm a weirdo." Mrs. Chatelaine cocked one eyebrow at her niece.

"Let's say unconventional," Angela replied.

"I attended a webinar on geriatric issues in mental health about a year ago. Polypharmacy does mimic the early stages of dementia." Charmaine nodded.

Mrs. Chatelaine sighed. "Geriatric. I loathe that word being thrown around concerning *me*. I feel the same as when I was in my thirties. Well, maybe my forties."

"You're young at heart and still... what is the word y'all used?" Angela asked.

"Foxy." Mrs. Chatelaine lifted her nose in the air. "In the right soft lighting I still turn the heads of men a good fifteen years younger than me."

Charmaine and Angela laughed at them. When her telephone chimed, Mrs. Chatelaine went to answer her landline. She launched into a spirited conversation about lunch with friends at a local restaurant.

"My family and I are so grateful to you for everything. We got Auntie the right medical care because of you. And you saved property that belongs to us. My little cousin and her fiancé will build their first house on one of Auntie's lots." Angela became misty-eyed. "I don't know how we can ever repay you."

"Taking care of our last invoice should do it," Jessi said.

"Jessi!" Charmaine gave her sister a sharp side-eye.

Angela burst into laughter. "No, no. I agree. Excellent service deserves compensation. I'm going to miss you. Jessi is so like Auntie in a lot of ways."

"Ah, I didn't know she was on the pole back in the day," Jessi teased.

"In her day they were called burlesque dancers. She never performed officially. But I've eavesdropped on a few family elders. She dressed up in skimpy outfits for more than a few private costume parties."

"They swore I was 'besmirching the good family name.'" Mrs. Chatelaine rejoined them. She sank onto a stuffed chair, waving one hand with a flourish. "Fortunately, I had dignified siblings to balance things out."

"Yeah. I benefitted from Charmaine being the straightlaced bougie girl." Jessi smirked at her sister.

"Another way of saying I'm boring," Charmaine tossed back.

Mrs. Chatelaine grew serious. "Oh, no. Nothing about you is dull or ordinary. You saved a big part of our generational wealth. You know how much that means for our community especially."

"For sure," Jessi replied. "So, I sent more documents to your lawyer. Hopefully she won't have any problem establishing your ownership to the three lots in question. Kayla sent her report on the forged signature. The taxes on the two other properties have been caught up."

"Yes, and we reimbursed Gina Shaw's real estate firm for the payments she made plus interest," Angela added. "I hear she was not happy."

"I'm pretty sure she didn't think anyone would notice or look into your family. If she had, she would have known you're not without resources," Charmaine said.

"True, but we got a bit complacent. If Andre hadn't been the one paying closer attention, things might have turned out a lot differently. He's become the family hero for getting you to investigate," Angela replied with a grin.

"Yes, quite a change from being one source of embarrassment for our less tolerant kin," Mrs. Chatelaine joked. "I'm the other one."

"Let's be real. You're not the only two, Auntie." Angela and Mrs. Chatelaine shared a high five.

"Sounds like there's more hot family tea." Jessi leaned forward as if eager to hear.

Charmaine spoke up before Angela or Mrs. Chatelaine, both eager to share, replied. She held up her cell phone angled so only Jessi could read the screen. "We have to get going."

"But the stories are about to get juicy." Jessi frowned as she read and then her eyebrows went up. She patted Mrs. Chatelaine on one shoulder. "I'll be back for the details."

"Thanks again." Mrs. Chatelaine stood. She insisted on giving Jessi and Charmaine a hug.

"I sent information on how to get your court hearing expedited on clearing up that forged title filed," Jessi said as they walked to the front door.

"I'll email our final summary in the next couple of days with the invoice." Charmaine waved goodbye.

Once they were in her Kia SUV, Jessi blew out air. She took Charmaine's phone again to read the text message. Then she handed it back. Twenty minutes later they arrived at the offices of Fannie Wilkens. A legal assistant led them to a small conference room. Built-in shelves were lined with law books. Neither the attorney or Diamond had arrived yet.

"So, she texted you instead of me. Guess we haven't made up enough yet," Jessi muttered. Her glared at the wall of books as if they were the enemy.

"Check your phone. She said you didn't answer."

Jessi took out her cellphone. "No, she didn't... Oh, right. I blocked her after the last squabble we had."

"Okay, Queen of Petty," Charmaine side-eyed her. "Friends since you were sixteen and that's how you act."

"It wasn't exactly a fight over who won at spades. There. I put her number back in." Jessi saved the number. "She probably doesn't even know."

Charmaine was about to reply when the door swung open. Fannie Wilkens strode in first. She wore a crisp light gray button front shirt tucked into a charcoal gray pencil skirt. Her dark brown braids were pulled into a neat bun. Diamond, dressed in chunky navy-blue sweater over denim slacks, followed her in. She wore a tense expression as she looked from Charmaine to Jessi. She murmured a soft hello before she sat in a chair next to Charmaine.

"Thanks for coming right over." Fannie nodded to them by way of a greeting. She sat and opened a slim file folder. "Diamond wanted you to hear about the latest development in her case. Before I forget, thanks for doing legwork. Information you gave really made my job easier."

"It's what we do," Jessi said..

"They're the best private detectives in New Orleans. Probably the state," Diamond said in a subdued voice.

"We'll always have your back. You're family." Charmaine gave one of Diamond's hand a quick squeeze.

"We always knew them charging you was a setup," Jessi added.

"Well, it seems the DA's office isn't so confident about their case, too. First, I told the ADA handling Diamond's prosecution that the plea deal was off the table. A source told me about the news story the day before it was to come out. Bernard Kennedy and his real estate company have been under investigation for well over a year. The feds got involved because some of the alleged illegal activities crossed state lines. Wire fraud is one possible violation." Fannie showed them a copy of one online news article she'd printed out.

Charmaine scanned the first two paragraphs of the Yahoo! News article. "Whoa, the story has gone national. Wouldn't the fact that the suspect is dead put an end to the whole thing? I mean, they can't dig the guy up and sentence him."

"He had business partners. Plus, they could go after the assets of Uptown Realtors, LLC, for any fines or penalties." Fannie tapped another part of the file. "His wife is part owner, at least on paper. Doesn't matter if he's dead. If the business assets can be seized," Fannie explained.

"But killing him wouldn't stop the investigation. No point in risking a murder charge for nothing." Jessi frowned as she read a sheet Fannie had handed her.

"You would think so, but..." Fannie sat back. "Here's where things get interesting. The DA had to share the full details with me not yet released to the press. Word is Bernard Kennedy was considering taking a deal."

"Let me guess. His always-high ass got sloppy and careless," Jessi said with a snort of disdain.

Fannie shrugged. "I don't know the who or how, but obviously somebody slipped up. The feds haven't shared specifics. They probably won't until they're ready to request a grand jury be convened."

"So, what does this mean for Diamond?" Charmaine asked.

"Fannie says it strengthens her defense to..." Diamond looked at Fannie.

"I can offer credible alternative theories as to motive and opportunity. Who's to say Kennedy didn't take drugs or a doctored drink before he saw my client that night? Several who were there said he seemed 'tipsy' before he got there." Fannie made air quotes with her fingers.

"Also known as reasonable doubt. But can you bring up the investigation?" Jessi frowned.

"Federal agents will resist being called as witnesses. They don't want to give away info about an on-going investigation. I can subpoena an agent who will confirm certain facts that won't compromise their case," Fannie replied.

"And that Buddy wasn't the only suspect," Jessi added.

"Exactly. Additional motives and people who might have had a reason to harm Mr. Kennedy. I also learned something else. I've already informed the DA." Fannie sat forward again with a gleam in her eyes. "Mr. Kennedy consulted a divorce attorney back in late 2022. He didn't know about the investigation back then. At least not according to the attorney I spoke to."

"How'd you find that out? I didn't see where a petition for separation or divorce had been filed?" Jessi asked.

"A friend of a friend passed on the information. The guy at first balked at talking to me. Attorney-client privilege survives after the death of the client," Fannie replied.

"Damn, that's right. So, you can't use it in court and get your friend in trouble. Hmm, but maybe Buddy told somebody about it," Jessi said.

"Which is another good reason I called you to meet with us. You're already investigators on the case for me." Fannie smiled at Jessi and Charmaine in turn.

"I'll be surprised if Buddy didn't run his mouth to someone. The question is who," Jessi said.

"Based on what we know, he was sloppy in his personal life and business," Fannie agreed.

"But will they talk to us," Charmaine said.

"We'll find a way. One way or another." Jessi looked at Charmaine and then at Diamond.

"I couldn't ask for a better lawyer. Or friends. I finally feel like I can breathe, like maybe my life isn't over." Diamond sniffled as she accepted a hug from Charmaine.

Jessi stood. "Girl, you a pain in the ass. But you're *our* pain in the ass."

Diamond blinked at her for a second and then broke into a grin. They hugged tightly with Charmaine putting her arms around both. Fannie gathered her papers together as they talked. She left one page on the table.

"You can keep the copy of that article." Fannie pointed to it.

"Thanks," Jessi said as she disentangled herself from the ball of sister love.

"So, what happens next?" Diamond asked Fannie.

"The DA's office is evaluating the case in 'light of new information available.' If I don't hear from them by Wednesday of next week, I'll call," Fannie replied.

"Yay, it's over." Diamond did a little dance.

"I didn't say they would drop the charges. The system hates being wrong or looking foolish." The lawyer wore a grave expression.

"Oh, we might still go to trial then." Diamond's bright smile faded.

"We'll see. But things are looking up. I'll hammer home the issue of wasting taxpayer money given these new facts," Fannie said.

"I'm sure there's more to find out," Jessi said.

"Yes. Loreen Kennedy has more secrets." Charmaine thought back to the attractive middle-aged widow. Beneath that sweet magnolia charm lay cold calculation. "I wonder how far she'd go to keep them hidden."

"Be careful. The Kennedy family's powerful friends haven't abandoned them yet," Fannie warned.

Charmaine glanced at Jessi. "Then let's find reasons for them to jump ship."

The weekend went by with Charmaine resting as insisted by both Jessi and Scotty. They, like the rest of New Orleans, wanted nothing but normalcy after the past few hectic weeks. Although their excitement had included rowdy poltergeists and the spirit of an eighteenth-century Rougarou. The calm after their storms inspired a nesting urge in Charmaine. She added the last touches to the nursery on Saturday morning. The afternoon was spent cooking casseroles and freezing them. Sunday, Scotty joined her at church. Jessi, Diamond, and Indyah came over to Charmaine's house for dinner. Everyone's mood was lighter. Scotty insisted that they not talk about anything heavy. Monday, Jessi and Charmaine were back on the case. They'd both taken the morning off from work for their mission, a visit to the offices of Gina Shaw Realty.

"How do you think she'll react?" Charmaine said as she fastened the seat belt of Jessi's Jeep Compass.

"I expect she'll catch an attitude at first; try to bully us. But she didn't follow through on the stay-away order. That tells me something."

"She doesn't want any more police attention maybe." Charmaine studied the scenery as they drove down St. Charles Avenue. A streetcar rumbled alongside on the tracks that went down the center.

"Maybe. More likely she just wants us to go away. Fast."

"So, the plan is to get her talking," Charmaine said.

"Yeah, and nervous."

Jessi steered them through the increasingly busy traffic onto Canal Street. She found a parking space in the small lot adjacent to the building. Then she took out her cell phone. She looked at a text message. Jessi had asked a fellow paralegal to call Gina on the pretext of looking for a rental. "Tara just called to make sure she's at her office. So, here we go."

"Yeah. Into the lion's den," Charmaine murmured.

"Nope. We're the lions." Jessi got out of the Jeep. She waited for Charmaine to join her.

The building had a glass front that gave a view into the lobby. Two desks were visible. Chairs for visitors lined a wall to the right. When they entered, a young blond man was on the phone. He used his best salesman's voice, presumably talking to a client. A slim Apple laptop was open, showing the interior of a home. Charmaine stood waiting for him to notice them. Jessi strolled around looking at prints on the wall showing scenes of New Orleans neighborhoods. After a few minutes, the young man gestured at them in acknowledgment.

"Of course. We can set up a tour of the Bayou St. John property. Wednesday evening? Yes, perfect. Thank you, Mr. Benedict." The young man hung up. The keypad gave off soft clicks as his slim fingers few over them. Seconds later he faced them. "Good morning. How can we help?"

"We're here to see Gina," Charmaine said.

"Oh. You have an appointment?" His fingers moved again over the keypad.

Charmaine craned her neck until she saw the calendar display. She beamed at him when he looked at her again. "No."

"Umm..." His hazel eyes blinked as he gazed from Charmaine to Jessi with a look of mild confusion.

Jessi walked over to stand next to Charmaine. "She'll see us."

The young man seemed to sense trouble might be on the horizon. "I'm not sure she's in the office."

"Her car is parked outside. I checked. Plus, she just answered her phone," Jessi said.

"Umm. Right." The young man looked uncertain of his next move.

"Don't sweat." Jessi tapped the screen of her cell phone. "Hey Gina, we're in your lobby. Let's chat."

Moments later they heard the tap-tap of high heels on the white oak laminate floors. Gina appeared in the short hallway. Four doors, two on either side, led to offices. Dressed in brown slacks and a tweed jacket, she marched in with a tight frown. The young man wore a deer in headlights expression when she glanced at him.

"Thanks, Tyler," Gina clipped, her tone empty of gratitude.

"I'm off to a closing at ten." Tyler opened a desk drawer as he spoke. He grabbed a set of keys and headed for the front door.

"Have a great day," Jessi said as he went by. His only reply was a short nod. When the door whisked shut behind him, Jessi faced Gina. "He seemed in a hurry all of a sudden."

"Our business is done. I thought I'd made that clear," Gina snapped.

"You owe us one last payment," Charmaine replied in a mild voice.

"The fee is over the amount in our contract. So, it's a breach and I owe you nothing," Gina replied.

"Yeah, about the cost. See, we didn't factor in being ambushed when you added that last property." Jessi's playful expression turned to stone.

"Harold stayed to check on finishing work. If he mistook you for trespassers and overreacted, sorry. Must have been a miscommunication. I thought for sure I'd told him we'd stop by." Gina affected a cold smile that pulled her face into a rictus.

"That's the new story you're going with now. You told Detective Harrison we weren't even supposed to be there," Jessi said.

"You tried to file a restraining order against us. Not very nice. Or honest." Charmaine glared at her.

"I'm not alone. Two other agents are in in the office and..." Gina took a step away as if ready to flee down the hallway.

"We didn't come to threaten you. Look at me. Do I look like I'm ready to rumble?" Charmaine smoothed a hand over her baby bump. Her sweater jacket was open over the pink maternity sweater she wore.

"Harold is talking, by the way. A police interview could be in his future. Anybody's guess." Jessi spread out both hands.

Gina's defiant façade softened. "We can negotiate a reasonable rate. I understand why our last encounter might have upset you. Let's just call it a misunderstanding."

"Let's not," Jessi tossed back.

Before Gina could reply, a white couple entered with a toddler. She stammered a greeting to them. Once they told her who they'd come to see, Gina used the desk phone to make a call. A middle-aged woman with a neat reddish-blond bob appeared seconds later. She gushed a hello to them, commented on the child's cute outfit, and led them to her office. The door closed.

"What do you want?" Gina spoke through tight lips in a hush-hush voice.

"Deed fraud. Title theft. The truth is a super nifty place to start." Jessi replied in a normal conversational volume.

Gina winced and glanced over her shoulder. "My office."

"Should have done that in the beginning. We accept your invitation." Jessi grinned waved a hand at her to lead the way.

Two days went by before Harrison called them. Late Thursday afternoon, Jessi and Charmaine arrived at the police station. When Harrison greeted them, he seemed harassed and intrigued at the same time. His handsome brown face was pinched with exhaustion. Still, the veteran detective looked put together. He wore a dark blue suit well, and a white dress shirt with a green silk tie. The buzz and beeping of landline phones in the NOPD District 1 office added to the harried atmosphere. By contrast, Ricky looked fresh and rested. His red hair, combed back, framed his pale complexion. The dusting of faint freckles across his straight nose added to his attractiveness. The only hint of tension showed in the faint crinkles on his forehead.

The news about an investigation into Bernard Kennedy's business affairs didn't make immediate waves. Rumors that Kennedy had negotiated to cooperate brought the slow simmer of media attention to a boil. Jessi and Charmaine studied the detectives. Obviously, they were feeling the heat.

Witnesses present at the party the night Kennedy died were being questioned again. Including Diamond, who fidgeted nervously between Jessi and Charmaine. When her turn came, she stood, gave the sisters a nervous smile, and followed her attorney.

"I don't see any of the partygoers. Just people from the catering staff." Charmaine looked at the crowd.

"I'm sure they were either interviewed at the lawyers' offices or the privacy of their homes. You know, the power of privilege." Jessi followed Charmaine's gaze.

"At least they're interviewing Diamond first."

"She's still their most acceptable suspect," Jessi retorted. "I'll bet Harrison is being pressured to pin the murder on anybody but the posh Porsche set."

"They can't ignore the new facts that have come out." Charmaine felt a nervous flutter in her stomach that wasn't the baby.

"The system does it all the time. They'll say Kennedy's shady business deals don't change the evidence pointing to Diamond."

"We won't let them off the hook though." Charmaine put a hand on Jessi's arm. She could feel the emotion radiating from her sister. Memories of her past encounters with corrupt or cruel cops had left scars.

Jessi turned to Charmaine with a more relaxed expression. "Don't worry. I got a clear head."

Ricky walked into the lobby and gestured to them. "Hey, come on back."

Charmaine and Jessi exchanged matching surprised expressions. Charmaine looped her arm through one of Jessi's as they walked. Ricky, his cop demeanor firmly in place, didn't look back at them as he strode ahead.

"What do you think this means?" Charmaine whispered.

"No clue," Jessi mumbled low.

"In here, please." Ricky pointed to an open door.

They entered an interview room with a metal table and chairs. Ricky gestured they could sit. Charmaine took him up on the offer while Jessi remained standing. Diamond and Fannie were side by side in two other chairs. Harrison sat across from them.

"Ms. Phillips asked that you be present," Harrison rumbled in answer to the obvious question. "The DA has decided not to go forward with the first hearing in her case. In light of the new information we've discovered."

Jessi grunted. "After we forced you to keep looking."

"Jessi..." Charmaine squinted at her volatile sister. "Let Detective Harrison finish."

"The bottom line; he won't drop the charges yet because of the evidence implicating Ms. Phillips. But—" Harrison raised his voice. His narrowed gaze on Jessi warned her to quiet. "We're actively pursuing other avenues of inquiry."

"Translation; the circumstantial case against Ms. Phillips is now weaker than water. Bernard Kennedy had enemies. He almost got into a fist fight twice with two business associates. His wife hated his guts, too. She thought his behavior would harm the political ambitions of both their sons." Fannie spoke in a mild voice. She remained unruffled despite the heated look on Harrison's face. "It's going to come out soon, detective. If it's not already online."

Harrison's stiff expression didn't change. Official police demeanor firmly in place, he stood. "Thanks for coming in again, Ms. Phillips. Ms. Wilkens."

"No problem at all." Fannie placed a hand on Diamond's shoulder after she stood.

Harrison waved at Charmaine and Jessi to stay in place. "I need to talk to you two. If you don't mind."

Jessi exchanged a look with Charmaine. "Okay."

Diamond had also stood to leave but paused and turned to Fannie. "I'm going to wait outside for Charmaine and Jessi."

"Detective Ward will show you to a smaller, less busy lobby," Harrison replied.

Fannie glanced at him sharply. "As long as you don't attempt to question my client without *me*. You know, suddenly remember one more thing she needs to clear up."

Harrison's jaw tightened as he spoke; his voice was tense yet controlled. "We don't operate like that."

"Just making it clear." Fannie turned to Diamond, who nodded she understood.

Ricky left to show them out but returned moments later. At a look from Harrison, he nodded. "Statements are moving along smoothly."

Harrison let out a slow breath. He sat and motioned for Jessi to do the same. "I knew the investigation into Bernard Kennedy would produce a shit show."

Jessi chuckled as she sat. "Yeah, well. I tried to warn you. I'll bet chasing street dealers and regular gangstas looks real good right about now."

"Let's go over what you told me in detail. And by the way, you were supposed to stay away from Gina Shaw," Harrison said.

"Gina asked to see us," Jessi spoke up before Charmaine could reply.

"She'll say so if I question her?" Harrison squinted at Jessi and then glanced at Charmaine.

"She admitted the fraud scheme," Charmaine, sidestepping his question. "Harold Green would put her on to properties owned by families with few or no financial resources. Struggling to pay the property taxes," Jessi said.

"Black people who still haven't been able to rebuild since both hurricanes," Jessi added.

"Humph." Harrison pursed his lips.

"They'd offer to pay the taxes and split profits from development. Shady contracts with a load of legalese allowed them to use the land as collateral. Then change the title to make themselves owners," Jessi continued.

"If the real owners complained, Gina and Kennedy would point to clauses in those contracts to prove their ownership claim. Most of them were older people who didn't understand what they'd signed," Charmaine said.

"Several of them died within a few years. Their family members left behind were poor. They were too pressed trying to make it from day to day to follow up. Bernard and Gina's partner decided to seal the deal by forging signatures on deeds. A risky move, but Kennedy got away with it for almost a decade after Hurricanes Katrina and Rita. But they made a big mistake picking one target," Jessi said.

Ricky looked at notes on his phone. "Lydia Chatelaine."

"Her three lots are in prime locations with post-storm high prices. A gentrifiers dream," Jessi replied. "She hired us to research ownership. That's how we uncovered the real estate funny business."

"Why did Gina Shaw hire you? She must have known she was taking a chance," Ricky asked.

"She had no reason to think we knew Mrs. Chatelaine. Let alone that she was our client, too," Charmaine replied.

"Loreen Kennedy told her about us. They cooked up a plan. Gina would hire us to keep us distracted and find out what we knew. They both figured we were fake or crooked. Either way, they could gather ammunition against us," Jessi said.

"Undermine our credibility in case we dug up dirt to clear Diamond.

"So, there weren't any haunted houses. Your contract was just a ploy. I'm not surprised." Harrison remained a skeptic about their paranormal side of their business.

"Neither one of them believed in spirits, no," Charmaine agreed.

"Bet they do now. That side business of keeping valuables antiques or historical documents found in old homes stirred up negative energy. Resident spirits or AEBEs—"

"Stop right there." Harrison held both palms. "I don't need or want to know about woo-woo crap."

Ricky smothered a laugh by putting a hand over his mouth. Then he cleared his throat. "Kennedy's homicide is our priority. Our property crimes section will work with the feds on the fraud."

"I wish Loreen Kennedy and Gina would get dragged into a NOPD station." Jessi smiled as if picturing their humiliation.

Harrison stood. "That's all for now. We still have to figure out who killed Bernard Kennedy. Now we have to wade through a whole new set of suspects."

"You're welcome." Jessi smiled and opened her arms as if waiting for a hug.

The peeved senior detective waved a large hand at the door, a silent order for them to leave. Charmaine gave him a conciliatory smile. When Harrison's stone face didn't relax, she murmured a thanks for his willingness to listen and followed Jessi out. Ricky and Jessi had a brief hushed exchange in the hallway. Charmaine pretended not to notice the discreet kiss they shared. Minutes later they were back in the lobby.

Diamond sprang from a chair to meet them halfway. "I hope y'all not in trouble because of me. Damn it, I should have cut Buddy off a long time ago. I knew he was trouble when he started with the prescription pills."

"Harrison just wanted more information about our other case. We're good." Charmaine glanced around. "I have to pee. Where are the restrooms?"

A young, fresh-faced blond woman who had been seated to Diamond's right pointed. "The short officer over there will have to let you in. They keep it locked because it's not open to the public. I'm sure she'll let you in since you're preggers."

"Thanks." Charmaine hurried off.

"First time in a police station. I've been waiting over an hour to be seen." The woman gazed around with a nervous frown.

"They're moving pretty fast, Zoe. You should be next," Diamond said.

"I hope so." Zoe didn't look encouraged.

Diamond tried to put the young woman at ease with chit-chat. Jessi glanced around at the potential witnesses. A few were older folks, but most looked like Zoe—college students working side jobs for extra cash. Charmaine rejoined them five minutes later. Diamond gave Zoe a consoling pat on the shoulder before she turned to Jessi again.

"Damn, they pulled in the catering staff. They ain't playin' around," Diamond said.

"They sure aren't. You might get your wish after all," Charmaine whispered to Jessi as she dug through her huge purse.

"Huh?" Jessi looked at her.

"Maybe Gina and Loreen have been 'invited' to explain themselves, too." Charmaine pointed to a tall man who stood out in the crowd. She zipped the pocket of her bag closed.

Diamond glanced in the direction Charmaine had indicated. "Yes, the cops are going all in. They even pulled in

Harry. I doubt he knows anything since he dipped almost an hour before shit popped off."

"No, I'm talking about the wallpaper guy that works for our other client." Charmaine nodded toward Harold Green.

"I don't know what other gigs he has, but Harry was one of the waiters at the party. Only he left early. The manager was pissed. That's why I offered to help out and ended up being a suspect. Hey!" Diamond yelped when Jessi gripped her arm.

"You sure?" Jessi pulled her close.

Diamond peeled Jessi's fingers off. "Yeah, and stop clawing me with those long acrylics. Why are you—"

Jessi hissed a string of profanity. She glared across the space to where he stood. Harold Green turned away and headed for the exit. Jessi strode toward him and then broke into a jog. She pushed her way through a knot of three people blocking her path. They complained loudly and the rest of the crowd became restless. A uniformed officer tried to impose order. Ricky appeared seconds later.

"Everybody settled down." Ricky turned to Charmaine. "What's going on and why is Jessi running across the parking lot?

Chapter 15
Foreclosure

Charmaine pawed through the jumble of items in her satchel purse. She finally found the object of her frantic search. The hip hop ringtone that signaled a text from Jessi shrilled nonstop. "It's him; he was there!"

"Who?" Diamond and Ricky blurted in unison.

"Tell Harrison. Jessi is chasing the murderer." Charmaine started for the door, keys in hand.

"Oh no you don't." Diamond grabbed the back of Charmaine's sweater jacket and yanked her back. "You ain't runnin' after no crazy killer. Not on my watch."

Ricky grabbed Charmaine by both shoulders to further restrain her. "Slow down and make sense."

Breathless from excitement, Charmaine shot out the most succinct explanation she could muster. "Harold Green was in on the thefts with Gina. He knows about the title fraud. He was at the party that night posing as a waiter."

"Party..." Ricky's eyes went wide as he quickly connected the dots.

"She's following him. Here, see." Charmaine held up her cell phone. Jessi had shared her live location. A moving dot traced her path.

"Ricky rubbed his forehead. "The hell?"

"We have to follow her," Charmaine shouted.

"Not *you*, pregnant woman." Diamond kept her grip on Charmaine. She spun to face Ricky. "Do your effing job, dude. Tap his ass as quick as y'all came for me!"

Her words seemed to slap Ricky out of his confused daze. He sprinted off and yelled over one shoulder, "Stay here."

"Damn it." Charmaine huffed in frustration. Before she could react, Diamond took her keys.

"You're not going anywhere. Don't even ask." Diamond dropped the keys into her shoulder bag.

"She needs my help," Charmaine protested.

"You and the baby gone throw hands? I don't think so, ma'am," Diamond shot back.

"I have ghost weapons in my SUV. What if the séance guy calls up some nasty ghosts she can't handle alone? The police won't know what to do. You can drive. I'll stay in the car if it makes you feel better." Charmaine scurried to the glass doors.

Petite Diamond, still holding on tight to Charmaine's sweater, couldn't stop being hauled along after her. Minutes later they sped down the streets of New Orleans with Diamond at the wheel. Charmaine had put her cell phone in the dashboard holder. They both tracked Jessi's position on the dynamic map. Ten minutes seemed to pass with agonizing slowness as Diamond drove. The dot, Jessi, moved toward New Orleans East.

"Where the heck are they going?" Charmaine's rhetorical question hung in the air as Diamond shrugged. Her phone rang and she swiped to answer it.

"Tell me where you are," Ricky said. They heard sounds of traffic and his police radio in the background.

"Heading down Jefferson Avenue right now. She's headed away from Uptown. Maybe to Tchoupitoulas. Is he running to his house?" Charmaine frowned at the map.

"The address we have for Green is in Central City," Ricky replied.

"Oh, okay." Charmaine tapped her contacts icon and found Ricky's number

"No, no. Take a right on Magazine and—" Charmaine sucked in air as she gripped the door handle.

"I know this city. I'm going down Jefferson instead." Diamond spun the steering wheel as she hit the gas pedal.

"Holy mother of... Are we driving on two tires?" Charmaine managed to gasp out.

"My cousin used to shoplift. She'd rent a car, she was eighteen see, but I could drive at fourteen. I learned all kinds of ways to get around." Diamond smiled as if the memory brought back good times.

"Somebody must have wondered about a kid driving," Charmaine managed to gasp.

Diamond gunned the engine while waving a middle finger at an angry guy in a delivery truck. "I sat on pillows to look taller. Plus, I wore makeup and sunglasses. Mesha got caught but never when I was with her."

"Charmaine, share your location," Ricky said.

"Right. Right." Charmaine sent him several cryptic texts. Her mind in a whirl, sharing their real time movements hadn't occurred to her.

Charmaine clenched her teeth as they approached an intersection. She sighed when Diamond hit the brakes at a stop sign. The front bumper extended a few feet into the cross street.

A Honda Civic blew its horn. A woman passenger in it scowled at them and mouthed something that probably wasn't a compliment. Charmaine tapped the contacts icon, found Ricky, and shared their location using the map.

"Harrison must be so hot smoke is coming out his ass." Diamond grinned. She didn't take her eyes off the street.

"Oh, Lord," Charmaine mumbled. She held on tight to the grab handle.

"We're good, lil' mama." Diamond used one hand to pat Charmaine's knee reassuringly. "She's stopped on Dufossat Street. Weird."

Charmaine tapped the cell phone screen. "At 2208. Maybe a relative he thinks will let him hide out."

"Don't approach," Ricky said.

"And you're right. I'm not happy." Harrison's deeper voice rumbled from the speaker. "Stay put once you get to the location or I'll put you both in handcuffs."

"He wouldn't do that to a pregnant woman," Diamond said low to Charmaine.

"Try me," Harrison retorted.

Diamond parked around a corner on Coliseum Street. She switched to the phone controls and hit the mute icon on. "Shit. You think he heard me about driving Mesha?"

"Don't worry. Statute of limitations." Charmaine unbuckled her seat belt.

"Nope." Diamond grabbed the sleeve of her sweater before Charmaine could open the passenger door.

"We both know Jessi is probably following him inside." Charmaine yanked free. She took her phone from the mount first. Then she got out of the SUV, went to the back of it, and lifted the hatch.

"I don't get why you think she needs ghostbusting stuff," Diamond said when she hurried to Charmaine's side seconds later.

"The guy set us up at least twice to be attacked by spirits. I'm guessing it's a property he knows is haunted. For lack of a more scientific term. Jessi would probably not approve." Charmaine reached into the cargo area. She pushed aside the folding chair she used for outdoor festivals. The dark gray duffle bag that matched one of Jessi's sat under a blanket. "Here we go. Thank goodness I made her give me a backup."

"I thought you didn't like Jessi spending extra." Diamond peered into the SUV.

"Yeah, well. She has a tendency to barge into danger. Hold it while I do the settings." Charmaine shoved the rectangular box with straps at Diamond.

"What is this?" Diamond took it.

"The first prototype of the EMF neutralizer we, well Jessi, had made. It disrupts electromagnetic energy." Charmaine twisted dials as she spoke.

"Okay." Diamond wore a baffled expression.

"Jessi's theory, which has proven to be true, is that what we call ghosts are forms of electromagnetic energy. Devices have been used for years to disrupt it." Charmaine looped both belts through Diamond's arms like a backpack.

"So, it zaps them until they're gone?" Diamond allowed Charmaine to adjust the straps.

Charmaine entered one last setting. "It's on, so you won't have to hit a button or anything. Let's go."

"Hold up. You're not going. Hell, I'm not even sure *I'm* going. Harrison said—"

"When you approach the house, go to a side window and take a peep in. This has a range of up to fifty feet. You won't have to go inside." Charmaine strode down the sidewalk.

"Hey!" Diamond yelped. It took her a second to react. She locked the SUV and followed. She caught up with Charmaine. "Think about the baby, girl. Stay your hardheaded ass away from that house!"

Charmaine stopped at the corner. She stared down Dufossat Street toward the house. "You're right. I'm just getting an idea of what's-what. I don't see Jessi's Jeep."

"She went down Soniat. I'm pretty sure she parked there and walked."

"Yeah, because Harold has seen her Jeep. If we get a little closer..." Charmaine glanced around just as Diamond grabbed for her again. "Fine, fine. I'll wait here."

Look, I don't know what I'm doing with this thing." Diamond jumped when the neutralizer let out a soft beep.

Two different ringtones sounded. Diamond's phone trilled a chime. Charmaine's played the hip hop tune she'd assigned to Jessi. They both stopped in their tracks to read the message. Jessi sent a group text to them. Harold Green had gone inside the house. Jessi didn't think he'd spotted her.

"Damn it. There's a second story. You may have to go inside. It'll be fine," Charmaine added when Diamond's mouth dropped open in protest. "Let the neutralizer do the work. All you gotta do is keep moving."

"This thing works one hundred percent of the time, right?"

"Yeah. Well... pretty close. Get moving!"

"I hope them prayers Pastor Evans said over me the other Sunday still workin," Diamond whispered as she walked away, adding her request for protection.

Jessi crouched as she went along the narrow path leading to the rear of the house. She paused to put the address into a search. As suspected, the house was for sale on a real estate website, described as a camelback charming Victorian built in 1923 by a member of the Soniat extended family. The listing had Gina's company and one of the agents that worked for her. An expansive primary suite was on the first floor. Jessi took a few more seconds to look at the layout. Then she tucked the cell phone into a zip pocket in her jacket. Best to make sure she didn't drop it. Jessi wore a telescoping baton stuck in the back of her jeans. She had a pretty good guess why Harold made a beeline for the place.

She looked through the glass back door before she eased inside. Harold apparently was in too much of a hurry to lock himself in. The security panel had a green light. Jessi froze for a minute but the alarm system didn't ping an alert that it had opened. Connections for plumbing were to her left. She guessed this would be the laundry room once finished. She carefully stepped around building materials scattered on the floor. A narrow kitchen with brick flooring lay to her right. Rustling behind her made Jessi spin around. Diamond's head slowly came into view in a west window of the kitchen. Jessi put a finger to her lips and then pointed up.

"Okay." Diamond mouthed the word. Then she made a series of hand gestures; improvised signed language.

"What?" Jessi mouthed back. Then she shook her head and mouthed. "No time. Stay."

Diamond half-turned so she could see the disrupter backpack, Jessi grinned then grew serious. She mouthed, "Charmaine?"

Diamond flapped both hands animatedly to reassure her Charmaine was far away. Jessi considered going outside again to stop this weird pantomime conversation. A solid thump from above drew her attention instead. She held up a palm at Diamond, a final instruction for her to stay outside. Then she found the staircase and climbed the steps. As she suspected, Harold had gone to the attic. But to be sure, she tiptoed along the second story hallway. Three bedrooms had no furniture. They were in various stages of being refurbished. Jessi moved quietly up the flight leading to a finished attic. In most historic homes, attics had been used for storage. Belongings like decorative items or documents sometimes got shoved into nooks and crannies. Forgotten or no longer visible, they ended up in walls later covered by drywall. Or concealed on purpose by previous owners. In this case, Jessi figured Harold used this house to hide his own secret stash. Something to fund an escape maybe.

"Damn it!" Harold's muffled exclamation was followed by a soft grunt and soft scraping.

"You will not get away with your treachery," a whispery voice said.

"Not now," Jessi murmured low to the voice. She didn't need the complication of a vengeful spirit.

Sounds from the attic stopped. Stillness became almost palpable. Jessi could almost feel Harold holding his breath. The presence in the Dufossat House felt different. Heavier somehow. She only had a few seconds to wonder about the history of the location when the scraping started again. Harold let out a strangled cry.

"Yes," he said, followed by the clinking of items being moved.

Jessi took advantage of his preoccupation with the loot to move with stealth to the attic door. She risked a look around the frame. Harold, his back to her, stuffed items into a long military type duffle bag. Sunlight through a window created flashes of light. One polished silver platter vanished into the bag. A second, more tarnished one followed. Jessi watched as he put a vase encased in bubble wrap in last. Finally, Harold put the bag down. A large square of drywall had been removed from the wall. Inside the unfinished original wood was visible. Grunting, Harold reached into the opening until the upper half of his body disappeared. He brought out a small object.

"There you are." Harold kissed a bag tied at the top with twine or rope. He spun around, coming face-to-face with Jessi. "How did—"

Before Jessi could react, Harold dropped the bag and rushed her. She reached for the baton but dropped it. Harold stopped a second, looked at it on the floor and smiled. He pounced but Jessi had already hopped to his right. While he stumbled to regain his footing, Jessi dived for the baton. His hulking frame blocked the door. With no other option, Jessi had no choice but to fight. He had a good fifty pounds on her and desperation fueled motivation.

"You gone learn to mind your own fucking business today," Harold said, his voice a low growl. "That little twig won't help you this time."

Jessi, her back against the south wall, pressed a button. The baton opened to full length. "Let's find out then, big boy. The police should be here any minute to pick up the pieces I leave."

"One thing for sure, you know how to talk trash. You're alone so it's you and me."

"I was at the station." When Harold's eyes went wide, she smiled. "Oh, so you didn't see me. Well, I saw you, asshole." Jessi sliced the air with her baton.

Harold's eyes narrowed. He cocked his head to one side. "No sirens. Rushed over here without a Plan B. Cocky meddling bitch."

When he lunged Jessi tried to evade him, but his body crashed into her. Before she could twist away, one huge hand closed around her throat. She pressed a smaller button on the baton. When he grabbed it, a crackle made him squawk in surprised pain. His grip loosened but not enough. Jessi tried to bring a knee up to his groin, but he pressed her flat against the wall. Her vision grew cloudy as she fought to breathe. Suddenly his weight was gone. Harold gaped at her, his mouth a wide circle. Then his body jerked away. He was lifted up until his Wolverine boots cleared the floor by one inch. Jessi blinked at him but recovered from her surprise. She swung the baton and delivered a solid whack onto his torso. At the same time, Jessi pressed the button to deliver a shock. Her baton doubled as a stun device.

Harold's lips twisted into a grimace of agony. A wet stain appeared on the crotch of his khaki pants. "Oh no! Please! I didn't mean—"

Ricky appeared in the doorway, gun in one hand. Whatever he was about to say seemed to be snatched from his lips. Instead,

Ricky stared in astonishment at the sight of Harold hovering. The tall man's boots swung about six inches off the oak plank floor. Then as if a string snapped, Harold dropped. He landed on his feet, wobbled for two seconds, and crumpled into a heap.

Harrison arrived a minute later, also gun in hand. He glanced at Harold before holstering his gun. He walked inside a few steps. His gaze swept the attic until he saw the bag. Then Harrison glanced at Ricky, who stood staring at Harold. A uniformed female cop appeared behind Harrison.

"Cuff him," Harrison barked over Ricky's shoulder.

"Sir."

The officer went around Ricky. She rolled dazed Harold onto his side. In a matter of seconds, both Harold's wrists were secured. She motioned to a male cop to help her. Between them they got Harold up. His eyes popped open along with his mouth.

"I can explain," Harold croaked.

Harrison looked at Harold with an implacable expression. "Take him downstairs. Ricky and I will transport."

Ricky watched the officers leave with Harold stumbling between them. He shook his head as if to clear it. "Did you see..."

"The suspect on the floor. Nothing else." Harrison turned to Jessi. "And I'm going to assume that's a normal baton used *only* in self-defense.

Jessi realized she still held the baton in battle ready position. She lowered her arm. "For sure. He came at me. More than once."

"Full statement. At the station." Harrison glared a silent warning at her not to argue.

"Yes, sir." Jessi snapped her heels together and saluted.

"If you don't... Oh never mind." Harrison strode off, muttering to himself.

"You okay?" Ricky took a step toward Jessi with a frown of concern.

"Yeah. He didn't hurt me much." Jessi rubbed her neck.

"Jesus, you've got bruises. Let's get you checked out." Ricky put the safety on his service pistol before he holstered it.

"I'm good." Jessi voice shook as she spoke.

"Just in case, alright?"

Ricky put an arm around her. He made soothing sounds when Jessi leaned into him. They walked down the stairs to the ground floor and onto the backyard deck. Charmaine and Diamond rushed over to them, both babbling questions. Jessi gave each of them a hug in turn. The same two uniformed officers could be seen through the windows. They searched for a minute or two before moving on. Medics appeared from the alleyway. At Ricky's insistence, they examined Jessi. Once sure she didn't want to go to the hospital, the two men left. But not before reporting that they'd checked out Harold and he didn't require a trip to the ER either.

Harrison seemed to be less irritated by the time they arrived at the Fifth District station. He allowed Jessi to give her statement without being interrupted. He let Diamond go as well after a short interview. Three hours later, Jessi was home. After a warm shower, she lounged on her sofa. Charmaine and Scotty brought takeout Chinese; her favorites. Sesame chicken, stir-fried broccoli, and spring rolls. By eleven o'clock that night all three were dozing in front of the television. The doorbell tinkled close to midnight. Scotty, yawning widely, went to the door and looked out before opening it.

"It's the cops," he said.

Jessi stretched and let out a groan. She was still sore thanks to the fight with Harold. "Very funny."

Scotty chuckled as he exchanged a handshake with Ricky. "Peace, bro."

"Good evening, everybody." Ricky slapped Scotty on the shoulder before he walked in. He glanced at his smartwatch. "Well, almost morning."

"Hey, babe." Jessi wore a sleepy smile as she accepted a kiss and hug. She swung her legs from the sofa to make room for him. "You should be in bed resting after the day you've had."

"I should say the same for you. But I'm glad you've got company." Ricky pulled Jessi's legs across his lap. He massaged her calves until she sighed.

Charmaine sat straight against the cushions of the smaller sofa. "I'm staying the night in case she needs me."

"Um, maybe not." Scotty tipped his chin toward the other couple.

"I'm going home to clean up, nap for a couple of hours, and head back to the station. A lot of paperwork. Plus, the boss needs me to help shovel the shit that's about to hit the fan," Ricky replied.

"What did Harold, aka Harry, have to say for himself?" Jessi asked.

"He claims Gina and Loreen Kennedy arranged for him to be on the catering crew. He went with a bottle of Bernard Kennedy's favorite brand of champagne. Nobody noticed when he slipped it in the crate with the rest of the liquor," Ricky replied.

"They were willing to poison more than one person to get at him," Charmaine said.

"And risky," Jessi added.

"The drug wasn't in the bottle. He handed a glass with the drug in it to a server. A drunk woman dressed in a harem costume bumped into the guy and the glass tipped over. He finally got another chance later."

"Let me guess. The same glass Diamond handed to Kennedy," Jessi said.

"He's not sure. All the tipsy partygoers in costumes confused him, but yeah. That's what we figure. He didn't know Diamond had been hired to entertain the guys, Kennedy in particular. That was a lucky coincidence," Ricky explained.

Charmaine frowned. "But wait a minute. Y'all tested the glasses."

"Yes, we did," Ricky said. "The theory was Diamond managed to get rid of the glass somehow. Turns out Harold took it with him when he slipped off. He crushed it into a fine powder and threw it in Bayou St. John."

"Can't be found because it no longer exists. Pretty smart." Jessi let out a low whistle of admiration.

"Evil, and nothing pretty about it," Charmaine said. "So, Harold killed Bernard Kennedy to help Gina and Loreen?"

"He denies it. We've spent hours of him sniveling about being set up. Green claimed at first that he was only supposed to spy on Kennedy; make sure he didn't get intoxicated and talk too much. Which Kennedy had a habit of doing," Ricky said. "Then he admitted to knowing about the drug, but that Gina told him it would only knock him out. Again, to keep him from being indiscreet."

"Like he did with Diamond, which made her even more of a perfect scapegoat." Charmaine shook her head.

"Loreen and Gina didn't know Diamond would be there either. They figured the cause of death would be put down to a heart attack due to a combination of drugs and alcohol," Ricky replied. "They knew folks would be passing out pills like party favors."

"And they wanted him dead because of the investigation," Jessi put in.

"Harold says he didn't know about the investigation." Ricky shrugged when Jessi rolled her eyes. "Yeah, we don't believe him either."

"Poor Harrison. He's gotta tell his bosses that two of the city's elite Southern belles are murder suspects." Jessi giggled.

"You can imagine what kind of mood he's going to be in for months," Charmaine said.

"A little advice. Keep a low profile for a good long while. And stay out of trouble. No weird cases that lead to a dead body or two." Ricky looked from Charmaine to Jessi.

"We'll do our best, but shit happens," Jessi joked. Her grin widened at his pained expression.

Ricky patted Jessi's legs until she swung them to the floor. He stood and rolled his shoulders. "I better get going. I'll send updates when I can. Don't be surprised if Harrison calls you two for more questioning."

"We're gonna be solid citizens willing to cooperate." Jessi rose to stand next to Ricky. She tiptoed to kiss him on one cheek. "Sleep more than a couple of hours, babe. The city won't go to hell that fast without you."

Once Ricky had left, Scotty decided to head home as well. But not before he tidied up and put leftovers in the refrigerator. Once he made sure the sisters had everything they needed, he left. Charmaine would sleep in Jessi's guest bedroom. Ricky's account has chased away any thoughts of sleep for them. Charmaine insisted on preparing chamomile ginger tea.

"This will calm the nerves and help us drift away. Oh, and I said a prayer of thanks to the good Lord for protecting us, too." Charmaine snuggled onto the small sofa again, a plush throw blanket around her. She sipped tea.

"Humph, Sky Daddy had nothing to do with it. You and Diamond had my back. I better check that EMF neutralizing disrupter. A poltergeist showed up even though you'd turned it on," Jessi retorted.

"No need. I had her turn it off. Madame told me you didn't need EMF protection."

"Wait, you talked to Madame Laveau's spirit without me? Charmaine, that's huge!"

"I didn't hear her voice. More like a strong feeling. Madame's presence washed over me. That's the best way I can describe it." Charmaine frowned as if searching for the right words.

"She tried to communicate. And you've seen or heard spirits a few times. You might have latent medium characteristics. I mean, we share genes," Jessi said.

"Plenty of 'normal' people experience ADC, Charmaine replied, using the acronym for After Death Communication.

"Still, very interesting." Jessi left the sofa and padded to the small hall closet. She took her laptop out of a bag and sat again. The keypad clicked as she typed in notes.

"Just because I have telepathy doesn't mean I'll be like you one day. Please no, God. Bad enough I get mental pollution from other people's thoughts. The things I've heard when I didn't want to."

"Anyway, I'm glad it was pissed at Harold instead of *me*. Probably because he was stealing its belongings," Jessi said.

"Poltergeists usually can only move or manipulate relatively light objects, and for short periods. You say Harold hung in the air for minutes? And he's definitely not little."

"Right, I almost forgot that part." Jessi tapped more notes into the laptop. She put it down and picked up her cup again. She snuggled in a corner of the sofa. "This gentrified tea ain't hittin' on nothin.'"

Ten minutes later, Charmaine smiled as she tucked a blanket around her sleeping sister. "Thanks, Madame."

"De rien, mes enfants," came the faint reply, delicate as mist over Manchac Swamp.

Sunday afternoon sunshine slanted through the windows of Charmaine's living room. After church services, Scotty and Charmaine had hosted dinner. Jessi brought dessert courtesy of Mama Etta Ray. A sour cream pound cake with lemon glaze sat on the kitchen island. Indyah had made a valiant effort to keep her eyes open. The Nap Spirit won. Diamond took her to the nursery to sleep. The scent of fresh-brewed coffee filled the house. The adults exchanged chit-chat over cake until half of it was gone.

"Girl, can't nobody do cake like your grandmomma." Diamond licked a spot of glaze from her thumb.

"You better not say that in front of your aunt," Jessi replied.

"I love her, but Tee-Tee can't throw down like Miz Etta Ray LaMotte. Period," Diamond replied. "But you got a point. I wouldn't dare tell her so."

"Remember when Mama Etta Ray won the baking blue ribbon at the church fair? I thought your aunt was gonna throw hands with the judges!" Jessi burst into a laughter at their childhood memory.

Jessi's comment started a round of familiar anecdotes from days gone by between the friends. Having known each other since childhood, they had plenty of them. Another hour went by before Indyah woke up. Diamond packed her up to go home.

"Thanks for everything. And I do mean *everything*. I'm closer to y'all than my family. I love some of my cousins, but they be trippin'." Diamond tilted her head to one side as she thought for a second. "Come to think of it, I be trippin' myself sometimes. All the mess with Buddy and stuff."

"Listen, if nobody else got you, *we* got you." Jessi pointed to Charmaine and Scotty.

They shared hugs. Indyah, still groggy, accepted their attentions as she clung to her mother's hip. When Diamond went out the kitchen door, Detective Harrison strolled in. He wore a forest green pullover sweater against the chilly February wind outside. Navy-blue slacks matched his loafers.

"Afternoon all. Ms. Phillips." Harrison nodded to her. He smiled at Indyah and the little girl returned it with a shy smile of her own.

"You look relaxed." Diamond leaned to the side and looked down the driveway.

"No police raid. I stopped by to give y'all an update," Harrison said.

"Oh, I'm staying to hear this since you ain't here to..." Diamond's voice trailed off. She glanced at Indyah who looked on with curiosity.

"No worries. For you at least," Harrison reassured her.

Diamond took Indyah back to the nursery with her purple kid's tablet. They heard the strains of a song from Gracie's Corner playing seconds later. The soft thud of the door closing came before Diamond rejoined them.

"She don't need to hear about killing and stuff," Diamond said.

"Have some cake and coffee, detective." Charmaine pointed to the cake.

"No thanks. I have pastries from Brocato's for my wife." Harrison sat in one of the chairs across from the sofa. "A peace offering."

"Mrs. H. got beef with you, huh?" Jessi grinned at him.

"I missed a few social events working overtime the last few weeks." Harrison waved a hand. "Isabelle gets it even though she's annoyed right now. Now if I can survive you two until retirement."

"We help you close weird cases though," Jessi reminded him.

"Emphasis on weird." Harrison sighed. "A lot of people in authority are unhappy. But hell, the evidence leads where it leads."

"Media attention helps. No sweeping the dirty details under a rug. Reporters and true crime vloggers are all over the story," Charmaine said.

"Yeah. Bad idea trying to protect their faves. No matter how much money or connections they have," Jessi added.

"All the juicy bits. Sex, drugs, and shady business deals." Scotty grinned at Harrison. "People love getting the tea on rich folks' mess."

"They've got *a lot* to guzzle down when it comes to Bernard Kennedy and friends," Harrison said. "Anyway, to quote an old cliché, Harold Green is singing like a bird. His story changed a few times. He's sticking to the part about not knowing they intended to kill Kennedy though. *They* meaning Gina and Loreen."

Charmaine leaned forward. "So, what do they say?"

"Nothing on advice of their high-priced attorneys. Here's the scenario I've presented to the DA. Bernard is up against it with the criminal investigation. He decides to cooperate. How much? We don't know yet. The feds are guarding their case because it's ongoing," Harrison explained.

"Probably because they're after more people," Jessi put in.

Harrison nodded. "And said people have money. Enough money to get out of the country fast. On PJs."

"Huh?" Diamond blinked hard.

"Private jets, girl. Something we don't know anything about and most likely never will," Jessi wisecracked.

"Like I was saying, Loreen Kennedy despised her husband. She put up with his behavior for years. Why? Obvious answer—because of the money, influence, and lifestyle he provided. But his addiction to porn, kink, and drugs made him careless. He became a liability, including to his son's political future. The other adult children as well, but mainly it's about the son. Said bad habits provide the perfect way to get rid of him. Years of excessive booze and drugs took a toll. So, get rid of him using those same vices? Not even his friends would be surprised." Harrison sat back.

Charmaine frowned for a few moments and then said, "But I don't get how they roped Harold into the plan."

"Gina made it plain that Kennedy knew about Harold's side business in stolen valuables. Plus, Harold helped them in the deed fraud scheme as well. They had a good reason to want Buddy gone gone." Harrison stood. "Anyway, that's it. Harold is definitely going to get charged."

"I almost feel sorry for Harold. He played out of his league. Loreen and Gina probably always planned for him to be their fall guy," Charmaine said.

"He gets no sympathy from me," Diamond said. "I hope those evil females get some jail time, too."

"At least Loreen and Gina are sweating under the heat right now. We'll give NOPD any ammunition we can dig up," Jessi replied.

"Absolutely not. Stay far away from my investigation. You two have done enough 'helping' already." Harrison pointed a finger at Jessi and then Charmaine. "Far, far away."

"The only reason y'all caught Harold is because of us. Our excellent investigation skills led us to the séance circle." Jessi grinned at Harrison's puzzled expression.

"Say again?" Harrison glanced at Scotty as if looking for a source of reason.

Scotty shrugged. "Hey man, it's wild."

"Oh right, we didn't tell you about Mathias and the others. See, Harold is, or was, a member of Le Cercle Harmonique. They conduct séance sessions on the regular. That's how he knew where to find hidden treasure in old homes," Charmaine said.

"From the spirits of past occupants," Jessi added. "Here's what you'll find interesting."

"I doubt it," Harrison's mouth turned down.

"With their help we have a good chance of getting property returned to the descendants." Jessi wore a pleased smirk.

"Good for them."

"Guess who their ancestor is? Madame Glapion, aka the famous *Marie Laveau*! Ta-da!"

Harrison pinched the bridge of his nose. "Jesus, take the wheel."

Jessi didn't let his reaction dampen her enthusiasm. "The Circle contacted a spirit which led me to find documents in the Notarial Archives. Two lots were taken by eminent domain, but the city never put them into public use. Instead, they ended up in private hands. Based on a similar case in California, the Glapions have a chance to get them back. Great, huh?"

"Wonderful. You're going into civil court with a goblin for a witness." Harrison wore a sour expression as he fished his car keys from a pocket. "I just hope it keeps you too busy to bother me."

"You mean a ghost. Obviously, we won't bring up the séance to a judge," Jessi said.

"Good idea," Harrison agreed.

"Ghosts are electromagnetic energy with a biological origin. Different from goblins, sort of. But that's a discussion for another time. Anyway, the Circle..." Jessi stopped when Harrison glared at her.

"Enough. Harold Green renovated old homes. He stumbled on antiques and decided to steal them. I don't want to hear anything about ghosts, séances, or fortune tellers." Harrison headed for the nearest exit.

Jessi followed him like an eager puppy. "Don't you want to hear about Madame Laveau and how she helped—"

"I *do not*!" Harrison barked as he jerked open the door. "Enjoy the rest of your Sunday. Bye."

Jessi laughed as she turned around after the door thumped shut behind him. "Wait until he finds he's one of Madame Laveau's lucky heirs."

Don't miss out!

Visit the website below and you can sign up to receive emails whenever Lynn Emery publishes a new book. There's no charge and no obligation.

https://books2read.com/r/B-A-YISG-LZCUC

BOOKS 2 READ

Connecting independent readers to independent writers.

Also by Lynn Emery

Dr. Zen Mystery
The Lodestone Puzzle
The In Situ Murders
The Titan Paradox

Joliet Sisters Psychic Detectives
Smooth Operator
Hunting Spirits
Dead Wrong
Dead Ahead
Die Trying
Spirited Sisters
Dead End

LaShaun Rousselle Mystery
A Darker Shade of Midnight
Between Dusk and Dawn
Only By Moonlight

Into the Mist
Third Sight Into Darkness
Devil's Swamp
Blood Bayou
LaShaun Rousselle Mysteries Books 1-3

Triple Trouble Mystery
Best Enemies
Devilish Details
Pretty Dangerous

Standalone
After All
Louisiana Love City Girls Boxset
A Time to Love
One Love
Sweet Mystery
Night Magic
Good Woman Blues
Gotta Get Next To You
Soulful Strut
Tell Me Something Good
Tender Touch
Louisiana Love Box Set

Watch for more at www.lynnemery.com.

About the Author

Mix knowledge of voodoo, Louisiana politics and forensic social work, and you get a snapshot of author Lynn Emery. Lynn has written over twenty novels so far, one of which inspired the BET made-for-television movie AFTER ALL based on her romantic suspense novel of the same name. Holly Robinson Peete and DB Woodside starred as the lead characters.

Her romantic suspense titles have won and been nominated for several awards, including Best Multicultural Mainstream Novel by Romantic Times Magazine.

Get exclusive offers each month in Lynn's newsletter and a free short story when you sign up! Go to:

https://www.subscribepage.com/s1y8j8

Visit www.lynnemery.com to see a full list of Lynn Emery novels.

Read more at www.lynnemery.com.